Praise for Emma Miller and her novels

"This is truly an enjoyable tale overall."
—*RT Book Reviews* on *A Love for Leah*

"The concept of having two suitors…provides a fresh twist. It is fun trying to figure out who [the heroine] will choose."
—*RT Book Reviews* on *The Amish Bride*

"A captivating story."
—*RT Book Reviews* on *Miriam's Heart*

Praise for Diane Burke and her novels

"It is carefully plotted, leaving the reader to actively participate in all the twists and turns."
—*RT Book Reviews* on *The Marshal's Runaway Witness*

"Alternating points of view add to the suspense, and [the hero's] character is well researched and well crafted in this terrific, touching tale."
—*RT Book Reviews* on *Silent Witness*

"A fascinating story of hidden identities and forbidden love, creating a page-turning mystery."
—*RT Book Reviews* on *Double Identity*

Emma Miller lives quietly in her old farmhouse in rural Delaware. Fortunate enough to be born into a family of strong faith, she grew up on a dairy farm, surrounded by loving parents, siblings, grandparents, aunts, uncles and cousins. Emma was educated in local schools and once taught in an Amish schoolhouse. When she's not caring for her large family, reading and writing are her favorite pastimes.

Diane Burke is an award-winning author who has had seven books published with Love Inspired Suspense. She won first place in the Daphne du Maurier Award for Excellence in Mystery and Suspense and finaled in the ACFW Carol Award for book of the year. When she isn't writing, she enjoys taking walks with her dog, reading and spending time with friends and family. She loves to hear from readers and can be reached at diane@dianeburkeauthor.com. She can also be found on Twitter and Facebook.

EMMA MILLER

A Groom for Ruby

&

DIANE BURKE

The Amish Witness

⬧HARLEQUIN®LOVE INSPIRED®

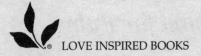 LOVE INSPIRED BOOKS

Recycling programs for this product may not exist in your area.

ISBN-13: 978-1-335-46350-0

A Groom for Ruby and The Amish Witness

Copyright © 2018 by Harlequin Books S.A.

The publisher acknowledges the copyright holders of the individual works as follows:

A Groom for Ruby
Copyright © 2017 by Emma Miller

The Amish Witness
Copyright © 2017 by Diane Burke

This edition published by arrangement with Love Inspired Books.

® and TM are trademarks of Love Inspired Books, used under license. Trademarks indicated with ® are registered in the United States Patent and Trademark Office, the Canadian Intellectual Property Office and in other countries.

www.Harlequin.com

Printed in U.S.A.

CONTENTS

A GROOM FOR RUBY

Emma Miller

And be ye kind one to another, tenderhearted,
forgiving one another, even as God
for Christ's sake hath forgiven you.
—*Ephesians* 4:32

Chapter One

❧

Kent County, Delaware

"I'm sorry we couldn't have had a nicer day to greet you," the matchmaker said as she guided her driving horse onto a curving country lane. "We usually have beautiful weather in September."

Seated beside Sara Yoder on the buggy seat, Ruby nodded and clutched her black purse on her lap. She was too nervous to think of a sensible reply that wouldn't make her hostess believe she was a complete gooseberry. She'd been eager to come to Seven Poplars and had counted the weeks and days until her *mommi* and *daddi* had put her on the bus. But now that she was finally here, she was suddenly struck dumb.

Thunder rumbled overhead and heavy rain beat against the thin roof and sides of the buggy. It was raining too hard for her to see much through the window over the dashboard. Sara's buggy was black, rather than gray like the ones she was used to, but otherwise it seemed completely familiar to be rolling along to the sound of the horse's hooves and the creak of the iron wheels. Her father had warned her that Seven Poplars was a more conservative Old Order Amish than their own community, but so far nothing in Sara's dress or manner of speaking had proved severe.

Still, Ruby had plenty of reason for concern. What if Sara didn't like her? Worse, what if Ruby didn't like any of the potential husbands that Sara offered? What if none of the men were interested in Ruby? She was twenty-five, a quarter of a century old. In a community where all of her friends and cousins her age had already married and were mothers or expecting babies, she was practically an old maid. If she failed to find someone, she'd be letting her parents down as well as herself.

All Ruby had ever dreamed of was a good husband, her own home and the opportunity to practice her faith under the loving eyes of her parents. But there would be no plump and laughing babies, no grandchildren for her mother and father, and no future for her if she couldn't find a husband. And not just any husband would do. She wanted one who would love her with all his heart because, seeing the special relationship her parents had and the way each one had always put the other first, she wasn't willing to settle for less.

"We'll give you a few days to feel at home here, meet the other girls who are staying with me and then we'll talk about some possibilities," Sara explained.

Ruby nodded. She, who was rarely at a loss for words, felt as though she had a whole shoofly pie stuck in her throat. She swallowed, thinking she might be coming down with something. It had been raining since she'd left home; she'd gotten wet when she'd changed buses in Philadelphia and again when she'd gotten off in Dover. It wasn't cold out, but she felt damp and chilled, and her stomach had an ache that was either the greasy foot-long chili dog she'd bought from a cart in Philadelphia or she'd caught an ague. She pressed the back of her hand against her forehead, hoping that she wasn't feverish. Instead of being hot to the touch, her skin felt clammy, so it had to be nerves.

"I've already got someone in mind for you," Sara went on. "A widower only a few years older than you. He has a son, but your mother assured me that you would welcome a stepchild."

"Ya," Ruby managed. "Children are a heritage from the Lord, offspring a reward from Him." She winced. Was that all she could say? Now she was imitating her bishop's wife, who was never content to speak for herself, but always had to be quoting proverbs so as to appear wiser than she was.

Not that Ruby didn't love children; she adored them. Since she had been young, she was always mothering orphaned animals, birds, even hapless insects that crossed her path. Once, she caused a ruckus during church service when the mouse she'd rescued from a cat wiggled out of her apron pocket and ran up Katie Brunstetter's leg.

"Here we are," Sara announced as she drove the horse into a yard. "And I promise, it all looks cheerier in the sunshine."

Through the rain, Ruby could make out a sprawling Cape Cod–style house and a white picket fence. Behind the house stood a tidy stable, painted white, and several well-kept outbuildings.

"This rain isn't going to let up. We'll have to make a run for it," Sara told her. "Leave your suitcase in the buggy. I'll have my hired man bring it in when he un-harnesses the horse. Hiram won't mind and there's no sense in your struggling with it now."

A figure in a dark coat and hat dashed from the house toward them. "That must be Hiram now," Sara said as she climbed down from the driver's seat and hurried toward the house. She paused only momentarily to exchange words with the man, then turned and waved. Ruby opened the door, peered down and saw a huge puddle.

Sara's hired man ran up to the buggy. He shouted something and held out his arms, but Ruby couldn't make out what he'd said above the din of the thunder and the rain pounding on the buggy's rooftop. "I don't need help, thanks," she called. The buggy was high. She wasn't very tall, so she knew that she'd have to give a little leap or she'd land smack in the middle of the mud puddle.

She forced a smile and hopped down.

At least, *that* was her intention. But the heel of her shoe caught on the edge of the buggy frame, and when she tried to catch her balance, her other foot caught in the hem of her dress. Having already reached the point of no return, her graceful hop to the ground became a lunge.

Which became a fall and Ruby felt herself sail through the air.

Sara's hired man darted forward and threw out his arms in an attempt to catch her. They collided. Hard. One second, Ruby felt herself hurling through the air and the next, she slammed into something solid. Her head smacked into the man's chin. His arms went around her, and the two of them crashed to the muddy ground with her on top of him. As they landed, there was a loud thump and a groan, and her would-be rescuer sagged backward with her full weight on top of him.

Arms and legs akimbo, Ruby rolled off the hired man into the puddle. Instantly, cold water soaked her stockings and skirt. She tried to get her balance by supporting herself with her left hand, but it slipped and she went facedown into the muck. Gasping, she scrambled up, intent on putting distance between her and Sara's hired man. She was mortified. She'd never live this down. How would she ever look the man in the eye? How could she face the matchmaker? Had any potential bride ever made such an embarrassing entrance to Sara's home?

Ruby glanced down at the man on the ground, steeling herself to meet an angry expression. But there was none. He hadn't moved. He lay there stretched on the ground with his eyes closed, his features slack, and the rain beating against his face. Ruby's heart leaped in her chest. Had she killed him? Crushed him beneath her weight? Ruby had what her mother called a *sturdy* frame. All the women on her mother's side were short and stocky.

"Are you hurt?" she yelled. And immediately felt a deep flush wash up her throat and face. Of course, he was hurt. Otherwise he wouldn't still be lying there in the pouring rain.

He lay there as motionless, as lifeless as the granite mounting block standing beside Sara's hitching post.

"Ach," Ruby wailed.

She dropped to her knees and lifted his head. His crumpled wool hat fell away. His face was as pale as buttermilk. His thick brown hair felt sticky to her touch. She jerked her hand back and stared at it, watching the rivulets of red rain. Not red rain. Blood. He was bleeding. A lot. Trickles of blood were running down out of his hair onto the grass. "Sara!" she shouted over her shoulder. "Sara! Come quick! I think I've killed your hired man!"

Joseph groaned and opened his eyes. A woman's beautiful face loomed over his. He gasped and let his eyes fall shut again. Where was he? He must be dreaming. He felt as if he were spinning and there was a throbbing ache in the back of his head. But he wanted to see those warm brown eyes again... He had to know if she was real or just his imagination.

"Hiram, wake up. You have to wake up," A melodic, feminine voice urged. "Please don't die." He felt her hands on his chest. "You can't die."

Hiram? Hiram was dying? Joseph drew in a deep breath and forced his eyes open again. What had happened to Hiram? And why was he dreaming about Sara's hired man? Joseph parted his lips and tried to speak, but soft fingertips pressed against them.

"Hush, don't try to talk. Save your strength."

Save his strength? What for? He started to try to sit up, but another wave of dizziness came over him.

A cool hand pressed against his forehead. "Everything's going to be all right," the voice said. But who was this lovely girl? And why was she so concerned about him?

"Who...who are you?" he managed to whisper.

"I'm Ruby. It's nice to meet you, Hiram."

What beautiful eyes she had. He'd never seen such beautiful eyes. They were a warm brown, almost the color of cinnamon, streaked with darker ribbons of walnut. They radiated compassion. He could feel himself melting under her gaze.

And her voice...

"Hiram?" he repeated thickly. "I'm not Hiram."

"Oh, Sara," the lovely girl said, speaking over her shoulder. "He's hurt bad. He can't remember his own name."

Sara's chuckle cut through the fog in Joseph's head like a fresh breeze.

"That's not Hiram," Sara exclaimed. "This is one of my clients, Joseph Brenneman." The matchmaker came to stand over him.

Her voice faded and then came back to him. Joseph wasn't certain if only a moment had passed or an hour. But it was still raining. "I've called Hannah's daughter, Grace," the matchmaker said, holding an umbrella over him. "Emergency cell phone came in handy. You've got quite a bump there. Hit it on the edge of the brick flowerbed. I think you need to go into town for stitches. The immediate care clinic should be open. Be cheaper and faster than the hospital. I don't think you need an emergency room." This last statement seemed to be as much for herself as him.

"I need stitches?" Joseph reached back to gingerly touch his head, but all he could feel was cloth.

"Yes, you need stitches," the sweet voice chimed in. "Don't fuss with it. The towel is to stop the bleeding."

He blinked, trying to focus and then she was there again, the beautiful woman. "You're Ruby?" he asked. Where had she come from? Could this be the one Ellie had said that Sara had gone to pick up at the bus station? And then in bits and pieces, he remembered going out into the rain to help the women out of the buggy. The

girl with the sweet voice had been getting down and…
Had she fallen? She must have. Apparently, somehow,
they'd fallen together. He stared at her, then lowered
his gaze, overcome with shyness.

"I'm so sorry," she said. "It's all my fault."

"Ne." He slowly sat up, holding the wet towel against
the back of his head. He wondered where his hat was.
It wasn't proper for him to meet this lovely girl without
his head covered. "I… I should have…have caught you."
Joseph tried to remember what Ellie had said about
her. Ruby. Even her name was special. Had Ellie said
Ruby was coming to marry someone? Was she already
spoken for?

Not that it would matter. Ruby would think him a
hopeless woodenhead now, a klutz who'd slipped and
broken his skull.

"Here's Grace now," Sara said. "We were in luck.
She was just next door. She'll drive you into Dover and
get you patched up." And then to Ruby, Sara explained,
"Grace is my cousin's daughter. She's Mennonite and
drives a car."

"I don't think I need to see a doctor," Joseph protested. "It's just a little bump on the head." He raised
his gaze to Ruby again.

Sara scoffed. "Nonsense. You cracked your head like
a melon. You need more stitches than I'd like to put in
you. And you're not to worry about the cost. You fell
in my yard, and I'll pay for everything."

"Do you feel well enough to walk?" Grace appeared
at his side, taking his arm.

"I can walk," Joseph said.

"I'm going with him." Ruby grabbed his other arm
to help him to his feet. "It's the least I can do."

Sara looked at her. "Are you certain? Not sure how long the wait will be."

"*Ne*, I want to," Ruby insisted.

"Well, then, go and change your dress and stockings. There's no need for you to go out with your things wet and dirty," Sara replied. "You look as if you've been swimming in a mud puddle."

"I'll hurry," Ruby said.

Walking to Grace's motor vehicle took more effort than Joseph expected. Every step he took was a shaky one. His stomach churned and his head throbbed. He felt foolish with the towel on his head. As they made their way to the black SUV, he remembered his horse and buggy. He'd come to see Sara, and his horse was still harnessed and tied in her shed. "My horse," he began, but Sara patted his hand.

"Don't worry. Hiram will take care of him. Plenty of room in my barn."

"He's wet," Joseph said.

"I said you're not to worry." She peered into his face. "Hiram can rub him down and give him a nice ration of oats."

Joseph slid into the back seat and leaned back, gratefully resting his aching head. He thought he only closed his eyes for a moment but then the door on the other side opened and Ruby climbed in. "It will be all right," she said soothingly.

A short time later, they arrived at the urgent care facility and Joseph, Sara and Ruby got out of the car.

"I'll call you when we need a ride home," Sara told Grace. "No telling how long a wait we'll have." She turned to Joseph as they went through the automatic doors at the entrance. "You two just find a seat in the waiting room. I'll check you in. Hopefully, they'll see you soon."

But the walk-in facility was busy and it was obvious he wasn't going to see a doctor right away. Instead, Ruby guided him to a corner of the crowded room while Sara checked him in. Ruby found two empty seats side by side and proceeded to convince another waiting patient and his mother into moving to the far wall so that Sara could sit with her and Joseph. As Joseph watched Ruby, he couldn't help but be surprised a young woman could be so assertive with *Englishers* in a strange town.

"You'll be able to see the television better from over there," Ruby assured the woman who was wearing a tight Superman T-shirt, cut-off denim shorts and cowboy boots.

Her child, a stout, red-faced boy of about eight, didn't appear to be too sick to Joseph. In one hand the boy clutched a can of soda, in the other a bag of chips. But he was whining that he was hungry and needed a candy bar from the vending machine. The kid's head was shaved except for a standing ridge down the center, two inches high and a thin braid hanging down the back of his dirty shirt.

"You'll be closer to the snacks, as well," Ruby said with a cheery smile as she scooped up the woman's rain jacket and handed it to her. The boy's mother reluctantly gathered her belongings and moved toward the other vacant seats. "Terrible, isn't it, how you have to wait?" Ruby went on. "We're so grateful that you were kind enough to allow our friend to sit with us."

"I want a candy bar!" the boy whined.

"All right, all right," the woman said as she and her son walked away.

Joseph glanced at Ruby as she plopped her black purse on the empty seat on one side of him and sat down in the other one. He wanted to tell her how much he admired her ability to deal with the situation, but as usual, words failed him. All that he could manage was, "Your English is *goot.* I mean *good.*"

To his delight, she turned that sweet smile on him. "Thank you."

Joseph felt his face grow warm and he averted his eyes.

"My *mommi* and *daddi* thought it was important that I learn English early on. Most parents from our church send their little ones off to school not knowing a single word, but not my *mam* and *dat.* Not my parents. No, indeed…"

Joseph stole a glimpse of Ruby as she chattered on. Usually, when he was with a girl, he was too nervous to get out a sensible word. He liked girls; he desperately wanted a wife. A family. He just wasn't good at meeting girls. Talking to them.

Ruby asked him a question, but then thankfully went on, not waiting for him to come up with a clever reply. She just kept talking and he kept staring at her, not even trying to hide his infatuation now.

Joseph couldn't believe this was happening. If he'd known that falling and cracking his head would have gotten him the attention of a beautiful young woman, he would have done it long ago. Best of all, Ruby wasn't blaming him. She seemed to think that it was *her* fault. And she didn't appear to care whether he talked or not. She seemed to have no problem talking for them both.

Joseph glanced up and saw Sara, who had taken the seat Ruby had saved for her, looking at them. He wondered what she was thinking. Did she think he was slow-witted because Ruby was talking and he wasn't? Some people who didn't know him well thought he was slow. Even his mother agonized over his lack of knowing what to say when girls were nearby. "Speak up," she always told him. When he was a boy, it was "Stand up straight, Joseph. Look people in the eye when they speak to you. Do you want the teacher to think you have an overripe cucumber for a brain?" And now that he was a man full grown, it was "God gave you a mind. Why can't you show it when it matters most?"

Joseph became aware that Ruby had stopped speaking. He looked into her eyes and was rewarded with another compassionate smile. She was waiting for him to say something, but what? He tried to think. What had she been saying? He was so overwhelmed by her presence that he was at a total loss. And just when he thought the floor would open and swallow him up, Sara came to his rescue.

"Ruby comes to us from Lancaster County in Pennsylvania," Sara said, handing Ruby her purse. "I've promised her parents that I'll find her a match."

"Who is it?" he blurted. Was it Levi King? Jason Bontrager? If she'd set her *kapp* for either of them, he wouldn't have the chance of a pullet in a fox den. Levi could charm the birds from the trees. And Jason had a blacksmith's shoulders and a father with more farms than he had sons.

"She's not spoken for yet," Sara said. "But I'm certain it won't be long before we'll all be invited to her wedding."

Ruby blushed prettily.

Then Sara added icing to the cake by saying, "Our

Joseph is looking for a bride. He's a master mason, and is a credit to his mother and community."

"Is your father living?" Ruby asked. "*Ach*, maybe I shouldn't have asked that. I have a wonderful father." Without taking a breath, she switched from smooth and perfect English to *Deitsch*. "He's so good to me. And he loves to laugh. Everyone says I look like my mother but I'm most like my father. I hope that if I do find someone to wed, we won't live far from my parents. I'm devoted to them."

She paused and looked at him expectantly. What was he supposed to say?

"Joseph's father died when he was very young," Sara said. She reached into her bag and pulled out a Christian romance novel. "I hope the two of you won't mind, but I'm dying to see what happens in my book."

"Do you like to read?" Ruby asked Joseph as Sara settled in her chair.

He nodded. Instantly, his head began to throb again and it was all he could do not to reach up to touch the towel. But he didn't want her to think he was a complainer or that he wasn't tough.

"Don't move," Ruby cautioned, brushing her hand against his wet sleeve. "I don't want you to start bleeding again. I feel so terrible that you were hurt. And I'm entirely to blame. I'm such a klutz. You may as well know it. I've always been a klutz."

"I read," he managed. "The Bible. And *The Budget*."

"Your injury will probably be written up in *The Budget*. I hope no one mentions my name. It's so embarrassing. And you'll probably miss work. Will your boss be angry with you?"

"*Ne*. I… I'm sort of an independent contractor."

"You are? That's wonderful." She clasped her hands together. They were nice hands. "What kind of masonry do you do? Bricklaying? Stonework? Cement?"

"*Ya.* All."

"And you're a master mason already? You must do fine work."

"I try."

She smiled at him. "Listen to me. When I'm nervous, I talk too much." She chuckled. "Truth is, I always talk too much. Are you thirsty? Hungry? There are vending machines over there. The least I can do is to buy you a drink. Wait, I'll go see what they have." She got up, taking her purse with her, and threaded her way through the waiting people to the corner.

Sara glanced at him. The corners of her mouth were drawn up in a "cat that swallowed the cream" hint of a smile. "Ruby talks a lot, doesn't she?"

"Not too much," Joseph defended, watching Ruby. "Just the right amount, I think."

Ruby returned. "They have Coke, orange, lemon-lime and root beer. Then there's bottled water and iced tea in a can. What would you like?"

Joseph reached for his wallet.

"*Ne,*" Ruby said firmly, patting her purse. "This is my treat. I insist."

"All right." Feeling bold, he returned her smile and said, "Next time, I pay."

"But what would you like?" she asked.

"Soda is good."

"But what kind?"

He shrugged. "Anything wet."

She giggled. "*Ne,* you have to tell me what you like best."

"R-root beer," he managed. "I like root beer."

The smile spread across her face, making her even more beautiful. "Me too. I love it. My *daddi* says that I like it too well. It's not good for my teeth. But I drink it anyway."

Her teeth looked fine to him. White and even and sparkling.

"And now you get to choose a snack. Pretzels. Chips. Candy. Or peanut butter crackers."

"Crackers," he said. "I like…crackers."

"Me too." She laughed, looking down at him like he was the cleverest man she had ever met. "Isn't that funny? We both like the same treats. Sara, I'm not forgetting you. What would you like?"

Sara glanced up from her book. "I'm fine. Too many treats and I'll grow out of my clothes. You young people enjoy your snacks."

"If you're sure," Ruby said, turning back to Joseph. "I'll be right back with your soda and crackers."

As she walked away, he noticed that she was wearing a green dress. He liked green. He smiled to himself as he watched her. His head hurt and he was still feeling a little dazed, but it didn't matter because this was turning out to be the best day of his life.

Chapter Two

Joseph pushed back his plate. He'd eaten only a few bites of potato salad and nibbled at a fried chicken leg. The truth was the back of his head where he'd gotten the stitches stung and he didn't have much of an appetite. And he had more on his mind than eating.

"Joseph, you've barely put a thing in your mouth." His mother's delicate forehead wrinkled with concern. "I knew you should have stayed in bed this morning. Does your head hurt? Are you dizzy?" She fluttered her hands helplessly over her plate. For a small woman, Joseph was always amazed at how much his mother could eat and never gain an extra pound.

He forced a smile and took a sip of the glass of buttermilk next to his plate. Normally, he loved buttermilk, but today, it tasted flat on his tongue. "Now, don't fuss. A few stitches. Nothing for you to worry yourself over."

His mother rose, came around the table and pressed a cool palm to his forehead. "You feel a little warm to me. You might be running a fever."

"*Ne*, no fever," he protested. "It's a hot day. Near ninety, I'd guess. And you've made enough food for two families." It was stifling there in the kitchen. All the windows were open, but no breeze stirred the plain white curtains. It made a man think longingly of cool autumn mornings.

His mother, Magdalena, nibbled at her lower lip. "It wouldn't hurt for you to go back to the doctor."

Joseph raised a hand in protest. "Mother, *ne*, really. There's no need for you to be concerned. I slipped in the mud and knocked my head. It's nothing. I've had far worse. Remember when I fell out of the hayloft?"

"And landed in the pile of manure your father had just forked out of the cow stall," she finished for him with a chuckle. "At least you had no stitches then."

"No stitches, but I broke my arm in two places."

"We felt so awful." She shook her head ruefully. "My only *kinder*, my precious seven-year-old son in so much pain. We rushed you to the hospital and there you were all covered in muck and stinking like an outhouse with all them *Englishers* staring at us. Such a bad mother, they must have thought, to have no care for her child."

They traded smiles at the shared memory. He'd long ago forgotten the hurt of the broken arm. What he remembered was that he'd gone all that summer unable to swim in the pond with his friends, and that his father and mother had churned ice cream for him every Saturday. He wiped his eyes with the napkin, rubbing away the tears of laughter and maybe something more. That summer and the taste of that sweet ice cream on his tongue were some of the last memories he had of his father. His *dat* had been killed in a farming accident that September.

His mother was still hovering, something she had a tendency to do. "Maybe you could manage a slice of pie?" she coaxed. "Peach. Your favorite. I made it especially for you."

Which was what she said of most meals... "Save it all for supper tonight," Joseph answered. "I've got an errand to run this afternoon, and I'll be sure to be hungry later. We'll have everything cold, and you won't even have to heat up the kitchen by turning on the stove." His mother pursed her lips and began clearing away the dishes. Her silence and the pained expression on her face was an obvious sign of her disapproval.

"Can I help you clean up?" he offered.

She shook her head. "This is my job, Joseph. It's the least I can do, being a widow and dependent on your charity."

Joseph bit back the retort that this house was hers as long as she lived and he loved her and would never consider her a burden. He'd said that many times before. Instead, he rose to put the milk and chicken into the refrigerator.

Theirs was a small kitchen for an Amish house, but it provided everything his mother needed to cook and preserve food from her garden. He'd worked hard since he was fifteen to provide for the two of them, and his *mam* had done her share by keeping their home as shiny as a new penny. The Bible said to honor your mother and father, and he tried to always remember that when she was being difficult.

There'd never been any doubt in Joseph's mind that she loved him and wanted what was best for him. Twice she could have remarried, but both times she'd refused, even though both prospective husbands could have given her a more spacious home and an easier life. "A stepfather might be harsh on you," she'd said. "And your needs might be lost in a large family of stepbrothers and stepsisters. We're better on our own."

Joseph smiled at her as he crossed the room to take his hat from the peg near the door. It fit a little snug because the emergency room doctor had shaved the back of his head and covered the six stitches with a thick bandage. But he could hardly show up at the matchmaker's without his head covered. It wouldn't be proper.

"Where are you going?" His mother removed the plate of chicken from the refrigerator where he'd just put it and covered it with a clean length of cheesecloth before placing it back in the refrigerator. "I think you'd best put your errand off for a few days," she said. "No need for you to go out in this afternoon heat."

"I'll be fine," Joseph assured her. "I won't be long."

"Where did you say you were going?" She dropped her hands to her hips and tilted her head in that way she always did that reminded him of a curious little wren. Her bright blue eyes narrowed. "Joseph?"

"I didn't say." He opened the back door. "I'll be back in plenty of time to milk the cow before supper."

"But Joseph—"

He closed the door behind him and kept walking. He loved his mother dearly, but if he let her have her way, she'd treat him as though he was twelve years old and not in his late twenties. He was blessed to have a mother who loved him so much, but she had a strong will, and it was sometimes a struggle as to who was the head of their house. She was sensitive, and if he was too firm with her, she'd dissolve in tears. He couldn't stand the idea of making his mother cry and he felt relieved that she hadn't wept when he hadn't done what she'd wanted and stayed home.

Turning to a matchmaker to find him a wife had been his mother's idea, and after hearing her talk about it for nearly two years, he'd weakened and agreed to let Sara Yoder see if she would have more success than he had on his own. He'd been reluctant and more than a little nervous because he'd always been tongue-tied around young women. He'd never imagined that he'd meet anyone like Ruby so quickly or in such an unusual way.

Whistling, Joseph descended the porch steps. Glancing back over his shoulder, he caught a glimpse of white curtain moving at a window. As he'd suspected, his mother was watching him. He strode around the house to his mother's flowerbed, out of her sight, and quickly picked a bouquet of colorful blooms. A girl like Ruby probably had lots of fellows saying sweet stuff to her, but girls liked flowers. Maybe they could speak for him.

Everyone talked about his mother's skill at growing flowers. She had beds of them that brightened the front yard and clustered around the house. She rarely cut them for the house, but from early spring to late autumn she had beautiful bouquets to sell at Spence's Auction. He didn't claim to know much about them other than to turn over the soil when she asked him or to fertilize and weed the beds, but he'd seen her create enough bouquets to know what flowers went with each other. For Ruby, he chose a rainbow of cosmos, sweet peas, zinnias and asters. He cradled the stems in peat moss and wrapped them in green florist's paper just as he'd seen his mother do for her stand at Spence's Market. He still had the headache, but he was whistling as he hitched up his driving horse to the cart.

All the way to Sara's house, Joseph tried to think of something sensible to say to Ruby when he gave her the flowers. He even practiced saying the words aloud. It wasn't difficult to be clever when there was no one to hear him but the horse. Should he speak to her in *Deitsch* or English? She'd told him that she was from Pennsylvania. Those Amish up there were less conservative. Maybe she'd think he was old-fashioned if he spoke *Deitsch*. So English. But what did he say?

"A little something to welcome you to Seven Poplars." That was good, but should it be "*welcome* you" or "welcome *you*"? What word should he emphasize? Or maybe that would sound too put-on. They'd talked a lot in the urgent care waiting room. If he welcomed her, it might appear that he was acting like she was just another of Sara's clients and she wasn't special.

Joseph's stomach flip-flopped. He felt a little light-headed. His head still hurt, but he didn't think that was the cause of his distress. The truth was, he was scared. His mouth was dry and it was hard to think straight. He'd always heard of love striking a man like lightning cutting down a tree, but he'd never believed it until now. Ruby Plank falling into his arms was the most exciting thing that had ever happened to him and he didn't want to mess it up.

The trouble was, when it came to girls, he always did. And he was terrified that this time would be no different. Joseph was still going over and over in his mind what he would say as he approached Sara Yoder's back door. The yard had been quiet, without anyone in sight, and he couldn't hear any talking from inside. Sara's house was usually bustling with young people coming and going, but today he didn't see so much as a dragonfly hovering over the flowerbeds along the drive. What if he'd come to find that some other fellow had taken

Ruby buggy riding? Or worse, what if she'd changed her mind about making a match after yesterday's disaster and returned to Pennsylvania?

Gathering his courage, he knocked on the wooden screen door. No one appeared, so he knocked again, and then called out in *Deitsch*. "Hello? Is anybody to home?" Again, there was only silence except for a bee that had gotten trapped on the screen porch and was buzzing loudly as it attempted to escape.

Joseph's stomach turned over. Now his head was really hurting. He was hot and sweaty, and he'd crossed his mother and come here hoping to see Ruby again. All for nothing. But he wasn't ready to give up yet. Maybe they were in the garden and hadn't heard him. He left the porch and circled around the house. In the side yard, farthest from the drive, was a wooden swing, a brick walk, a fishpond and a fountain. "Hello?" he called again.

And then he stopped short. There was a blanket spread on the clover near the tiny pond. A young woman lay stretched out on her stomach, bare ankles crossed, apparently lost in a book. But the most startling thing to Joseph was her hair. Among the Amish, a woman's hair was always covered. Little girls wore pigtails with baby caps or student *kapps*. Teenage girls and women of all ages pinned their hair up in a bun and covered it with a scarf or a prayer *kapp*.

This woman was clearly Amish because she wore a sky blue dress with a dark apron over it. Black leather shoes stood beside the blanket with black stockings tossed beside them. But the woman's hair wasn't pinned up under a *kapp* or covered with a scarf. It rippled in a thick shimmering mane down the back of her neck and over her shoulders nearly to her waist.

Joseph's mouth gaped. He clutched the bouquet of flowers so tightly between his hands that he distinctly heard several stems snap. He swallowed, unable to stop staring at her beautiful hair. It was brown, but brown in so many shades…tawny and russet…the color of shiny acorns in winter and the hue of ripe wheat. He knew he shouldn't be staring. He'd intruded on a private moment, seen what he shouldn't. He should turn and walk away. But he couldn't.

He inhaled deeply. "Hello," he stammered. "I'm sorry, I was looking for—"

"Ach!" The young woman rose on one elbow and twisted to face him. It was Ruby. Her eyes widened in surprise. "Joseph?"

"Ya. It's me." He struggled to think of something else sensible to say.

Ruby sat up, dropping her paperback onto the blanket, pulling her knees up and tucking her feet under her skirt. "I was drying my hair," she said. "I washed it. I still had mud in it from last night."

Joseph grimaced. "Sorry."

"Ne." She shook her head. "It was all my fault."

"An accident," he said.

"And you had to get stitches. Are you in pain?"

He shook his head.

"Goot. I was worried about you."

He tried not to smile, but the thought that she'd worried about him filled him with hope.

"Everyone else went to Byler's store." She blushed prettily and covered her face with her hands. "But I stayed home. To wash my hair. What must you think of me without my *kapp*?" Her words were apologetic, but her tone was mischievous, rather than guilty. Dropping her hands, she chuckled.

She had a merry laugh, Joseph thought, a laugh as beautiful and unique as she was. She was regarding him with definite interest. Her eyes were the shade of cinnamon splashed with swirls of chocolate, large and thickly lashed. His mouth went dry.

She smiled encouragingly.

He shrugged. A dozen thoughts tumbled in his mind: he could comment about the color of her dress or ask her what she was reading or say something about the weather, but nothing seemed like the right thing to say. "I… I never know what to say to pretty girls," he admitted as he tore his gaze away from hers. "You must think I'm thickheaded." He shuffled his feet. "I'll come back another time when—"

"Who are those flowers for?" Ruby asked. "Did you bring them for Sara?"

"*Ne*, not Sara." Joseph's face grew hot. He tried to say "I brought them for you," but again the words stuck in his throat. Dumbly, he held them out to her. Several of the asters in the bouquet had broken stems and they hung down awkwardly. It took every ounce of his courage not to turn and run.

She scrambled to her feet, her smile as sweet as sunrise on a winter day, her beautiful eyes sparkling with pleasure. *"Danki,"* she said as she reached for the bouquet. "I love flowers. Nobody ever brought me flowers before." She clutched them to her. "I think they're wonderful."

For a long moment, they stood staring at each other. Ruby's hair tumbled down around her shoulders, still damp from the washing, the thick locks gleaming in the sunlight. Her hair looked so soft that he wanted to touch it, to feel the curls spring between his fingers.

Joseph stepped back another step and sucked in a breath of air. They were practically strangers. He shouldn't be here with her without a chaperone. He shouldn't be looking at her unbound hair. It was scandalous. If anyone found out, there would be talk. He couldn't do that to Ruby. "I g-guess I should go," he blurted. "I shouldn't… We shouldn't—"

"Ne," she said. "Don't go yet. Wait here. No, sit there." She waved toward the wooden swing. It was fashioned of cedar, suspended on a sturdy frame and shaded by a latticework canopy. "Where it's cooler. Wait there. I'll be right back." She ran several yards, then turned and ran back. "Stay right there," she repeated before grabbing up everything in the blanket and dashing around the house.

Stunned, Joseph did as she said. Truthfully, it was good to get off his feet and when he gave a small push, the motion of the swing eased the tension in his neck and shoulders. What had he been thinking to come here this afternoon? To bring flowers for Ruby? But he'd had to come. He couldn't get her off his mind. But he'd never expected her to be so sweet. He closed his eyes and thought about how pretty her unbound hair was.

Ruby slammed the kitchen door shut behind her. *"Ya!"* she exclaimed joyfully. *"Ya!"* Laughing, she spun around in a circle and buried her face in the flowers. Joseph had come back! She'd been certain that knocking him nearly senseless and sending him to the hospital had ruined any chance she might have had of attracting the respectable young mason. But, in spite of her clumsiness, he'd returned and brought her flowers. It was almost too good to be true. She couldn't wait to tell her mother.

But Joseph had caught her in the yard, sprawled out on a blanket with her hair wet and hanging instead of being decently covered with her *kapp*, she reminded herself. He'd been shocked. Probably he'd come in search of one of the other girls and only given her the flowers to be kind. But he was kind. And not only good-looking, but sweet natured and clearly in search of a wife. She didn't dare let herself hope that he might choose her, but neither could she throw away any opportunity she might have.

Her mother's words of advice came to her as clearly as if her *mommi* were here in this room with her. *You will find someone who will see your inner beauty, Ruby. And he will be the one who deserves you.*

Coming to Sara Yoder's and asking the matchmaker to find her a husband had been an act of desperation. Her parents had believed that the only way for her to find someone was to go to a place where no one knew her. And now Joseph had fallen into her lap. Or, rather, she'd fallen into his. She couldn't let him slip through her fingers. He might not be someone that she wanted to marry, but she couldn't know that until they were better acquainted.

Dropping the flowers into the sink, she searched for a container to put them in. Spying an old blue-and-white-speckled bowl and pitcher on a table in the adjoining room, she snatched up the pitcher, dumped the flowers in and filled the pitcher half-full of water. She left the arrangement on the counter and ran upstairs to her bedroom to make herself decent.

Grabbing a brush, she raked it though her damp hair, twisted the mass into a knot and pinned it securely at the back of her head. She snatched up her *kapp* and took the stairs to the first floor two at a time. What if Joseph hadn't stayed in the yard? What if he'd examined the book she'd been reading and discovered that it was one of Sara's romance novels? Would he think she was flighty?

Breathlessly, she filled glasses with ice and lemonade and hurried back outside. "Let him still be here," she whispered. "Please let him be here." She felt as though she'd swallowed a double handful of goose feathers. She liked Joseph; she really did. And she wanted him to like her. She stopped short, seeing the empty swing. Her heart sank and her knees went weak.

And then she saw him on his knees beside the fishpond. "Joseph!" she called too loudly. She gave him her best smile as she hurried toward him.

"Ruby." He rose and stepped back from the lip of the pool. "Her fish are getting big," he said. "I saw an orange-and-black one." Joseph's hat was crooked, and she could see that it was too tight due to the bulky bandage.

"I brought you a drink," she said. "It's hot out here. I hope you like lemonade."

Joseph nodded. "*Ya*, I do." His lips curved in a tentative smile.

She'd been with him all evening, here at the house and at the hospital, but she hadn't really gotten a good look at him. She'd remembered his amazing eyes, but memory wasn't as good as looking at him here in full daylight. They were as blue as cornflowers, intelligent, and they inspired trust. They were *Deitsch* blue eyes that seemed lit from within. He wasn't a huge man, but neither was he small. He was exactly the right size, she decided, tall enough without being gangly, and broad at the shoulders without appearing muscle-bound. Joseph's nose was straight and well formed, and he had a smattering of freckles across his rosy cheeks.

Was this the man her mother promised her would come?

Joseph reached for the glass.

Suddenly, she was aware that she'd been staring at him, lost in her own thoughts while he was waiting for his cold drink. She shoved the lemonade at him with too much force. As his hand closed around the glass, ice and liquid splashed across the front of his shirt.

"Ne!" she protested. "I'm so sorry."

Joseph looked down at his shirt and laughed. "That's one way to cool me off."

"It's all my fault," she said. "I'm such a klutz."

"My fault. I was looking at you and not the glass."

Ruby shook her head. She felt sick. "You might as well know I always trip or drop or knock over things. I always have. When I was in school, the teacher called me stumble-bumble. I never got to write on the blackboard because I either snapped off the chalk or dropped the eraser and then kicked it when I leaned over to pick it up or—" She gestured, showing him the hopelessness of the situation.

"Yeah, well…did you ever get up in front of the whole school and the parents and…and…not be able to say your own name?" Joseph asked.

"You didn't," she exclaimed.

"I… I did." He paused and then went on. "It was

our Christmas party. I was supposed to recite a poem. It was short, just six lines. But I couldn't get past my name. I just stood there like a block of wood with my mouth open, trying not to cry."

Ruby pressed her lips together. "I know what you mean. It's bad when I tip over the milk bucket or catch my apron in the barn door, but it's worse when people are watching."

He shook his head. "Anyone can have an accident."

"But I make a regular habit of it."

"Then I'd best take that other glass before you dump it over my head," he teased.

For an instant, she thought he was mocking her, but when she saw the expression on his face, she was certain she'd made a friend. She gave him her lemonade and followed him sheepishly to the swing.

"You...you sit first," Joseph said.

She could feel herself blushing, but she didn't feel as though she was going to throw up anymore. She felt happy. She'd sent him to the hospital with a broken head and she'd tried to drown him in lemonade, and he didn't seem to care. He was smiling at her the way she'd seen other boys smile at the girls they wanted to drive home from singings.

"Admit it," he said. "You've never been at a loss for words."

Ruby shook her head as he handed her lemonade to her. "Words I have aplenty," she said. "Too many according to some people. My grandfather used to say that I talked faster than a horse could trot." She sighed. "I've tried to stop and think before I speak, but the words bubble up inside me, and when I open my mouth they fly out."

"I don't think you talk too much," Joseph pronounced solemnly. "I like to hear you talk." He chuckled. "It keeps me from having to try and keep up my end of the conversation."

She gazed down at her drink and considered what he'd just said. She took a sip of the lemonade. It was a little tart.

Joseph took a seat beside her. There was a gap between them, not too much, and not too little. They were far enough apart to satisfy propriety. "I have more work than I can do," he said. "Bricklaying. Cement. Fireplaces."

She held her breath.

"I asked Sara to try to find me a wife."

Ruby's heartbeat quickened.

"And...and I know that's why you're staying with Sara." He met her gaze. "To...to find a husband, I mean, not to find a wife."

She smiled at him, thinking he was the cutest thing she'd ever seen.

"If you don't have anyone either, maybe—" he swallowed, and his fingers tightened on the glass "—I thought... I mean... I hoped we..."

"Could see if we suit each other?" she finished for him.

Joseph nodded eagerly.

"I'd like that," she said. "I'd like that very much."

"Me too," he agreed. He looked down. "But... I suppose I... It's only fair I should tell you I... I have a good trade and I work hard, but I'm far from well-off. And... and you should know that I have a widowed mother that I'm responsible for." He spread his hands. "I'm a plain... plain man, Ruby. If that's not what you're looking for..."

She clapped her hands together and smiled at him. "That's exactly what I'm looking for, Joseph Brenneman. I think we'll suit each other very well."

Chapter Three

"It...it's early. I... I know," Joseph said, hat in hand at Sara's back door. It was Wednesday morning, and he was starting a foundation for the Moses King family's addition today. He had a lot of work to do. But he couldn't wait any longer to speak to the matchmaker. "Could I? That is...is..." As usual, the words he wanted to say caught in his throat, choking him. He could feel his face growing hot. Sara would think him a fool. Maybe she was right.

Sara stepped out onto the porch in her bare feet. She was a round, tidy woman with crinkly dark hair, and dark eyes that seemed to bore through him. "Ruby isn't here," she said. "She went off with Ellie to the schoolhouse. Ellie's our teacher. Today is their first day, and Ruby offered to give her a hand getting the first graders settled in."

"Didn't come to—" He broke off when he realized that he was practically shouting at Sara in an effort to get the words out. "Came to see you." The last bit came in a rush, like shelled peas popping out of a shell all at once. He groaned inwardly. Why was this so hard?

Words rolled off his cousin Andy's tongue so easily. Tyler never seemed to have trouble talking to women. Joseph took a deep breath. "I want…" He swallowed the lump in his throat. "Ruby. Make a match. You. With us."

Sara's shrewd face softened. "This sounds serious, Joseph. Maybe you'd best come to my office. I don't like to discuss business in front of other people. I like to keep things confidential until matches are formally announced. To give everyone privacy."

Joseph nodded and tugged on the brim of his straw work hat. He'd shaved and showered that morning. It was important to look his best. He might sound like a hayseed, but there was no need to look like one. He'd even worn a new shirt his mother just made him, but he had an old one in the buggy that he could change into when he got to the King house. If he ruined this one with concrete, his mother would not be happy, and when she wasn't happy, home could be an unpleasant place. But the shirt didn't matter now. It was what he had to get straight with Sara.

"Ruby," he blurted. Her name came out in a whisper, which he corrected in a deep and more insistent tone. "Ruby. I… I want to talk to you about…" He looked down at his boots. "Her," he finished in a rush of breath.

When he looked up, a hint of a smile lit Sara's almond-shaped eyes, but her mouth remained firm. After a second's hesitation, she held open the door and motioned him into the kitchen.

A tall girl in a lilac dress was washing dishes at the sink while an even prettier one dried. The tall one turned to smile at him. "Arlene," Sara said, "This is Joseph Brenneman. Leah, I think you know each other."

"Hello, Joseph," Leah said. "It's good to see you

again." And then to Arlene, "Joseph's from another church district, but we used to see each other at auctions and work frolics."

Arlene nodded. Smiled.

"Ya." Joseph's cheeks burned with embarrassment. Leah had once hit a home run when he was pitching at an interschool game. She'd married a Mennonite and gone to South America to be a missionary. He'd died and now Leah had come back to Seven Poplars; she was staying with the matchmaker. Leah had always been known as the beauty of the county and she'd been nice too. But he'd never been drawn to her, not even as a boy still wet behind the ears. "Ruby," he managed. "I… came for Ruby. About Ruby," he corrected. "A match… with Ruby. Maybe," he added. "I hope," he clarified.

Arlene chuckled. "I see," she replied in *Deitsch*.

She wore a different-style *kapp* than Leah and the other local girls, a shape of prayer covering Joseph wasn't familiar with. Ruby did too, but hers wasn't like Arlene's. Ruby's was heart shaped. He decided that he liked Ruby's *kapp* better.

Thankfully, Sara rescued him from having to say anything else by leading him through the kitchen to her office. Sara gestured to a chair in front of and facing a desk. She closed the door and took a seat behind the desk. The desktop was empty except for a spiral notebook and a black pen.

Joseph leaned forward in his chair. The windows were open, but with the door closed there wasn't any breeze and it was warm in here. Unconsciously, he ran a finger under his collar. Sara was just sitting there, looking at him. He couldn't have been more uncomfortable if she'd caught him chopping wood without his shirt. "I want…want to court Ruby," he declared bluntly.

"So I gather." Sara sat back and smiled. "This is a little sudden, don't you think? You've known each other, what? Three days? And that's including today, and I don't think you've even seen her today." Her eyes sparkled with amusement rather than disapproval.

Joseph shifted in his chair. It was straight backed, oak and had probably been made at the chair shop not half a mile away. His mouth felt dry and he was slightly light-headed. "*Ya,* but…" He exhaled. But what? How did he explain to Sara that how long they'd known each other had nothing to do with anything? That he'd known the moment he'd opened his eyes, lying flat out in Sara's driveway, that Ruby was the girl for him.

Sara's chuckle became a full-throated laugh. It was a jolly laugh for a woman and it came up from deep in her chest and bubbled out with genuine mirth.

Joseph stood up. He wasn't going to sit here and be laughed at.

"Sit down, sit down," Sara insisted, waving her hand at him. "I wasn't laughing at you. I was surprised. But in a good way, Joseph. I'm just not used to young men being in such a hurry." She laced her fingers together, leaned forward and rested her hands on the desktop. "Don't you want to get to know Ruby a little before you start talking about marriage?"

"*Ne.*" He shook his head, settling in the chair again. "She's the one. For me." He forced himself to meet Sara's piercing gaze. "I like Ruby."

"You've made that clear." Sara's attitude grew kindly as she slipped on a pair of wire-frame glasses she'd retrieved from her apron pocket. "And it's clear that you're uncomfortable here with me. I'm sorry for that. I hope you can come to think of me as a friend, maybe a favorite aunt. I like you, Joseph. You appear to be a fine man and an excellent candidate for one of my brides-to-be. You're just the sort of man I like to find, someone who isn't wishy-washy, someone who knows his own mind." She paused and opened her notebook. She thumbed through until she'd reached a page about halfway through and picked up her pen. She jotted something down and then made eye contact with him again. "Sorry. I have a system, and if I don't keep to it, I'd forget who was who."

"Ruby's not spoken for, is she?" That was the question he'd been dreading to ask. He knew he'd asked Sara that before, but he was afraid that someone had snapped her up since then. Because if there were another suitor, there'd be a whole lot more trouble before things could get worked out. He wasn't going to give up. Sara had promised she could find him a wife; he just had to make her understand that Ruby was the one for him.

"Well…" Sara tapped her notebook with her pen. "I'd planned to introduce her to a blacksmith." She looked up. "And I'd wanted you to get to know Arlene. I think you'd be very compatible. But if you've seen Ruby and you're taken with her, there's no reason why the two of you shouldn't—"

"Then you have no problem matching us?"

Sara separated her hands and raised them, palms forward. "Now, just slow down, Joseph. It's customary for my couples to take this one step at a time—get to know each other before a match is actually made. Usually couples attend some singings together, have meals here at the house and see each other at church. Picking a wife or a husband is a serious matter."

He dropped his straw hat onto his knee and balled his hands into fists. They seemed clumsy, like two clubs rather than hands and he tucked them under his knees. His right foot wanted to bounce on his heel like he did when he was nervous but he forced it firmly to the floor and held it there by force of will. He was sweating. He could feel tiny beads of moisture trickling down the back of his shirt. Sara was looking at him expectantly. She was waiting for him to respond. "I… I know it's a serious matter. I told you when I first came to you that…that I was serious about finding a wife. And I'm ready. Ruby and me… Ruby and I," he corrected. "We've talked and we both want to court. Each other."

Sara raised an eyebrow speculatively. "Ruby told you that she's interested in courting you?"

"*Ya*, she did. She and I… We…we agreed."

Sara sat back in her chair. It was an oversize office chair, crafted of oak and comfortably cushioned. The chair swiveled and rocked. It was a chair that Joseph had seen at the chair shop and greatly admired, but it was big for a woman of Sara's size. She resembled a great-aunt of his, someone who'd always sneaked him cookies when he was a child. The thought of Aunt Rose made it feel a little easier talking to Sara.

Her smile widened. "Your mother said you were shy and that you had a difficult time expressing yourself. That doesn't seem to be the case at all. I'm impressed. And frankly, young men rarely impress me."

"I can support her… Support Ruby. And my mother. Mother has to live with us. But I told Ruby, and she's fine with it. As a mason…a master mason, I can always get work. I'm working with James now. His construction company, I mean. He says he's got plenty of work for me. And…and I have a house. In my own name."

Sara wrote something in her notebook. "It's good to know that you are financially solvent. That you can take on the responsibility of a household as a husband and father, if God blesses you and your future wife with children."

"I will. I mean… I expect to." He could feel perspiration trickle down his back. He needed to hurry this along, otherwise he'd be late to the job site and James would be disappointed. He liked to start on time. But this had to be settled first with Sara. About Ruby. He'd lain awake half the night worrying. He couldn't do that again. He realized that Sara was saying something about a dowry and he jerked upright, giving her his attention again.

"Do you mind?" she said.

"M-mind what?"

"Financial wealth of a girl's father." She peered over her glasses at him. "Is that something that's important to you?"

"Ne." He shook his head. "I don't care. Money… money isn't important to me. I mean…it is, but I don't expect… It doesn't matter. Ruby could be penniless. It's fine." He took a breath. "So, are we courting? Officially?"

"Ne. You are not. Not yet. It's simply not the way I operate," Sara said firmly. "I'm happy that you're committed, but I've had a lot of experience with matching couples. Often young people form attractions, infatuations, if you will. But marriages, *good* marriages are not built on infatuation. There has to be more, things

like mutual respect, compatibility and an equal commitment to faith. Think of it as laying a foundation." She indicated him with her hand. "You're a mason. You understand the need for a solid foundation."

"A house won't stand without it."

"Exactly. And for an Amish couple, the foundation is even more important. We marry for life. There's no divorce. Whoever you choose and whoever chooses you, chooses until death parts you."

"I—" A knock at the door interrupted what he was going to say.

"Ya?" Sara asked.

The office door opened and a man in a patched blue shirt and raggedy straw hat in his hand peered in. "Mule's thrown a shoe," he said. "What do you want me to do?"

"Take him to the smithy, Hiram. A mule can't work with three feet, can he?"

The door opened wider and Hiram stepped through. He was the man that Joseph had seen unloading a bag of feed from a wagon when he'd driven into Sara's yard. "Planning on cutting hay in that little field."

"Then it will have to wait. Tend to the mule first."

Hiram scratched his head. "Thought you'd say that."

"I'm in the middle of an appointment," Sara explained. "Close the door behind you."

"What do I do for money?" Hiram asked.

"The blacksmith will send me a bill." She raised a hand and waved at him. "Goodbye, Hiram. Thank you."

Hiram grimaced. "Leah said don't bother you. You got somebody in the office."

"That's right," Sara said. "When I'm with someone, I

don't like interruptions unless it's important. *Extremely* important."

"But the mule threw a shoe," he said doggedly.

She smiled. Her tone was kind when she spoke. "And I trust you to take the mule to the smithy and have a new shoe put on."

Muttering to himself, Hiram backed out of the room and pulled the door shut behind him.

"My hired man," Sara explained. "I'm sorry. You were saying?"

Joseph stared at the toes of his work boots. "I was saying that I...that I think we're compatible. Very... compatible. Ruby, she...she's kind. She cares about people. I always wanted a kind wife, somebody who... would love me." The last three words came out as a whisper. It wasn't that the idea of love that embarrassed him, only saying it out loud. Because he *did* want a woman who would love him, someone he could love. Not just like. Once, when he was *rumspringa*, his running-around time before he'd been baptized, he'd seen a romantic movie at an *Englisher*'s house about a man and woman who were in love, and a message one of them had written and put in a bottle. The movie had been sad. It had made him tear up. But it had been a notion he'd remembered. He didn't think his mother and father had loved each other like that. Was it greedy to want it for himself?

"Marriage isn't just about a man and a woman," Sara was saying.

He wondered if she'd heard what he'd said. What he meant about wanting romantic love in his marriage.

"Marriage is about family," she continued. "Family and faith, respect and friendship."

"And love?" he asked, daring to repeat himself and reveal his inner hope.

"Sometimes a couple will be fortunate enough to find love ahead of the marriage, but usually it comes later. That said—" she held up her finger "—there's nothing wrong with searching for love. At least I don't think so. But to get back to you and Ruby, we have to go slowly."

He fiddled with the brim of his hat. "And what if we don't want that? Ruby and I?"

"I insist. Who is the expert here, Joseph? There's a lot to consider. In your case, one issue is your mother. What do you think she would say if you rushed into an arrangement and started talking about marriage to a girl you haven't even walked out with?"

"I don't suppose she'd like that." He looked down and then back at Sara. "But Mother wants me to marry. She's the one who told me to come to you. She said I'd never find someone on my own."

Sara got up and came around the desk to stand only a few feet from him. Hastily, he got to his feet again.

"I'm sure Magdalena wants the best for you," Sara said. "But it's never easy for a woman to welcome another woman into her home. To give up her son to a wife."

"She'll have to accept Ruby. I can deal with my *mam*." He shuffled his feet. "But what if we want to marry and *you* don't agree? Do you have to approve of the match?"

Sara straightened her shoulders. "I can tell you that I once stopped a wedding on the morning of the marriage. I told the bishop and the elders that the couple was not right for each other. They called off the wedding."

"What did the couple do? Were they unhappy with you?"

"They were. At the time. But a few months proved that I was right. I told you—I know what I'm doing. I don't make careless matches. I make marriages that are strong and loving, marriages that will only grow stronger through the years. Do this my way, Joseph, and you'll never regret it."

"I suppose you're right," he admitted. "But I really… like Ruby. And she likes me." He considered for a moment and then asked. "What happened to the couple? Did…did they ever marry?"

Sara chuckled. "They did, but not to each other. The man married his almost bride's older sister and the girl married his younger cousin. Both marriages that I arranged. And they have worked out beautifully. Between the four of them, they have nine children, and it's only been seven years."

He glanced longingly at the door. "So what happens next? With me and Ruby? About, you know… taking it slowly."

"We'll start with a simple supper. Tomorrow night. Be here at six thirty, and bring your appetite."

"*Mother* will want to meet her. Can I bring her?"

Sara shook her head firmly. "Too soon. I'll invite Magdalena when it's the right time." She glanced at the schoolhouse clock on the wall. "And now I suppose you want to get off to work." She opened the door. "Have a good day, Joseph. And don't be late for supper. I hate it when young men keep my girls waiting."

Gratefully, he hurried out. He hadn't gotten all he'd wanted, but neither had Sara rejected him. He wasn't going to worry. Sara would see how perfect he and Ruby were for each other. He was certain of it. He couldn't wait to see Ruby tomorrow night, and he couldn't wait to tell his mother that he'd found the girl he'd been waiting for.

School was a half day, so Ellie and Ruby were back at Sara's by twelve thirty. After the midday-meal dishes were cleared away and the kitchen spotless, the two young women went into the garden to pick tomatoes. Leah and Arlene had gone to Fifer's Orchard to pick apples and Sara was catching up on her sewing.

Despite spending the morning together at the schoolhouse, Ruby was still shy around Ellie. The little schoolteacher seemed nice, like someone Ruby would like to have as a friend. But Ruby had never known someone with dwarfism before and was afraid that her habit of saying whatever popped into her head might cause a problem. She feared she'd blurt out something offensive that would ruin their prospective friendship.

At school, it had been easy to concentrate on the children and forget worrying about saying or doing something awkward. Children always had a positive effect on Ruby. She adored them, and they seemed to respond well to her. If things had been different at home, maybe she would have liked to have been a teacher herself.

The best way to keep from putting her foot in her mouth was to keep it closed, but being quiet never came easy to Ruby. So before she knew it, a question slipped out. "Why aren't you married, Ellie?" She tried to stop herself but it was too late. There it was, bobbing between them as obviously inappropriate as a mule in a kitchen. "I'm sorry," she said quickly. "I didn't mean—"

Ellie responded with a peal of laughter. "You mean

why hasn't Sara been able to find me a husband? My fault, entirely. I'm too picky. I've had two marriage proposals since I got here, and I turned them both down."

Ruby plucked a tomato from a plant and carefully placed the fat tomato into the basket. If you bruised them, tomatoes could go soft before you could get them canned, and that would be a waste. "You did? Were the boys awful?"

Ellie tossed a rotten tomato into the space between the rows. "*Ne*, they were very nice. And one was very handsome." She giggled. "He was the hardest to refuse because I really liked him."

"But you didn't want to marry him?"

"Nope. I'm not even sure I want to marry. Maybe I like being single." Ellie ducked down behind a big tomato plant and all Ruby could see were the leaves shaking. "Ha. Thought you were hiding, didn't you?" Ellie reappeared, brandishing a perfect tomato. "The heritage tomatoes are the hardest to pick because they're not always that red color that gives them away. But they are delicious."

"I know," Ruby agreed. "I love them. They have more taste than the commercial varieties." She stood to her full height and rubbed the small of her back. Picking tomatoes was hard work because of all the bending. "The boys you turned down," she said. "Joseph Brenneman wasn't one of them, was he?"

Ellie giggled again. "*Ne*, not Joseph. But he's cute, don't you think?"

"He is." Ruby blushed and busied herself in searching for ripe tomatoes. "Was it awkward? Saying no?" she ventured after a few minutes of picking. "Refusing a man's proposal?"

"Not particularly. Only one of them seemed to take it hard, but he's found someone else, so I couldn't have broken his heart." At this, they both laughed together. As they reached the end of the row, Ellie brushed the dirt off her skirt, glanced up at Ruby and sighed. "My current problem is with a certain blacksmith that I know Sara would like to fix me up with."

"You don't like him?" Ruby furrowed her brow. "Or you don't think he'd like you?"

Ellie shook her head. "It's more complicated than that." She lowered her voice and moved closer. "I know Sara means well, but he's *little*."

"Little?" Ruby asked.

"Like me," Ellie said, throwing up her hands. "A little person. Jakob obviously likes me. But he's a pest, always trying to wrangle an invitation to dinner or showing up at the schoolhouse with some excuse or another. He's even trying to get my friends to put in a good word for him."

"Is that a bad thing?"

Ellie picked a tomato up from the ground, examined it, and then threw it hard against a fence post. The rotten tomato burst, sending a red-winged blackbird skyward in a flurry of tomato bits. "I would never date someone just because he's little like me." She gave a little huff. "Right now, I don't even want to think about it. I'm happily independent. I don't want to marry anyone. I love teaching at Seven Poplars School. I'm having the best time of my life and I don't have to do a man's laundry. But if I *do* decide to marry, it will be because he's the one and I can't live without him. Does that make sense to you?"

"It does," Ruby agreed. She wondered if Ellie might

like this Jakob more than she let on or if it was smart to rule out a person just because of his height, but she didn't say so. For once, she was able to keep her mouth shut.

"How are you two doing?" Sara called from the garden gate. "Finding many ripe ones?"

"Lots," Ruby answered. "I need to start another basket. This one's full." She picked up the basket with the tomatoes she'd just picked, but when she turned to carry it down the row, she tripped. The basket tipped and half of them rolled out onto the dirt. "Sorry," she said, making haste to recover the fallen tomatoes.

"Let me help." Ellie began putting tomatoes back into the basket.

Ruby was mortified. "Sorry," she mumbled again.

"Don't worry." Smiling, Sara walked toward them. "We'll start another batch of canning tomorrow. It won't matter if some of them are bruised." She stopped and made eye contact with Ellie. "*Ach.* I forgot my soup on the stove. Ellie, would you mind running in and stirring it? Just turn off the flame."

"I can do it," Ruby offered.

"*Ne*, let Ellie go," Sara said.

"But I don't mind," Ruby said, eager to help.

Ellie looked to her. "What Sara is trying to say politely is that she needs to speak to you alone."

"Oh," Ruby declared.

"It's how it works when you live in a matchmaker's house," Ellie explained. "Watch out, Ruby, she's about to have a serious conversation with you." She giggled. "And unless I'm mistaken, it has to do with a certain bricklayer named Joseph." As she walked out of the garden, Ellie called back over her shoulder. "Remember what I said about the laundry, Ruby. Don't make any hasty decisions."

Nervously, Ruby looked back at Sara. "You wanted to say something to me that you didn't want Ellie to hear?"

Sara turned over an empty five-eighths basket and sat on it. She smiled at Ruby. "No need to fret. What I have to tell you isn't bad news. *Ne*, not bad at all. You have an offer of marriage. Quickest ever, for me." She shook her head in disbelief and folded her arms. "So fast and easy that I might not feel right collecting a fee for it."

Excitement bubbled up inside Ruby. So Joseph really had spoken to Sara, just like he said he was going to. She didn't know whether to jump with joy or drop to the ground in shock. She'd had offers before, but none she was so eager for. "Joseph?"

Sara rolled her eyes. "Of course, Joseph. What other available man has laid eyes on you since you arrived? Other than Hiram, and he doesn't count." She chuckled. "Well, he counts. He's a sweet enough man under all that laziness, but he's certainly no match for a young girl like you."

Ruby shivered with delight. A young girl. The matchmaker had called her a girl. Sara knew she was twenty-five but didn't consider her over-the-hill. It was probably pride that made her take pleasure in hearing it, but she did. "Joseph really wants to marry me?" she asked, still unable to believe her ears. "He wasn't joking?"

"Not a joke," Sara assured her. "And not a match, not yet. There's much we need to discuss. Your parents made it clear to me that I was not to share your circumstances with any possible prospect. Now that Joseph has made his intentions clear, how do you feel about that? I've never counseled a would-be bride to keep such a big secret from her might-be groom."

She exhaled softly and considered. "I've worried about that. But I gave my word to *Daddi* and *Mommi*. They didn't think it would be wise to tell and asked that I not say anything. But that was before—" She chewed hard on her lower lip. "I don't want to be dishonest with Joseph, but I promised them. I feel as though I have to keep my word. What do you think?"

"I agree that this is unusual, Ruby. Your father explained that he doesn't want you judged for your circumstances. I don't often condone misleading a suitor, but I understand your parents' concern."

"My father is a wise man. And I know both he and *Mommi* want what's best for me."

"Mmm, *ya*." Sara picked a potato bug off a tomato leaf and dropped it into the dirt. She squashed it with the heel of her foot. "Nasty things," she said. "I'll never understand why the Lord created them, unless it was to teach us something I haven't learned yet." She met Ruby's gaze. "You might as well know that I'm a woman who says what she thinks. And I have to tell you that the swiftness of Joseph's proposal worries me."

Ruby made a sound but was able to keep herself from interrupting.

"I'm sure he's sincere, but these matters usually go at a much gentler pace. I had intended to introduce you to someone else." Sara narrowed her gaze. "Are you certain you wouldn't like to meet him before we proceed with Joseph's suit?"

Ruby shook her head. "*Ne*. I think Joseph is wonderful, perfect even."

Sara pursed her lips. "A perfect man I have yet to meet, although my former husbands all had excellent qualities. I'd be of an easier mind if you and Joseph would just date one another before you consider a formal courtship."

"Ne." Ruby sighed. "I've been to enough taffy pulls and barn frolics. I'm tired of *dating*. If Joseph is willing, I am too. I would love to have him court me."

"Courtship is a serious matter. You'll be strictly chaperoned and the community's eyes will be on you. When you go out with Joseph, you'll be in at a decent hour and you will not be alone with him in any private place. And there will be no physical shows of affection. Do you understand?"

"Ya, ya," Ruby replied, feeling herself blush. "I understand. That's fine. So what happens next? When can I see him?"

"Well…" Sara sighed as if resigned, though still not totally in agreement. "Joseph is coming to share supper with us tomorrow night. We'll see how that goes. Fair enough?"

"Fair enough." Ruby grinned. Tomorrow night! How could she wait that long? What would she wear? What would she say to him? She clasped her hands together. "I can't believe this is happening," she managed.

"Neither can I," Sara admitted, coming to her feet.

Chapter Four

It was close to six o'clock when Joseph got home from work that night. He'd been laying a line of blocks on a house foundation and wanted to use the last of the mixed cement so that it wouldn't go to waste. It had been a hot day and he wanted to shower before supper. "I'll be quick," he promised his mother as he cut through the kitchen. "I've got something exciting to tell you."

"Your clean clothes are in there," his mother said, waving in the direction of the bathroom. She was her usual neat and tidy self. She didn't appear to be a woman who'd done a day's work and prepared supper on a warm evening. Her *kapp* and apron were spotless, her complexion was smooth and without blemish, and her shoes were newly shined.

Hair slicked and dressed fit to sit at the table, Joseph took his seat twenty minutes later. He was so excited to share his news that he could hardly keep from tapping the tabletop or bouncing his heel up and down, both of which always made his mother unhappy. She didn't scold him the way she had when he was younger anymore, but she had a way of expressing her displeasure without words.

"Aunt Milly stopped by today and left us a carrot salad," she said as she placed a platter of cold ham and cheese in front of him. "So hot today, I thought we'd eat light. But if you're really hungry, I can fry some chicken."

"Plenty here," Joseph said. Which was an understatement. Besides the lunch meat and carrot salad, there was a platter of deviled eggs, coleslaw, sliced onions and tomatoes, Kaiser rolls, homemade applesauce, peanut butter, raisin bread and three quarters of a chocolate pie. "Maybe we should invite the neighbors."

His mother's eyes lit up as she poured lemonade from a crockery pitcher and handed him a glass. He had a weakness for her lemonade. His mother always froze her ice cubes with fresh mint or bits of fruit in season.

Joseph wondered if Ruby was a good cook. He knew that young women often had much to learn in the kitchen, but he didn't care. If he could have her to wife, he would gladly eat cold cereal three times a day. Even if he had to fix it himself. Of course, they would all be living together, and his mother, an excellent housekeeper as well as cook, could teach Ruby whatever she didn't know yet. *"Mam,"* he began, unable to contain himself any longer. "This morning, I—"

She silenced him with a slender fingertip to her lips. "Grace," she reminded him gently. She bowed her head and closed her eyes. Joseph did the same, willing his thoughts of Ruby to recede during silent prayer. Before long, his thanks to God for the food before him led naturally into gratitude for finding Ruby. So intent was he on expressing his joy that such a gift could come to him that he lost track of time and was surprised when he heard his mother's voice.

"Joseph? Are you listening to a word I say?"

He opened his eyes. *"Ya."*

"Goot. I was saying that Milly's neighbor Pauline has a daughter."

"That's nice." He picked up his fork to reach for a slice of ham, then put the fork down without retrieving the meat. "So I stopped at Sara Yoder's house on the way to work this morning."

"Something wrong with the ham? Too fatty?" She got to her feet and picked up the platter. "Here, let me trim it. It's delicious. I had a slice at lunch. Did you want mustard on that or mayonnaise? I didn't put the mayonnaise on the table. You never want to leave it out when it's warm. But I can get it."

He took the plate of cheese and meat from her hand and set it back on the table. "Mustard is fine. Now, sit down with me. I want to tell you about my talk with the matchmaker."

"I'm glad you brought that up. That's what I want to tell you!" She raised a small hand. "No need to waste your hard-earned money on Sara's fee. Aunt Milly's neighbor Pauline has a daughter in Indiana. Widowed, with three children, all boys. And the word is she's looking for a new husband. Aunt Milly says she remembers the woman well, very pious, makes excellent *hasen pfeffer.* Heda's a few years older than you, but that's no problem." She slipped back into her chair." It's always good for a young man like you to have a more experienced wife to guide him."

He glanced at her. "What do you mean, *a man like me?*"

"Oh, Joseph, hush. I'm not criticizing you. But you and I are both aware that you've never been forward. And Heda is the exact opposite. She knows how to get things done. She's run a household for ten years. She's frugal and understands how to manage money. Aunt Milly said her last boy was born in three hours. Can you believe it? And Heda was on her feet in time to cook dinner. Doesn't she sound perfect for you? I think that between us, we could arrange for you to go out and meet her. I was thinking—"

Joseph had picked up his glass of lemonade and now set it down sharply. "Mother, will you please stop talking long enough for me to get in a word?"

She crossed her arms over her chest, looking peeved. But at least she was quiet.

"You wanted me to hire a matchmaker," he said, gentling his tone. "You told me that my best chance for finding a wife would be to let Sara Yoder find me someone. And you were so right, because she has!" He went on quickly, before she could interrupt him again. "I've met the most wonderful girl. And the best part? She likes me too. I'm so certain that she's right for me that I went to Sara's this morning and asked for permission to court her."

His mother popped out of her chair again. "Court her? How can you possibly court her? How many times have you seen this girl?" Clearly flustered, she looked frantically for the paper fan she always kept nearby. She found it on a chair and began fanning herself. "You can't court a stranger. I haven't even met her. That's not the way it's done." She shook her head. "What can Sara be thinking? I knew I should be the one to speak with her first."

"Mam," he said quietly. "We've been together twice, but…but I knew the minute I laid eyes on her. She's the girl for me, the one I've been waiting for. And when you meet her, you'll see it too. I know you'll—"

"It's not right." She fluttered her fan in front of her face. Two bright spots of color bloomed on his mother's pale cheeks. "I can't give my permission."

He decided not to bring up the fact that he didn't need her permission to court anyone. Instead, he said, "Just wait until you meet her. You're going to love her. She's smart and she's beautiful and…and she can talk about anything."

His mother whipped the fan back and forth faster. The red spots had spread so that her entire face had taken on a flush and beads of sweat formed at her temples. "You can't really be courting this girl. You must be mistaken, Joseph. I'm sure you mistook what the matchmaker said. Nothing happens this fast. It *shouldn't* happen this fast. Not without consulting me. And what kind of a girl would agree so quickly?" She began to pace behind her chair, fanning her face furiously. "I know what you need. It's not this upstart but a sound prospect like Heda. Did I tell you that she's well set up? Her husband had a nice little farm, and now that belongs to Heda. When she sells it to move here, it will bring a good sum."

"Mother, please, listen to me." It was all Joseph could do to keep from losing his patience. He hadn't expected this response. He'd been so certain that his mother would be glad to hear about Ruby. "I'm not marrying Heda King," he said.

"She's not Heda King any longer. I think her married name is Miller but I could find out. I could ask—"

"Mother, you aren't listening to me. I know Heda. Remember? She went to school with me. And not only is she five or six years older than me, but she's a shrew. She was unkind to all the younger children. And she used to tease me about not being able to speak in class. And she can't be too good with finances because she kept failing the seventh grade. She was terrible at multiplication."

"That was years ago." She waved her fan in his direction. "I'm sure she's changed. That's the trouble with you. You're not willing to give a suitable young woman a chance. I'm sure if you go out to Indiana and meet with Heda, you'd find her just the woman for you."

"Ne." He shook his head, reaching for his lemonade again. "I'm not going to Indiana to meet Heda. No Heda."

"But Aunt Milly assures me she'll make a perfect wife for you."

He took a sip of lemonade. "No Heda," he repeated. "The girl that Sara introduced me to…" He chuckled. "The same girl that sent me to the hospital with a cracked head. We suit each other. I've spoken to Sara and she's invited me to have supper with them tomorrow night. We'll get to know each other better, and Sara will give us the okay to begin courting. Officially." He reached for the tray of meat and cheese. "Now, please don't upset yourself. I'm handling this."

His mother sighed heavily. Her eyes reddened, and for a few seconds he was afraid she would start crying.

She waved the fan back and forth, stirring the warm air. It was an old fan and had once been painted with the date and the words *Delaware State Fair*, but they had faded and peeled away. Now it read "ware air" in faint lettering. The bouquet of roses had also faded to a smear of pink-and-yellow coloring, but his mother would not part with the fan even though he'd offered to buy her a better one. "What time are we expected for supper?" she asked weakly.

Joseph shook his head, not looking up at her. "Not us, *Mam*. Me."

"That's ridiculous. No young man from a decent family starts courting a girl her family hasn't even met. If your father were alive, Sara Yoder wouldn't think of trying such a thing." She picked up her plate to carry it to the sink. She'd never put anything on it. "The proper thing would have been for Sara to invite me. And I won't hesitate to tell her so."

"I'm sure Sara will ask you to come soon, but tomorrow night, it's just me." He'd lost his own appetite, as well, but he had no intentions of allowing his mother to see that. He cut off a small piece of ham and picked it up with his fork. "Once the arrangements are settled, I'll invite my girl to come here and meet you." He put the meat into his mouth and forced himself to chew. It was tasty.

"I don't know anything about this young woman. Where is she from? Who is her family? Is it anyone I know?"

Joseph took a little of the tomatoes and onions. He'd make himself eat a little. After all, his mother had gone to the effort to prepare and serve the meal. "All I'm going to tell you is that she has a kind heart and she's from Lancaster County. I don't think you know her family."

"A stranger? Not even local? What church does she belong to? You have to be careful. You're baptized. You can't go around courting girls from liberal churches. What if she's too good for a horse and buggy and expects you to drive a car? They do, some of those Amish in Pennsylvania. Not Amish at all, if you ask me."

Joseph took a spoonful of the applesauce. He hadn't seen his mother get this worked up in a long time. But it didn't matter. No one, not even the matchmaker could persuade him that Ruby wasn't the one for him, the one he wanted to make his wife.

"I trust Sara not to introduce me to a young woman who isn't Old Order Amish."

"What's her name?" His mother's voice was softer now, coaxing. "You can at least tell me her name. I hope it isn't Swartzentruber. We have Swartzentrubers way back in the family on your father's side, and she could be related, a cousin even."

"Her name isn't Swartzentruber." He started to speak her name and then realized he didn't want to. Not yet. Because for the first time in his life, he felt as if he had something that was his and his alone. And he wasn't ready to share it. He wasn't ready to share Ruby with his mother.

She stopped the motion of her fan. "You won't tell me her name?"

"All in good time." The applesauce was sweet on his tongue. He could taste the spicy tang of cinnamon and just a hint of nutmeg. Delicious. He helped himself to more.

"Well, I never." His mother fanned herself again. "I'm hurt, Joseph. I have to be honest with you. I'm hurt."

"I'm sorry, *Mam*. I wouldn't hurt you for the world. I didn't plan for things to go this way. I didn't expect to meet her so quickly. But that's what's happened. Now, sit down with me and eat something."

"I couldn't possibly eat." His mother stood behind her chair, resting her hand on it. "A wife becomes part of the family. Marriage is all about family." She shook her head. "This isn't a good beginning for what should be a happy occasion."

"It will be a happy occasion, I promise you." He took another piece of ham. "You and my girl are going to love each other."

"We'll see about that, won't we?"

He took a Kaiser roll and began to make a sandwich.

"Well," she exclaimed, looking away. "I suppose this means that I'm not going to Sara Yoder's with you tomorrow night."

He grinned to himself. "*Ne*, Mother. You aren't."

"I won't be able to eat a bite," Ruby said to Ellie as she drew aside the curtain and peeked out the kitchen window to see Joseph talking with Hiram at the long picnic table under the trees. It was cooler today than the day before, so pleasant that Sara suggested they take advantage of the lovely weather and eat supper outside. "I'm as jumpy as a hen on ice. I'll do something silly, I know it. Either that or I'll say something silly. If he hasn't already come to tell Sara he's changed his mind, he will then."

"Ruby, Ruby, no need to get yourself in such a state," Ellie soothed. "We're just having supper together." Her blue eyes sparkled with amusement. "There's no reason to fret. If you don't say much, Joseph will just think you're shy."

Ruby grimaced. "He already knows better than that.

I talked his ears off the other day." She pressed her hand to her midsection. "I think I feel sick. I might get sick."

Ellie laughed. "You're not going to get sick. You're going to help me carry out the rest of the supper, and you're going to enjoy our meal. You like Joseph, and he likes you. There's nothing to worry about. It will be fine."

"You can say that," Ruby replied, "but that doesn't make it true. You don't know me. I'm a klutz and I say whatever comes to mind. I can mess up anything."

The back door opened partially and Sara popped her head in. "Girls, the men are getting hungry. Let's move this along."

"We'll be right out," Ellie called as she opened the refrigerator. "The ham's not sliced," she told Ruby when Sara was gone. "I think one of us was supposed to do it."

"I'll slice it and bring it out," Ruby said. "You carry the pickled beets. I might spill those on Sara or Joseph, and beets stain." The ham was heavy. She wasn't sure if Ellie could manage it, but didn't want to say that.

Ellie took the bowl of beets in one hand and the peppered cabbage in the other, and then used her hip to push open the screen door. "Ruby, don't look as if you're going to a funeral," she called back. "This will be fun."

"*Ya*, fun," Ruby agreed half-heartedly. She found a sharp knife and moved the ham from the refrigerator to the counter to cut it. At least Sara was serving ham and not fried chicken. Ruby had a vivid memory of once carrying a plate of fried chicken to the men's table at a barn raising. She hadn't done a thing wrong all day, and she'd been feeling quite sure of herself. "Here it comes!" she'd called to the bishop just before she'd tripped over a cat and sent the pieces of chicken flying—literally flying—through the air.

A thigh had landed on the bishop's head, while a breast had knocked the visiting preacher's hat into the Jell-O salad. The cat had made off with a drumstick, and the rest had scattered on the ground. The only positive note had been the single wing that bounced onto the bishop's plate. He liked wings, he'd assured her, which made everyone laugh all the harder. Ruby's mother had tried to console her by reminding her that no one went away hungry. There was always plenty at a barn raising. But she'd never been able to live it down. And even her father had teased her about it whenever they were having chicken.

Ruby wished her mother were here now. Her *mommi* always knew how to put things into perspective. Ruby had attempted to write to her last night to tell her about Joseph and how much she liked him, but she couldn't find the right words. After three starts, she'd given up and dropped the torn-up sheets of paper in the trash. Maybe it would be better to wait a few days and see what happened, she reasoned. By tomorrow, Joseph might have realized what she was like and moved his attentions to another prospect. She didn't think he would though. And if things did go well tonight, she'd have more to tell her parents.

Ruby picked up the knife to start slicing and then hesitated, remembering all too well the flying pieces of chicken. Maybe it would be better to carry the ham out to the table and cut it up there? After a moment's hesitation, she picked up the platter and pasted a smile on her face. *Please, please*, she prayed silently. *Keep me from making a fool of myself in front of Joseph.*

Everyone was at the table, and as she crossed the lawn, their faces turned toward her: Hiram, Sara, Leah, Ellie and Joseph. Ruby walked slowly, carefully balancing the ham on the platter. *I won't stumble*, she told herself. *I absolutely won't—"Ach!"* she cried as the ham suddenly slid forward on the plate. Ruby stopped short, fighting to keep the plate level. The ham had slid across the plate like a hockey puck on the ice on her father's pond. She stood there, frozen, afraid to move.

"Need some help?" Joseph offered. He rose and strode toward her.

Gratefully she looked into his handsome face. *This can't be true*, she thought. *It has to be a dream. This wonderful man can't be asking to court me.* Joseph reached out for the platter, and somehow, in the exchange, Ruby tilted the right side and the slippery ham slid off and landed splat in the dirt.

Ruby stared at the ham on the ground. *"Ne,"* she groaned. "Not again."

"My fault," Joseph said. "I… I distracted you." He was looking right at her. Right into her eyes.

Ruby shook her head.

"Not to worry," Sara said, appearing beside Ruby to scoop up the ham off the ground. "Come on, Ruby, let's just get the other one. It's already sliced."

"Should…should I…help?" Joseph took a step forward and Sara waved him back.

"Ne, ne, we cooks can tend to this. Sit down. We'll be right back. Ruby?" she called as she walked away, the big ham in her hands.

Mortified, Ruby followed Sara into the house. "I'm so sorry," she said, once they were inside. She clutched the empty plate. "I don't know how it happened." It was all she could do to hold back the tears welling up in her eyes. And the knife. She'd left the knife in the grass somewhere. What if someone stepped on it? What if it went right through Joseph's foot? He wouldn't want to court her if he had to go to the hospital a second time in one week on her account.

"It's not a problem," Sara said. "I did the exact same thing myself last Christmas. Now, just get a hold of yourself. Joseph Brenneman doesn't want to court you because you can serve at the table. What he *does* want is a smiling face. You have to laugh off the small things, Ruby. Life is too full of big things to worry yourself over the small." She turned to the sink. "Now, put down the plate and go change your apron while I wash the dirt off this ham so I can slice it."

"But I thought you said…" Ruby stared at her wide-eyed. "You don't have a second ham?"

"Don't I?" Sara chuckled as she patted the ham dry with a clean kitchen towel and set it on a cutting board on the counter. "Foolish of me. I must be getting forget-ful in my dotage." Her dark eyes lit with mischief. "I won't tell if you don't. Now, you make yourself pretty while I slice up this *other* ham. Hurry, or your Joseph will starve to death before he ever gets the chance to propose to you."

Minutes later, Ruby and Sara were back at the table under the trees, silent grace had been shared and they were passing the old pewter platter of sliced ham around. Ruby thought it had been clever of Sara to change service dishes, but then, she was coming to realize that the matchmaker was a wise woman on so many levels.

Once the meal commenced, Joseph had little to say,

but he ate plenty, and twice Ruby caught him smiling shyly at her. She smiled back, still uneasy after the ham incident, but with Ellie, Sara and Leah keeping up a lively chatter, Ruby began to relax.

"Have another biscuit," Ellie told Joseph. "They're light as air."

"Ya." He nodded and reached for another biscuit.

Ruby blushed with pleasure and looked down at her plate.

"Ruby made them," Sara proclaimed to everyone at the table. "Her grandmother's recipe. She won't tell us what makes them rise so."

"You'll have to give me some pointers," Leah said. "When I was in Brazil, we could rarely get baking powder that hadn't already expired. Some of my biscuits were more like crackers."

Sara rose and refilled Joseph's iced tea glass. "Our Leah will be marrying soon. She'll need that help or her new husband will be complaining that she's not the cook his mother was."

Leah and Ellie giggled. "Good thing he couldn't come for supper tonight," Leah teased. "From the taste of these biscuits, he might have dropped me and started courting Ruby."

"You couldn't possibly make biscuits as bad as my aunt Anna's," Ellie put it. "Hers were so hard that her kids wouldn't eat them. They would sneak them out to the chickens, but they were even too tough for the chickens."

Laughter and more lighthearted stories flowed across the table. Joseph took a third biscuit, buttered it and devoured every bite. Hiram ate doggedly, not speaking and rarely looking up from his plate. And before Ruby knew it, Leah and Ellie were bringing out the pies.

Soon the meal was over and Ruby began to worry that she'd cause another disaster clearing away the dishes. She rose and began to gather the plates, but Sara took them from her. "Plenty of hands to make this work light," she said. "You young ones need to go and sit and talk a little. Joseph, would you mind taking Ruby over to the gazebo?" She indicated the one in the side yard. Under the roof were porch swings, benches and chairs for relaxing. "You go on. I'll join you shortly."

Joseph flushed but got to his feet and looked expectantly to Ruby. "Will you come? W-with me?" he stammered.

"Oh, yes," she agreed. The gazebo was on the opposite side of the house from the fishpond and it was near the driveway. The sides were latticed wood, open enough so that a couple could be seen inside, but closed in enough so that there would be a feeling of privacy.

Shyly, she walked beside him across the yard. He stood back and let her step up into the gazebo. "Good… good supper," he managed as she took a seat on the nearest swing.

"Good ham," she said, and they both laughed.

"A second ham," Joseph said and laughed all the harder. He sat down beside her and gave the swing a slight push. "And the—the best biscuits… I ever tasted."

As she looked up at him, Ruby sighed and all the worry seemed to slip away.

Chapter Five

Joseph looked at Ruby sitting beside him under the gazebo and his heart knocked against his ribs. It was pounding so loud that he was certain Ruby must hear it. He had so much he wanted to say to her, but as usual, he couldn't turn his thoughts into words. "Good…good supper," he squeaked out. Heat washed up his throat, burning his cheeks. It was all he could do to keep himself seated there in the swing beside her.

All of his insecurities chipped away at his confidence. Why would this wonderful woman choose him? He'd wanted to date other girls over the years. Not *date* exactly, but drive home from a singing or a frolic. Most of them had turned him down flat. Why should Ruby be any different? She'd told him she wanted to court him, true, but maybe she was simply too kind to hurt his feelings. Maybe that was why she'd come out here with him. Maybe she was preparing to tell him that it was all a mistake and she didn't want to court him.

His hands were damp and he rubbed them on his trousers. Beads of sweat trickled down the back of his neck. He was going to ruin any chance he had of having her for his own through his confounded shyness. And then, he realized that she was saying something.

"I was so embarrassed that I dropped the ham," Ruby said. "I feel like such a silly—"

"Ne," he said abruptly, cutting her off. He turned toward her and looked directly into her large, beautiful eyes. "You shouldn't—shouldn't worry about things like that."

"That's what Sara said."

"And she—she's right. The food was delicious. No one minded."

Ruby smiled at him. "Sara said she would get the other ham. But there wasn't another one. She washed the dirt off and we sliced the one I dropped," she confided. "I wouldn't want you to think that I was trying to trick you."

"Really?" He started to relax. "That was smart of her."

"So you don't think it was wrong?" she asked.

He chuckled. "It's what my mother would do. Maybe not say she had a second ham, but she'd sure wash it off and serve it. It would be wasteful to just throw away good meat." He paused. "And who knows what goes on in restaurant kitchens?"

Ruby giggled. "Maybe the cooks play soccer with the hams."

"To make them tender," Joseph suggested. When Ruby laughed at the idea, he felt quite clever. And he began to feel a lot better about being here. "Ruby… I don't talk much," he admitted. "In front of people. Like at…supper. I hope…you don't care." He made himself look at her.

"Ne. Of course I don't care. I didn't even notice. I'm

just the opposite." She chuckled. "You've probably already noticed. I open my mouth and I can't seem to stop talking."

"It's not that I don't think of stuff to say," he explained. "It—it just won't come out."

Ruby thought for a moment before she responded. "My father always says that it's better to be quiet and be thought wise than to open your mouth and prove to be a fool. I try to remember that, but I guess not often enough." She laughed, and Joseph found himself chuckling with her.

He sat up a little straighter. Ruby was easy to talk to. He liked being with her. No matter what happened, they ended up laughing together. He looked down at her and gathered his courage. "I—I was afraid you'd had second thoughts. After you…you know, thought about it."

"About us?" She shook her head. "*Ne*, I haven't." She offered a shy smile. "But I was afraid you'd changed your mind."

"Not at all. In fact… I—I couldn't wait to come here tonight. To see you again." He exhaled slowly. Things were definitely looking up. He gave a small push with the toe of one shoe and the swing began to move. "I guess Sara told you, but I talked to her about—about you and me courting. I told her that we both wanted it."

"I did too."

"You did?" He looked down at her pretty face again. "So, are we? Courting? Each other?"

Ruby blushed and covered her face with her hands. *"Ya,"* she whispered. "I think we are." She lowered her hands and looked up at him. "If it suits you, Joseph."

Happiness bubbled up inside him. "It does," he answered. "It suits—suits me fine."

He was still looking into Ruby's eyes when he heard Sara coming across the lawn toward them.

"I don't hear any shouting, so I suppose you two are still getting along," she said as she entered the gazebo. Joseph leaped to his feet but she motioned him back with a quick wave of her hand. "Sit, sit." She perched on the arm of one of the wooden chairs and glanced from one to the other. "I take it you two have talked and that you both wish to proceed with this arrangement?"

"We do!" Ruby cried, clasping her hands. "We're perfect for each other."

"*Ya,*" Joseph agreed. He removed his straw hat and held it tightly. "Perfect."

"So what's next?" Ruby asked. "Do we introduce each other to our families? We'll get to spend time together, right?" She glanced at him and back at the matchmaker. "Because we want to spend time together. As much as we can."

Again, Sara raised a hand. "I'll explain it all," she said. "You have to understand that these are unusual circumstances. Normally I ask, or rather, I allow my couples to get to know one another before entering any kind of formal agreement. If you're just riding home from singings together and such, there's a lot more privacy. Folks tend not to pay attention too closely to couples just dating. A young couple just dating, or maybe *rumspringa*, might be sneaking out of the house after dark to go for a buggy ride. It's only right that young men and women meet lots of people so that they can pick the one right for them. The community understands this, and the rules are loosened for this special time. That way, if the match doesn't work out, no one needs to feel any embarrassment."

Joseph exchanged smiles with Ruby. This was going smoother than he'd hoped.

"But with official courtship," Sara said, "it's very different. I need to be sure you two understand that courtship is serious. Couples who court think that they want to marry each other."

"We do," Ruby said, placing one hand very closely to his on the swing. "Don't we, Joseph?"

He nodded. "*Ya.* We—we do."

Sara fixed them with a cautionary gaze. "I just need you both to understand that courtship will be more restrictive than dating would be. When my couples are courting, I'm conservative, which means I expect you to have an escort when you go somewhere together."

"You mean, like a chaperone?" Ruby asked. "But at home in Lancaster County, courting couples are free to come and go as they please. As long as…you know, they behave themselves."

"Which is why I'm suggesting maybe you should just date for a few weeks, a few months."

Ruby met his gaze questioningly. "Do you just want to date? I don't want to just date, do you?"

Joseph swallowed hard, moving his gaze to Sara. "We don't want to… We don't need to date. We want to… We're ready to court."

Sara looked at them for a moment. "I just want to be sure this is what you want. This isn't a lighthearted game. Many young people fall into infatuation, sometimes more with the *idea* of marriage than with a particular person. None of us is perfect. You have to get to know each other so that you can decide if your partner's weaknesses are ones you can accept and love."

Joseph wanted to say that he already knew that any

of her weaknesses didn't matter to him. Just like she said that his inability to talk in public didn't matter to her, but he couldn't quite bring up the words.

Sara turned to Ruby. "Are you certain you don't want to discuss this with your parents before agreeing to a formal courtship with Joseph?"

Ruby shook her head. "They trust me. I'm twenty-five, almost twenty-six. I know my own mind, and I can see what a good man Joseph is. They will be happy with him."

Sara glanced back at Joseph. "And you? You don't think you should take a little time to think on this?"

"Joseph knows his mind. He's older than I am." Ruby took a deep breath and rattled on about Joseph's qualities and maturity until Sara spoke up.

"I need to hear Joseph's opinion from his own mouth," the matchmaker said. "Are you certain, Joseph? This is your decision?"

"Ya." He nodded.

"And do you think your mother will approve of this haste?"

"My mother will be happy that—that I'm happy," he assured Sara with more enthusiasm than he felt. His mother could be difficult at times, and she was deeply attached to him. But once she realized how perfect Ruby was for him, she would welcome her into the family. Ruby would be the daughter his mother had always wanted.

He and Ruby reached for each other's hand at the same time. Her warm fingers closed around his, and a sweet sensation flowed up his arm. "Is—is it all right?" he asked Sara, looking over to her. "To hold hands?"

Sara grimaced. "Most of my couples wait more than

a few minutes after declaring their wish to court before moving on to intimacies such as hand holding. And I'd strongly suggest that you two do the same."

Joseph let go of Ruby's hand and felt himself flush. He couldn't mess this up. He had to do this right, for Ruby's sake. Everyone must see what a great match they would make. And nothing could sully her name.

"So we're officially courting?"

"It appears that you are," Sara answered, getting to her feet.

Ruby squealed with delight and leaped up and threw her arms around Sara. The older woman almost lost her balance and Ruby had to grab her with both hands to keep her from tumbling back. But Ruby was still bouncing with excitement as she righted the matchmaker and hugged her. "Thank you, thank you," Ruby said breathlessly. "You're wonderful. And Joseph—Joseph is the—"

Ruby turned to him as he rose from the swing, and for a second he thought she was going to hug him, as well. Drawn by her vibrancy and caught up in the excitement, he opened his arms. But Sara's voice cut through their exuberance.

"Indeed not," Sara scolded. "There will be no embracing in my presence or out of it. You two will conduct yourselves properly. I do have a reputation to protect. And I've given my word to your parents, Ruby." She waggled her finger at him and Ruby. "So I'm warning you both, behave yourselves."

"Ya," Joseph agreed, tucking his arms behind him. He couldn't stop grinning. "We will."

"Absolutely," Ruby agreed, meeting his gaze again. "But it won't be easy."

* * *

Later that evening, when the house was quiet, Ruby removed the cap from her pen and began her letter to her parents in English.

September 5,
Seven Poplars, Delaware

Dearest *Mommi* and *Daddi*,
I pray that all is well on the farm and that you both remain in good health. Everyone here is nice to me. You would like Sara Yoder, the matchmaker. As Aunt Ellen would say, Sara has an old head on her shoulders. I have already made a new friend here at Sara's house. Her name is Ellie, and she has blond hair and blue eyes and is pretty. You would not guess what is special about her besides that she is the schoolteacher. Ellie has dwarfism but Sara calls her a little person, and I think Ellie likes that best. Ellie is such a happy and busy person. We laugh together all the time. She is a little older than me and has a suitor, but she wants nothing to do with him. I think maybe she protests too much and likes him a little. Ellie is funny and smart, and she can do anything I can do, even though she's short. Usually better. Certainly without dropping the ham. That is a long story and I will tell you about it when I see you, which I hope is soon because I miss you all so much.

Does Bretzel miss me? I miss him. I keep looking for him to come around the corner, wagging his tail, or coming to curl up on my feet as he always does. Has Polly had her foal yet? I can't wait to see if it is a bay or piebald like the *fader*. Did you get rain? I hope the garden is still producing well. I'm sorry I'm not there to help with the canning. I remember my prayers as you told me, and I pray for you both every night.

I saved the best news for last. Sara has made a match for me. His name is Joseph and you will love him. He is a hardworking mason and is kind and sweet. He is also shy but doesn't mind that I am not or that I am a klutz. *Mommi*, I don't think he cares that I am plain even though he is not. *Ne, Daddi*, I will not say that Joseph is as handsome as you, even if I think it. I am so glad that you talked me into coming to Seven Poplars because I now have a beau who knows nothing about me. I feel bad not to tell him, but not so bad as to break my word to you. We will have to talk about when to tell him.

My heart is so full that it is hard to write my thoughts. I think I love Joseph and we are officially courting. I hope you will meet him soon. That's all I have to say. Tell Aunt Ellen that I miss and love her. Remember me in your prayers.
Your obedient daughter,
Ruby

"This is Spence's Bazaar and Auction," Sara explained as she guided the mule and wagon through the crowded parking lot. "It started off years ago as a traditional livestock and farm produce market, but now we sell Amish and Mennonite food and vegetables, and there's a giant flea market that draws locals and tourists. They sell everything from furniture to hammers. Lots of people come, Amish and English."

Automobiles and trucks filled the haphazard rows, and throngs of people wandered between the vehicles, headed toward the buildings and stalls or back to their cars. "I don't imagine that you have any trouble mixing with the English, Ruby," Sara continued. "You have a lot of tourists in Lancaster. So you can help Arlene if she needs it."

Arlene, wide-eyed, nodded shyly. Her home was a small rural community in the Midwest, and she seemed a little awed by all the *Englishers*.

"Of course I will," Ruby said, taking in all the sights and sounds. "I think we have more traffic on the roads than here. Lots of buses from all over. In summer, if you go into Bird In Hand or Kutztown, it can be hectic. Tourists everywhere." It was Friday morning and she had come with Sara and Arlene to Spence's. Joseph had promised to meet her here, and she was excited to see him.

"You girls go on," Sara said as she found an open space in a row of buggies to hitch the mule. "I'll catch up with you. You'll find Leah at the far end. Her betrothed's vegetable stall is on the east side. The awning is blue and white."

"We'll find her," Ruby said.

Leah's sister Grace, who was Mennonite, had picked her up early that morning to drive her to Dover. Leah had a big family in Seven Poplars, and her husband-to-be was from the area, as well. Together, they were starting an organic-vegetable business with plans to supply restaurants and specialty markets. Leah had asked Ruby and Arlene to give her a hand today as her beau was busy in the field.

As Sara predicted, the two of them quickly located Leah. "Oh, good, you're here," Leah called in *Deitsch* when she saw them. "I'm swamped. Arlene, could you restock while Ruby helps me wait on customers?"

Ruby circled the table. She removed her black bonnet, put it and the spare apron she'd brought along in Leah's buggy and hurried to take a place beside Leah.

An English woman with a toddler in a stroller pointed at the potatoes Leah had placed in a wooden crate. "This is all grown without pesticides?" she asked.

"Absolutely," Leah assured her. "Everything on the table is grown organically."

"I'll take five pounds of the potatoes and a quart of those striped tomatoes," the woman said. "I have my own bag." She held up a green cloth sack that read Fresh Veggies.

Ruby smiled at her as she carefully packed the vegetables. "Thank you. Come again," she said when the woman paid her and tucked the produce into the bottom of the stroller.

As the customer walked away, a gray-haired man in a cowboy hat stepped forward to take her place and the line lengthened behind him. Ruby quickly learned the prices and soon felt more at ease as she, Leah and Arlene laughed and chatted between customers. Leah seemed to know everyone, and she introduced sisters, friends, aunts and cousins from the Seven Poplars community. Before Ruby knew it, more than an hour had passed and then another.

When the next lull in business came, Leah asked if they wanted anything to eat or drink. "It's always busier as it gets closer to lunchtime, so you might want to grab a bite now."

"I'm expecting Joseph," Ruby said. "I told him that I would be here. We're having lunch together. But you go ahead. Arlene and I can manage until you get back."

"That works," Leah agreed. "I'll just grab something I can bring back here. Then you can go whenever you're hungry, Arlene. When Joseph comes, Ruby, take your time. Arlene and I will be fine."

Ruby wrinkled her nose. "Am I supposed to take Arlene with me? Sara was pretty adamant about me having a chaperone."

Leah chuckled. "I'm sure he'll bring his mother. I think Magdalena Brenneman will be chaperone enough to suit anyone. Be right back." She gave a wave and hurried away.

Ruby wondered about Leah's remark, but she didn't have long to think about it. Not five minutes later, she spied Joseph walking through the crowd. With him was a petite, slim, neatly dressed Amish woman, so youthful in appearance that at first, Ruby wasn't certain that she was his mother. The woman wore a dark blue dress, black apron, bonnet, shoes and stockings. She had light brown hair just like Joseph's. It framed her petite face, small straight nose and delicate chin.

Ruby waved wildly. "Joseph! Over here." Ruby was so excited that she could hardly keep from bouncing up and down. As she leaned forward on the table, she knocked into the bin of onions and tipped it. *"Ach!"* Some rolled over the front of the table, others rained around her feet.

Ruby ducked down to snatch the fallen onions just as Joseph reached the table and announced, *"Mother,* this—this is Arlene and this," he let out in a rush, "is my Ruby."

Ruby stood up and smiled at Joseph and Magdalena, her arms full of onions. She dropped one, grabbed for it and managed to drop two more.

"I'm so happy to finally meet you," his mother said to Arlene, clasping the young woman's hand in hers. "You're just a lovely girl."

Magdalena's voice was as sweet as her face, Ruby decided. It fit her perfectly.

"Joseph has talked of nothing else but you all week," Magdalena continued. "And I can see why. You're just perfect for him. Such a pretty girl."

Realizing Magdalena's mistake, Ruby looked from the older woman to Joseph's quickly reddening face and back to his mother again.

"Ne," Arlene protested. "I'm not—"

"And modest too!" Magdalena clapped her hands together. "My dear, we will get on—"

"Mother" Joseph protested. "That—that isn't…"

Arlene tried to back away from Magdalena. "You don't understand," she said. She was blushing too as she pointed. *"That's* Ruby."

"Ya, of course," Magdalena agreed. "That is Ruby." She nodded in Ruby's general direction. "Nice to meet you, Ruby." She returned her attention to Arlene. "But of course you're the one I'm here to meet, Arlene. I can't tell you how pleased I was when my Joseph told me he was courting." Apparently taking no notice of Joseph's distress, she beamed at him. "You've done very well, Joseph. I couldn't have picked a lovelier bride for you myself."

Arlene shook her head, her eyes now round with

dismay. "*Ne.* Not me. I'm not—it's her." She pointed at Ruby and then turned sharply and made a beeline for the back of Leah's buggy.

"*Mother*, you…" Joseph insisted, clearly distraught. "You've…misunderstood. This—this is…*my*—my Ruby."

Magdalena's vivid blue eyes turned on Ruby. "You?" she said.

"Yes." Ruby let the last of the onions she'd picked up fall from her arms into the bin and stood as tall as she could. "Me. Ruby Plank. I'm… Joseph and I are courting." She extended a hand, streaked with dirt and onion skins, across the table. "It's nice to meet you, Magdalena."

"Oh. I see." Magdalena's perfectly shaped mouth, her naturally pink lips firmed into a thin line as she returned a limp handshake. "Joseph said you were beautiful and I naturally assumed that…" She looked pointedly in the direction Arlene had fled.

Ruby withdrew her hand, dusted off the onion skins and folded her arms over her chest. Lifting her chin, she said, "If he said that, I can see how it would be an honest mistake to think Arlene was Joseph's bride-to-be." She cleared her throat and forced a chuckle. "I know what I am, Magdalena. I am as plain as a turnip. But Joseph doesn't seem to mind. And so neither do I." She met his mother's gaze with one she hoped was just as strong and just as determined. "And I am so pleased to meet you. Joseph speaks of you so highly."

"That's nice to know," Magdalena said tersely. She patted his arm. "There, there, Joseph. Breathe. You look as though you've swallowed a fishhook. There's no harm done. Had you told me her name as I asked, it would never have happened. And Ruby doesn't look to be the type to hold a grudge." She looked up at Ruby, meeting her eye to eye. "Are you, dear?"

Ruby stubbornly held the woman's gaze. "Of course not."

"Magdalena!" An Amish woman in a green dress waved to her from two stalls down. "Magdalena! This is the chowchow I've been raving about. Come and see."

"Coming," Joseph's mother answered. "I'll be right back. Don't go off without me, you two." Back straight as a fence post, black handbag on her elbow, Magdalena walked away without another word.

"I'm so, so sorry," Joseph said the moment his mother was out of hearing range. "She's right. That was all my fault."

Ruby shook her head. She'd had such high hopes that Joseph's mother would take to her at first sight. She'd hoped they'd become the best of friends at once, but she suspected that had been naive of her. And now some comments she'd heard from Leah and others who knew Magdalena made more sense. "Don't worry about it," she said softly.

"I should have warned you. I should have…we should have talked about this. *Mother*, she says whatever comes into her head. Sometimes, not as charitable as it should be. But…but her heart is in the right place. She's going to love you. I promise she will. She just takes…takes some getting used to."

Ruby swallowed back her hurt. "I've been accused of saying whatever comes into my head, as well," she admitted. "But I don't think she likes me."

"Nonsense," he protested. "She's just embarrassed over what happened."

"If you say so. You know her better than anyone." Ruby began picking up the onions and putting them back in the bin.

"Ruby, we haven't really talked about this but…but it's—it's important to me that you like her. That she… That she likes you. She means so much to me. She's a wonderful mother. You don't know how she's sacrificed, being a widow all these years. You've seen her. She could have married a lot of times, but she didn't. She didn't want me to have a stepfather that might not treat me well."

Ruby waited for him to look at her. "But what if she doesn't?"

He looked uncomfortable. "Doesn't what?"

"What if she doesn't like me, Joseph?" She picked up an onion she'd missed from the ground and tossed it to him. His hand darted out to catch it. "You said it's important that I like her. What if she doesn't like me?" she asked him. "Is it over between us?"

For a moment he seemed so taken by surprise by her words that he didn't respond. Then his words came in a rush. "*Ne*, don't say that. Why would you say that?" He gently put the onion back in the bin. "Doesn't the Bible tell us to respect our parents? To honor them?"

Ruby nodded. She knew she should just be quiet right now. She should let this subject go until a later time. Later, down the road when they knew each other better. But she couldn't just let it go. Joseph had to know how she felt. She looked up at him, hoping she wasn't making a terrible mistake by speaking her mind. "*Ya*, the Bible does say to honor our parents. But it also says that a man should put his wife first. Ahead of everyone." She rested her hands on her broad hips. "I'll do all I can to help Magdalena accept me. I'll give her the respect she deserves as your mother and as an older person. But if she doesn't give me the same respect, you may have to choose between us. Because I will never come into a household where I won't be welcome. Not even for you, Joseph."

Chapter Six

Ruby was still standing in front of Joseph, the produce table between them, when Leah returned with a can of soda and two slices of pizza. "Hi, Joseph," Leah greeted.

He mumbled a hello in her direction.

"I can take over for a while," Leah said. "It's not too busy inside right now. So go, have a nice lunch together."

"Ya," Ruby agreed. "That would be nice. I'm getting hungry. You?" She smiled up at Joseph, sorry that she'd been so blunt about his mother. She didn't regret stating her position, but she didn't want to cause him any grief. Clearly, he was caught between the mother he loved and a growing affection he felt for Ruby, an affection that Ruby hoped might blossom into real love.

"I invited Mother to—to lunch," Joseph said. "If—if that's okay." His high cheekbones were dusted with a dusky red and Ruby could read the uncertainty in his eyes. She'd noticed that Joseph's shyness was more evident when others were present.

"Wonderful. We'll go find her." Ruby untied her

work apron. "Let me get my good apron out of the buggy, and we'll go find her and ask her to join us."

Leah placed her pizza on the table and walked around to the other side. "There are picnic tables over there under the trees," She motioned toward a cluster of white tables not far away. "It's warm inside the restaurant area, even with the fans. You might want to get something and eat outside."

"Ya," Joseph agreed. "Outside is…good."

Ruby came around the table to Joseph's side. She smiled up at him. "Don't worry. I'm sure your mother and I just got off to an awkward start. Everything will be fine. I'm sure we'll become the best of friends."

He nodded, his features revealing both gratitude and wistful hope. Ruby's heart went out to him. He really was a very gentle man. In some ways, he reminded her of her father, although no one would ever accuse Solomon Plank of being shy. But they shared a genuine kindness.

"Looks like the picnic tables are filling up pretty quickly. Should I get us a seat?" Ruby asked.

"Sure, and I'll get mother," Joseph agreed.

Ruby found a good spot in the shade and Joseph and Magdalena soon joined her. "I'll get our lunch and you two can sit," Joseph said, clearly feeling awkward. "What would you like, Ruby?"

"I'd like a hot dog and water," Magdalena said, opening her small black purse. "Get us all hot dogs, the nice beef ones from the stand just inside the door."

She pulled out a ten-dollar bill and held it out to her son.

Joseph flushed and lowered his gaze to his boots. "I have money," he said under his breath.

"Ne, ne," his mother insisted, shaking the bill. "I won't let you spend all your hard-earned paycheck on me." She smiled up at him. "You know you have to count every penny. No one ever pays you what you're worth."

Joseph shook his head again, and Magdalena tried to push the money into his hand. He stepped back.

"You see what I have to put up with," Magdalena said over her shoulder to Ruby. "He's stubborn, just like his father." She turned back to him. "Fine. Have it your way, Joseph. But I'd feel better if you'd at least let me buy my own lunch. Then you'll just have to pay for yours and Ruthie's. We want mustard and relish on the hot dogs. No onion."

"R-Ruby, Mother." Joseph's tone was sheepish. "Her name is… It's *Ruby*."

If Ruby didn't know better, she would think Magdalena had purposely called her by the wrong name. "Ruby," she repeated, hoping her smile looked more genuine than it felt.

"Oh, I'm sorry. Of course. Ruby." Magdalena chuckled. "And your last name, dear?"

"Plank." Ruby looked to Joseph. "A hot dog would be fine, but I like mine with onion and ketchup. No mustard, please."

Magdalena chuckled, glancing at Ruby. "Onion? Didn't your mother ever tell you that a girl with onion on her breath will never catch a beau?"

"Ketchup and onion," Ruby repeated, thinking that if Joseph really wanted to marry her, he might as well know now that she liked onions. "And water will be fine for me, Joseph."

Magdalena held out the ten-dollar bill once more, but

Joseph walked away, leaving Magdalena to join Ruby on the picnic table bench.

"Well, well." Magdalena set her purse on the table and sat down beside Ruby. "Isn't this a nice opportunity for us to get to know each other?"

Ruby could hear insincerity in the woman's voice. But she truly *did* want to be friends with Magdalena, so she forged ahead. "I've been wanting to meet you. And…well, I just want to tell you that I know this must be difficult for you. Joseph and me courting. He told me that you're very close. I wouldn't want you to think that I'd ever try to come between a mother and her son."

"Never crossed my mind." Magdalena smoothed an invisible wrinkle in her skirt. "Because that would be impossible. Joseph and I share a special…" She sighed. "It's difficult to explain to someone who hasn't had children. But a son, especially a first and only, is very dear to his mother." She patted the bench between them. "Come closer, dear. Let me see the stitching on your dress and apron. It's very well-done. You must be an accomplished seamstress."

Ruby slid over and turned over the hem of her black apron so that Magdalena could inspect the tiny, neat stitches. "My mother made my dress and apron," she admitted sheepishly. The fact that she wasn't much with a needle and thread or a sewing machine didn't usually bother her, but having to admit it to her mother-in-law-to-be was a little daunting.

"Oh." Magdalena put a forefinger to her lips. "You have hook-and-eye fastenings on your dress, don't you? We don't see much of that. Hooks and eyes, buttons, zippers on women's dresses." She indicated her own dress. "We use straight pins."

Ruby started to assure Magdalena there were no buttons nor zippers on her clothing, but the older woman went right on talking.

"Of course, our church communities are quite conservative. Probably more so than…" Magdalena frowned, her forehead wrinkling. "Where is it you come from, my dear? Out west?" She opened her black bag, removed a folded fan, opened it and began to fan herself.

Ruby bit down on her lower lip, then winced. This first meeting with Magdalena wasn't going at all the way she'd imagined it would. Ruby had gone over and over this meeting in her head, planning what she would say. What they would talk about. Showing Magdalena the best of herself and setting her at ease, letting her know what a good wife she would make for Joseph. It had never occurred to her that Magdalena might not like her. Or might not be all that likable herself. Joseph had said his mother would live with them after they were married and suddenly she was worried. Was that even going to be possible?

"Iowa?" Magdalena asked pointedly. "Wisconsin?"

"Pennsylvania." Ruby forced another smile. "Lancaster County."

"Ach," Magdalena exclaimed. "No wonder. You *Pennsylvania Dutch* are quite liberal, aren't you? Lancaster County, you say? I'm sure we have a few mutual acquaintances."

Ruby certainly hoped not. Someone who knew Ruby might inadvertently tell things that Ruby's parents didn't want told. At least not yet. Suddenly Ruby wished fervently that she'd never agreed to her parents' plan. She didn't like keeping secrets. Not even from someone as ungracious as Magdalena. But she couldn't think about that now. And she couldn't allow Joseph's mother to put her on the defensive. She was supposed to make the woman like her, so that she would give her approval of the wedding.

"Where in Lancaster County?" Magdalena nudged. "Exactly?"

"Oh…out in the country. Nowhere that you'd know, I'm sure," Ruby said. "A little town called Bee Bonnet. It's really not much more than a crossroad."

"Bee Bonnet? How quaint." Magdalena's eyes narrowed. She stared. "Have you joined the church?"

"I—I have," Ruby assured her, taken aback by the sudden change in the conversation. "When I was eighteen. Just like Joseph," she added.

Magdalena frowned. "Your father isn't one of the automobile-driving Pennsylvania Amish, is he?"

Ruby chuckled, imagining her father driving a car. "*Ne.* A horse and buggy."

"Rubber tires?"

Ruby shook her head, fighting the urge to laugh. "Just like Sara's. Only, our buggy is gray instead of black."

"Magdalena!" a man called.

Ruby looked up to see an Amish man carrying a cardboard box crossing the street toward them. "Magdalena, I was hoping to see you here today," he called cheerfully in *Deitsch*.

Magdalena smiled and waved and then said to Ruby, "Elmer Raber. A lovely man. He has a butcher shop. You may have seen his stand inside."

Elmer was a short, solid man in his early fifties. He had a medium-length, curly beard that might have originally been auburn but now was a dull rust color. He was dressed in a black coat, blue shirt, black trousers and suspenders. "Magdalena," he repeated, a little out of breath. He nodded to Ruby. "Afternoon."

"Elmer, this is Ruthie Plank."

"Ruby," Ruby corrected. "*Ruby* Plank."

Magdalena covered her mouth and chuckled. "Did I say Ruthie again? Forgive me. Just a slip of the tongue. Elmer is a widower." She nodded in his direction and then her eyes suddenly widened. "Elmer's a widower," she said again. "And would be a fine catch for any single woman." She popped up off the bench. "Elmer, you should join us for lunch. My Joseph will be right back. Have you had your lunch? We were just about to have a bite."

"Already ate. I can't stay long, have to get back inside. Lots of customers today. Abe is a fine young man, but the stall runs smoother when I'm there. Just went back to the wagon to get more paper bags." He indicated the cardboard box under his arm. "People have questions about the cuts of beef." He smiled at Magdalena, and Ruby noticed one discolored front tooth in an otherwise pleasant, bespectacled face.

"Ruby is staying with Sara Yoder," Magdalena explained, sitting down again. "She's come to Delaware to find a husband." She patted Ruby's hand. "Don't be embarrassed, dear. Nothing wrong with it. I urged my Joseph to ask for Sara's help. She has great success with making matches."

"Good ones, so I hear," Elmer said.

"And I'm sure Ruby won't be looking long. She's a fabulous cook, and she sews beautifully. Such a delicate young woman. She'll make someone a wonderful wife." Magdalena looked to Ruby. "Elmer's a widower. I mentioned that, didn't I? Two years now, isn't it, Elmer? So sad to lose a life companion. But he has the blessing of children to fill his home."

"Not quite," Elmer said. "Blessings, true. Two sons and a daughter. But they're all grown, married and out of the house. I'm on my own, and I can tell you, I don't like it much." He looked to Magdalena again. "A house isn't a home without a woman."

"Joseph and I—" Ruby began, but Magdalena cut her off.

"Here he comes with our hot dogs." Magdalena popped off the bench again. "Joseph, Elmer Raber's here. You remember him." She flashed Elmer a smile. "I should get Joseph to stop by your stall and get a nice roast for Saturday dinner. You pick me out a good one, Elmer. Something about three or four pounds with just a smidgen of fat in it."

"I have just the thing for you, Magdalena," Elmer promised, smiling down at her. "Angus beef. The best. Aged to perfection. And maybe I'll tuck a pound of scrapple in with it. Just for you."

"Good to see you, Elmer," Joseph handed Ruby a hot dog. "Did you meet Ruby?"

"We're walking out together. Joseph and I," Ruby explained, glad to clear up any notion Magdalena might had given Elmer that she might still be looking for a beau.

"Well, not quite," Magdalena amended. Then she laughed. "You know young people today, Elmer. Always in such a hurry. But I've advised my Joseph to go slow. Marriage is for a lifetime. It's important to pick the right person."

"And to know her when you see her," Elmer said, grinning, his gaze on Magdalena again.

"Ya," Joseph agreed as he set his mother's hot dog down in front of her.

"You really should join us for lunch, Elmer," Magdalena told the butcher. "Joseph can run and get another hot dog."

"Like to." He shifted the box from one arm to the other. "But I better get back to work. Might have time for a soda after the lunch rush though. If you'll still be here, Magdalena. Good weather to sit outside here and chat."

"And a perfect day for—for Mother and my Ruby to get to know each other," Joseph said awkwardly.

"Magdalena is a fine woman." Elmer grinned at Joseph's mother. "I know you'll like her, Ruby. Everyone speaks so highly of her."

Again Ruby opened her mouth to say something, but wasn't quick enough.

"Don't," Magdalena protested. "You'll make me proud." She fluttered her fan and looked down at her plate. "Such things to say to an old woman."

"Not so old." Elmer winked. "You know what they say. A new broom sweeps clean, but the old broom knows all the hiding places. For the dirt," he added, and then chuckled at his own joke.

Just then, Sara walked up to the table. "There you are, Ruby." She set her shopping bag on the bench. "Afternoon, Magdalena, Joseph, Elmer." Her gaze met Ruby's and she smiled. "How nice to find you all having such a lovely time."

It was all Ruby could do to look down, bite her tongue and not say what she was really feeling.

* * *

"That's just what I was thinking!" Ruby exclaimed, turning on the stepladder.

"Whoa!" Joseph shot out his hand and caught the tipping paint can inches from the floor.

"Oops." She grimaced. Then they both laughed.

It was a Wednesday afternoon and she and Joseph had come to a work frolic for young couples organized by Leah's sister Miriam and her husband, Charley. Eight couples, including the sponsors, had gathered at the Seven Poplar Schoolhouse to paint the interior of the building and have a picnic outside afterward. Arlene and Leah were there as well as several girls Ruby hadn't met yet. Everyone seemed friendly, and conversation and laughter filled the schoolroom.

Since Joseph had promised to have her home before dark and they were riding in Joseph's wagon in full public view, Sara had allowed them to ride the short distance to the school unchaperoned. It was the first time they'd been alone together since Joseph had found her drying her hair beside Sara's fishpond, and Ruby had been enjoying every moment.

"Sorry," Ruby told Joseph. The paintbrush in her hand was dripping white paint down her arm.

"I'd better take that." He reached for the paintbrush. "Why don't I finish up this window trim?"

"Good idea." Ruby looked down at the spots of paint on her dress and stockings. "I warned you," she told him. "I'm prone to accidents."

"Ne." He shook his head. "Painting trim is tricky." He took her hand and steadied her as she descended the stepladder.

A thrill shot through Ruby. Had he held her hand a

fraction of a second longer than was necessary? His touch was warm and strong, exactly like the personality that radiated from his bright blue eyes. "Not for Leah or Arlene," Ruby said looking at the two of them working on the opposite side of the schoolhouse. "They don't make a mess when they paint."

He smiled down at her. "Maybe not so much. But I don't mind." He released her hand and stepped back, but his gaze remained locked with hers.

How handsome he was in his short-sleeved blue shirt and dark trousers, Ruby thought. She wondered what he would look like with a beard. He'd always been clean-shaven when she'd been with him. But, of course, that would change if they married. *When* they married, she told herself. Nothing was going to go wrong with this courtship. She wasn't going to let Magdalena get in the way, or anything else. No matter what, she'd find a way to smooth the small wrinkles in their relationship. That was her job, wasn't it? As a woman, she would be expected to be the one to adjust, to bend to her husband's will. That's what the preachers said.

"I was happy that you came to church with me, Sunday," Joseph said as he swept the small brush over the trim in smooth strokes to even up her painting.

"*Ya*, I enjoyed your bishop's sermon. He seems like a down-to-earth kind of bishop."

"He is," Joseph agreed. "Easy to talk to. In fact, I got a chance to talk to him about an idea I've had for a while. About a new kind of windmill," he explained, moving along the window with his brush. "The kind *Englishers* are putting up. No Amish around here have one, but the bishop said he didn't see why it would conflict with our values. He promised to take it up with the elders at their next meeting."

"Wonderful," she said, beaming. She liked that they had plenty to talk about. That Joseph felt comfortable telling her things. It was funny how he seemed to have no trouble getting his words out, without stuttering or stammering, when they were alone.

"And Mother said lots of people asked about you," he added. "I hope you had a good time."

"I did." Ruby perched on the corner of the big teacher's desk. She noticed that it wasn't nearly as high as most desks and remembered that Ellie had explained it had been built to fit her small stature. "Everyone was so nice and welcoming. I like your friends."

"And they like you."

Around them, the other couples were also painting or scrubbing and polishing the paneled wainscoting. They were using latex paint so that it would be dry by morning. It was amazing how much could be done when there were a dozen willing hands. One of the men, a bearded widower named Joel began singing a fast hymn and soon everyone joined in. Ruby, who knew she had a tendency to get carried away and sing too loudly, kept her voice low so that her spontaneity wouldn't embarrass Joseph. His voice was rich and sweet, and Ruby was delighted to discover this talent of his.

"What did you think of Elmer?" Joseph asked when they'd sung the lively spiritual through twice and the schoolroom had become quiet again, except for the conversations of the various couples.

"Elmer?" She had to think for a moment to realize who he was talking about. "You mean your mother's friend we met at Spence's?"

"*Ya.* Mother told me she was thinking of inviting him to supper one evening. I think he likes her."

"I think he does too," Ruby agreed, with a giggle. "But I'm not sure that your mother realizes it."

"She must. She speaks so well of him. She went on and on about what a good husband he would make."

"Did she?" Ruby laughed, recalling how Magdalena had been extolling his virtues when she introduced them.

"Girls," Miriam called from the doorway. "It looks like we're almost finished in here. Could you come out and help me set up the food?"

It was amazing to Ruby how much Miriam resembled her sister Leah. Miriam's face was a little rounder and her hair a darker auburn, but like Leah, she looked younger than she was. Ruby liked her, and she liked Miriam's husband, Charley, as well. Both of them went out of their way to include everyone and make the event fun.

"*Ya,*" Arlene said. "We're coming."

"We'll be right there," Ruby replied.

"I'll be finished in two minutes." Joseph turned his attention from painting to Ruby. "Mother sent a dozen poppy-seed rolls and a jug of cider for the picnic. I'll have to run and get them. They're in the split-oak basket in the back of the wagon."

"That was kind of her." Ruby stood up from her perch on the desk. "We'll have plenty, I'm sure."

Every girl had brought food, which they'd combine and share, potluck-style. Sara and Ellie had prepared fried chicken and apple fritters. Ruby, who knew she would have burned them both had her hand been in the pot, had contented herself with packing the basket and making certain there were enough utensils and napkins to share. She wasn't ready to chance her cooking skills on Joseph or any of the other hapless couples.

Ruby glanced up at Joseph. "See you soon?"

"I'm right behind you." The way he looked at her made her face flush and she hurried for the door.

"What do you think of Joel?" Arlene whispered to Ruby as they walked out of the classroom. The other couples had filed out, leaving only Joel and Joseph still in the schoolroom.

"He seems nice," Ruby said.

"He is. Widower. He has an adorable little boy. I met his son today." She caught Ruby's arm and the two lingered for a moment in the addition that served as both a storage room and cloakroom for the small school. "I met Joel's mother too. Very sweet and welcoming."

"That's a good sign," Ruby whispered. "I don't think he would have introduced you to his child and family if he wasn't interested in you."

"That's what Sara says." Arlene beamed. "She's introduced me to two others, but I like Joel the best."

They exited the outer door and walked down the steps single file. Along the side fence line of the schoolyard were an assortment of horses and buggies. Ruby and Joseph were the only ones who'd come in a wagon. But there was a buggy that hadn't been there earlier. Oddly, the horse was hitched to the back of Joseph's wagon.

"What's *my mother* doing here?" Joseph asked, coming up behind Ruby.

She looked back over her shoulder. Joseph and Joel were walking side by side. Joel nodded to her and strode to catch up with Arlene.

Ruby fell back to walk with Joseph. "Your mother?" Ruby said. "I didn't know she was coming."

Joseph was frowning. "I didn't either. I hope nothing's wrong at home."

When they rounded the schoolhouse, Ruby saw that Magdalena was standing beside Miriam, talking and pouring lemonade at the long serving table.

"She seems fine," Ruby whispered.

"There you are, Joseph," Magdalena called, waving. "You'd better hurry. I'm not sure there's enough chicken."

"Mother," Joseph said quietly, as they approached the buffet table. "What are you doing here?"

"I realized that I'd made two pies for the frolic and had forgotten to remind you to put them in the wagon. I thought the best thing to do was to bring them myself and see if Miriam could use my help." She looked to Miriam, who was busy removing foil from covered dishes.

"Always glad of another pair of hands at a frolic," Miriam said cheerfully.

Charley, standing beside his wife, grinned mischievously. "Oh, *ya.* Especially a mother."

Miriam elbowed him, but Magdalena didn't seem to notice.

"Men, find a seat for you and your date on the blankets spread around the yard," Charley announced. "Each couple gets their own spot. I'll come around with drinks. The women will make up plates for the men's suppers, and all of us fellows will do the cleaning up after dessert. How does that sound?"

"Goot," Joel called.

The other men joined in with a chorus of *"ya"* and "sounds good."

"And don't eat too much," Miriam reminded them. "Because we're playing softball afterward, and it's men against the women."

"Are you pitching, Miriam?" a boy Ruby didn't know called out.

"She sure is," Charley said. "So watch out for her fastball."

"Do you play softball?" Joseph asked Ruby.

Ruby nodded.

"Good. Because I love it. I catch," he said. "What position do you play?"

"First base," she answered. "But I don't mind out-field."

"Can you hit?"

She chuckled. "Just wait and see."

"Where would you like to sit?" he asked.

"You pick," she told him. "I'm getting the food."

Ruby watched Joseph walk across the lawn to a mul-ticolored quilt spread out near the swings, and then she got in line with the other young women at the serving table. For a light supper, there were more choices than could possibly fit on one plate. She wondered what Jo-seph liked, then decided to choose what she liked and hope for the best.

A few minutes later, walking carefully and balanc-ing several of his mother's poppy-seed rolls on top of the plate, Ruby joined Joseph at the quilt where he was sitting. "I wasn't sure what you'd want," she said as she held out the plate.

"Ach," came a familiar voice from behind her. "Jo-seph, I picked out your very favorites." Magdalena

nudged Ruby aside with her hip. "Joseph can be particular about his likes and dislikes," she said sweetly. "I'm afraid I've spoiled him."

Blushing, Joseph got to his feet. "*Mother*, Ruby already—already... I have a plate."

"Nonsense," Magdalena said. "You can just give that plate to her. I've brought—"

"Your plate looks wonderful," Ruby said to Magdalena as she pushed the plate in her hands into his. "And Joseph can eat every bite just as soon as he finishes what I've picked out for him." She smiled up at Joseph. "You *did* say you were hungry," she teased.

He nodded, looking obviously uncomfortable. "I—I did."

"Good. See, Magdalena—" Ruby turned to his mother "—now I won't have to go back for seconds for Joseph. Now, if you'll excuse me, I'm going for my own supper." She smiled sweetly. "If you like, Magdalena, I can bring you one, as well."

Magdalena stood there, holding the plate of food. Her mouth opened but nothing came out.

"No?" Ruby said, still smiling. "Well, I'm starved." And with that, she headed back to the serving table, leaving Joseph to deal with his mother.

Chapter Seven

Andy Troyer pumped the handle and cool water gushed out of the spout behind Joseph's house. Andy removed his hat and thrust his head under the flow, letting the icy well water wash away the sweat and grime from his head and neck. He stepped back, sputtering, shook his shaggy, blond head and clamped his straw hat back on. "Whew, that feels better." Water streamed down his shirt and dripped into the dust around him, and a few chickens ran over to investigate and stirred up the ground with their scratching.

Joseph laughed and patted his cousin's generous mid-section. "You're getting soft," he observed. "Maybe you're eating a little too much of your mother's pie. Pitching a little hay into the loft too much for you?"

"Ne," Andy protested, patting his own belly. "This isn't fat. It's muscle." He adjusted a faded, black suspender and eyed the barn loft they'd just come from. "Heavy bales, them. And it's a warm day for late September. Been a hot summer too."

Joseph stepped up to the pump and drew a cupful of water. He drank it down, wiped his mouth and then pumped more. The well was deeper than most Delaware farm wells and it had always produced sweet, clear water without the hint of sulfur that sullied some sources. "I appreciate your coming over to help me get the hay in the barn. It's starting to cloud up in the west. I was afraid that we'd get rain before I could get it all under cover."

"Good timothy hay like this, I can see why you'd worry. I heard thunder a while back. A storm's heading this way, for sure. Maybe a little rain will ease this late heat wave." Andy removed his hat again and slicked his damp hair back. "Violet asked me to check with you. You'll be there for the wedding? To help out with setting up tables and such?"

Andy's sister was marrying in late October. Her fiancé was from Ohio but the wedding would be held at her parents' house.

"I sure will. Wouldn't miss it. I'll take the whole day off."

"Good. Violet is afraid to leave the setup for the midday meal in my hands." He chuckled. "I guess she doesn't think I know how to set up for a wedding."

"Well, tell her I'll be there. And…" Joseph hesitated. "Looks like I'll be bringing someone along. If that's all right."

"All right? It's better than all right." Andy playfully clamped his hand around Joseph's arm. "When am I going to get to meet this girl of yours?"

"Ruby?" Joseph smiled. "Soon enough."

"Whirlwind romance, so your mother told mine."

Joseph didn't respond.

"*Mam* says you haven't known Ruby long enough to

be getting so serious," Andy went on. "She had some ditty about a marriage in haste."

Andy's mother was a sister of Joseph's father, and she'd always been a favorite aunt of Joseph's. He had no doubt that Aunt Frieda had his best interests at heart, but he was certain she'd change her mind about him and Ruby once she saw how wonderful she was.

"The time you've known someone doesn't always matter. It's like we've always known each other."

Andy sighed. "As much as I hate to do it, I have to agree with my mother and yours. My advice is to go slow, cousin. Marriage is for a long time. And you don't want it to be with the wrong woman." He leaned against the hitching rail and wiped his face with his blue-and-white handkerchief.

Joseph chuckled and pointed at Andy. "I think you're making it worse. You've smeared something black across your forehead."

"Figures." Andy took another swipe at his forehead with the handkerchief. "Look, I'm not trying to put my nose in your business. Knowing Aunt Magdalena, I imagine you have enough of that already. I'm just looking out for your own good." Andy motioned to the cup that dangled from a string, and Joseph pumped a cup of water for him. Andy drank it slowly and then went on. "Seriously, Joseph. You can't know Ruby that well in what? Two weeks since she's been here? How do you even know if you really like her?"

"Almost four weeks," Joseph defended, though it was closer to three. "Almost a month. But I do like her. A lot. I—I think I love her. I love her enough to ask her to be my wife," he added with a firm nod.

Andy gave a low whistle. "My *mam* says your mother

isn't happy about that. Not that she doesn't like the girl, but your mother is concerned about the rush. Especially since Ruby is from somewhere else and no one knows the family. No one knows Ruby. She's a newcomer. *Mam* says your mother's afraid Ruby might not be all she pretends to be." He scuffed the ground with his boot and looked up. "And I understand her point."

Joseph frowned. "A lot of advice from another single fellow. I don't see you finding anybody you want to spend the rest of your life with yet."

"True words." Andy chuckled. "But you don't have to be a farrier to know a driving horse goes better with four shoes than three."

"Besides," Joseph said, not sure he liked the idea of having to defend Ruby to Andy. Andy was his best friend. He didn't think it ought to be like this between best friends. "Ruby hasn't pretended to be anything. She's…she's…" He could feel exasperation growing in his chest. He never had trouble speaking his mind to Andy. They'd been friends since they were babies. They'd been together through school and all the church affairs and family get-togethers so long as he could remember. He'd been planning to ask Andy to be part of the wedding.

"Come on, I'm not picking on you. Or your girl," Andy said. "Just telling you what's on my mind. Now tell me what it's like, courting? Picking someone that you like better than all the rest?"

That was an easier question to answer and Joseph felt on solid ground again. "It makes me humble," he exclaimed. "Ruby is the prettiest, the kindest, the funniest, the smartest girl I've ever known. Just being with her makes me…makes me want to stand up in worship service and lead a hymn of thanks."

"And you think she feels the same way about you?" Andy asked.

"I think she does." Joseph nodded. "*Ya*, I'm sure of it."

"And you can talk to her? Because I know… I know words don't always come easy to you."

"We talk all the time. I never get tired of talking to her. Sara has to come out and chase me off her porch when it's time for Ruby to go in. And if she'd let me, I'd be at her supper table every night just so I could look at Ruby."

Andy grimaced. "Sounds like you've got it bad. Like you were struck by a lightning bolt."

"It's what it feels like." Joseph was surprised by how easily he could voice his thoughts on Ruby. "I think about her first thing when I wake up in the morning, and I think about her all day. She's special, Andy. I know she's the one God wants me to choose for my wife." A black-and-white barn cat came over and rubbed up against Joseph's leg and he bent and stroked it. Joseph scratched it behind the ears and it began to purr loudly.

"So why doesn't Aunt Magdalena think she's a good match for you?" Andy asked. "I know she wants you to marry. She's always telling my mother how she wants you to settle down, find a good wife and give her grandchildren."

"I don't know why Mother doesn't approve of Ruby," Joseph admitted. "I think maybe she isn't happy because she didn't do the arranging."

"But it was *her* idea to go to the matchmaker, *ya*?"

"Right," Joseph agreed. "But I think she had it in her

head that Sara was going to parade girls in front of her and she was going to pick for me."

Andy laughed. "Sounds like Aunt Magdalena."

"Anyway." Joseph gave a shrug. "Everything's going to work itself out. Mother invited Ruby to supper this evening." He looked down at his hay-flecked clothing and dirty shoes. "Which means I'd better get cleaned up. I know for certain that neither of them will allow me to sit at the table looking like this."

"And I'd better get on home," Andy said as they started across the barnyard.

"You know you're welcome to stay for supper."

Andy laughed. "Looking like this?"

"I can loan you some clean clothes," Joseph offered. "And it would give you an opportunity to meet Ruby. See, I'm not trying to hide her."

"Not tonight, thank you. I promised my younger brothers and sisters I'd take them for pizza in Dover. Maybe another night we could go out together. You bring Ruby, I'll find a date, and we could go out to the mall and just walk around. Have a bite at the food court?"

"Maybe. I don't know how Ruby's parents feel about her going to malls and such."

Andy walked backward and shrugged. "I think Josie King might be having a singing next week. Maybe we could double-date for that?" The sound of a dinner bell rang out from the back porch.

"Joseph," Magdalena called. "Supper."

"Guess you best be going," Andy said.

Joseph thanked Andy again, then watched him stride off in the direction of his family's farm, before heading to the house. There, he found Ruby on the back porch waiting for him. Sara must have dropped her off while he was in the back field. "I'm glad you could come," he said. Just seeing her made him smile.

She grinned, clasping her hands together. "Glad you invited me."

They just stood there looking at each other until Joseph began to feel awkward. "Well, I—I better get washed up before we eat," he told her.

She was still smiling at him, which made him feel good. Capable. "You must be exhausted after throwing all that hay up into the barn."

He shrugged. "It's hard work, but it feels good when the barn is full and you know you have good hay for the horses and the cows for the winter." He gestured toward the door. "How is she? Is she in a good mood?"

It was Ruby's turn to shrug. "As good as mine."

He met her gaze questioningly.

"Don't worry." She gave a wave. "It's fine. There is bound to be a little—" She broke off at the sound of buggy wheels. "Expecting someone? Another girl maybe?" she teased.

"Never."

A buggy pulled by a gray horse was coming up the driveway. It was Elmer Raber. He waved with enthusiasm. "Not late for supper, am I?" he shouted as he rolled by.

"*Ne*. Just in time," Joseph replied. He glanced at Ruby and lowered his voice. "Did you know Elmer was coming?"

She shook her head. "Your mother didn't mention it."

Elmer drove his horse to the hitching post and climbed down from his buggy. "Joseph, come give me a hand. I've brought your mother a roast, a half-dozen steaks and some prime rib."

The back door opened and Magdalena came out. "Elmer!" she called, wiping her hands on her apron. "How pleasant to see you." She looked at Ruby. "Isn't this nice? Elmer's come to join us."

"Nice," Ruby repeated.

"You brought meat?" Magdalena called to Elmer. "Now, you know that wasn't necessary, but we do appreciate it."

"I can't bake a pie." Elmer wrapped the reins around the hitching post. "But I know a good roast when I see one."

Joseph's mother was all smiles, positively twittering as she said to Joseph, "Those two got along so well last time, Elmer and Ruthie—"

"Ruby," Joseph interrupted.

Magdalena gave a quick smile in Ruby's direction and went on talking. "I thought I'd invite him for supper. You never know. Men and women plan, but the Lord decides. Give Elmer a big, big welcome."

Joseph glanced at Ruby as he headed for the buggy to take the box Elmer was unloading from his buggy.

"You heard your mother, Joseph," Ruby said sweetly. "Let's give Elmer a big welcome."

"Ya," Magdalena waved her guest in. "Come right in and sit down, Elmer. You too, Ruby. Joseph can put the horse and buggy in the shed. And while I get supper on the table, you two can have a nice talk."

"Thank you for the meal, Mother." Joseph rose from the kitchen chair he'd carried into the living room after the meal. "You outdid yourself as usual."

"Ya," Elmer agreed. "I don't know when I've eaten better." He stood up from the couch and scooped up the last few kernels of popcorn out of a bowl and put them in his mouth. "Good cooking, good talk and a good game. I can't think when I've enjoyed myself more."

Joseph picked up the last of the playing pieces and put them back into the box, relieved the evening was coming to an end. After they'd eaten, the four of them had played Settlers of Catan, a board game that Ruby and Elmer seemed to enjoy as much as he and his mother did. The thunderstorm that Joseph had worried over when he'd been getting up the hay had finally materialized. Now the thunder and lightning had moved off to the east, but a light rain continued to fall, which meant that he could couldn't drive Ruby home in the open wagon as he'd promised Sara. He wondered if he should ask his mother to ride with them in the buggy. It was the right thing to do; he just didn't know how Ruby would feel about it.

"Elmer, you know where the matchmaker lives, don't you? Would you mind dropping Ruby off at Sara's?"

"Um…sure," Elmer said, looking from Magdalena to Ruby and back to Magdalena again.

Ruby, who'd been carrying the empty popcorn bowl to the kitchen, let it slip through her fingers. The aluminum container hit the floor with a bang and bounced. Unpopped kernels rained on the floor. *"Ne,"* she managed as she grabbed the fallen bowl. The kernels rolled. "I wouldn't want to put you to the trouble."

"It wouldn't be any trouble," Elmer protested. "I just—"

"I… *I'm* taking Ruby home," Joseph interrupted.

"Thank you… Elmer, but… Ruby is… She's my responsibility."

Ruby blushed and looked distressed. "I don't want to cause any problem," she said. "I can walk."

"Nonsense." His mother moved to Ruby's side and slipped an arm around her waist. "You'll not walk home in a rainstorm. There's no good reason you can't accept a ride from Elmer. The rules of courtship don't apply to friends. And Elmer is certainly in that category."

"I hope I'm a friend to all of you, Magdalena," Elmer said, looking to her.

"There." His mother released Ruby and put her hands together with a smile. "It's all settled."

"It is *not* settled," Joseph managed. "Ruby, Elmer, if you'll excuse us for just a moment, I need to speak to my mother. Alone."

"Certainly," Elmer replied.

Ruby looked as if she were about to burst into tears. Joseph met her gaze. "Just give me a moment," he said quietly to her. "I'll hitch up the buggy and take you. Sara will just have to understand."

"If you're sure," she said, glancing from him to his mother.

"I'm sure," Joseph said, and then he looked to Elmer. "Maybe you could take Ruby out on the back porch for me. I'll be right along."

Elmer nodded and motioned to Ruby. Together the two hurried into the kitchen and then out the back door.

"I never!" His mother crossed her arms over her chest. "How could you be so disrespectful to a guest in our house? And to me?"

Joseph bit back the hot retort that rose on his tongue.

"Mother, for once will you just stop talking and let me speak my mind?"

"Joseph Brenneman. What would your father say if he heard you talking to me in such a tone?"

"He'd probably say that it was high time I stood up for myself."

"Where's the respect the Bible says you should show your mother?" She covered her face with her hands and began to weep softly.

The sound cut him sharply. He wanted to beg her forgiveness and tell her not to cry, that he'd do anything if she didn't cry. But he thought of Ruby standing on the back porch, he thought of her crying, and he stiffened his spine. "I do respect you, Mother."

"All I've ever done is love you and try to do what is best for you," she said into her hands.

"I know that. But you have to realize that I'm a man grown. Some things I have to decide for my own. And choosing a wife is one of those things." He wanted to put his arms around her and comfort her, but he didn't.

Another big sob. Her narrow shoulders trembled. "This isn't—isn't the way it was supposed to go."

"You are the one who urged me to go to Sara Yoder and find a wife." Joseph exhaled slowly and took a clean handkerchief from his pocket. He passed it to her and she blew her nose daintily. "Mother, you should be happy for me," he told her. "I've found the most wonderful girl, the sweetest—"

"Ugly," she whispered.

"What?" He drew back. "What did you say?" He couldn't believe what he'd just heard.

"She's—she's not even pretty. You'll have thick, unlovely children."

He blinked, still in disbelief. "Mother. How can you say that? Ruby's beautiful."

"You see?" She shook her head. "I believe you've lost your wits. She's as plain as an old shoe. Her mouth is too big, and her nose looks like a lump of biscuit dough. And her chin…" She gave another wail. "Stubborn. A stubborn chin."

"Don't ever speak about Ruby like that again. Do you hear me, Mother?"

She sniffed and blew her nose again. "Very uncharitable talk for a son to his widowed mother."

"We're not going to talk about charity, Mother. That you would say such things about the girl I love, the girl who is going to be the mother of your grandchildren, it—it hurts me more than I can tell you. I won't have it."

"And what about her cooking? Did you ever taste such terrible macaroni and cheese as what she brought tonight? Have you?"

He almost smiled. "I can't say I'm in love with her mac and cheese, but I am in love with her."

His mother wiped her eyes. "Not yet. Please tell me that you aren't marrying her yet. You haven't even been to the bishop."

He sighed. "*Ne*, I haven't, but I will as soon as Ruby tells me that she's sure of me."

"You mean *she* hasn't agreed yet?" Suddenly she perked up. "So she's not sure?"

"We're courting, Mother. That means that we're trying to find out if we're right for each other, but both of us feel we're headed toward marriage. Now, I want you and Ruby to get to know each other, but if she isn't welcome here under your roof—" he took a breath "— then I'm not either."

"Not my roof," she said. She began to fan herself with her hand. "Yours, strictly speaking. I'm the dependent one, the widow with only one son to care for her. Helpless in my old age."

"Mother, you are far from helpless. You're strong and smart, and to me you've always been loving and charitable. I'm asking you to show some of that charity to the girl I want to marry."

"So you haven't set a date for the wedding?"

"*Ne.* Not yet, but—"

"Good, good. That's as it should be. Take your time. That's all I ask. Get to know her better. Find out something about her. Go and meet her family. See if she's all you think she is."

"That's the best advice you've given me all evening," he said. "Now, I'm driving Ruby home and then I'll be back. Don't wait up. I think you and I will both be in a better mood if we say good-night now and see each other fresh in the morning."

She brought a hand to her mouth. "I never meant to hurt your feelings, Joseph. You must know that. And it was never for myself. I could get used to plain grandchildren if—"

"Mother," he warned.

"Sorry. It just slipped out." She gathered her dignity around her and raised her chin higher. "That was ill said. I suppose we all have different ideas of beauty."

"Apparently." He headed for the door.

She followed him. "And beauty is fleeting. Not worth much compared to grace."

He didn't turn around. "Good night, Mother."

"Good night, Joseph."

Grabbing his hat, he stepped onto the porch and

pulled the back door closed behind him. The rain was coming down harder, but Ruby and Elmer were standing far enough back that they were dry.

"Sorry about…that," Joseph murmured.

"It's fine." Ruby smiled up at him. "Elmer and I were just talking about the rain. He thinks it's going to be off and on for a while yet."

"Why don't I drive the both of you to the matchmaker's and then bring you back home," Elmer suggested. "My horse is already hitched up in the shed, and it would be the least I can do in exchange for that fine supper."

"Thank you," Ruby said, "but Joseph and I can manage in the wagon." She motioned to the rain slickers hanging on the porch wall. "The horse is going to be wet no matter what."

"Ne," Joseph said. "That's silly. I'll hitch up my buggy."

Ruby frowned. "I'm afraid Sara will be disappointed in us for breaking her rule. She wanted us to be chaperoned if we rode in a closed buggy."

"Then it's settled," Elmer chimed in jovially, bringing his hands together. "I've got no one waiting for me at home but my gray cat. I can be your chaperone and bring Joseph back." He chuckled as he adjusted his hat before stepping into the drizzle. "Who knows? I might even be invited back in for another slice of your mother's fantastic chocolate pie."

Chapter Eight

"Stay where you are," Joseph said, rising from his chair. "I'll get you a refill on your lemonade."

With a handful of napkins, Ruby mopped at the lemonade on the table and hoped that no one in the fast-food restaurant had noticed she'd spilled her drink. It was a Friday evening and she and Joseph, Leah and her beau and Joseph's cousin Andy and a young woman named Nancy had hired a van and driver to take them to Dover. They'd gone to an indoor produce market and then come to the restaurant for supper.

Joseph had just brought up the subject of visiting her parents. Again. And she wasn't sure what to say to him. For once her clumsiness had come in handy. When she'd knocked over the cup so hard that the lid popped off, both of them had jumped out of their chairs to keep from becoming covered in lemonade, ending the conversation. Or at least putting it off.

She watched Joseph walk away and when he turned to look at her, she couldn't help but smile back.

She supposed he was right. It probably *was* time he met her parents, but it made her nervous just thinking about it. So long as she was in Delaware, and her *mommi* and *daddi* were in Pennsylvania, she could almost forget that she wasn't being totally honest with Joseph about who she was. She *did* want them to meet Joseph. Of course she did. She wanted them to see how wonderful Joseph was and to agree that he would make the perfect husband for her. But when they met him, it would be time to tell him her secret and she wasn't looking forward to having to admit to him that, while perhaps she'd not been dishonest with him, she'd certainly not been as forthcoming with some information.

When they'd first met and she'd gotten to know Joseph at the hospital, she'd been instantly attracted to him. For her, it was love at first sight, the love that her mother talked about finding with her father. But with each day and week that she'd known Joseph, her feelings for him had become deeper, so much deeper that she'd realized her first infatuation had been a feeble emotion compared to how she felt now. Just the sight of him made her giddy. She thought about him all the time, and she dreamed about him at night.

They'd been eating their chicken sandwiches and fries, laughing and talking when Joseph had asked her if she'd contacted her parents about the two of them coming for a visit. She'd become so flustered that she'd spilled the large lemonade.

Ruby watched an English father walk by the table. He was carrying a small boy about two years of age, and he held the hand of a little girl a year or two older. The children were blond and blue-eyed and dressed alike in blue jeans and striped shirts. The girl's hair was pulled up into a ponytail and tied with a pink ribbon.

The little girl stared at her and pointed before breaking into a big smile. "Daddy, look. That lady has a bon-net like my Polly doll."

"She does," the father agreed, ushering her by.

Ruby smiled at the little girl. Ruby had worn her best go-to meeting clothes tonight, her good black bonnet and cape. No wonder the little English girl had thought she looked like a doll. Old Order Amish clothing did stand out in the outside world. But Ruby didn't mind. She liked being unique. It was part of who she was. Didn't the Bible instruct them to remain apart from the world?

She glanced around to see what had happened to Jo-seph. He was standing in line behind a man in a military uniform and a woman with three half-grown children. Joseph smiled at her and she smiled back. How hand-some he looked. A small wave of joy rippled under her skin and she hugged herself. How could a man like Jo-seph have chosen her? It had to be God's doing. Never had she ever expected, when she'd agreed to seek out a matchmaker, that she'd meet anyone like him, and not only *meet* him, but have him ask her to become his wife. Joseph was the answer to her prayers.

Ruby's *daddi* had always told her that the right man would come along and would love her despite her clum-siness and her plain face. Her *mommi* said that she was beautiful; it simply took a man with a pure heart to open his eyes and see. Until her teens, Ruby had never thought much about the way she looked. She knew she had her mother's square chin and her father's nose. But she was sturdy and bursting with energy and good health. As her mother said, she'd been fortunate enough to be born with two eyes that worked, two ears that heard the word of God, two good arms and two legs

that carried her through the day. What did it matter if
Mary Mast had flaxen hair and skin like new-skimmed
cream? And many was the person with beautiful eyes
who couldn't see a hand in front of their face. But when
Ruby had blossomed from child to woman, being plain
and sturdy rather than pretty suddenly mattered. It mattered when her friends all paired up and began to marry.
It mattered when her mother's friends whispered behind
their knitting and called her "poor Ruby" and said "too
bad she didn't take after the other side of the family."

Ruby straightened and smiled, realizing that she
wasn't "poor Ruby" anymore. Joseph loved her for who
she was rather than what she looked like. Her parents
had been right all along. When the right man came
along, he didn't see a snub nose or a thick waist and
wide feet. Knowing that Joseph thought she was beautiful made her feel beautiful and cherished. And if her
mother and father had been right about this, maybe they
were right about what they'd asked her to promise them.

The man and his children joined a fair-haired woman
at a booth a short distance away. The little girl looked
back and waved and Ruby waved back. She couldn't
help thinking that maybe she and Joseph would be
blessed with children. Maybe they would have a girl
who looked like the English child, all blonde and blue-
eyed and dimpled. Boy or girl, it wouldn't matter to her.
They would welcome whomever God sent, and they
would love the child, sick or well. If a baby were born
to them who was little, like Ellie, or with Down syn-
drome like Susannah, Leah's sister, it wouldn't matter.
Every baby, quick or slow, pretty or plain, was a bundle
from heaven. All children came from God, and a special
child would be cherished all the more. Still, she hoped

Joseph's child might look like him, not because he was so attractive, but because she loved him so.

Joseph returned to the table with her drink refill and two ice-cream sundaes. "Sorry," he said. "There was a line at the counter."

"It's fine." She accepted the cup, setting it down on the table carefully. "I was watching that little English girl. She's adorable. She waved at me."

Joseph glanced at the booth she indicated. *"Ya,"* he agreed. "She is cute." And then he gave Ruby a smile that made her toes curl, but then he frowned. "Um. I... need to talk to you about something because... Well, I haven't been entirely honest with you, Ruby."

Her eyes widened. "You haven't? About what?" Her heart suddenly fluttered in her chest. "Oh, no, is this bad?"

"No, no, not bad. Not terrible. Just..." He looked down at the table, slowly sliding her sundae to her. "It's just that earlier, when I brought up visiting your parents, I was hoping you'd say you were ready for me to meet them and we'd make plans. But actually..." He pressed his lips together. "I sort of already arranged for a driver to take us to Lancaster next week."

"You *sort of* arranged it?"

"I did. I made the arrangements, but we can... I can cancel." He grimaced. "I might have gotten a little ahead of myself. But, I *really* do want to meet your parents. And...and I think it's time." He met her gaze. "I'm sorry. For, you know, hiring the van before you and I... Well, before your parents agreed they wanted to meet me."

"Of course they want to meet you, Joseph. It's only that—" She was flustered. Not because she was nervous about her parents meeting him, but because that would make all of this real. And for it to be real, she'd have to tell him her history. All of it.

"Charley and Miriam, the couple that sponsored the schoolhouse painting frolic, said they could chaperone us on Saturday. I thought we could drive up together, and then Charley and Miriam will visit friends in the area. You and I can visit with your parents. We could take them out to eat, and we'll come back to Delaware in the evening."

"Oh," she said. "I'm sure they'd rather have dinner for us. I just… I'll have tell Sara."

"You should tell your parents," he said. "If you think you're ready for me to meet them, of course. I just thought… I think we agreed that we both want to marry soon. Right?"

She looked down at the table. *"Ya."*

"So is that a yes? Can we go next Saturday?"

"Ya. I'm sure it will be fine. I just need to call and let them know. Leave a message on their answering machine. *Daddi* has a phone in the barn. For…emergencies and such. They can't wait to meet you," she added quickly.

"Good, then it's settled." Joseph laughed and scooped up a spoonful of vanilla ice cream with chocolate fudge sauce poured over it. He took a bite and said, "Don't look so worried. I'll be on my best behavior. But I'll warn you, we're not leaving until your father and mother give their blessing for us to marry." Then he slid his hand across the table and took her hand. "I'm not that bad of a prospect, am I?" he teased.

She shook her head. "They'll love you." She pulled her hand away and giggled self-consciously. Her hand still tingled from his touch. "Joseph, what will people say?" she whispered, glancing around the restaurant, but the other customers seemed to be concentrating on their own chicken and fries.

He chuckled. "I don't care. I'm not ashamed of letting them know how I feel about you."

As Ruby took a big bite of her own sundae, she couldn't help thinking that this Joseph Brenneman was so much more assured than the young man she'd nearly crushed when she'd fallen on him the first day they met. He hardly ever stammered when they were alone together, and he had no problems stating to her what he thought and how he felt. And being able to talk to each other was important in a marriage. She knew that from watching her parents.

"Hate to interrupt you two, but it's time to be heading back," came a raspy English voice behind her.

Startled, Ruby looked up to see their driver, Gene, standing beside the table. He was an older man with salt-and-pepper hair, a potbelly and a blue ball cap that read Niagara Falls. "The others are ready and my wife will be looking for me," he said heartily. "Early to bed, you know."

"Ya," Joseph agreed. "We'll be right behind you." He waited until the gentleman had walked away, then turned back to Ruby. "So it's settled, right? We visit your parents and as long as that goes well, we set a date for our wedding."

Ruby took a deep breath, almost feeling light-headed. Dreaming of a wedding was one thing, but the reality of it was quite another. Still, it was what she wanted more than anything. To marry Joseph. "It's settled," she agreed.

* * *

Ruby pressed her cheek against the cool glass window at the back of the van. It was raining, and the windows were steamed up and she was slightly carsick. She'd never particularly liked traveling by automobile, especially on gray days. She hoped it wasn't raining in Bee Bonnet, but she'd awakened to rain on Sara's roof, and so far the skies showed no signs of clearing.

It worried her that she hadn't had time to speak with her parents yet. She had hoped to talk to them and get their permission to tell Joseph what needed to be told so there would be no secrets on visiting day, but it had not been meant to be. On Monday, she'd walked to the chair shop and tried to reach them by phone. Like many folks in Bee Bonnet, they had a phone in the barn, which was used for business and emergencies. She had thought she might catch her father, but she hadn't and his answering machine hadn't been working. She'd then sent them a letter telling them she and Joseph were coming to visit, which was a good thing because on Wednesday she'd made a second attempt to call with the same results.

So Saturday had come, and here they were on their way to meet her parents in Pennsylvania. But it wasn't Miriam and Charley accompanying them; it was Magdalena.

"I wanted to surprise you," Magdalena had declared when Ruby had gotten into the van. "Won't this be fun? I can't wait to get to know your parents."

Helplessly, Ruby had looked at Joseph for an explanation, but he'd only rolled his eyes and given her a half-hearted smile.

"Already the first week of October," Madeline had proclaimed. "And harvest in full swing. You know

Charley Byler has better things to do than tag along with you two to Lancaster County. They're a charitable couple, always thinking of others. But they have responsibilities. And Sara certainly can't object to Joseph's mother as a chaperone, can she?"

So the lovely trip, or what *should* have been a lovely trip, had been dominated so far by Magdalena, who'd gone so far as to plant herself beside her son in the middle bench seat, leaving Ruby to sit alone in the back. Magdalena hadn't stopped giving Joseph advice since they'd left Sara's.

"You need to be firm," she was saying. "Make it very clear that Ruby will be coming to live with you in Delaware. On no account will you be moving to Pennsylvania. You will be the husband, the head of the household. It's important that they respect you."

"*Ya*, Mother" Ruby heard Joseph reply.

"And ask questions about the family. What church community do they attend? How big is it? Are there any chronic illnesses in the family that we should be aware of?"

"*Ya*, Mother."

Joseph had barely said anything else in the first hour of the trip and Ruby wondered how he could be so agreeable. Yes, Magdalena was his mother, but he was a grown man. Ruby couldn't help but wonder if she was making a mistake in marrying Joseph. Was this what their marriage would be like? Would Magdalena always be at the center of their decisions? Would what his mother wanted come ahead of what she wanted?

"You know, Joseph," Magdalena continued, her voice growing louder and more insistent. "If you're not totally happy with what the Planks have to say, it's not too late to break this betrothal. Better safe than sorry, I always say."

"Coffee stop," Gene called from the driver's seat. He slowed the van and turned in to a convenience store. "Good doughnuts, clean restrooms. I always stop here when I'm passing through. Take your time. No hurry."

Joseph was waiting for Ruby when she stepped down out of the van. "Would you like coffee or something cold to drink?" he asked. "Are you hungry? Would you like a doughnut?"

"A soda would be nice," Ruby answered. "But I don't want to eat anything. My mother will be certain to have dinner waiting for us. She'll be disappointed if we don't sit down with big appetites."

When they returned to the van, Joseph motioned her to the rear bench seat, but this time, he followed her and sat beside her. "What's wrong?" he asked. "You're being quiet. I thought you'd be excited to be seeing your parents today."

"I am," she said.

Magdalena stood on the step the driver had put out for them and looked into the van at the two of them. "Joseph? Aren't you sitting with me?" she called.

"*Ne*, I'm riding back here with Ruby."

"Suit yourself." Magdalena frowned and slid into the middle seat.

"Everyone buckled up?" Gene asked. He started the ignition. Soon they were back on the road and heading north.

Ruby and Joseph exchanged glances. Ruby slowly let out the breath she hadn't realized she'd been holding.

"So tell me what's wrong," Joseph said quietly.

"She wasn't supposed to come," Ruby whispered.

"Miriam and Charley were supposed to be our chaperones." She wanted to say "This was supposed to be fun." But she didn't.

Joseph nodded. "I know, and I'm sorry. She didn't tell me that she was going to cancel on them and come herself."

"We should just have asked my parents to come to Delaware," Ruby said, glancing out the window. She knew there was no sense being upset with Joseph. He hadn't done this, but she didn't see why she couldn't be at least a little upset about the situation.

"What did you want me to do, Ruby? If I'd known, I would have stopped her. But I didn't. I didn't know until the van arrived and by then, she'd already canceled on Charley and Miriam. There was no way Sara was going to give her approval for us to travel by ourselves. What was I supposed to do?"

"Your mother doesn't like me," Ruby said, keeping her voice low. "She'll never like me."

He shook his head. "That's not true. How could she not learn to love you?"

"You agree with everything she says."

"*Ne*, Ruby, I don't. But I'm caught in the middle here. Think of how much you love your parents. I feel the same way about my mother." Their hands were side by side on the seat and he lifted one finger and stroked hers. "You'll have to learn to get along with her. You can speak up for yourself. I've seen you do it. And believe it or not, she admires a woman with spunk."

"I didn't plan for this," she replied. "I didn't tell my parents that your mother was coming."

"From what you've had to say about them, I'm sure they'll be fine with it," he said. "Now this is what it is.

There's no reason to let her ruin our day. Let's make the best of it." He looked at her hopefully, sliding his hand over hers. "Please?"

Ruby stared at the front of the van where Magdalena was leaning forward and talking loudly into the driver's ear. Joseph was right. They would have to make the best of it, but she didn't feel much like being reasonable. She wanted to feel sorry for herself, to have Joseph take her side against his mother. But that wasn't the way she'd been raised. "I'm sorry for being out of sorts," she murmured, slipping her hand out from under his. If Magdalena saw them holding hands, there was no telling how she'd respond. "I'll try harder to be more understanding."

"Thank you," he said quietly. "I appreciate that. I know she isn't always charitable toward you, and that's wrong. But you have to put yourself in my place. I'm all she's got. It must be difficult for her. Everything will change when I marry you. She won't be the center of my world anymore. It will be you, Ruby. Because… because I love you."

Her eyes grew moist. It wasn't the Amish way to make such declarations.

She looked up into his handsome face. "Do you mean that? Because I love you too." Her last words came out in a whisper.

"I do mean it," he said. "I promise you that this will all work out. Because we do love each other. I just ask that you don't ask me to hurt her or make her feel unneeded. Once she comes to realize what you mean to me, she'll treat you the way you deserve to be treated. You haven't always seen the best side of my mother, but she's a wonderful person. And she has a loving heart."

"Like I said, I'll try to be more understanding," Ruby promised, her heart still fluttering from hearing him say he loved her. "And I'll pray harder," she added.

"Ya," he agreed. "And so will I. I love you both, and I want you to become close."

"What are you two whispering about back there?" Magdalena called.

"Prayer, Mother," Joseph answered.

"Goot," Magdalena answered. "We should all pray for guidance. We need to know if this marriage is God's will or if you two aren't just infatuated with each other."

Ruby and Joseph looked at each other.

"It isn't," he mouthed and she smiled.

"I'll try harder," she repeated.

And the way he looked at her made her realize she'd do anything he asked, just so she could be with him forever and always.

The landscape out the windows of the van had become hilly with fields of corn shocks, stone farmhouses, red barns and the occasional gray buggy pulled by a high-stepping horse. Sometime after they'd crossed the state line into Pennsylvania, the sun had come out from behind the clouds and the day had turned from gloomy to glorious and sunny.

Ruby sat up straighter and stared out at the familiar sights. Soon there were signs for Bird in Hand and Lancaster and Strasburg. "You go toward Strasburg," she called to the driver. "Then when you reach the crossroads just east of town, you make a left turn on Green Willow Road."

"I've got the address in my GPS. They live on Bee Bonnet Road, right?"

"Once you reach Bee Bonnet Road, it's about four miles," Ruby explained. "The place is on the right, back a long lane, but there's an old mill just off the road. You can't miss it. There are two houses. One is stone and the other smaller one is frame."

What would her parents think of Joseph? Surely Magdalena would like them. Who wouldn't like her *mommi* and *daddi*? Everyone in Bee Bonnet said how pleasant they were.

At last Gene drove around a bend and down a hill beside a rocky creek. Ahead was the old stone mill and just before the mill, the driveway that led to the farm where she'd grown up. Ruby was so excited she could hardly stand it. Without realizing what she was doing, she reached over and gave Joseph's hand a squeeze.

Gene turned into the long driveway.

"Quite some farm," Magdalena remarked.

And it was, Ruby thought. White fence posts enclosed herds of dairy cows, horses and beef cattle. Sheep grazed on the slope that ran down to the creek. Straight rows of corn shocks stretched as far as the eye could see. And nestled against a rise of ground stood a big stone house that had been there for nearly two hundred years. It was flanked by a slowly turning windmill, two massive barns, a half-dozen outbuildings and a smaller house.

"Your parents live here?" Joseph asked as he took in the bounty of rich land and fertile fields.

Before she could think how to answer, the side door opened on the smaller house and out came her parents, her father pushing her mother's wheelchair. Both of them were waving, smiles from ear to ear.

Ruby wiggled past Joseph and jumped out almost before the van had stopped rolling. *"Mommi!"* she cried. *"Daddi!"* She ran to them and threw her arms around first one and then the other.

"Where's this young man of yours?" her father demanded, grinning.

"So you got my letter. I called, but—"

"Of course we got your letter. Been looking forward to this all week. So where is he?" her father asked. "You didn't lose him on the way, did you?"

Ruby was laughing and weeping with joy at the same time. *"Ne*, I didn't. This is my—" She broke off as she saw that it wasn't Joseph climbing down from the van but a stern-faced Magdalena. "This is Magdalena," she corrected herself. "Joseph's mother."

"Welcome to our home," her father said. "What a pleasant surprise."

Joseph stepped out behind Magdalena and gave an uncertain smile.

Ruby could see that he was nervous, and she prayed silently that his words wouldn't lodge in his throat nor that his shyness would make this meeting uncomfortable. "And *this* is my—" she began again.

"My son, Joseph," Magdalena finished for her. "He's a little backward when it comes to strangers, but I assure you, the boy has all his wits."

"Joseph! A good name for a young man," Ruby's father exclaimed. "An excellent name. You see, *Mommi*, he's all our Ruby said he was." He extended a hand to Joseph and the two shook hands vigorously.

"Mommi, you look wonderful." Ruby hugged her mother a second time. "How I've missed you and *Daddi*. I've so much to tell you."

"Gracious, child, don't they feed you in Delaware?

Look at her, Solomon. I believe she's lost twenty pounds since she's been away," her mother proclaimed.

Ruby laughed. "I wish. And you know I haven't." She kissed her mother's cheek. "Magdalena, this is my mother, Ina." She turned to smile at Joseph's mother. "I hope you two will become friends," she said.

Magdalena's eyes narrowed thoughtfully. "Well, certainly, certainly we'll have a lot to talk about. I've much to ask you, Ina."

"Ask away," her mother replied. "Questions are free, but I warn you, answers cost a dollar."

Magdalena looked puzzled, but Ruby's father laughed. "That's my Ina," he said. "Always teasing. Now, you behave yourself, wife. What will our guests think of us? And worse, what will they think of our daughter?"

What indeed, Ruby wondered as her mother clapped her hands and ushered them all around the house to the picnic table where a huge lunch was waiting. She'd hoped to speak to her parents in private before the visiting began. She really felt it was time to tell Joseph the truth about her situation and her past, but she wanted their permission. Obviously there would be no time for that now. She'd just have to hope for the best. *Ne*, she thought, not hope but pray. She'd pray everyone had a good afternoon and that everything would work itself out, including her secret. Because if her marriage to Joseph was meant to be, it was meant to be.

God's will, she told herself. *God's will.*

Chapter Nine

Joseph took a seat at the picnic table under the poplar tree and tried not to show how nervous he was. Ruby's parents seemed welcoming and pleasant, but he was still sweating beneath his hat's brim. He wanted to make a good impression, and as his mother had reminded him in front of everyone, he wasn't at his best with strangers. But he was determined that this would be different. His and Ruby's future was at stake. She was depending on him, and he couldn't let her down. One way or another, he would fight through his shyness and be the man she deserved. He'd ask her father for her hand in marriage. God willing, he thought and offered a silent prayer.

Joseph suddenly realized that Ruby's father was speaking to him, and gave the older man his full attention.

"...heard so much about you," Solomon went on heartily. "*Hallich* we finally get to meet you."

Joseph nodded and opened his mouth to make some kind of proper response, but when nothing came out, Solomon went right on talking without missing a beat.

The older man didn't seem to notice that he was the only one speaking, which was fine with Joseph.

Ruby's father was a solid man in his late sixties with a full beard and bushy gray eyebrows that arched up at the outer corners. He had full red cheeks, a wide mouth and a nose much like Ruby's. Solomon was clearly a man who liked his food and liked to laugh, and he obviously was as fond of his daughter as his wife seemed to be because both of them kept smiling at Ruby with genuine pleasure.

"It's good of you…to have us visit," Joseph managed when Solomon stopped talking long enough to catch a breath.

Solomon grinned, slapped Joseph on the back and shoved a huge mug of cider into his hand. "Taste that. Cider. Sweet. Not hard. I don't hold with spirits. What do you think? Secret recipe. You have to marry into the *familye* to get it." He chuckled, a deep, rumbling belly laugh that threatened to pop the buttons of his old-fashioned, long-sleeved blue shirt. "And even then, maybe not until we have a few grandbabies."

"Solomon, no need to talk of *kinner* yet," Ruby's mother said. "You'll frighten the young man away."

"I don't think so," Solomon replied. "He's smitten. Look at him, *Mommi*. He can't take his eyes off our Ruby."

Ina laughed, a loud, jolly sound. Joseph hadn't expected the wheelchair. Ruby hadn't mentioned that her mother had health problems. But Ina didn't look sick or feeble. Her cheeks were full of color, her skin clear and her hair, although streaked with gray, was thick and shining, framing a square, pleasant face. He wondered why Ina couldn't walk but didn't want to ask such a personal question.

"*Buwe* or *maed*, we don't care," Solomon continued merrily. "Boy or girl. We're not getting any younger and we'd like to bounce some *kinner* on our *gnie* while we've still got the energy. Not that we expect you to have more than five or six. Families aren't as large as they once were, not even in Bee Bonnet. Why, when I was a tad, it was nothing to see a family of fourteen kids. But things are different now. Six would be *goot*. Excellent. Maybe three boys and three girls. What do you think?"

"*Daddi*, please," Ruby pleaded jokingly. "Don't run Joseph off before he's even had his dinner." She didn't seem in the least embarrassed by her father's remarks.

"She's right, Solomon." Ina waved a finger at her husband. "Give Ruby's young man a chance to eat his dinner before you start naming their firstborn. And speak English or *Deitsch* but not both at the same time. Our visitors will think this is an uncivilized household Ruby comes from."

"Whatever you say, *Mommi*." Ruby's father's reply was so meek that even Joseph couldn't keep a smile off his face, because even he could see that Solomon wasn't in the least repentant, and Ina wasn't in the least offended.

A cement sidewalk and patio made it easy for Ruby's mother to whip around the picnic table, directing everyone to seats and rolling up to take her place at the end of the table opposite her husband. There seemed to be nothing frail about Ina. Rather she appeared quite hearty with her ample girth and cheery countenance. Had she been standing upright instead of sitting in the wheelchair, he guessed she was taller than her husband. And she had the arms of a blacksmith.

Joseph glanced at his mother, who'd ignored the chair Ina had pointed to and taken a place smack-dab between him and Ruby. His mother was smiling her practiced smile and taking in the yard and the small house and neat garden with a calculating eye. He knew she was comparing the Plank's home to the larger stone house that stood not far away. *Be nice*, he wanted to say to her, but of course, he couldn't.

But his mother had turned her attention to Ina. She'd always had compassion for the sick or handicapped. And she was always the first to respond to a neighbor or friend's health crisis. Nothing was too much to do for someone in trouble. His mother had so many admirable qualities. Why couldn't she show them to the woman he loved?

"You have a fine garden," his mother remarked to Ina. "How do you manage?"

"*Ach*, goodness. *Ne*, that isn't my garden," Ina answered. "I wish it was. I've been after Solomon to build me one of those raised vegetable beds so that I can keep my hand in. The garden belongs to my twin sister, Ellen. She lives here with us, though she's gone today. She has a fair hand with anything that grows. Just don't put her in a kitchen. She cooks like a bishop's wife."

"The bishop's wife—that's a family joke," Solomon explained with a chuckle. "You see, the last two bishops we've had, their wives were good-hearted for certain, but they couldn't boil water." His ample belly quivered with suppressed laughter. "So, I always say Ellen—"

"If you can't say anything *goot*," Ina interrupted.

"Is a kindhearted woman," Solomon finished with

a nod. "That's what I was going to say." He exchanged glances with Ruby and both chuckled. "You're too quick to judge me," he told his wife. "And me as innocent as a deacon on the Sabbath."

"Your words maybe, but not your thoughts." Ina shook her head. "You will have to excuse my husband," she went on good-naturedly. "Sometimes, he acts as though he's never grown up."

"I like to have a little fun." He winked at Joseph. "And what's wrong with that? Especially on this special day with Ruby's Joseph and his mother?"

Joseph looked at his mother, who seemed to him anything but at ease among these lighthearted people. She was sitting primly, hands folded in her lap, mouth turned up in a polite smile. She always admonished him about being easier with strangers, but he knew her well enough to see that she was nervous too.

"So let's get down to business. When will you be taking this girl off my hands?" Solomon asked Joseph the moment they'd finished the silent grace.

"Daddi!" Ruby blushed, this time definitely embarrassed. "Please. Not during dinner."

"Solomon," Ina admonished. "I told you. No talk of that at the table."

"Oh, all right," he responded, passing the potato salad to Joseph. "But we'll talk about it after, won't we, young man?"

Solomon laughed again, but from the look on Magdalena's face, Joseph was afraid that she hadn't understood he was joking with them.

Ina pushed a large platter of roast beef into his mother's hands. *"Picalilli,"* she said, dismissing the subject. "The young ones haven't said they are absolutely settled on the match yet. Have they, Solomon? They're only courting."

Solomon looked at Ruby. "Now, Ina, have you looked at our girl? Has she taken her eyes off him? Remember how you were when I went to your father to ask his blessing? Head over heels for me." He patted his stomach. "You wouldn't believe it, but I cut quite the figure when I was *rumspringa*. But that's all in the past now." He buttered a sweet-potato biscuit. "Some thought I was the catch of Lancaster County."

Ina laughed and shook her head. "Shame on you for saying such things."

He sighed. "No harm in telling the truth. But as I was about to say, our Ruby's just like her mother. A long time to decide on a man, but when she does, she won't be moved." His tone grew serious. "And a *goot* thing, I should say. Ina and me, we've knocked along pretty good, haven't we, wife? Through sickness and health, loss and God's bounty. A good match is a good match." He met his wife's gaze, his tone softening. "I knew it the day you said you'd marry me, *Mommi*."

"I... I can see you've had your share of troubles," Joseph's mother said, clearly uncomfortable with this tender exchange between husband and wife. "But all the more reason these two shouldn't rush into any commitment. It's plain that you need your daughter's help around here. I don't know how you've gotten along these weeks without her. And it's a child's duty to care for a parent. There's no question of my Joseph leaving his home and business. I'd not want her to marry him, move off to Delaware and leave you—"

"Ham, Magdalena?" Ina's eyes twinkled with mischief as she interrupted, plopping a wedge onto his mother's plate. "And do have some of those baked beans. They're Solomon's specialty. He made a fresh batch this morning."

"Your husband cooks?" his mother asked, drawing herself up in surprise.

Little beads of perspiration began to pop up above her upper lip and Joseph feared it would only be a matter of time until she began fanning herself with whatever she could find available.

"Some things better than me," Ina admitted.

"You're better than you were when we first married," Solomon teased. "And I don't cook too much, but what I do, I do *goot*. Best baked beans you ever wrapped your teeth around. I wanted to be certain there was plenty to eat."

Joseph surveyed the table. There were only five of them, but there was enough food to feed half the neighborhood. It smelled delicious, but he was too nervous to have much of an appetite. He sipped at the sweet cider, wishing that he and Ruby were anywhere else. Alone. He never felt ill at ease when it was just the two of them. Unconsciously he tapped one heel nervously against the cement deck. It was cool here in the shade of the trees, but waves of heat still radiated under his skin. He wondered if Ruby's parents could see him sweating. He hoped they didn't think him a complete clod.

"Raisin bread!" Solomon practically threw the bread trencher to Joseph. "Have some. And don't short yourself on Ina's cream cheese. She makes it herself from her grandmother's recipe."

"I have a good recipe for cream cheese too," Magdalena said. "I like to add herbs to mine, chives or sometimes rosemary."

"That sounds lovely," Ina said. "And do you make chowchow in Delaware?"

"*Ya*, we do. But Ruby brags on yours," his mother replied. The two women chatted about recipes and the benefits of an extensive herb garden for both cooking and medicinal needs for a few minutes. They were almost through the meal when Magdalena excused herself from the table. Joseph couldn't hear what she whispered to Ina, but the older woman pointed to the house.

"Just through the kitchen," Ina said. "You can't miss it. It's the only room with a bathtub."

"So tell the truth, you are talking about marriage, you and my daughter, aren't you?" Joseph heard in his ear as he watched his mother disappear into the little house.

"What?" Blinking, Joseph turned to Solomon. "I'm sorry. What were you saying?"

"Solomon," Ina warned. "Enough with that talk."

Her husband laughed like a boy caught with his hand in the sugar bowl, and she and Ruby chuckled with him. No one at the table but Joseph seemed surprised that Ina would repeatedly admonish her husband in public or that he would take it without offense. "My fault," Solomon said, holding up both hand, palms out. "Finish up, young man. We've lots to discuss over *apfelstrudel* and *krum kuchen*."

"You can have one or the other, but not both," Ina cautioned. "You know what the doctor told you about your weight." She smiled at Joseph. "Of course, you can have as many desserts as you can hold. A trim young man like you. No need for you to worry about putting on pounds."

A sound came from inside the house like a piece of

furniture being moved or maybe a door being opened. Joseph glanced nervously in that direction, then at Ruby.

She didn't seem to have heard the sound. "Joseph works hard," she put in. "He's busy all the time."

Joseph gathered his courage and looked up at her father. "I have a—a trade," he managed.

"You like to trade, do you?" Solomon asked, straight-faced. "Horses or cows?"

"Ne," Joseph replied. "I mean—"

"Daddi! Please. You know what Joseph was trying to tell you. He's a master mason. He's saying he can provide for a wife. Financially."

Joseph nodded gratefully. Where had this beautiful girl been all his life? Then another sound came from the house. Definitely a cupboard door being closed. Where was his mother? Why hadn't she come back outside?

"Glad to hear it," Solomon said, seeming to take no notice of the sounds coming from the house, sounds that should not have been heard if someone was just using the bathroom.

"A man who won't work isn't worth his salt," Solomon went on. "He's certainly not worth my Ruby." He threw his daughter an adoring look. "One chick is all we have. Came later in life than we expected. God was good enough to spare us this one, and we cherish her. Not just any husband will do for our girl. I'm just saying…if you're considering marrying our Ruby."

"Daddi, I brought Joseph here so you could meet him. So you could get—" Ruby broke off as the sound of breaking glass came from inside the house. She and her mother both looked toward the house.

Joseph closed his eyes, not sure what to do. What to say. There was no way Solomon and Ina hadn't heard that. And they had to have realized that Magdalena was snooping. He cringed inwardly. How could she?

There was another clunk and the creak of a door. For an instant, Joseph thought he caught a glimpse of a face peering through an upstairs window. Hadn't Ina directed his mother to a bathroom downstairs? He hoped he was wrong and that someone else was inside.

"Ruby," Ina said. "I think Magdalena must be lost. Excuse us," she said. "We'll go and show her the way out."

Ruby nodded and rose. She took hold of her mother's wheelchair and pushed her back along the sidewalk.

"I'm sorry," Joseph blurted. "My mother, she…" He didn't know what to say.

"Nothing to be sorry for," Solomon answered kindly. A large, red-combed rooster strolled up to the table, stopped by Ruby's father's chair and ruffled his feathers. "All right, all right," Solomon said, throwing the bird a handful of bread.

Joseph glanced at the house again. With the women gone, this was his opportunity to speak alone with Ruby's father. It might be his only opportunity today and, as he told Ruby, he wasn't leaving without bringing up his intentions. Formally. But his palms were sweaty and… "I want—want you to know, Solomon, how…wonderful Ru-Ruby is. I—I think she's wonderful."

Solomon beamed. "She is, isn't she?" He arched a bushy eyebrow. "Of course, she's can't cook very well— takes after her aunt Ellen. And she's not much of a seamstress either. Takes after her mother on that one, I'm afraid. For years I walked around looking like I'd sewn my own trousers with a pitchfork."

"I—I don't care," Joseph managed, feeling sweat

bead on his forehead under the brim of his hat again. "I—I think she's—she's perfect."

"And so you should." Solomon chuckled. "At least in the beginning years."

"I…" Joseph's mouth went dry and he could feel sweat trickling down the back of his neck. "I… While we're alone, I wanted to…" He took a deep breath and went on faster than before. "I—I'm asking for—for your permission…to marry Ruby."

Solomon's hazel eyes grew serious. "Your mother doesn't seem too pleased with your marrying. Or maybe it's Ruby she doesn't like. Does that matter to you?"

"*Ne*, it doesn't. But—but I don't think she dislikes Ruby." Joseph concentrated on what he wanted to say, trying not to stammer. "They just have to get to know each other, and—and learn to appreciate how special they both are. I know…" He glanced toward the house. "Maybe you haven't seen the best side of my mother. But I can tell you that she's a fine woman, and the most—most selfless mother any child could have. It's been just the two of us, the two of us since my father's death, and she—she's sacrificed a lot for me."

Ruby's father seemed to consider that. He took a slice of raisin bread and spread it with cream cheese. He took a bite, chewed and then nodded. "You and my daughter are of age. You don't need my permission to marry. And you certainly don't need your mother's." He took a bite of the bread. "Ruby has a good head on her shoulders. And you seem a sensible lad, as well. I trust Ruby's decision." He looked up at Joseph and broke into a kind smile. "But, for what it's worth, son, you have my blessing."

* * *

Ruby pushed the wheelchair to the door but stopped short of the entranceway. "Do you like him?" she asked her mother quietly. "Can you see how wonderful he is?"

From inside the house came the sounds of rustling and a scraping drawer.

"Are you sure this is what you want?" Her mother placed a soft hand over hers. "Dealing with that one in there may not be easy," she replied, indicating the house. "You can tell she's used to having things her way. And clearly she's nosy. You said she'll be living with you."

"We'll be fine, *Mommi*." Ruby nodded. "I'll win her over, you'll see. Magdalena's not a bad person. She's just strong-willed. But so am I. We'll find a way to make it work. We have to because we both love Joseph."

Ina eyed the door, then looked back at her daughter. "Best do it before you wed."

"But you see why I picked him, don't you?" Ruby rested her hand on the back of her mother's wheelchair. She wanted to talk about Joseph, not about Magdalena. "Don't you think he's perfect?"

Her mother smiled up at her. "I can see you're in love."

Suddenly, Ruby was worried. Her smile fell. "You don't object to him, do you?"

"Of course not. If you're happy, Ruby, so are we. I think you've done exactly what we hoped you would do, find someone who would love you for yourself."

She let out a sigh of relief. "*Ya*, isn't it great? And he's going to ask *Daddi* for his permission to marry me."

"If your father will let him get a word in sideways."

She leaned close to her mother's ear and whispered. "So, now is it all right if—"

"Ruby!" The door opened, and then closed. "I… I…" Magdalena peeked through the screen. "I got quite turned around."

"But did you find what you were looking for?" her mother asked sweetly. "Upstairs?"

"What?" Magdalena pushed open the door again and stood staring at them. "I couldn't… That is, I was thirsty. I'm afraid I brushed against a canning jar…on the kitchen counter. It broke. I had to search for a…"

"A broom?" her mother suggested.

"Ya," Joseph's mother agreed. "A…a broom. And a dustpan."

"But you found the bathroom?" Ruby asked. She wondered how much of her conversation with her mother Magdalena had overheard. None of it, she hoped. But Magdalena had managed to appear at exactly the wrong time.

"No need for the two of you to leave your lunch. I was coming right back," Magdalena said.

"Of course, of course," her mother soothed. "We don't want to leave the men folk alone too long. They'll be talking business at the table again. You know how they are." She waved her hand and the three of them headed for the backyard.

When they reached the table, Ruby looked at Joseph, trying to see if she could tell if he'd had the nerve to ask her father for permission to marry and if he'd been successful. But her *Daddi* was telling a funny story about a deacon and an *Englisher* who'd gotten his car stuck in the cow pasture, and Joseph was giving him his complete attention.

Ruby's mother tried to engage Magdalena in small talk about the advantages of making coleslaw with lemon juice rather than vinegar, but Joseph's mother seemed determined to remain aloof. Maybe because she'd gotten caught snooping in the house. Ina, however, refused to take offense and launched into a long recitation of the bishop's last sermon and how well it was received by a visiting family from Ohio. Before Ruby knew it, they'd finished dessert and everyone chipped in to clear the table and carry the dirty dishes and the remainder of the food into the kitchen.

Ruby tried to get her mother alone again to ask about telling Joseph their secret, but Magdalena remained stuck to her side like glue. Time seemed to fly and the next thing Ruby knew, she heard a horn beeping and saw the van was rolling up the driveway.

"Here's your ride," Ruby's mother announced. "It seems like you just got here. Next time you and Joseph must come and stay with us for the whole weekend."

"They have to have a chaperone," Magdalena reminded her. "It isn't decent, otherwise. We keep by the old ways. People will talk, and it will do your daughter no good to get a name for being fast. Delaware isn't Lancaster, you know."

"So true. It isn't," her mother replied with a smile. "And thank the good Lord for it."

Feeling emotional at the idea of leaving, it was all Ruby could do to hold back her tears as she said her goodbyes and got into the van. Seeing her parents had been wonderful, but leaving them was difficult. She worried about their welfare, and she hadn't even gotten to see Aunt Ellen, who'd always been a big part of her home life.

She leaned close to the back window and waved at her parents. Her father was standing behind her mother's wheelchair, one hand on her shoulder. Her mother was doing her best to remain cheerful, but her smile was a mixed one. She knew they were happy for her and that they approved of Joseph, but she also was aware of how much her absence affected their daily life.

Joseph followed his mother into the van, gave a final wave and slid the door closed behind them.

"Why don't you sit here, Mother?" Joseph waved to the seat in the middle of the van, behind the driver. "It's not so bumpy here and you can see out the windows." He glanced over his mother's head and met Ruby's gaze, silently conveying that he was coming back to be with her.

But Magdalena had other ideas. "*Ne*, I'd rather sit with the two of you," she informed him. "It's nicer than sitting all alone. That way we can all chat." And with that, she moved to the back and plopped down on the bench seat beside Ruby.

"Would you like to sit by the window?" Ruby offered.

Magdalena shook her head and smiled. "*Ne*, I'll just sit between you. That way I won't have a bit of trouble hearing what's said."

Disappointment flickered briefly across Joseph's features, but then he smiled at his mother. With a slight shrug and an embarrassed smile, he slid his tall frame into the seat.

Ruby pressed her forehead to the window and stared out as the van rolled down the drive and away from her home and parents. She would have to write to them. She'd tell them how happy Joseph made her and how he was the answer to her dreams. Surely, that would be enough for her parents to release her from her promise. It had to be, because she couldn't go on like this. She couldn't keep deceiving Joseph. He was too fine a man to deserve such treatment, and she couldn't continue with the courtship without being completely honest with him.

That decision made, she felt a little better. She even managed a smile when Joseph caught her attention. Of course she would have managed an even bigger smile for him if he hadn't left her to sit beside his mother.

Chapter Ten

"There." Sara tightened the last lid on the second batch of perfectly halved pears and added them to the ten quarts already cooling on the kitchen counter. "Don't they look nice?"

"Ya," Ruby agreed. Sara's canned pears were as pretty as a picture, all topped with colorful, strawberry-patterned lids. It was the week after her nerve-racking trip home to Bee Bonnet with Joseph, and she was helping Sara and the girls can.

Of all a woman's traditional chores, canning was Ruby's favorite. And canning with Sara and her new friends Leah and Ellie added to the enjoyment. Ruby didn't mind that canning was heavy, labor-intensive work because, unlike scrubbing floors, which had to be done over and over if you wanted to keep a decent kitchen, you could enjoy the results of a day's canning for months to follow. There was something so satisfying about knowing that the pantry shelves were stocked with good, nourishing food to share with friends and family.

Plus, she loved canned pears, especially in the dead

of winter. There was something about the taste of pears that satisfied her sweet tooth without making her feel guilty for having a second helping of dessert. And best of all, when she was canning, she rarely dropped or broke anything. Today had been no exception—as long as she didn't count her stumble coming in from the porch when she'd sent a peck of Seckel pears rolling all over the kitchen floor.

But Sara, Leah and Ellie had only laughed and Ellie said it was a good thing no one sent her to gather the eggs. Everyone had taken her clumsiness so calmly that she'd found herself laughing with them as she crawled under a table to retrieve the last of the runaway pears.

Ellie was home this afternoon to help because she'd declared half days for the school all week. Ruby had come to be very fond of the woman from Wisconsin. Wherever Ellie was, there was always laughter, singing and fun. Normally, Ellie would be busy teaching at midday on a Wednesday, but so many of her older students were needed at home for harvest, canning and child care that Ellie thought it seemed wiser to start class an hour early and let all the children out at noon. A stern reminder to parents on the importance of regular attendance on the half days had so far proved successful. No one was falling behind in lessons and the families had the extra hands they needed so badly at this busy time of year.

"Ruby, stir that pear butter, will you?" Sara asked. "And taste it. I put in a little orange zest. See if it needs more." As usual, Sara was a bundle of energy, buzzing around the kitchen, directing the operation, cutting vegetables for a lamb stew for supper and planning the menu and activities for Saturday's upcoming haying day.

Leah and Ellie began singing a fast hymn as they worked together to fill the clean jars with fruit and pear juice. Some cooks used a thin sugar water to cover the fruit for canning, but not Sara. She preferred using not-so-perfect pears to make juice. She had told Ruby, "The good Lord has blessed me with a full head of good teeth. I mean to try to keep them. Too much sugar ruins a sweet smile."

Ruby joined in the praise hymn with Ellie and Leah as she stirred the bubbling pear butter. She knew the words by heart, and even though the kitchen was steamy and warm despite the crisp fall day, she was having a wonderful time. The smells coming from the kettle were amazing. In fact, the whole house smelled delicious.

There was only one thing keeping her day from being perfect and that was her worry concerning Joseph. Since they'd returned from visiting her parents, he'd been pressing for her to set a wedding date. Becoming his wife would be a dream come true, but there was still the concern that she hadn't been entirely forthcoming with him. She'd tried to call her parents the previous day and then she'd sent a letter asking them to release her from her promise. To add to her worries, somewhere in the back of her head, she kept thinking about Magdalena and Joseph's relationship with her. He told her that she would come first and his mother second after they were wed, but she wondered if she was being naive to think that was true.

"Look who's coming up the lane," Sara observed loudly. "Unless my eyes are getting as rusty as my knees, that's Joseph Brenneman's horse and buggy."

"Somebody's beau's come calling in the middle of a workday," Leah teased.

Ruby dropped the long-handled wooden spoon and ran to the window. Joseph's buggy was almost in the barnyard. She dashed to the bathroom. "Tell him I'm coming!" she sang, excited and giddy. She splashed water on her face, retied her headscarf and gave a quick glance into the small round mirror over the sink. She didn't have time to change her oldest dress for something nicer, but she could take off the pear-stained apron.

"You don't have to rush," Ellie said as Ruby hurried back through the kitchen. "That one's not going anywhere until he sees you."

"What are you doing here in the middle of the workday?" Ruby asked as the porch door banged shut behind her. She took the two bottom steps in one leap and met him halfway to the buggy.

"I needed to order extra bricks and was passing by Sara's so I thought…" Joseph was grinning shyly. Glancing toward the house, he motioned to her. "Come around to the other side of the buggy."

Curious, Ruby followed him. "Why? What is it?"

Joseph leaned in and picked up something. When he turned back to her, he was holding a bunch of black-eyed Susans. "I saw these in a field," he said, his voice husky. "It's late for them to still be blooming, but it was a sheltered hollow. I thought they were pretty. And—" he swallowed and handed her the flowers "—they reminded me of you. Because—because you're so beautiful."

Emotion made her throat tickle and brought tears to her eyes. No one but Joseph and her parents had ever called her beautiful. She knew it wasn't true. She was ordinary, not gorgeous like Leah or cute like Ellie. But it was so sweet to have Joseph say she was beautiful, and it made her feel all warm and fuzzy inside. "Thank you...for the flowers. They're wonderful." It wasn't enough. She wanted to say that she loved him more than hot raisin bread, but before she could get up the nerve to say it, he was swinging up into the buggy.

"Got to run," he said. "The guys are waiting for me. But I'll see you soon. And we'll set that date, won't we?" He threw her an adoring look, clicked to the horse and flicked the leathers over the standard bred's back. She stood there clutching her flowers and feeling so happy that she could almost float off the ground as the buggy rolled away.

Ellie's voice came from the porch. "Ooh, somebody got flowers. Pretty fancy."

"Ya," Ruby answered. She glanced down at the black-eyed Susans in her arms.

"You'd better get those in water," Ellie advised.

"What did he want?" Leah asked when Ruby returned to the kitchen.

She looked helplessly at Sara. "He wants to set a wedding date."

Ellie found an empty canning jar and filled it with water. "Here, put those in here. They wilt fast if they dry out."

"And there's something wrong with setting a date?" Sara asked. "Not having second thoughts, are you? Because if you have the slightest doubt, now's the time to speak up. I already told you I think this is fast for a couple who've only known each other as long as you two have."

Ruby shook her head. "Not having second thoughts about Joseph. I couldn't ask for a finer man."

"Very romantic for an Amish boy." Ellie took the flowers from Ruby to arrange in the jar. "Who would have thought he had it in him?"

"It's the shy ones who can fool you," Leah said.

"Ah, what's that smell?" Sara exclaimed. "Don't tell me the pear butter is burning." She darted to the stove, grabbed the spoon and stirred the mixture. "Just in time," she pronounced as she turned off the burner under the pot.

"*Ach*, it's getting warm in here," Ellie said. "Anyone for a cold glass of cider?"

"And some ginger cookies?" Leah suggested, grabbing a container from the cupboard.

"Absolutely," Sara agreed, going into the refrigerator for the glass jug of cider. "We've earned a break. The stew is on, the next batch of pears is ready to go in the hot water bath and we've plenty of wheat bread left over from yesterday's baking so we don't need to make biscuits for supper."

"You have to tell Leah what you told me and Sara about Magdalena using your mother's bathroom." Ellie eyes were full of mischief as she retrieved two glasses and carried them to the table. "She won't believe it."

Ruby grimaced, accepting the glasses from Ellie. "I hope this doesn't qualify as gossip," she said. "That wouldn't be very charitable to the woman who's going to be my mother-in-law."

"It's not gossip if it happened and you witnessed it," Ellie said, bringing two more glasses over.

Ruby kicked her shoes off and settled into a chair.

"Thanks. The cider will hit the spot. It seems to me that this is extra delicious this year."

"Don't change the subject," Leah urged, pouring everyone a glass. "Now that you've dangled this tidbit in front of me, you've got to tell me all."

"All right, you asked for it," Ruby replied, and she launched into the tale of Joseph's mother's *investigation* of the house during their visit. "I actually saw her looking out the window from my aunt's bedroom," she said.

Ellie began to giggle, followed by Leah. Sara tried to keep a straight face but couldn't quite manage it.

Telling it to them was funnier than it had been at the time. "And that's not all," she went on. "When we headed home, I sat in the back of the van so that I could talk to Joseph, but she managed to wedge herself in between us."

"*Between* you? What did you do?" Leah asked.

"What could I do?" Ruby shrugged and took another sip of cider. "She's Joseph's mother. I spent most of the ride looking out the window and listening to her tell him what he should have said to my father and what he should do with his life."

"That woman needs a hobby," Leah quipped, taking another cookie. "If she has time to try to run her grown son's life, she has entirely too much time on her hands."

Ruby rolled her eyes. "What she needs is her own beau."

Ruby met Ellie's gaze and they both burst into laughter.

Sara just smiled, but there was a twinkle in her dark eyes that made Ruby wonder what she was thinking.

Saturday morning was bright and crisp with the scent of autumn leaves and fresh-cut hay as dozens of friends and neighbors gathered for an old-fashioned haying. Sara's field was a relatively small one, and she, like many others, kept to the traditional ways. The hay had been cut and raked using horsepower, and now many willing hands would join together to pile the drying hay into fragrant stacks and pile them on a wagon for storage in the barn. Most in the neighborhood with larger farms baled their hay, or even had their English neighbors come in with tractors and pack the timothy and clover into huge round bales that could be covered with weatherproof wrap so that it could be left in the field until needed. But with such a small field and so much help, harvesting the loose hay was a reminder of the rich past and all the wisdom that had been passed down from generation to generation.

After the hay was safely stored in the loft to feed the stock through the winter months, the workers and their families would sit down to a big harvest dinner. Sara had organized games for the younger people, and Samuel Mast had brought his team of trained sheep with bells on their harnesses to give the little children rides in a bright green cart with yellow wheels and bells. There would be apple bobbing, corn husking, wood-chopping contests for the men, a pie-tasting event and a few surprise tests of skill. Everyone would eat their fill and end the evening with a singing attended by young and old.

But first, as Sara reminded her guests, there was hay to get in. She'd hitched her team of mules to one hay wagon, and Charley and Miriam had brought another. Usually Miriam liked to drive the horses, but she was in the family way again and Charley wouldn't hear of her climbing on and off a wagon or spending hours in the field. Eagerly, Ruby offered to step in for her. Sara had been a bit dubious, but after the first few minutes, it was obvious to everyone that Ruby Plank was used to handling a team of draft horses.

For Ruby, helping with the haying was much more fun than cooking or setting up the tables for the noonday meal. And it was a beautiful day, cool without being chilly and sunny without a cloud in the sky. Shrieks of running children, barking dogs and mingled voices added to the excitement. Ruby had to guide the team up and down the field at a walk while men and women, their voices joining in "Amazing Grace," forked hay onto the wagon. At times she had to bring the horses to a complete stop, and when they started forward again, she had to take care that they didn't break into a trot. When she reached the fence at the far end, it took some skill to turn the animals and wagon without endangering the growing mound of fragrant hay.

"You're turning that wagon too tight!" Magdalena called to her. Joseph's mother had come out to the edge of the field with another woman to watch, and apparently to offer suggestions from the sidelines.

Ruby laughed and waved. Charley's team of gray Percherons were well trained, the wagon was new and she'd been driving horses for her father since she was ten years old. The hay had been properly stacked by men who knew what they were doing and was in no danger of tumbling off. She felt a lot safer driving across Sara's field with these animals than riding her push-bike on the road with all the motor traffic.

"Better let Joseph drive!" Thomas leaned on his pitchfork and grinned at her.

Ruby paid him no mind. She knew Thomas, Leah's beau, was a tease, especially where girls were concerned. He said something to Joseph; Joseph handed him his pitchfork and came to run alongside the wagon. Ruby's heart filled to the brim and spilled over as she watched him leap up and find his footing. He was so beautiful…so strong. Joseph was everything she'd ever wanted, and she could hardly believe he wanted to marry her.

"I think that's a full load," Joseph said lightly. "Want me to take it back to the barn for you?"

She laughed, looking up at him. "You think I want you to take the reins?"

"I think you're doing just fine," he said, moving to stand behind her. "But maybe you could take up a little slack on right leather." He reached around and covered her hand with his.

"Joseph. What will people think?" She twisted her hand out of his grasp. Her fingers tingled from his touch, and she could feel the joy bubbling up inside. This was the best day, and she was having a wonderful time.

He laughed. "They might think I was giving you some help with the team. They're pretty powerful animals. We wouldn't want a runaway hay wagon, would we?"

"And we wouldn't want to give your mother an excuse to say we were acting inappropriately either." She smiled over her shoulder at him. Just then, the left front wheel rolled over a bump and Ruby lost her balance. For just a second, she struggled to regain her stance, and he steadied her shoulder. She reined the horses a little to the right and the floor of the wagon leveled out.

"Nice," Joseph said.

Ruby tried not to feel pride for the good job she'd

done with an unfamiliar team. She might be less than perfect with a needle, but this she could do. It made her feel good to be a vital part of the haying and even better that Joseph was pleased enough with her that he'd dare impropriety to put his arms around her in public.

"As for my mother, maybe I don't care what she thinks," he said.

Ruby didn't respond. Her feelings on that were mixed. She understood that he loved his mother and had to show her respect, but sometimes she wondered if this was something they could work out between them. Magdalena was proving to be a tougher nut to crack than she'd expected.

The second hay wagon, pulled by the mules, passed them going in the opposite direction. Jakob, the blacksmith in the community, had replaced Ellie as driver on the last trip to the barn. Jakob waved and Ruby waved back at him. One of Samuel Mast's twins was standing in the back of the wagon, forking hay into the center, but he was concentrating on his task and didn't look up.

"You think Ellie has her eye on Jakob?" Joseph asked Ruby.

"She wants nothing to do with him." Jakob was a little person like Ellie, and it was no secret to anyone under Sara's roof that he was definitely interested in courting Seven Poplars's schoolteacher, but, despite his popularity in the community, Ellie seemed immune to his charms. "I think Ellie likes being single."

"I'm glad you don't," he said. "You're sure you don't want help with the team?"

"*Ne*, I'm doing fine on my own."

"Guess who I ran into on the way here this morning?" Joseph asked, but didn't wait for an answer. "Our

bishop. He asked me if I was going to need his services
this fall. He's said that if we want to be married before
Christmas, we'll have to let him know soon because his
Thursdays are filling up. He said he had to have a few
weeks' notice to call the *banns*, so we really should—"

"Joseph Brenneman!" She reined the Percherons to
an abrupt halt, nearly sending Joseph head over teacups.
"You talked to your bishop about our wedding without
asking me first?" she asked him.

"I told you I was going to."

"I know, but…" She looked up at him. "Are you absolutely positive you want to go through with this? You
don't care that I'm a klutz and a terrible cook, not to
mention—"

"Hush," he said, grinning at her in a way that made
her knees go weak. "I don't want to hear it. I don't care
if you spill the cream and sour the butter and make pancakes like Frisbees. None of that matters to me. From
the first day I met you, you never tried to hide your
faults. Honesty and caring for each other are what's important to me in a marriage. That's all we need, isn't it?"

Dumbly, she nodded. Should she tell him the truth
now? Here in the middle of the hay field? She hesitated for only a moment, but then the chance was lost
because Charley was striding through the hay stubble
toward the wagon.

"Something wrong?" he called. "That left front
wheel isn't loose, is it?"

"Ne," Joseph shouted back. "We're good." He looked
down at her, smiling. "We're great, aren't we, Ruby?"

She nodded, a lump in her throat. *"Ya*, great," she
agreed.

Chapter Eleven

Joseph waited patiently as Ruby settled two toddlers into a single seat in a little sheep wagon, and then, when she nodded to him, led the wooly team on the path around Sara's hospitality barn. Ruby walked beside the wagon, watching over her two charges, a girl and a boy.

Ruby was good with children. They liked her and took to her quickly, even when she was a stranger. And it was easy to see that she adored them. She was patient and kind. That made Joseph happy, because he knew that Ruby would make a wonderful mother. He could imagine her with their own children. That thought made him smile. All he'd ever wanted was going to be his: a home, a loving wife and children to care for and bring up in the faith. His mother had always said that he had to choose someone who shared his values, a woman he could trust who would put family first, ahead of her own wishes. And he'd done just that.

Ruby glanced up at Joseph and smiled, and his pulse raced. He smiled back at her and wondered why his mother couldn't see what a treasure Ruby was. Couldn't his mother realize that just being near Ruby filled his heart with laughter? When he was with her, he felt a foot taller and able to face any obstacle. If this was what people meant when they joked about being struck by the love thunderbolt, then so be it. He was content to be stricken. The fact that the two most important people in the world to him bristled like grumpy hens when they were together was the only gray cloud on his horizon.

But now wasn't the time to dwell on what had to be resolved. It was time to relax and have some fun. After the hay was all in, he and the other men who'd worked in the field had ducked into the shower at Sara's bachelors' quarters to wash away the results of hard labor. Sara had insisted they all bring a change of clothing. "Can't have you smelling like a barnyard," she'd told them plainly.

Joseph's mother had thought that a little foolish. "What's wrong with a man smelling like good, honest work?" she'd said. "I was never so fancy that I would find fault in your father when he came in from plowing." Joseph had only smiled. But he'd been more than rewarded for his trouble when he'd returned to the yard to find Ruby waiting for him in a fresh, sky blue dress, navy apron and crisp, white *kapp*. She was so pretty that he could feel his throat tighten. God must have sent Ruby to him, because otherwise, he never would have had a chance with her.

Traditionally, men sat together for the communal harvest meal and the women served. Sara didn't try to alter that practice, but once the men had finished and the tables cleared and reset for the women and children, she suggested that the men take a turn at serving. It might not have been what they were accustomed to, but every one, including the Seven Poplars bishop, fell to it with good humor. And after the meal, it was the men who gathered and washed the dishes, the only exceptions being those too old or infirm to take part.

Then the games had begun. Joseph and Ruby had teamed up in the egg-and-spoon race where they'd not done so well because she kept dropping her egg. In the three-legged race, they'd come in a tie for second with Leah and Thomas. They'd helped out with musical chairs, a game played with clapping rather than instruments, and been soundly beaten in several rounds of corn hole. It was clear to Joseph that he had his work cut out for him in teaching Ruby how to toss the bean bags, because she was terrible. But it didn't matter, because she even made finishing last fun.

After the games, they'd found a quiet corner of the yard and shared a slice of lemon-meringue pie, followed up by one of raisin and one of apple cranberry. They'd talked and talked. He was never at a loss for words when he was with her. And even if he couldn't think of something to say, sitting in comfortable silence with Ruby suited him just fine. When they couldn't hold another bite of dessert, the two of them had wandered over to the horseshoe pits and watched Thomas taking on all comers, until Sara had called Ruby to help the little children with the sheep-cart rides. Honestly, he didn't care where they went, what they ate or what they did, so long as he could be with Ruby. Just being near her made him want to shout for joy.

"I like your friends and neighbors," Ruby said to him as they made their way back to the starting point so the children next in line could have a chance to ride in the cart. "They're so welcoming."

"And why wouldn't they be?" he replied shyly. "You're easy to like."

"I hope so. My mother was afraid I'd be homesick. I've never been away from *Mommi* and *Daddi* before. Does that make me sound immature?"

"Ne." He smiled at her again. "It shows you love your family, which is as it should be."

They returned the children to their waiting grand-mothers and then stepped aside to let another set of volunteers take their places with the cart. "Thirsty?" Joseph asked. "I think I could go for some of Anna Mast's lemonade. She freezes slices of lemon rind into the ice and makes her drink tart, the way I like it."

"Sounds good," Ruby agreed. They started walking toward the refreshment tables when Sara approached.

"Having fun?" Sara asked.

"We are." Ruby looked up at Joseph and smiled.

"I have something that I need to discuss with Joseph," Sara explained. "Maybe you could help pour drinks for a few minutes, Ruby, while Joseph and I talk in private?"

Ruby glanced at him again. "Of course," she replied.

"If it concerns me, it concerns Ruby too," Joseph protested. "There's no need for her to leave us."

Sara pursed her lips. "It's about your mother."

"Mother?" He frowned. "And us?"

Sara shook her head. *"Ne,* nothing to do with you and Ruby, although it might affect you in the future." She looked around. "We'd better go into the house. This isn't something for public knowledge, at least not yet."

"Maybe I should just let the two of you—" Ruby began, but he tucked her arm in his.

"I want you with me," he said.

Ruby nodded and followed him and Sara inside to Sara's office.

"Close the door." Sara waved them to seats in front of her desk and settled into her chair behind it. "I like to keep my matchmaking confidential."

Joseph leaned forward, suddenly very curious. Had she just said *matchmaking*?

"I'll be frank, Joseph. Elmer Raber came to see me in hopes that I could arrange a marriage for him." She folded her hands on her desk. "He's interested in your mother."

Joseph was so stunned that it took him a moment to respond.

Ruby gave a little squeak of surprise.

"My—my mother?" he managed when he found his voice.

Sara chuckled. "Don't look so shocked. Magdalena is still of marrying age. I've negotiated marriages for couples in their eighties. Being alone isn't natural for a man nor a woman." She leaned forward on her desk. "So tell me, what do you think of Elmer? He's financially sound and in good standing with his church. Marrying him would be an advantageous match for your mother. Do you think she'd look favorably on the proposition? I know she's turned down several suitors over the years, but now that you're marrying, perhaps she'd look at the idea in a new light."

Joseph sat back in the chair. He wouldn't have been more surprised if Sara had called him in to make a match for his milk cow. "You're certain it's *my* mother he's interested in? Not some other Magdalena?"

"Joseph." Ruby laid a hand gently on his wrist. "Your mother is still a very attractive woman."

"Exactly." Sara smiled at Ruby. "Attractive, industrious and a credit to the neighborhood. Who cooks *schmitz un knepp* like Magdalena? Or sews such a neat seam?" She picked up a pencil and tapped the point lightly against a yellow legal pad. "Normally, I wouldn't consult a son about his mother's match. But I know how close the two of you are. And you *are* the head of the household." She looked at him, obviously waiting for an answer. When he didn't say anything, she went on. "Do you think she likes Elmer? It's common knowledge that they're friendly, but have you seen any sign that she might feel more for him?"

It hadn't occurred to Joseph that his mother would ever want to marry again. She had always said that she didn't want to bring a stepfather into the house to rule over him. But maybe Sara was right. Now that he had someone of his own, maybe his mother... He removed his hat and balanced it on his knee. It was a lot to think about. Elmer Raber was a good man, and his mother *did* seem to like his company. Hadn't she invited him to supper? Maybe he'd been so concentrated on courting Ruby that he hadn't noticed what was happening in his own house.

"I'll tell you the truth." Sara rocked back in her chair. "When Elmer sent a boy to tell me that he wanted to meet, I thought it was Ruby he was interested in."

Ruby's eyes widened in surprise. "Me?"

Sara chuckled. "*Ach*, if I had a dollar for every person in the last two weeks who told me that Elmer liked Ruby and hoped to win her away from Joseph, well, that would be nice. But when I tracked down the rumor, I discovered it originated from one source. And that wasn't Elmer."

"Who was it?" Ruby asked. "Oh! Did Magdalena tell you that?"

Sara shook her head. "I do not repeat gossip. Not unless I know that the knowledge would do a great deal more good than evil, and that I absolutely know the information to be fact. In any case, it doesn't matter where the rumor started. It's not true. I asked Elmer right out. He made it clear that he thought you were a lovely girl and perfect for Joseph, but that his hopes were set on Joseph's mother. He believes that they are well matched, of an age to be sensible and young enough to look forward to many contented years."

Joseph frowned, trying to wrap his head around what the matchmaker had just said. "I can't think that my mother would start a rumor about Elmer and Ruby. She knows I intend to marry her." He glanced at Ruby. "And it hurts me that you'd assume that of her."

"I'm sorry," Ruby said with a shrug and an apologetic smile. "It just popped into my head."

"And out of your mouth." Sara shook her head. "Young people. You, Ruby, should learn to think before you speak. And you, Joseph," she said turning her attention back to him, "should realize that your mother is having a difficult time accepting your leaving the nest. It's not necessarily a fault—it only proves how much she loves you. Change isn't something that comes easy to us older folk."

"I suppose you're right," he agreed.

"So do you have objections to Elmer?" she pressed. "For your mother, not your betrothed."

He couldn't resist a smile. "*Ne*, so long as it's what she wants."

"Good." Sara slapped her hand on the desk. "That's

what I wanted to hear. Your mother deserves a life and a house of her own. She needs someone to take care of, someone other than a son. I was afraid that you might oppose the match. If you did, I'm sure Magdalena would balk at the whole idea. But if you see it as a good thing, then I think your mother will be more open herself to the notion of being courted."

"How can I help?" Joseph asked.

"Just be supportive. I'll arrange a supper and invite them both. And I'd like you and Ruby to be here. I'd like to get you all together and see how it goes. We'll go from there. Agreed?"

Joseph hesitated. "So…do you want me to say something to Mother?"

"*Ne.* Elmer's not quite ready, though I think he will be soon enough. He just wanted me to see how you felt about the idea."

Joseph glanced at Ruby. She was beaming.

He turned back to Sara. "I—I think it's a great idea, and Ruby and I will do anything we can to help."

His mind was already rushing ahead to the possibilities. If his mother married Elmer, she could move into Elmer's house, two church districts away. As Sara had said, marriage would give his mother something else to focus on, which would give him and Ruby time and privacy to settle into their new marriage. It might be the answer to his biggest problem. "*Ya,*" he said, breaking into a grin. "That sounds like a plan."

The following Friday, Joseph, Magdalena, Elmer and Ruby enjoyed a tasty supper at the matchmaker's house. So far, the evening had gone better than anyone could have expected. Magdalena seemed on her best behavior, and Elmer, smiling and witty, had actually gotten and held her attention. Sara's pot roast had been excellent, and Ruby and Joseph had eaten more *kartoffel kleesse* and corn bread than she suspected was wise, even if they did go easy on the green beans with bacon and the slaw.

Sara had Ruby and Joseph help themselves to fat squares of gingerbread heaped with whipped cream and go out on the porch where they could enjoy the mild October weather. Dusk was settling over the house and farmyard, the autumn air smelled of apples and hay, and crickets were keeping up a merry chorus. Ruby loved this time of the day, and she loved this season. It had always been her favorite, and this year she could share it all with Joseph.

"It's a *goot* thing you can't cook like that," he teased as they carried their dessert outside. "I'd soon be too fat to climb the hay ladder."

Ruby chuckled. "I'm not sure if that's a compliment or not, but it's true my cooking skills are limited. I *do* make excellent scrambled eggs though."

"Throw on some cheese and it will do just fine for suppers for me," he answered, taking a seat in one of the chairs on the porch.

She glanced toward the kitchen door and wondered if Sara was telling Magdalena about Elmer's offer of marriage. They'd heard no screaming or crash of broken china so far. Was it selfish to hope that Joseph's mother would surprise them all and be flattered by Elmer's attention? If she *did* accept the offer, that would leave Joseph's home just for him and Ruby. And that would be wonderful. The idea of beginning their marriage alone in a home appealed to her. Of course someday she'd want to move back to Bee Bonnet to care for her parents as they aged but they had made it clear they didn't expect her to return home anytime soon. She and Joseph would have to work out the details. She just liked the idea that they had options, and the option of some time alone with her husband without his mother or her parents would be more than she could hope for.

Maybe it hadn't been Magdalena who'd been spreading the rumor that Elmer was interested in her. It was wrong to suspect someone without proof, but it would be so like Magdalena. *God forgive me*, she thought. *I promised Joseph that I'd try harder to get his mother to like me, and I'm not living up to that promise if I'm suspecting her of trying to sow discord between us.*

What was it her father always said? "Take the log out of your own eye before you worry about a splinter in someone else's." It wasn't quite the same as the verse the preachers quoted from the Bible, but close and just as wise. And her mother was wont to say that you couldn't change another, only yourself. Needless to say, she had a lot of maturing to do to live up to their standards and learn to be charitable.

Ruby sat down and placed her plate of gingerbread on the small table between them. Seated the way they were, her knee almost touched his.

Joseph's gaze met hers and he smiled. He had such a beautiful smile. Whenever he turned it on her, she could feel her bones turn to butter. She averted her gaze, feeling a little shy, realizing that the time had come to spill the beans. For weeks she'd been worrying about keeping something from him, and all for nothing. He'd be pleased, so maybe it wouldn't be such a bad thing to surprise him. It would be like an unexpected gift.

The long-awaited letter from her parents had arrived on Wednesday and she'd been looking for an opportunity to explain everything to Joseph ever since. "Of course, tell your Joseph about your situation," her mother had written in her beautiful, flowing script. "Your father and I are surprised you waited this long. He has every right to know. Our only stipulation was that you and Sara not reveal your true circumstances until we could all be certain that it wouldn't make a difference to him. We were so disappointed in the Noffsinger boy, and I suspect Jason Zehr's motives were less than *goot* ones, as well. But that's in the past. It's easy to see that Joseph is a fine young man, worthy of being your husband."

Ruby lifted her lashes. "Joseph, I… I need to talk to you about…something." Suddenly, she was nervous, and she had no idea why. This was her Joseph, her betrothed. There was no reason to be nervous with him, not ever.

"Okay." He took a bite of gingerbread.

Ruby nibbled at her bottom lip. How to say this without sounding *hochmiedich*? Pride was considered a sin, but the truth was, her secret was a thing to make a girl feel valued and of worth. "It's nothing bad," she said in a burst of words. "It's a good thing, a wonderful thing. I just…" She stared at her lap.

He chuckled, setting his plate down. "What's going on? Have you learned to sew a straight seam?"

"*Ne*, better than that." She clapped her hands together, looking up at him. "You won't believe it."

"Okay…"

She pressed her lips together and barreled forward. "Remember when we met my parents at their house?"

"Of course, I do." His eyes narrowed.

"Well, that wasn't exactly my father's house," she said. "Well, it was, is…but it…isn't."

"I don't understand."

"It's…" She reached for his hand. "You see, the little house, it's my aunt's house. I mean my aunt lives there. Not *Mommi* and *Daddi*."

He looked confused. "So where *do* they live?"

"In the stone house next door." She grimaced and watched him for his reaction. "The big one."

He sat back. "You're telling me that your parents live in that big house?"

"Ya." She exhaled with relief. "It's a long story. Funny, really." She laughed but it came out half-hearted.

All of a sudden Joseph looked uncomfortable. He let go of her hand. Embarrassed, she withdrew it and tucked it behind her back.

"I'm listening," he said, his tone stiff.

"You see…both houses belong to my parents. The houses and the farm. And the land."

He was frowning. Joseph rarely frowned. "Your father owns land? How much?" he asked.

"A lot," she admitted. "If you count the smaller farms that he rents out…more than a thousand acres." Again, she grimaced. "I think."

"A *thousand* acres?" Joseph's features tightened and his complexion paled. "So you're saying he's rich and you didn't tell me. *Your father is rich.*"

"Not rich, exactly." She chewed on her lower lip. This wasn't going the way she expected it to, not at all. "But he does have the dairy and a herd of milk cows too."

"Your father is rich," Joseph repeated. "What else haven't you told me?"

"That's all." She opened her arms. "Well… I don't know what else you want to know. He's got a hog lot too, and sheep and… I don't know. We don't talk about it. I think he has a business or two. Partnerships. I suppose we should count those." She tried to make a joke of it.

Joseph wasn't smiling and suddenly she felt dizzy. Afraid. She stared at him. "I guess this comes as a surprise," she said, her voice dropping to almost a whisper. "To find out that I'm going to inherit—"

He stood up suddenly. "Ruby, you were untruthful with me! You…you made me think you—" His voice was hard, a tone she'd never heard him use with her before, and the pallor of his face had been replaced with an angry flush of red. "You…you lied to me."

"No, no I never lied," she protested, coming to her feet. "It's just that… Joseph, it's complicated. I had to be certain… My parents and I had to know that you—"

"I think I've heard all I need to," he said abruptly. "You deliberately deceived me."

"*Ne*, I didn't. I mean I did, but—" She exhaled and started again. "Joseph, let me explain." She grabbed his arm, forcing him to look at her. "See…two different boys tried to marry me for *Daddi*'s money. They said they loved me, but they didn't. It was just *Daddi*'s money they wanted. So my parents wanted to make sure that didn't happen again. That's why they sent me here to Delaware. So…no one would try to take advantage of *Daddi*'s—what *Daddi* has."

"And you think I'm like that?" he demanded. "You think I would do something like that?"

"*Ne*, of course not." She looked up at him, but he refused to meet her gaze. She let go of his arm. "You're different, Joseph."

"And so are you, Ruby." He pressed his hands stiffly to his sides. "You—you're not the woman I thought you were. The woman I trusted."

"Joseph, you don't understand." She took a step toward him. "Don't you see, this… It's not a bad thing."

He shook his head. "I can't believe you'd deceive me this way, Ruby. I suppose Sara was in on it too. And who else? Leah? Ellie?"

"Joseph, please."

"I've heard all I want to hear from you today." He turned away from her and strode toward the kitchen door, his shoulders rigid. "Mother," he called sharply. "Let's go. We're leaving."

"What's wrong with you, Joseph?" Magdalena said from inside. "I'm not done with my pie."

"There's pie at home." He stepped inside the door to the house and took her dress bonnet down from the hook on the kitchen wall. He held it out to her.

Magdalena rose from the table, coming to him.

"Let's go," Joseph repeated, handing her the bonnet. "We're going home." Then he turned and went back out the door.

"Joseph," Ruby pleaded as he strode past her on the porch without stopping. "Don't go." Stunned, she watched with tear-filled eyes as he went down the steps.

"I don't know what's gotten into the boy," his mother fussed from the kitchen door as she tied her bonnet. "I never taught him to be rude. And such a lovely supper, Sara. I can't thank you enough." She opened the door and then turned back. "We'll be expecting you for dinner on Monday, Elmer!"

Chapter Twelve

The day of his cousin Violet's wedding, Joseph arrived at his aunt and uncle's house at seven in the morning. Normally on a Thursday, he'd be working and, considering what had recently happened to his own dreams for marriage, a wedding was the last place he wanted to be. But family had to come first, regardless of his own feelings.

Outsiders might believe that Amish life was one of dour sacrifice, a rigid code of behavior and unrewarding toil. That was as far from Joseph's experience as the moon. Family, worship, community and work filled his world and he loved every hour of it. If it were not for his unwavering faith in God and in the Amish path to salvation, he didn't know if he would have been strong enough to survive losing the woman he'd waited a lifetime to find. *Gelassenheit*. It was what was expected of him and what he must give. He must put his future in the Lord's hands and accept whatever came with as much grace as possible.

Joseph hadn't spoken more than a few words to Ruby since he'd left Sara's home the night of her supper two weeks ago, and only then to tell her he wasn't going to talk about what had happened. She'd come to him, apologizing, trying to get him to talk to her. But what was the point? The engagement was over.

Of course there wasn't an hour that had gone by that he hadn't thought about Ruby or a night that he hadn't lain awake tossing until the first rays of dawn. The previous night had been particularly bad. He'd barely slept a wink, going over and over in his mind what had gone wrong between him and Ruby and thinking about his cousin's coming nuptials. He prayed fervently that the match Sara had made for Violet and John Abbott was better than his own. He hoped they knew each other better than he'd obviously known Ruby.

Despite his mother's vigorous resistance to his betrothal, Joseph had never doubted Ruby. Not only was she beautiful, but he'd believed her to be completely honest, a trait he admired above all else. He'd believed Ruby respected him as a man and the future father of her children. But, apparently, he'd been badly mistaken. Ruby's confession had hurt him so badly that at first he'd been stunned, too numb to feel the pain. But that had soon been replaced by anger, and then by an empty ache that was impossible to shake off. He just couldn't get past the fact that his Ruby, his beloved Ruby, had deceived him.

Another two buggies pulled into the leaf-strewn yard and Joseph moved to take the bridle of the nearest horse. "Go on inside," he said to the couple. It was almost ten and the services would soon begin. "I'll tend to your horse." After the family got out of the second buggy, Joseph waved to the driver to follow him to a line of horses and buggies tied to a board fence on the far side of the barn.

Joseph's aunt and uncle were well liked in the neighborhood and the wedding would be well attended. Groups of men stood near the well, the shed and the windmill. They were talking crops, weather and the availability of fertile land for sale in upper New York State and western Virginia while the women gathered inside to exchange the latest news and help with the preparation of the meals.

Sara, Ruby and Leah had arrived early, as well, to help with the dinner preparations, but Joseph had stood back and allowed Andy to take charge of their buggy. Ruby had seen him when she'd gotten down from the vehicle, but had wisely averted her gaze and continued on inside without attempting to speak to him. If she had tried, he didn't know what he would have done. Walked away? He wasn't discussing their breakup; there was no point. And he wasn't ready to talk to her about the weather or what was being served for the wedding dinner with her. He didn't know when or if he'd ever be.

A few laughing children, dressed in their black Sunday best, came out the back door and proceeded to chase one another around the yard. Joseph assumed that they belonged to guests who'd traveled to attend, probably the bridegroom's relatives from Ohio. Local mothers had come with a few babies and toddlers, but fewer kids were present than would be at other Amish gatherings. Most youngsters were at school or at home today under the watchful eye of babysitters because weddings were usually adult affairs. There would be a morning sermon, the seated midday dinner and another worship service in the afternoon before the evening supper.

Some families would stay for the entire event, while others had been invited for one meal or the other. No matter what the hour, the food would be fantastic and plentiful, and the services long and serious. A marriage wasn't simply the joining of a man and a woman, but a joyous addition to the families, faith and community. This was the first of what would be a full wedding season for the Amish of Kent County. Although weddings were traditionally held in November, after harvest, Violet and John's was being held in October, due to the large number of marriage ceremonies scheduled this autumn.

Normally the wedding ceremony and morning services would be held at another home nearby while the bride's parents' house was prepared for the wedding dinner with the elaborate arrangement of table setups and the *Eck*, the traditional corner of the main room where the bride and groom and their attendants sat. But Violet's parents' house was a large one, and they'd decided to have the sermon and the exchange of vows here. It would require a quick change of seating and place setting to make the change from worship service to wedding feast, but there were many willing hands to help.

"Joseph! It's time!"

He looked up to see his aunt waving from the back porch. He glanced down the driveway and saw that there were no other arrivals in sight. His thoughts still in turmoil, he crossed the yard amid a flurry of swirling maple leaves in vivid shades of brown, red and gold. He entered the house to find most of the guests, and the bridal couple, already seated. Both the men's and women's sections were full in the main rooms, and half the chairs were taken into an adjoining chamber that normally served as a guest bedroom.

"Here." Andy waved him to an empty spot in a row of unmarried young men.

Joseph slid in and removed his hat, tucking it under the bench just as one of the elders stood and signaled for the opening wedding hymn. They were halfway through when the preachers and the bishop filed in from an adjoining room and took their chairs in front of the assembly.

Joseph glanced at John and Violet sitting side by side up front. Even though they'd only met a few months ago and spent only a short time together, they seemed content with the match Sara had made for them. John was smiling and Violet was positively radiating joy in her new apron, dress and *kapp*. Watching her and her new husband-to-be, it gave Joseph pause to realize that after today, she would carefully pack her clothing away, not to be worn again until the day of her burial, hopefully many, many years in the future. Violet was so full of life that it was hard to imagine her as an old woman, her plain but cheerful face lined with age.

Two hymns later, the first preacher opened with a sermon about the sanctity of marriage and the need for a man and wife to stand together, no matter the trials of life. Never must they consider the option of divorce, for marriage was a sacred institution and one entered willingly with loving hearts. Family, he insisted, was the foundation of their faith and vital to God's plan. He went on to speak of the necessity of putting aside self and of honesty in all matters concerning each other.

The words fell like cold rain over Joseph. Honesty. That was what he'd required above all else from his wife-to-be, and true to his mother's prediction, Ruby had been hiding something. It didn't matter that she might have been hurt by other suitors before. She should have trusted him. She should have been truthful. And how could he go into a marriage with her if she didn't think she could be honest with him? Marriage was a sacred union, to be broken only by death. If he made a mistake, he'd have to live with it for the rest of his life, and a house divided by something so important was too weak to survive.

"Joseph." Andy nudged him. "Stand."

He rose quickly, feeling his cheeks flush with embarrassment that others might have noticed he was slow to get to his feet for the next hymn. He didn't need the *Ausbund*; he knew the more familiar hymns by heart. By force of will, he devoted his attention not only to the singing but to the lengthy sermons that followed. This was Violet's day, and he was determined not to do anything that would detract from her happiness.

It was shortly after twelve when the actual marriage ceremony took place. The bishop invited the couple to stand and answer the familiar questions. With his people there was no elaborate wedding clothing, no rings, no music or flowers. Violet and John just promised to be faithful and to support one another in front of God and these witnesses. And when each had uttered the words and clasped hands, the bishop had given his blessing to the union, a blessing echoed in the hearts of the entire community.

There were final words from the bishop and one of the preachers and several more hymns before the service ended. Then everyone, including the bride and groom, hurried to change the seating arrangements and prepare the house for the wedding dinner.

Joseph found himself immediately pressed into service setting up tables and carrying boxes of glassware from a second bench wagon in the yard. As he passed through the kitchen, he caught a glimpse of Ruby and he felt a moment of panic. Their gazes locked, and he forced himself to turn and walk away, head down.

"Joseph?" A hand gripped his forearm and he looked down to see Sara standing in the doorway. "You can't go on avoiding me too," she said quietly.

"I don't want to discuss this with you," he answered. His throat tightened and he felt a stinging behind his eyelids. He stared at the floor, gripping the box of glasses he held. "Not here. Not today."

She exhaled impatiently. "You can't continue to refuse to talk to Ruby. You need to settle this between you, if only so that you can both move on."

He shook his head, glancing up. People were watching. Listening. "Excuse me." He gestured toward the living room. "They're waiting for the glasses."

Sara grabbed his sleeve. "Joseph, Ruby's devastated."

"And you think I'm not?" He shoved the box into another man's arms. "Can you take this in?" Then, leaving Sara standing there, he walked back through the kitchen and out into the crisp midday air.

His chest felt as though a great weight was pressing on it. He hadn't wanted to be rude to Sara, but she'd been part of the deception. Did she think he could just forget that? He needed fresh air. He needed to get away from the smiles and laughter of the wedding celebration.

Shaken, he ducked around the corner of the house and walked away between the rows of corn shocks that marched in neat rows away from the farmyard. A brisk wind had picked up, sending chaff and dust whirling through the air, making it easy for Joseph to tell himself that the liquid that filled his eyes wasn't tears.

"A good wedding," Sara said to Ruby as she guided the driving mule down the dark lane. "A good match. I think they will be very happy together."

It was late, after ten. She and Sara had stayed to clean up after the guests left. They were alone because Leah had ridden home with one of her sisters, where she would spend the night. Ruby was glad that it was only the two of them because she needed to talk to the matchmaker. And, as much as she liked Ellie and Leah, she didn't want any more of their advice.

"You're quiet," Sara said. "Are you tired?"

"A little," Ruby replied. She shivered in the damp night air as goose bumps rose on her arms. She'd worn her green wool dress and cape, but she'd not brought a wrap. Mist rose from the fields to cloud the road and make it difficult to see the road ahead. Sara's buggy had lights and large reflectors, but the fog made the mule's hooves echo eerily off the hard surface of the blacktop. Ruby was glad that they didn't have far to go. It wasn't a good night to be on the road in a buggy.

"I wanted to tell you, Sara, that…that I've decided to go home," she said, swallowing and trying to hold back her tears. "To Bee Bonnet."

Bright headlights poured into the buggy from behind. Sara didn't speak until the car had passed them and vanished into the gray void ahead. A dog barked in the distance, and the alarm was taken up by two more. Ruby hugged her arms tightly against her chest as the first tear escaped and rolled down her cheek, followed by another.

"So you're giving up on Joseph?" Sara made a harrumphing sound. "I thought you were more determined than that."

Ruby sniffed and searched in her pocket for a tissue. "He wouldn't even look at me today."

"Joseph's stubborn, I'll give him that."

"I… I don't know what to do." A sob escaped her and she covered her mouth with her hand. There was no stopping the tears. "I've made…such a mess of things."

A truck passed, coming from the other direction, but the mule paid it no heed. The buggy kept rolling through the darkness. "So that's it? You've giving up and going home?"

"I don't want to give up," Ruby admitted. "But Joseph doesn't want me anymore. He's made that clear."

Sara sighed. "I feel partially responsible for this. I tried to tell your parents that deception is never a practice I recommend for courtship, but I didn't refuse to participate. Trust lost isn't easily regained. But Joseph cares deeply for you. We just have to give him time. I think he'll come around, once he smoothes his ruffled feathers and calms down. It's no small thing for a young man to suddenly discover that the penniless *maedle* he planned to make his wife will be a wealthy woman."

"Not *wealthy*."

Sara scoffed. "*Ya. Rich* by our standards. Do you know the value of Lancaster County farmland? Some say it is the most fertile topsoil in the world. Your father's land is better than gold locked in a vault somewhere."

"The land isn't mine," Ruby argued half-heartedly. "It's *Daddi*'s and *Mommi*'s."

"But in the Lord's time, it will pass to you and eventually to your children, should you be so blessed. As it should be if you and Joseph are good stewards and you live as you should, following the right path that God has planned for you."

The mule pricked up his ears and quickened his stride.

"Sara, you're not listening to me. It's been two weeks." Ruby clasped her hands in her lap. "I've tried to apologize. At least three times, but Joseph doesn't want to hear it. He wouldn't even speak to me today. He's not going to get over this."

"Maybe not, but I'm not ready to give up on the two of you, not yet," Sara said. "What I'm trying to figure out is whether Joseph's problem with you is the fact that you led him to believe you were poor, or that his wife will be financially secure in her own right. Some men find it difficult to accept when a woman is well set up. That's a truth I've learned over the years."

"Joseph's not like that." Ruby sniffed. "We talked about how things would be when we married. What is his will be mine and mine his. He said my opinion on matters would be important to him. He said we would always make decisions together." A sob escaped her lips. "Sara, can't you try to talk to him for me?"

"I tried, but he wasn't any more willing to talk with me than he was with you. Probably less," Sara admitted. She was quiet for a moment and then went on. "But I don't think you should go back to your mother just yet. I still believe the two of you are a solid match.

Better than most." She nodded thoughtfully, gripping the reins. "We just need to figure out how to fix this."

"But how are we going to fix it?" Ruby whispered.

"I don't know yet, but if you'll stay, I promise you, I'll think of something."

Ruby took a deep breath. "All right. I'll stay another week, but if we've made no progress, I think I should go home."

"If you have the sense God gave you, you'll stay as long as I tell you to. A man like Joseph doesn't come along every day, and if you leave before it's settled, you may regret it for the rest of your life."

"It's good of you to give up your Saturday evening to chaperone us," Elmer said to Joseph as he pushed back from the kitchen table.

"It's our pleasure." His mother beamed as she re-filled Elmer's coffee cup. "And Joseph doesn't mind a bit, do you?"

"Ne," Joseph said. And he didn't, not really. Since he'd stopped seeing Ruby, he hadn't been in the mood to socialize with friends. Andy had been making him-self scarce on nights when the two of them used to go in search of a singing, volleyball game or birthday party.

"Goot. I'm afraid I'm making a pest of myself since this is the third time I've shared supper with you and your mother this week." Elmer patted his stomach. "And *goot* suppers they were too."

Joseph nodded, though he'd barely tasted his pork chop and scalloped potatoes.

"You're so quiet that I was afraid you were coming down with something," Elmer went on when Joseph didn't say anything. "You know Harvey Zook from over near Willow Grove has the walking pneumonia. Last Tuesday. Milking cows in the morning and sitting in a hospital bed in Dover by supper."

"You think Joseph is sick?" his mother asked. She came around the table and pressed the back of her hand to his forehead. "He doesn't feel too warm."

Joseph held up his hands in protest. "I'm not sick. I'm fine. Just… I'm fine."

Elmer stirred a lump of sugar into his coffee. "I thought maybe Ruby would be here tonight. Haven't seen her in ages. Have you two set a date yet?"

Joseph exchanged looks with his mother. He hadn't said anything about the breakup, but he'd assumed that she'd told Elmer. Apparently, she hadn't. She corrected that oversight within seconds.

"Ruby and Joseph aren't seeing each other anymore," his mother explained smoothly. "She'd been keeping a secret from him. I knew there was something. Call me suspicious, but she had Joseph fooled."

"I'm sorry." Elmer grimaced. "I didn't know. I didn't mean to pry."

"Ne." Joseph shook his head. "It's all right."

"Hardly." His mother's brows knitted as she leaned forward eagerly to share the news with Elmer. "She deceived us all. For what reason, we'll never know. But she's not a poor girl like she insinuated. Her father owns a lot of land, and he has many businesses. Ruby is the only child, so she'll inherit it all. You know what everyone would be saying from here to Lancaster County. That Joseph married a plain-faced girl just for her fortune." She pursed her lips and nodded in the satisfied way she did when she'd been proven right. "I think too much of Joseph to have him be thought of that way."

"Ruby's not plain," Joseph protested. "Please stop saying that. She's a beautiful person, inside and out."

"You see what I mean?" his mother interrupted, throwing up her hands. "You see, Elmer? He was so besotted by her that he couldn't see what was right in front of his eyes. I'd not be uncharitable by calling her homely, but—"

"That's enough, Mother," Joseph said quietly. "I won't have you talk that way about Ruby."

His mother got to her feet, snatched a butter dish and her empty coffee cup and marched back across to the sink. Her back was rigid as she busied herself with the dishes. "Sons. When they fix on a girl, they lose all their sense." And then she turned back and looked directly at Elmer. "I'm going to have a good talk with Sara Yoder. What was she thinking? She must have known the truth, and that makes her almost as guilty as Ruby. Sara can make up for it by finding a more suitable bride for Joseph. And this time, I'll be the one to decide if she's suitable before she and my son ever lay eyes on one another."

"Mother, please," Joseph said. He bit back the words that rose in his throat. He couldn't disrespect her, especially in front of the man she hoped to marry. But he wouldn't sit here and listen to this. If Elmer hadn't been there, he would have gotten up and walked out. He didn't want to seem to be having a childish tantrum, but neither could he let her go on about Ruby so.

"It's not my place to interfere in a family affair..." Elmer began.

"*Ne*, say what you have to say. Maybe you can talk some sense into Joseph. You saw her. Did *you* think she was beautiful?"

Elmer averted his eyes. "I never believed it was fitting for a man my age to talk that way about a young woman, and certainly not one who was betrothed to someone. She seemed a lovely girl to me. Young, of course, but that's what a young man needs."

"I see how it is," she replied. "You men stick together. But—" Joseph's mother shrugged "—I was proved right, wasn't I? There was always something about her that didn't sit right with me." She dropped a bowl into her dishpan and it splashed a tide of water over the edge of the sink and down the front of her dress. *"Ach,"* she cried. She ran her fingers over the soaked cloth. "We'll say no more about her, if it upsets you so, Joseph. Excuse me while I go and change into something dry." She wrung out her dishcloth, hung it over the faucet and headed out of the kitchen.

Neither he nor Elmer said anything.

His mother paused in the doorway. "I'm sorry if I embarrassed you, son. But you're better-off without her. Anyone can see that. And when Sara finds you a more appropriate match, you'll see it too."

Silence reigned in the kitchen for several minutes after she was gone, and then Elmer drained the last drop of coffee and pushed the cup away. "I can see that Magdalena had strong feelings about your betrothal. You know that I have a lot of respect and admiration for her."

He met Joseph's gaze meaningfully. They hadn't discussed Elmer's talk with the matchmaker, but he knew Joseph knew.

"But I have to tell you," Elmer went on. "I don't agree with her on this. It doesn't look to me as if you're better-off without Ruby. I'd say it's the other way entirely."

Joseph rose and began to pace back and forth. "I do

miss her," he admitted after a minute or two. "But I...
She really hurt me, Elmer. I feel—feel betrayed. She
didn't trust me enough to tell me the truth about her father's worth. She thought I was the kind of person who
would pretend to fall in love with her because she'll
come into money someday."

"I can see how it would be a shock, learning such a
thing about the woman you were going to marry. But
think about it for a minute. This isn't a bad thing. Not
a bad thing at all. Not like she had behaved inappropriately in the past. Or if she was thinking of leaving
the church. That would be worse." Elmer was quiet for
a moment and then went on. "Joseph, I know just how
difficult it is to find someone you look forward to seeing at the end of the day, someone you can feel comfortable with at evening prayers. I'd hate to see the two
of you make a worse mistake by letting something like
this divide you. I agree that there shouldn't be secrets
between a man and a woman looking to marry, but... I
expect Ruby thought she had a good reason."

Joseph sighed. "It was what her parents wanted.
Some other boys had courted her just for the money. I
guess her parents thought that if no one knew what they
had, a boy would see Ruby for who she is."

"So there you go." Elmer sat back in the kitchen
chair. "You can see how a father who loved his only
child might err on the side of caution."

"My mother said she was suspicious of Ruby from
the beginning. She never thought she was the right one
for me." Joseph came to stand behind his empty chair
and look across the table. "I don't know, Elmer. I don't
know what's right. What I should do?"

Elmer smiled at him. "You should pray, Joseph.

That's my advice to you. Take it to the bishop or one of the preachers if it seems too heavy a burden. Your mother is a good woman, devoted to her faith and family. You can't fault her for that. But she can't make this decision for you. I certainly can't." He hesitated. "The thing is, I wouldn't want you to lose out on someone you were meant to be with over bruised pride."

Chapter Thirteen

The following morning was bright and crisp, a beautiful fall day, so pleasant that Sara hadn't bothered to have Hiram hitch up the buggy, but had decided to take her scooter to Magdalena's instead. The exercise would do her good, she reasoned, after all the wonderful food she'd eaten at Violet and John's wedding and in anticipation of the wedding season. She loved the festive air of weddings, but she couldn't resist trying other women's biscuits and pies. If she didn't watch what she put in her mouth, she could easily be as plump as Anna Mast.

When Sara reached Magdalena's home, she was a little winded. Pausing to catch her breath and regain her professional composure, she scanned the small, tidy house. The curtains were pushed back at the kitchen window, a good sign that the woman she'd come to call on was present.

What lovely flowers Magdalena grew, Sara thought as she pushed her scooter up the drive. The beds were a riot of fall colors: red and orange zinnias, gold mums, purple monkshood and brown and green ornamental grasses. There was a big clay pot of herbs at the step with basil, oregano and rosemary, still healthy and green. The door was closed, but it would be if Joseph's mother was home alone.

Magdalena responded immediately to Sara's knocking. "Sara?" Magdalena's surprised expression quickly changed to one of welcome. She pushed the door open wide and peered around her to see if anyone was with her. "Come in. I was just thinking of you. I imagine you came on business. But Joseph isn't here. He's at work."

"Actually, it was you I came to see." Sara followed her into a cheerful yellow kitchen. Magdalena kept the neatest kitchen in Seven Poplars; there wasn't a dirty dish in the sink, a cup out of place or a flowerpot that wasn't a mass of blooms.

"Would you like hot tea?" Magdalena went to the gas range and turned on the flame under the teakettle. "I was just thinking I could use a cup of Earl Grey. Unless you'd rather have coffee?"

Sara nodded her head. Common courtesy meant that she couldn't launch into her reason for coming until they had shared a beverage and exchanged news about each other's households. "Tea is fine. I hope I didn't interrupt your work."

"I was just finishing up some baby gowns and a dress for Mattie Ann Troyer's children. What with Ezra being laid up with a broken ankle, money is tight. I thought her little ones could use some warm new clothes for the cooler weather."

"That's kind of you," Sara replied. "My cousin Hannah's sewing circle is going to auction off a quilt to help with the medical expenses."

"I know the family will appreciate it. Doctors come so expensive today, don't they?" Magdalena measured loose tea into a blue teapot. "I see you came on your scooter. It must be four miles. I do admire you, Sara. So energetic for a woman your size." Magdalena brought mugs and a cream pitcher to the table. It was wooden, with a scrubbed white pine finish, obviously old and well cared for. Hanging from the ceiling over the table was a lovely oil lamp that had been fitted for propane. Already on the table were a blue-and-white pottery sugar bowl and a small vase, shaped like a woven basket, filled with tiny yellow mums. "I thought we should have a talk about Joseph," she said. "Straighten out this whole mess and start over with a different—"

"My first concern today is you, Magdalena." Sara smiled at her.

"Me?" The teakettle whistled and Magdalena went to the stove to pour hot water into the teapot.

"I'll get to the point. Women our age don't have time to pussyfoot around." Sara folded her hands, resting them on the table. "Elmer Raber has made a request for a formal offer of marriage. To you," she added.

Magdalena was just putting the lid on the teapot. She dropped it and it rattled on the counter, but it didn't break. "He wants to… Did you say 'offer of marriage'?" she sputtered.

"I sure did. Now, Elmer understands you've been an independent woman for many years, taken care of your own finances. For that reason, he's willing to settle a nice little nest egg on you, payable at the time of the wedding." She removed a slip of paper from her dress pocket and slid it across the table to Joseph's mother. "This full amount will be deposited to your bank account if you agree."

Magdalena's eyes widened as she stared at the piece

of paper on the table. Her lips parted, but for once, she didn't seem to be able to speak. Finally, she inhaled and stammered. "Elmer wants to give me…" She picked up a paper fan from the table and began to fan herself rapidly. "He wants to give me money to marry him?"

"Well, not exactly to marry him. He wants you to marry him because he thinks the two of you would get on well together." Sara rose from her chair and went to retrieve the teapot, securing its lid as she walked back across the kitchen toward the table. "It's not unknown in other parts of the country. In other Amish communities. It's a sign of good will, so that you know you'll be well provided for and not be totally dependent on your new husband." She sat down and poured them both tea. "Furthermore, if and when you do marry, he'll put your name on everything he owns, share and share alike."

Magdalena gripped the back of her chair with one hand while fanning herself with the other. There was a bright spot of red on each of her cheeks. "I… I don't know what to say. Elmer wants to marry *me*?"

"He does. He tells me he respects and admires you, and enjoys your company. He hopes that you will consider him as a suitor with the object of holy matrimony, if and when you find it agreeable." Sara chuckled. "Those were his very words to me, and quite a mouthful for Elmer, I must say."

"Ach." Magdalena covered her mouth with slender fingers. "I thought… That is, I *hoped* he wasn't just coming for my pot roast, but…" She looked at Sara. "It's quite amazing, isn't it? That Elmer would think so highly of me?"

"And why wouldn't he? Now, sit and have your tea." She began pouring. "You're still a young and vibrant woman. No one makes better cakes, and you sew like a tailor. You are a fine catch, Magdalena. You look years younger than you are, and God has blessed you with good health. Why wouldn't Elmer want to marry you?" She slid Magdalena's cup across the table to her. "The question is, are you interested in Elmer? I know you've turned down other offers."

She nodded, slipping into her chair. "I have, but not for years. When Joseph was younger, I was reluctant to give over his welfare to a stepfather. Joseph and I always had a special relationship, and I was content to raise him myself. But now…" She fluttered the fan faster. "I don't know what to say."

Sara took a sip of the tea. It was good, fresh and sweet on her tongue. "Your son is a grown man. It's time for him to marry and become the head of his own family. It's not too late for you to enter a new relationship. Now, tell me, do you like Elmer?"

"I… I do," Magdalena admitted. "He's hardworking and soft-spoken. And he seems easy to please at the dinner table. The bishop speaks well of him. They are distantly related. But…this is all so sudden." She looked down at her tea and then up at Sara again. "Does he want an immediate answer?"

"Of course not. Elmer wants you to take as much time as you need. He did say that he hoped I'd be able to tell him that it's not out of the question, that you will consider his offer." When Magdalena didn't answer, Sara said pointedly, "So, will you consider his offer?"

"I—I'll have to speak with Joseph. This isn't a good time for him. He might want me to be here with him."

"I've already broached the subject with Joseph, and he thinks it's a wonderful idea."

"He does?" Magdalena nodded. "Well, I… I'll have to think…to pray on it. It's a big decision."

"It is." Sara smiled at her again. "So I can tell Elmer that he may hope?"

"*Ya*, he can." A blush tinted her cheeks. She set down the fan, then picked it up and began to fan herself again. "My goodness, what a morning. I didn't expect this."

Sara looked at her. "What did you think? How many times has Elmer been at your table recently? Attended your church services? Surely you didn't think that all those meetings were coincidence, did you?"

She let out a pent-up breath. "*Ne*, but I wasn't sure. I didn't want to get my hopes up and look foolish, so I told myself that he was just lonely and looking for friendship."

"He *is* looking for friendship. But also more."

Magdalena pressed her lips together, seeming to fight a smile. "I always thought that I'd remain single. Joseph's father and I had a good marriage, but he's been gone for many years. I've gotten used to doing things my own way."

"I understand perfectly." Sara picked up her mug. "But there are advantages for a woman with grown children to marry again." She glanced around the kitchen. "Once Joseph takes a wife, you'd have to share this home with her. And in time, it will be her kitchen and, God willing, her children's. I'm sure you'll always have a place here, but it won't be the same place it has been. A mother must come second to a wife."

"I never wanted to be alone," Magdalena admitted. "To come home to an empty house."

"Exactly. And in a second marriage, you would be mistress of the house. You and Elmer would have many years of active living ahead of you. This way you can visit with your son and go home to your own domain whenever the grandchildren get too loud. Elmer likes to travel. He has relatives all over the country, and he told me that if you married, he'd take you anywhere you'd like to go for a honeymoon. He's lonely too. I've made inquiries of his late wife's friends and family. It's something I do. And they have only the best to say of Elmer. If anything, his sisters-in-law say he's too easy-going and tended to let his wife make most of the family decisions. He stands in good stead with his church community, he's charitable and I've seen his financial statements. You'd be hard put to do better."

Magdalena reached for her mug. "I'll think on it," she agreed.

"Good. I will warn you though." She sipped her tea. "Another widow's family has already approached me asking questions about Elmer. If you refuse him, someone else wants me to arrange a match with him."

"Who? Is it Mary Jane Byler? She's sixty-five if she's a day. And old in her ways."

Sara tried not to laugh. There was no dust gathering on Magdalena's *kapp*. "I'm not at liberty to say who. Just that Elmer has other options."

She tugged at an imaginary loose strand of hair and tucked it over her left ear. "But he chose me."

"He did. Elmer thinks you're very attractive. And he says he's never tasted better gravy."

"Well, fancy that. A beau at my age." Magdalena beamed. "I'm not agreeing just yet, of course. I'll have to pray on it."

"That's always best. And you can speak to the elders on the matter. Their wisdom never fails."

"True, true." Magdalena held her mug between her hands and looked across the table at Sara. "Thank you so much for…" She glanced away. "Thank you."

"You're most welcome." Sara gave a nod, thinking that, while Magdalena could be off-putting at times, she truly was good woman. "Now, while I'm here, we might as well talk about Joseph."

"*Goot.*" Magdalena set down her mug. "I do hope you have other girls in mind for him. This time, I'd like to appraise them before you introduce anyone to Joseph."

"*Ne.* I wanted to speak to you about Joseph and Ruby," Sara said firmly.

"That's over." She pursed her lips. "It's clear she isn't the one for him."

"Magdalena," Sara said, taking care with her words. "No one is more devoted to a son than you are to Joseph. And I know that, in your heart, you want his happiness."

"It's all I've ever wanted. To teach him to walk in God's grace, to follow our teachings and to be happy."

Sara fixed her with a knowing look. "Then you know he's unhappy without Ruby. And if he persists in this stubborn behavior, she'll return to her parents and eventually find someone else."

"I think it's best if she goes home." Magdalena sniffed. "Joseph will find a more suitable wife, someone that I can get along with."

"A girl you can get along with or one that will make Joseph happy?" Sara paused and then went on. "You loved your husband. And even if you decide to marry Elmer, it will never be like that first love. It will be different, good, satisfying, but not the passion of young love. Am I right?"

Magdalena frowned, not meeting Sara's gaze. "I suppose you're right."

"Here's my question to you. What if Joseph never finds someone he loves as much as he loves Ruby? What if he never marries and never has children for you to bounce on your knee? Have you considered that in years to come, he may blame you for the breakup?"

"Me?" Magdalena's drew herself up. "Why would Joseph blame *me*? Ruby's the one who deceived him about her financial situation."

"True. But then she told him the truth. And she's apologized to him for not telling him sooner. And tried to talk to him, but Joseph will have no part of a discussion." Sara sat back in her chair. "Honestly, Magdalena, I've been surprised by his behavior. Not being willing to talk over differences is not very mature. And it's not the Amish way. Doesn't our Bible teach us forgiveness and compassion?"

Magdalena looked down at her hands, folded on the table. "*Ya*, it does."

"And tell me, how much of your opposition to Ruby has instigated this? How much have you influenced him in his decision to back out of this courtship?"

"That's silly." Magdalena got to her feet, her face flushed again, this time with distress. "I'm the one who sent Joseph to you. I *wanted* him to find a wife."

"*Ya*, you did. But is it possible that you never expected a woman to fall in love with your son and him with her? Did you think that an arranged marriage would be one of convenience? And that way, you would remain first in your son's heart?"

"That's a terrible thing to accuse me of," Magdalena said. She picked up a dish towel, then set it down on the counter again. "Do you think I'm that selfish?"

"I think you are a good mother and a good woman who may have judged a girl too harshly because you were afraid that she would take your only child from you. And I think that when your son reacted badly, you didn't give him a piece of your mind." Sara rose to her feet. "You are a strong person, Magdalena, and I know you have a loving heart. I only ask that you consider if Joseph's breaking off this courtship with Ruby is better for Joseph—or for you."

"Did he tell you that?" Now Magdalena looked hurt. "Is that what my son thinks?"

Sara shook her head. "No, he didn't say that. I think he's hurt and maybe a little confused. So hurt and confused that he doesn't know what to think."

"You want me to talk to him. Is that what you're asking me to do?"

"I'm asking you to consider what I've told you. I'm asking you to pray for guidance and do what is best for all of you, especially your son. Because if you can bring the two of them back together and she is what will make him happy, he'll thank you for it for the rest of his life."

Joseph scooped mortar on his trowel and slapped it on a concrete block. He was working on the third row of a foundation addition to Moses King's house. He used the trowel edge to smooth and tidy up the wet mix and then added the next block to the row. He settled the block in place and eyed the string line to be certain he was laying a straight course. Turning back to the board, he shaped and turned over the mortar, mentally gauging the amount of moisture in the mix. It was just right.

Too much water in the mortar would make a weak wall, and too little would make it difficult to work.

"Joseph!" James called to him. "Your mother's here to see you!"

Joseph laid down his trowel and climbed out of the foundation. His mother? What could be wrong that she'd come to his worksite? He noticed that James was grinning and realized that if his mother hadn't come for an urgent reason, he'd face teasing from his friends and fellow workers. Striding toward his mother's horse and wagon, he tugged off his concrete-smeared leather gloves. He dropped them on a stack of concrete blocks as he passed them.

"Is something wrong?" he asked as he approached the wagon.

She was climbing down. She was wearing her black church dress and her bonnet, full apron and cape. He was immediately perplexed. She hadn't mentioned needing to go into Dover for anything, and she rarely drove herself, claiming that traffic made her uneasy on the road.

"*Ya*, plenty is wrong," she said.

He stared at her. She was definitely giving mixed messages. She'd said there was a problem, but she didn't appear as if she was sick or the house was on fire or someone they knew was in the hospital. And she seemed calm. He'd told her that he was coming home for the midday meal, so what was so important that she couldn't wait? He glanced over his shoulder and saw that James and Amos had both stopped putting up cedar shakes on the main house and were watching.

"Where are you going?" he asked, torn between concern for her welfare and embarrassment that she'd interrupted his work. Once mortar was mixed, you had to use it or throw it away. He didn't have time to waste, but he couldn't fail to show respect for his mother in front of the work crew.

"I'm coming *here*." She looked back at the horse. "You should take her out more often, you know. She doesn't stand to be harnessed very well. I had a time hitching her up. And I think the left back wheel on this wagon is loose. It squeaks. Your father wouldn't approve. You know how careful he was with his equipment. A little grease saves—"

"Mother?" he said sharply, cutting off her lecture on the benefits of maintenance of farm vehicles, which he knew from experience could be quite lengthy. "I'm working. If nothing's wrong, what do you need?"

She turned back to him. "I've made a mistake."

"What are you talking about?" He took her arm and tried to steer her back to the wagon, but she planted her feet and wouldn't be moved.

"I just told you. I've made a terrible mistake." She hesitated. "About Ruby."

He stared at her.

"*Ya*, I admit it. I was wrong. I've thought about it and—" Her eyes suddenly filled with tears. "I didn't mean to interfere. You know I've always wanted what was best for you. I always—"

"Mother, better we talk about this at home." He threw another look back at James and Amos. They were talking to each other, and he didn't doubt that it was about him. "I'll be home in an hour. You go home now, and I'll be along soon."

"*Ne.*" His mother raised a finger and shook it at him. "*Ne.* Now. I'll talk to you now and you'll listen."

She sniffed and blinked. A tear escaped and trickled down her cheek and she brushed it away "Even though I know it's time for you to marry, maybe a part of me wanted to keep things the way they are. Just you and me. I never thought I was a jealous person, but I think maybe in this, I was."

"Mother, this isn't the time for such a conversation," he protested. Again, he tried to take her arm, but she pulled away from him.

"Joseph, you'll hear me out here and now because… because, maybe in an hour, I won't have the courage to say these things to you. Maybe I'll have second thoughts, and the jealousy will creep back in."

He glanced over his shoulder again and then at her. "Please, keep your voice down. I don't want James to hear you."

She brushed away his concerns with a careless gesture. "James is a good man. Surely, he understands that sometimes there are things only a mother can say to her son? That family matters are more important than concrete blocks? This is important, and you will hear me out."

"Mother, private matters are not for everyone to hear."

"And you think this is a secret that I didn't approve of your Ruby? That I didn't find fault with her when she tried to win my approval? Half of Kent County knows that I was pleased when you fell out with your Pennsylvania girl. And I am ashamed of my behavior. And of yours," she added.

"Mine?"

"You're behaving childishly. You and Ruby have had an argument and—"

"It was more than an argument, Mother. She—"

"And you won't interrupt me." Again, she held up her finger. "That girl came to you and tried to apologize. I heard the two of you on the front porch last week."

"You were listening in?" he demanded.

"That's not the point. The point is that she made a poor choice, and you made a poor choice by refusing to accept her apology and by not talking to her."

Joseph balled his fists at his sides. How could his mother come to his workplace and accuse him of— Suddenly his eyes filled with moisture. Embarrassed, he looked away. "What exactly are you getting at?" he asked when he found his voice. "What do you want me to do?"

"*Ach.* Finally, I get through that thick skull of yours." She clapped her hands together. "I want you to take this horse and wagon and go to the matchmaker's house and find Ruby. I want you to tell her that you have acted like a child and you're sorry."

"Sorry for what?" He lowered his voice to a harsh whisper. "She lied to me."

"She didn't tell you the whole truth. But what exactly did she say? Did she tell you that she was penniless?"

He thought for a minute.

"Did she?" his mother demanded.

He exhaled. "*Ne*, not exactly. But…we went to see them. She let us think they lived in that little house. The garden was small. I naturally thought—"

"*Ya.* You assumed they were poor. But maybe this is partly your fault too. Maybe you didn't ask the right questions."

"M—"

Yet again she held up her finger and cut him off. "I've

prayed on this. On my knees, I tell you. Sometimes I am too stiff-necked to listen when God speaks to my heart. We're human, Joseph. We make mistakes. Ruby made a mistake, but you made a mistake in refusing to listen to her. In hardening your heart against her."

"I was angry with her." He took a breath and then went on, quieter now. "I was angry and upset that she wouldn't trust me."

"And afraid that some fool would poke fun at you. Admit it." She took hold of his hand and gripped it tightly. "If our Father in Heaven can forgive our sins, how can you look at the woman you say you love and refuse to accept her apology? That is pride. And pride is worse than words. For such a human mistake, that a girl should listen to the advice of her parents and keep a secret from you, is that enough reason to ruin two lives?"

Heat crept up his throat. He could feel shame rising in his chest. Was it true? Had he let pride come between him and Ruby?

His mother was quiet for a moment and then went on. "You have to decide who was wrong. Ruby? You? Both of you?" his mother continued. "You have to talk about it and you have to fix it. At least try."

"But you said she was all wrong for me. You said it was better if it ended."

"*Ya*, I did and I'm sorry for that. I hope you can forgive me. Both of you. I hope that in time I will be able to forgive myself for my selfishness. All I can say is that I thought I was saying what was best for you, when really what I was saying was what was best for me."

Joseph wiped his forehead with the back of his hand. "I can't believe you're standing here saying this to me," he managed.

She shrugged and gave him a half smile. "I can't either. Now, you take this horse and wagon. I'll drive your buggy home. And you go and try to straighten out the mess you have made of your courtship with Ruby." And with that, she walked across the yard to where his horse was tied. "James!" she called, waving her hand at him. "Come over here and hitch up this animal for me. There's no sense in me doing it. You're standing idle."

James put down his hammer at once.

"And you, Amos." Joseph's mother pointed at Amos. "Put your eyes back in your head and get back to work. My Joseph has more important things to do today than be a joke for the two of you."

Stunned, Joseph climbed up onto the wagon seat and gathered the reins. But he just sat there. Was she right? Was he as wrong as Ruby for not accepting her apology? Was what he had done worse than what's she'd done?

"Don't just sit there like a scarecrow!" Amos called good-naturedly to Joseph. "Do as your mother says."

Joseph did what any self-respecting man would do. He shook the leathers over the mare's neck and got out of there as fast as she could trot.

Chapter Fourteen

"Come on, *boppli*," Ruby coaxed the tiny fawn-colored calf. "Just taste this. You'll love it." She crouched down in the deep, sweet-smelling straw and held out the bottle. "It's delicious." The previous day, Leah's sister Grace had given her the little Jersey calf. Grace's husband, the local veterinarian, had purchased it for ten dollars from a farmer who'd intended to put the animal down. The mother had rejected the calf at birth, and without constant attention, the fragile baby had no chance of surviving.

Not only was this the wrong time of year for new calves, but this one had so far refused the nutrient-rich formula in the bottle. Getting the little Jersey to eat and keeping her warm in Sara's barn in the crisp autumn temperatures required Ruby's constant attention and around-the-clock feeding. It was a task that she had, at first, reluctantly accepted, but then she'd then thrown herself wholeheartedly into it. The calf, Star, as she'd decided to name it, needed her. And she needed something, other than Joseph's rejection, to concentrate on.

Star was so weak this morning that she could barely

stand. Ruby had sat down in the oat straw and pulled the calf into her lap. With a clean towel, she rubbed the baby's coat, stroking and murmuring to the animal and scratching behind her ears. And when she felt the calf relax against her, she used up the last trick in her bag. From her pocket, she removed a half-pint mason jar of honey, dipped her fingers in it and rubbed the honey between Star's lips. For a moment, there was no reaction, and then a small rough tongue appeared.

"Ya," Ruby said. "It's good, isn't it?" The calf nudged her hand, seeking more of the sweet honey. Ruby dipped the nipple of the bottle into the honey and let Star suck on that. The tiny ears twitched and the tail wagged. The calf took the nipple and began to drink the formula. "Good girl, good *boppli*," Ruby murmured. She pressed her face into the calf's warm neck, and for a few minutes forgot Joseph and her heartache and let the peace of the small creature in her arms sweep over her.

Footsteps pulled her from her reverie. She glanced up to see Joseph standing at the edge of the stall. She blinked, not certain if he was really here, or if she'd imagined him.

"Sara said you were out here," he said.

She looked down at the calf. The bottle was half-empty. Afraid that Star would stop drinking if she got up, she remained where she was, concentrating on the calf in her arms. He pushed open the stall door and crouched beside her. She raised her head and gazed into his eyes. Her hand holding the bottle trembled.

"I've been a fool, Ruby," he said. "I'm so sorry. I… We should have talked. I should have listened to you. I should have…" He exhaled, gazing into her eyes. "Can you ever forgive me?"

She hugged the calf closer, wanting to believe that she was hearing what she was hearing. "*Ne*, Joseph, it was me," she whispered, tears filling her eyes. "I'm the one who was dishonest. It's my fault."

"Ruby, we were both wrong. You should have told me sooner. You should have trusted me. But I let pride and my mother's words come between us. My fault is greater."

"I didn't want…" she began. Then she stopped and started again. "I didn't know what to do, Joseph. My father said not to tell anyone. He said to find a man who would love me for me and not my father's dairy herd." She laughed because it sounded so silly now.

"It doesn't matter." He shook his head. "None of that matters. What matters is how we feel. About each other and…and I know how I feel. I love you, Ruby." He reached out and touched a wisp of hair that had escaped from her *kapp*. "I just hope you can see past my stupid—"

"Shh." Smiling at him through her tears, she pressed one finger to his lips. "No more," she entreated. "It was all a silly misunderstanding. If you really love me, it doesn't matter. None of it matters."

"I do, Ruby. I love you, and I want us to marry…to grow old together…to make our own family. If only you can…if only you could find it in your heart to—"

"Love you?" The bottle fell from her fingers. The calf bawled and scrambled to her feet. Ruby went to throw herself into Joseph's arms, but she leaned too far, hitting him in the forehead with hers. Down they both went into the straw. Joseph's hat rolled off, her *kapp* tilted to one side and her apron flew up over her shoulder, leaving one *kapp* string dangled across her face. "I do love you," she cried, laughing.

Joseph's lips, warm and firm, brushed hers, and sweet joy spread outward from his touch.

"Ruby! Joseph! What do you think you're doing? Rolling in the hay? Kissing? In my barn? Shame on you both," Sara admonished.

They parted as quickly as they had come together, struggling to get to their feet. He offered his hand to her and pulled her up. Ruby straightened her *kapp* and pushed down her apron. Joseph brushed the straw off his shirt and retrieved his hat from the corner where the calf was happily nibbling on the brim.

Sara's eyes flashed. Her fists pressed against her hips. "What possible explanation do you have for this behavior?" she demanded.

Ruby covered her mouth with her hand and tried not to giggle.

Joseph moved to stand beside her. He pulled on his hat and then snatched it off to shake the straw out of the brim. "We—we want to be married," he declared. "As soon as the *banns* can be called."

"And you think that's an excuse?" Sara demanded. "For putting my reputation at risk? Not to mention your own?" She shook an accusing finger at the two of them. "Good for the both of you that I came when I did."

"It was just a kiss," Joseph explained. "Our first kiss, and there won't be any more. You have my word on it. I have too much respect for the woman who will be my wife."

Sara huffed. "A good speech for a young man who not so long ago couldn't manage a single sentence without hesitating. Proof that all you needed was to find the right woman." She pursed her lips. "But a kiss has led to more than one regret. Kisses are best saved for the honeymoon. Do you understand, Ruby?"

"Ya," she said meekly.

"Are we quite clear on that?" Sara asked Joseph.

"Ya." He glanced down at Ruby, and his big hand closed over hers. "We'll try."

Ruby looked up, meeting his gaze, so filled with joy that it was hard to put two words together, let alone a sentence. "But maybe it's best if those banns are cried soon."

"My sentiments exactly," Sara said, turning and walking away. "Before your families cause even more mischief."

Epilogue

Ruby pushed aside the curtain to see the swirling snowflakes turning the fields and trees a wintry white. Outside, the temperature was dropping and the gray skies hung low over the house and barn, but she didn't mind. She liked winter. The small house was snug and toasty warm with its propane heat and the added comfort of the kitchen woodstove. The delicious smell of baking bread and simmering vegetable soup filled the downstairs.

She hoped Joseph would like the soup. Her cooking skills were not equal to her mother's and certainly not to Magdalena's, but they were improving. She and Joseph, together, had mixed up the yeast bread midday, and it had risen perfectly before she'd popped the loaves into the oven. It amused them both that Joseph had a real knack for making bread, biscuits and pancakes.

Baby Samuel, faithfully guarded by the tabby cat, was sleeping peacefully in his cradle. Ruby couldn't help smiling as she gazed at the small hand that had escaped the confines of his quilt and the tumbled mass of ringlets curled around his precious face. If she hurried, Ruby had just enough time to write a letter and put it out in the mailbox before Samuel woke from his nap and Joseph finished his wood chopping.

There were many things she could have been doing: diapers needed folding, the table had to be set for supper and there was that missing button on one of Joseph's work shirts that needed replacing. But keeping in touch with family was important, and she loved an excuse to sit at the small maple writing desk Joseph had given her on their second wedding anniversary. A horse and buggy passed the house on the road, the familiar rhythm of hoofbeats muffled by the falling snow. A family hurrying to get home before nightfall. That was another thing she loved about winter. Not that she didn't love her community and the constant coming and going, visiting and church services. She did. But days like this, when Joseph was home and it was just their little family, were special.

She took out a sheet of paper with a pretty flower border, found her favorite pen and began to write.

Apple Valley, Kent County, Delaware
February 14

Dearest Mother,
How good it was to see you last Sunday. I'm so glad that you were able to get home before the weather turned. It is snowing here today, but we never get as much as you do in Pennsylvania. Thank you for the baby clothes. As always they are beautifully sewn and the blue will look so nice with his eyes. Joseph and I were talking, and I think we are ready to move permanently to Penn-

sylvania next fall when *Daddi* retires. The good news is that we will be next door to my parents and only a half hour away by buggy from you. Joseph and I are so happy that you and Elmer decided to move to Lancaster to be nearer his daughter and grandchildren.

It is our wish that Samuel and any other children it pleases God to give us will grow up with both sets of grandparents nearby so that they will benefit from your wisdom and love. We have found such happiness in our marriage that we deeply want you and dear Elmer to be part of it.

I know that you and I have had our differences in the past. I think we got off to a bad start, but thankfully that is not the case anymore. Joseph and I have missed you since you married Elmer and moved to Pennsylvania. I do hope that you can give me some cooking lessons. I certainly need them. I made a vegetable-beef soup today, and I am hoping for the best. I remembered what you said and added a bay leaf and celery. I had red cabbage but no green, so...

The back door banged open and a red-cheeked Joseph stomped in amid a gust of cold air, his arms full of firewood.

Samuel startled in his cradle and let out a whimper.

"Sorry," Joseph called. He caught the door and pulled it closed before carrying the logs to the wood box beside the cookstove. "It's freezing out there."

Ruby jumped up and went to the cradle where Samuel was squirming. "Shh," she murmured soothingly as he opened one eye sleepily. "Hush, *boppli*. It's just your *daddi*." She rocked the cradle gently.

Joseph tugged off his gloves. "Did I wake him?"

She shook her head. "*Ne*, he's all right. He'll sleep a while longer."

"*Goot*." Joseph chuckled. "Let sleeping babies lie."

"*Ya*." She smiled at him. "Just look at our Samuel. He's growing by the day. He won't be a baby for long. Soon, he'll be trailing after you."

"And carrying wood." Joseph smiled at her as he shrugged off his flannel-lined denim coat. "Soup smells good."

She grimaced. "Don't say that until you've tasted it."

He returned the few steps from the living room to the kitchen and hung his coat on a hook by the door. "After living in this house, you won't know what to do in your father's big place," he said. "We'll rattle around like two peas in a pod."

"We'll have to fill it with children, I suppose."

He held out his arms and she went to him, laying her cheek against his chest and feeling the strength and goodness of him. *I'm truly blessed*, she thought. *I could not ask for a better husband*.

Joseph's arms tightened around her. "A round dozen, do you suppose?"

"Children?" She peered up at him. "A dozen?"

"Or more." He cupped her chin in his hand and raised it. "You remember what Sara told us?"

"What was that?" she asked. "I don't remember anything about twelve children."

"About the kissing," he teased as he lowered his mouth to hers.

Ruby closed her eyes and savored the tenderness in

her husband's caress. "She said that kissing is for the honeymoon. And marriage."

"I agree," he murmured huskily. "But the last time I checked, we were married."

"So kissing's allowed?"

"Absolutely." He kissed her again. "Not only allowed by the faith, but encouraged."

She wrapped her arms around his neck and stood on tiptoe to kiss him again, a slow, sweet kiss of absolute, contented joy. And then she caught a whiff of burning bread. "Joseph! The bread!"

"Let it burn," he answered, still holding her tight. "This is more important."

And, she decided, it was.

* * * * *

*If you loved this story,
pick up the other books in
The Amish Matchmaker series:*

A Match for Addy
A Husband for Mari
A Beau for Katie
A Love for Leah

*And these other stories of Amish life
from author Emma Miller's previous miniseries,
Hannah's Daughters:*

Leah's Choice
Johanna's Bridegroom
Rebecca's Christmas Gift
Hannah's Courtship

Available now from Love Inspired!

Find more great reads at www.Harlequin.com.

THE AMISH WITNESS

Diane Burke

To my granddaughter, Emberleigh Valcich.
You are deeply loved.

Behold, we count them happy which endure.
Ye have heard of the patience of Job,
and have seen the end of the Lord; that the Lord
is very pitiful, and of tender mercy.
—*James* 5:11

Chapter One

Elizabeth Lapp couldn't distinguish anything out of the ordinary in the shrouded stillness of the empty Amish landscape. She lifted her kerosene lamp closer to the windowpane, pressing her face against the cool glass, and stared harder. Still nothing but dark winter shadows sheltered by even darker ones stretching across the Lancaster farm.

He was out there.

She knew it.

If not today, tomorrow or the next day, but he'd be there. Every instinct told her he would come. She'd seen him standing over Hannah's dead body—and he'd seen her.

He'd come. If only to silence her...

Dear Lord, please keep me safe. Bless me with inner peace and wisdom as I face the days ahead. And thank You, Lord, for leading me home.

The first glow of morning sun would not touch the horizon for a few more hours. Elizabeth chastised herself. There was work to do, more than enough to occupy her mind, and she needed to get to it. Chores came early on an Amish farm, even in winters in Lancaster County, when the fields lay dormant under drifts of waist-high snow.

A finger of light from the quarter moon was the only thing illuminating the distance between the house and the barn. She studied the shadows. She dared one of them to move and prayed in the same moment that none would.

Where was he? How much longer would she be tortured with the wait?

She raised her face from the glass.

Enough. You're going to make yourself sick. Where is your faith?

"What do you look for, Elizabeth?"

Elizabeth startled at the sound of her mother's voice. Her left hand flew to her chest. She swallowed a small gasp and spun around.

"You frightened me, *Mamm*. I didn't hear you coming."

"Don't be foolish. I come down these stairs the same time each morning to fix breakfast and begin the day." Mary Lapp came close, smoothed a strand of hair beneath her daughter's white prayer *kapp* and smiled. "Why do you stare out that window? Tell me, child, what do you hope to find out there in the darkness?"

It was what she *didn't* want to find that frightened her so.

She returned her mother's smile. "I'm not hoping to find anything, *Mamm*. I guess I'm having trouble adjusting to how dark it is here. There's always light in the city. No matter what time it is. The city never seems to sleep."

A shadow flitted across her mother's face. "Do you miss it already? Are you sorry you came home?"

"I'm just sorry I stayed away so long." Elizabeth had only arrived home yesterday afternoon, but she knew she had made the right decision to return. She placed her lamp on the table near the front door and a soft light enveloped the room.

Seven years had added a few strands of gray to her mother's hair. The small lines etched at the edges of her mouth had deepened, and now there were crow's feet at the edges of her eyes, but her mother would always be young and beautiful in her eyes.

"I don't miss the city, *Mamm*, and I'm glad to be home."

Her mother gave her a warm hug. "I'm glad you're home, too."

Sadness wiped the smile from Elizabeth's face. "I regret I wasn't here when *Daed* died. I never got the chance to say goodbye."

Her father had died two years ago of pneumonia. Her mother's eyes still carried her grief. Elizabeth hadn't learned he was sick until it was too late.

"I am sorry, too, little one. Your *daed* would have been pleased to have you home again. Maybe the Lord has told him you are here now. If he does know, I am certain your *daed* is thanking *Gott* every day." Mary playfully pinched her daughter's chin. "*Kumm*. Help me with breakfast."

Elizabeth followed her mother into the kitchen and lit two more lamps, as well as the gas fixture over the table. She stared at the long wooden table and smoothed her hand against the grain. Her father had made this table as a wedding gift for her mother over thirty years ago and it still looked brand-new. A pang of loss filled her heart. She wished she could have seen him one more time before he died.

"I don't remember your head always being lost in the clouds. Is that something you learned to do in that fancy city of yours?"

Elizabeth returned her mother's smile. "Sorry, *Mamm*. Just thinking about *Daed*. Wishing I had been here…"

"No good comes from looking behind you. We can't change the past." Her mother turned from the stove. "He never stopped loving you. Never." Her mother smiled. "And he knew you never stopped loving him. He understood your decision to leave even if he didn't agree with your choice."

Tears filled Elizabeth's eyes.

Silence stretched between them.

She remembered the last day she had seen her father. It had been an early winter morning like today and they'd been talking in the barn. She remembered his look of disappointment, the pain and loss already reflected in his eyes, and the warmth and love of his final embrace moments before she left.

"Elizabeth, please, get that head of yours out of the sky. We have chores to do."

Elizabeth nodded, gathered plates, silverware and mugs and set the table.

The delectable aroma of bacon and freshly brewing coffee teased her nostrils. Her stomach growled. Because her stomach had been too twisted in knots with dread and fear, she hadn't eaten much at dinner last night. But this morning she was hungry and nothing was going to snatch away her appetite.

"Could you gather some eggs from the henhouse?" her mother called over her shoulder from her spot at the propane-powered stove.

"If I can bring in a jar of your strawberry jam from the pantry to smother on your homemade bread I like so much."

Her mother smiled and waved her away. "*Ja. Ja.* Now go."

Elizabeth decided not to bother with a coat. From the house to the barn was such a short distance and she would only be exposed to the elements for a brief time. She threw a shawl over her shoulders, grabbed the hurricane lamp and hurried out the door. She'd barely cleared the third step down from the porch when a prickling sensation raced up her spine and froze her in place. She threw her gaze in one direction and then another. Looking. Anticipating.

Nothing.

Just a foolish girl's imagination running wild. That's what city life did to you. You don't trust anything or anyone anymore, do you?

She held the lamp high. The only sound was ice cracking on tree branches. Her feet wanted to scamper across the yard, but she forced herself to step off the final stair and walk slowly and purposely toward the barn.

Dear Lord, please help me stop being so afraid. If he had followed me, wouldn't he be here by now?

She took one final look around the yard.

Darkness covered the objects and bushes like shrouds.

She knew she was being foolish. No one in the city except her best friend, Hannah, had known she came from an Amish background. And Hannah had never told anyone. Had she?

Mental images of the tall man standing over Hannah's dead body flashed through her mind. Who was he? And why had he killed Hannah?

When she reached the barn door, she lifted the latch and swung it wide. The pitch-black interior gave her pause. Holding her lantern high, she stepped inside and moved deeper into the barn.

The pungent smells of livestock, hay and manure were a far cry from the exhaust fumes of the city, but they pinged nostalgia, reminding her she was home once again, and it felt good. The cows bawled as she approached, indicating their need for milking. She'd have to hurry with breakfast and get back out here to tend to them so her mother wouldn't have to.

The clucking sound of the hens in the chicken coop drew her back to the task at hand. She rubbed her hands together and blew warmth into them. Maybe she should have worn her coat. She opened her apron, holding it with her left hand, and reached inside the coop with her right. Soon she'd gathered enough eggs for both breakfast and a pudding recipe she had learned from one of her friends. Her mother would be surprised to discover that life among the *Englisch* hadn't been all bad. She'd learned to cook some wonderful recipes. She nudged the door to the coop closed.

It wasn't a sound that caught her attention. It was a feeling, an innate sense that she was no longer alone. She swallowed and tried to calm the wave of fear threatening to drown her.

It's nothing, Elizabeth. You've been on edge. Seeing bad men in shadows like children see animals in clouds.

But the internal scolding did little to calm her sense of unease.

The squawking and clucking of the hens in the coop gave her pause. The chickens knew it, too. She wasn't alone. Someone was standing close behind her...too close.

Taking another gulp, she clutched the apron filled with eggs to her chest and turned around.

A man, his face obscured in the darkness, loomed in the entrance to the barn.

Elizabeth gasped. "Who are you?" she asked. "What do you want?"

The stranger moved into the light and Elizabeth's heart stuttered.

It was him. The man she'd seen standing over Hannah's body.

"I want what your friend gave you. It belongs to me." The coldness in his tone froze her in place.

Elizabeth's eyes shot around the barn. Where could she run and hide? What could she use as a weapon if she was forced to protect herself?

"You know who I am, don't you?" he demanded.

Elizabeth took a step back. "No, sir, I don't. Please... leave. I don't know who you are. I don't have anything that belongs to you." She straightened her spine and tried to exude strength she didn't feel. "If you don't leave this property, I am going to send for the sheriff."

Then her deepest fear became a reality. He moved toward her with such speed she barely had time to react.

Elizabeth's throat muscles froze and she couldn't scream. She backed up as fast as she could until her body slammed against a solid surface. Trapped against the chicken coop with nowhere to run, sheer panic raced through her veins.

No. No.

Elizabeth raised her hands to cover her face, dropping the edges of her apron. The eggs smashed on the ground and a few rolled across the floor.

Within seconds he was on her, his hands clasping her shoulders, his face inches from her own.

"You want me to leave? Then give me what's mine and I will." He shook her shoulders and banged her against the wooden piling behind her. "I'm not playing. Unless you want the same fate as your friend you will give it to me."

Spittle sprayed across her face as he screamed at her.

She kicked at his shins and tried to scramble from his grasp. "I don't know what you're talking about. Hannah didn't give me anything. Go away. Please. Leave me alone."

An almost evil sneer came over his face. "Hannah? So you do remember me." He dug his fingertips painfully into the soft flesh of her upper arms. "Don't make the same mistake she did. Just give me what's mine and we'll call it even. I'll go away and leave you to live your life in this forsaken place."

"Please, mister, I don't know what you want. I don't know who you are. Hannah didn't give me anything of yours."

He squeezed her arms harder and tears sprang to her eyes.

"She told me she did. She told me with her *dying* breath. I don't believe an Amish woman would pick that time to lie."

Trapped against the piling behind her, Elizabeth

twisted in his grip. "Leave me alone!" She reached up and clawed at his eye.

He yelped in pain and for a split second he grabbed his face and released his grip on her arms.

It was all she needed. She threw herself sideways. The sudden shift in weight threw her off balance. She stumbled over his boot and fell hard against the wooden floor of the barn, the breath temporarily knocked out of her.

He stood over her, just like she'd seen him standing over Hannah. His hands moved to her throat. "She told me you had the information I need. Do you really think I'm going to let you ruin my life? Unless you give it to me, I'll have no choice but to make sure you suffer the same fate she did. Is that what you want?"

His hands squeezed her throat.

"Please…" she whispered. "I don't have anything. I don't know what you want."

"Hey! You! Get away." Another man, an Amish man by the sound of his dialect, entered the barn and ran out of the shadows straight toward them. "Leave her alone."

Out of the corner of her eye, Elizabeth saw the man grab a pitchfork and continue toward them.

The stranger gave one long, hard squeeze to her throat and whispered close to her face. "This isn't over. I'll be back. And if you know what's good for you, you'll keep your mouth shut or I will permanently shut it for you."

He turned and ran toward the barn's open back door. Just as quickly as he'd come he was gone.

Elizabeth rolled to her side, coughing, trying desperately to draw oxygen into her lungs.

The Amish man, whoever he was, had just saved her life.

* * *

Thomas King kneeled beside the woman who was crumpled in a heap on the dirt floor.

"Mrs. Lapp?"

What had happened? Who was that man and why had he attacked Mrs. Lapp?

Thomas offered a silent prayer of thanksgiving that he had arrived when he did. He came to the farm at the same time every morning since her husband had died. He wished he could devote more time to help out on her farm, but it was all he could spare from his own farm and family. Mrs. Lapp had always been grateful and appreciative of his help. His body shuddered at the thought of what might have happened if he had arrived a few minutes later.

"Mrs. Lapp?" His hands trembled as he reached for the woman. Placing his hand on her shoulder, he gently turned her toward him. "Are you all right?"

The lantern light dappled across her face.

This wasn't Mrs. Lapp.

He stared into the woman's face and a shaft of pain shot through his chest. He knew this face all too well. It was a face he'd thought he'd put out of his mind and his life forever, a face he'd once loved.

Elizabeth.

His eyes quickly scanned her from head to toe for any obvious injuries and found none. "Elizabeth?"

The shock registering in her pale blue eyes must have mirrored his.

"Thomas?"

"Are you hurt?"

She shook her head.

"What are you doing here? Who was that man?"

"What am *I* doing here? What are *you* doing here?" She sat up and then allowed him to help her to her feet. Her hand felt tiny in his and her fingers trembled despite the outer calmness she tried to display.

Elizabeth gently pulled her hand from his. She brushed dirt and pieces of hay from her dress and apron. "I don't know what you are doing here at this hour but I am glad you are. I hate to think what would have happened to me if you hadn't come when you did."

"Who was he?" Thomas glared at her. He knew his emotions were flashing across his features, but he was too surprised at what had happened, too shocked at whom it happened to, too upset to gain control. "What did he want? Why was he trying to hurt you? And what are you doing back at your *mamm*'s house?"

"Let's go inside." She threw a nervous glance over her shoulder. "I don't know if that man is still around." She took a step forward and stumbled.

Immediately, Thomas reached out, clasped her elbow and steadied her. "Are you hurt?" he asked again.

"No," she whispered. "Just shaken up." She placed her head against his chest for just a second while she steadied herself. He could smell the fresh scent of her hair despite her prayer *kapp* covering locks he knew were silky and blond. He remembered her scent, fresh soap and lemon, from their *rumspringa* days, when he'd lie awake at night and think of her.

Before she'd betrayed him.

Before she'd abandoned him.

Pain and anger washed over him. Where had she been all these years? And why was she back?

She felt small and fragile leaning against him.

He couldn't help himself. He wanted to hold her

closer, tighter. Maybe if he did, she wouldn't run away this time.

But she was good at that, wasn't she? Running away. Leaving without a word.

"I'm sorry. I shouldn't have done that." She straightened and stepped away. "When I think of what could have happened if you hadn't come…if you hadn't helped." She stared at him, her eyes shimmering with tears. "*Denki*, Thomas."

What had happened between them seven years ago was ancient history. They both lived different lives now. He wouldn't let himself feel or remember or care. Not again.

But images of the man's hands around Elizabeth's throat filled him with rage. The possibility of what could have happened threatened to overpower him with a raw, primal fear. He had lost her once. He wouldn't be able to handle losing her again. Especially in such a heinous way.

Lord, everything happens in life according to Your plan. But this? Lord, help me understand and be strong enough to accept whatever Your plan entails.

Chapter Two

❧

"Elizabeth?" Mary Lapp called, presumably from the top of the porch steps. "Are you all right?" Her voice drifted into the barn. "Thomas, are you out there?"

"We're coming, *Mamm.*" Elizabeth picked up the few unbroken eggs she was able to gather from the barn floor and started toward the house. Thomas silently followed.

As they drew closer, Mary called out, "When you didn't return with the eggs I became concerned. I thought I may have heard a commotion. Is everything all right?" Her eyes widened in alarm when she saw her daughter's face in the lantern light. "Elizabeth, you look scared to death! What happened?"

Elizabeth kept shooting glances over her shoulder and staring into the shadows as she hurried up the porch steps to the safety of the house. As she brushed past her mother and entered the house, Mary shot a questioning look his way.

"Thomas?"

He cupped the older woman's elbow with his hand.

"Let's go inside, Mary, where it's warm. We'll talk there."

Without another word, Mary led the way. She set the lamp on the small wooden table inside the front door and followed the sounds of Elizabeth moving about the kitchen. Mary stood with Thomas in the doorway.

Elizabeth tried to appear calm and unflustered, but her hands shook as she tried to fill three coffee mugs without spilling any of the hot liquid, giving her away.

"Elizabeth? You're frightening me." Then she looked at Thomas. "What happened?"

"I'm not sure," he replied, his tone of voice grave. "There was a stranger in the barn when I arrived. I saw Elizabeth fall to the floor and the man put his hands around her throat…"

Mary gasped. Her hand flew to her chest and she rushed to her daughter's side. "What man? Did he hurt you? Are you okay?"

Thomas's eyes never left Elizabeth's face but he spoke to Mary. "I thought it was you. I knew you were expecting me so I didn't announce myself. When I saw what he was doing I panicked. I grabbed a pitchfork and raced over to help."

"Who is this man, Elizabeth?" Mary put her hands on Elizabeth's shoulders and turned her around. "Is that why you were staring out the window this morning into the darkness?"

Elizabeth nodded.

"How did this man find you? Do you know him?"

"No, I don't know him but—but I saw him. I saw him do something terrible. I am sure he followed me here. We are a small community, *Mamm*. You know it would be easy to find our farm once he came into town. He only had to mention my name and any Amish person would have been able to direct him."

Elizabeth collapsed into the nearest chair and hung her head. She couldn't seem to meet their eyes.

"I didn't know that Elizabeth had returned home," Thomas said into the uncomfortable silence.

"She only arrived yesterday afternoon," Mary replied. "There was no time to let you know."

"Did you tell her I *kumm* every morning to milk the cows and clean the stalls?"

"No. I—I couldn't seem to find the proper time to bring up the subject."

Thomas's eyes locked with hers. "You thought if she knew I worked this farm every day that she would run away again, didn't you?"

Mary looked away, but not before he saw a flash of guilt in her eyes. Her voice dropped an octave. "Of course not."

Before either of them could say anything more, Elizabeth spoke. "Please. Stop." She wrapped her hands around her mug, then squared her shoulders and looked directly at him. He saw the determination in her posture, the strength in her resolve. This was a different Elizabeth than the girl who had left years ago. This was a strong, independent woman staring back at him and Thomas found the changes intriguing.

"*Denki*, Thomas. I am grateful you were here to help me. I don't know what would have happened if you hadn't arrived when you did."

"Did he hurt you?" Mary asked. "Oh, my, look. Your throat is red. It will probably be badly bruised."

Elizabeth shook her head. "No. I'm okay. He frightened me. But I am fine now."

Mary gently touched her arm but asked no further questions, giving her daughter the time she needed to compose herself and tell the story in her own way.

"Gut." Thomas remained standing in the doorway. "I am glad you were not hurt." He lifted his flat-brimmed winter hat, ran a hand through his blond hair and put the hat back in place. As much as he wanted an explanation, he knew it wasn't his place to demand one. His heart slammed against his chest. His lungs threatened to rob him of breath. He hadn't seen Elizabeth in years and here she was right in front of him. To think that just a minute or two longer and she might have died at the hands of a stranger in her very own barn was more than he could handle at the moment. He'd get the details later. For now, he needed distance so he could breathe. "I will leave the two of you to speak in private."

Before either of them could respond, he nodded at both women. "Excuse me. I have work waiting for me in the barn." He strode as fast as he could from the room.

He worked for over two hours, refusing to let his mind whisper one single thought. He milked the cows and prepared the containers for the local man to collect and take to market. He cleaned the stalls and pitched fresh hay with such speed and force a sweat broke out on his forehead despite the freezing temperatures of morning.

And although he fought hard to keep Elizabeth out of his thoughts, she crept in softly and slowly, like the sun was doing now with the dawn. He doused the lanterns and, pausing for a moment in the broad opening to the barn, stared at the white clapboard house.

Who was that man? And why had he tried to harm Elizabeth?

He knew it was not his business. He had no right to question her, to demand answers. Their time together had passed long ago. But he couldn't seem to let it go.

He went to the tack room and washed his hands in the sink, then splashed water across his face and along the back of his neck.

Obviously, Elizabeth needed help. She must have come home looking for that help and trouble had followed her.

Thomas hung the wet towel on a rod, finger-combed his hair and put his hat back on. He sighed heavily.

She had to be terrified, even though she fought hard to make an outward show that she was in control and able to handle things on her own.

What had happened to her over the years? Where had she been?

It was none of his business.

She had made her choice years ago and it had not been a life with him. He had gone on and made a different life for himself. A happy life. One that had no room for her. He thought about his *kinner* and a smile caught the corners of his mouth. They were his joy. He couldn't help wanting to introduce them to Elizabeth. Foolish, he knew. But once she had been a friend…and so much more.

Thomas sighed again.

But if someone was terrorizing Elizabeth or trying to do worse, than he would have no choice. He wasn't the kind of man to walk away when someone needed help. And he would never walk away from Elizabeth when she needed him. He would be a friend to her. He would find a way to help.

Even when the shattered pieces of his heart silently wished he had never laid eyes on her again.

Elizabeth stood at the kitchen sink washing dishes when her mother came up behind her and placed a gentle hand on her shoulder. "I'm sorry, Elizabeth."

Elizabeth reached up and patted her hand. "For what? You did nothing wrong."

Mary turned Elizabeth to face her. "I'm sorry you had that frightening encounter with the stranger in the barn. I am also sorry I did not tell you sooner about Thomas. I am sure the shock of seeing him again was difficult for you."

"Why didn't you tell me, *Mamm*? Was Thomas right? Did you think I would run away again?" Elizabeth studied her mother's face. She'd known she would see Thomas sooner or later. She had tried to prepare herself for it before she returned to Sunny Creek. But she supposed no amount of preparation would have been good enough. The shock of seeing him again—leaning over her in the barn, standing in the kitchen doorway, his blond hair catching the glint of the lamp's glow—had made her heart seize despite all the self-talk and preparation that had gone before. There were no words good enough to dampen her feelings or assuage the guilt for betraying him.

"Never mind. It's all right, *Mamm*." She put an arm around Mary's waist. "Let's sit. We'll have a cup of coffee and talk this out."

"Go to the barn and ask Thomas to *kumm* in."

Elizabeth's eyes widened. That was the last thing she wanted or needed right now.

"Now that you have had time to compose yourself, you will sit and tell both of us the story of this man."

"I will tell you, *Mamm*, but I don't think we have to involve Thomas."

"Thomas is already involved. He deserves an explanation." Her mother smiled at her. "Besides, he is a smart man. He will be able to tell us what to do."

Elizabeth bristled. She'd lived independently and successfully for years. She didn't need a man, especially not Thomas, to tell her what to do.

But she was back in Amish territory and things were done differently here. Women listened to their men. Men listened to the bishop and the elders. This was what she wanted, wasn't it? To be home again? To feel safe?

For the first time, she wondered if coming home had been the right thing to do. She had come home to be with family and friends, where she had always felt safe. But had that decision been selfish? Was she inviting danger into the lives of the people she loved? Why hadn't she considered that possibility before she'd come back? Now it was too late. If anything happened to anyone in the community, it would be her fault.

Elizabeth looked at her mother. She should leave. Today.

But where would she go? This was her home. These people were her family. And she knew she needed their wisdom, their guidance and their love. She would tell them the truth, all of it. Then she would gauge their reactions and consider Thomas's counsel. But if she felt her presence would put her loved ones in danger she would not hesitate to leave.

"You're right, *Mamm*. I will call Thomas in for breakfast. He must be finished his chores by now."

"Gut." Mary moved to the stove and lifted a cast-iron skillet. "I cook for him every morning and he always brings a healthy appetite." Mary began fixing the meal.

"Thomas has a beard, which means he also has a wife. Doesn't his wife fix him breakfast?" She said it as nonchalantly as she could, but one glance at the smile on her mother's face and she knew she wasn't fooling anyone.

Her mother continued with her cooking and replied as nonchalantly. "He waited a year for you to return. Kept coming by the farm every week to see if we had heard from you. Finally, your *daed* took him aside and had a man-to-man talk with him. I don't know the details. I never asked. But I assumed he told him to stop waiting for you because shortly afterward Thomas married."

A kaleidoscope of emotions exploded inside Elizabeth's heart. What had she expected? For him to love her forever even after she'd left him? Of course he would marry. She had been gone for *seven years*. But when she'd seen him again those years had vanished and all she saw was the man she'd once loved.

She couldn't allow those feelings to resurface. They would only cause pain. He was a married man with a family now. Besides, the reason she'd left, the secret she couldn't share with him, still existed. She'd left for his good. She'd wanted him to be happy, to marry and start a family. But she'd never realized how deeply it would hurt both of them.

Tears trickled down her cheeks. She brushed them away before her mother could see her distress.

"Did he marry someone I know?" she asked, unconsciously holding her breath, not able to picture Thomas with one of her former friends.

"He married Margaret Sue Miller. You never met her. Her family moved to Sunny Creek from Ohio a few months after you left."

Elizabeth folded her hands in her lap and pondered the information.

"I think you would have liked her," her mother said. "She was such a happy, loving woman of *Gott*. She always had a smile and a kind word for everyone."

Elizabeth's head snapped up. "Was?"

"*Ja*. Poor Thomas. He lost Margaret two years ago. She died from complications during childbirth."

This new information rocked Elizabeth to her soul.

Oh, Thomas. How horrible that must have been for you.

"And the child?" Elizabeth asked.

"They had a beautiful little girl. Named her Rachel. She has a sweet disposition like her mother. She's a bundle of smiles. Not like that brother of hers. He is all boy. Skinned knees. Energy that doesn't quit. A dirt magnet, that one." Mary laughed. "I don't know how Thomas does it raising them on his own. His parents help when he is working the farm. But they leave to spend six months in Florida every winter. They left a few weeks ago. Margaret's parents help in their absence. And I step in now and then. But still the responsibility for their upbringing rests on his shoulders."

Mary carried her mug to the sink more, Elizabeth suspected, to steal a moment to collect her thoughts than to clean.

"Thomas brings the *kinner* here a couple times a month," Mary said. "He pays me to watch them while he goes into town for supplies. I think sometimes it is more to help me than to help him. He knows I love children. I am alone, and I can certainly use the little extra cash it brings. But the rest of the time he is both mother and father to those children."

"Two children?"

"*Ja.* Benjamin and Rachel."

"How old is Benjamin?"

"He just turned five."

A bittersweet smile twisted Elizabeth's lips. She was happy for Thomas. She had known years ago that he would make a good *daed* someday.

"Now, go. Get Thomas. He must be hungry by now." Mary crossed to the stove. "Tell him I have a hot breakfast waiting for him."

Elizabeth's heart fluttered. She could hardly wait to see Thomas again and yet knew she had to keep a distance between them. It wasn't just her heart that was in danger of being lost, but her life, too. She could not put Thomas at risk by being around him, especially when he had two little ones to raise. She wished she hadn't come back. She'd put her mother at risk, too, and she didn't know what to do about it. What had she been thinking? The Amish were not selfish people. They always put the community's needs before their own. Had living in the *Englisch* world changed her? Was she not Amish anymore?

She needed to rethink her situation. She couldn't bring evil here…unless it was too late and she already had.

I will be back. Keep your mouth shut if you want to live.

A chill raced over her bones as she remembered the stranger's words.

Maybe she should go to the sheriff and tell him what she knew.

But the Amish frowned on involving outsiders in their business. They handled things together as a community whenever possible. Besides, the murder had happened in Philadelphia. What could the local sheriff do here?

How could she convince this man that she didn't know his name and wouldn't be able to identify him so she wasn't a threat? And what did he think she had? Did Hannah really tell him she'd given something to her that this man was willing to kill for? If she could talk to him, convince him she was no danger to him, maybe he would believe her and go back to Philadelphia.

The memory of his dark eyes and threatening sneer seized her breath.

Or maybe she wouldn't talk to him.

Dear Lord, how have things gone so terribly wrong? Please guide me to make good decisions. Don't let my foolishness hurt others.

Stepping outside, Elizabeth paused at the top of the porch steps and took a good look around the farm now that daylight had arrived. It was beautiful here. Peaceful. Quiet. It seemed like millions of miles away from bottleneck traffic, talking on cell phones and witnessing her best friend's murder.

But was it far enough?

She placed her fingers gently against the tender flesh of her neck. She could almost feel her attacker's grip on her throat. She knew with certainty he would return. And now, because of her selfishness, she had led an evil man straight to the doorsteps of the people she loved most.

Please help me, Lord. Please give me wisdom and guide me. I don't know what I should do now.

She stood in silence and waited.

What? Did she expect some booming voice from heaven to start telling her what to do?

What was wrong with her? She knew better. *Gott* answers all prayers. He speaks quietly in the inner recesses of one's soul. Sometimes the answer is yes, sometimes no, sometimes wait. But He answers.

She needed to learn patience and to relearn trust. Maybe He'd be slow to answer because it had been so long since He'd heard from her. For seven years she had not gone to Him for guidance, or little else for that matter. Maybe He no longer recognized her voice.

I'm sorry, Lord. Forgive me.

Placing her fears in *Gott*'s hands, she stepped into the yard and headed for the barn.

Thomas had milked the cows, put the tall metal containers of milk outside the barn for pickup for market, moved the horses into the pasture, cleaned the manure from the stalls, laid fresh straw and finished sweeping the wooden floor. There was nothing left for him to do, but he couldn't make his feet carry him to the house. Elizabeth was in the house.

A flood of emotions—anger, guilt and something else he wouldn't acknowledge—tormented him.

It was not the Amish way to hold on to anger. He'd thought he'd forgiven her. But when he saw her again, anger simmered in his blood as fresh and strong as it had the day she'd betrayed him and left.

Guilt gnawed at his insides. How could he allow himself to have any feelings of any kind for Elizabeth? Wasn't that a betrayal of his dear Margaret? He'd have to keep his distance. He wouldn't let himself betray the memory of a wife who had loved him with all her heart…like he had once loved Elizabeth.

"Thomas?"

He froze. The soft tones of her voice caressed his nerve endings like hot caramel coating an apple in autumn. His emotions tumbled and fought each other for center place. Anger won.

"Ja?" He turned to face her. He grasped the pitchfork tightly and, barely noticing the whitening of his knuckles, tried to hide the anger flooding through his body. He knew he had failed when she glanced into his eyes and he saw guilt and sorrow looking back.

"Mamm wanted me to ask if you are almost finished with your chores."

He nodded. "They're done."

"Gut. She has a hot breakfast waiting."

"Denki." He knew the word of thanks hadn't hidden the iciness in his tone but he couldn't help it. He needed time to process his feelings. Time to ask the Lord to help him forgive. Time to figure out a way to be in her presence without his heart shattering into painful shards.

She nodded and turned to leave.

"Elizabeth," he said quickly.

She froze but didn't turn back toward him.

"Who was that man? Tell me. What are you running from?"

"I'm not running from anything."

He caught her arm with his hand and turned her toward him.

"Is that what the *Englisch* taught you? To lie?"

She didn't move a muscle. She couldn't meet his eyes, either.

When she didn't answer him, he threw more questions at her.

"Why did you leave with Hannah? How could you leave your church and abandon your faith?"

"I never abandoned my faith." She kept her eyes down. "I believe today as I have always believed."

"You left your parents and your community." His voice was filled with accusation and hurt before it broke into a hoarse whisper. "You left me."

Silence beat loudly between them.

Thomas murmured a prayer for *Gott* to forgive him for harboring these negative feelings and to give him the strength he needed to forgive Elizabeth. When he spoke again, he tried to soften his tone.

"I deserved more than that handwritten note your mother gave me, which said nothing more than goodbye. *We* deserved more." He stared at her slumped shoulders and continued to wait for an answer that didn't come.

Slowly she lifted her face. "Thomas…" Her eyes pleaded for understanding but her words offered no explanation. Pain stabbed through his chest.

What had happened to his Elizabeth? Who was this stranger standing in front of him?

"Why did you *kumm* back?" He glared at her, his heart holding such hurt he could hardly bear it.

"This is my home. Where else should I be?"

He recoiled in shock as if she had slapped him. He knew his face registered his surprise but he couldn't hide his emotions. "You're staying? This is not just a visit?"

She straightened her shoulders. "I'm not sure. When I came back, I planned to get baptized and remain here." Her voice lowered to a whisper. "Now I'm not sure that was a wise decision."

Thomas pulled her close, so only inches separated them. His breath gently fanned the loose tendrils of hair on her neck. "Why now? Why after all these years?"

She didn't answer.

He studied her closely.

"You used to be able to talk to me," he said. "We were friends…more than friends." A thread of steel laced his words. "We are not leaving this barn until you tell me the truth."

"You cannot order me around, Thomas. I am a grown woman and make my own decisions." Before he could ask any more questions, she eased her arm out of his grasp and hurried to put a distance between them. "I'll tell *Mamm* you are ready for breakfast," she called over her shoulder as she headed toward the house.

A short time later Elizabeth had just set a tray of spam, fried potatoes and scrambled eggs on the table when she heard Thomas enter the house. He joined them in the kitchen. He'd hung his hat on the rack by the front door. His face and hands were clean and water droplets glistened in his hair from cleaning up after doing his chores.

Elizabeth's pulse quickened. It was so good to see Thomas again—too good.

Thomas took a seat at the head of the table, as if he belonged there.

But why shouldn't he?

If he helped her mother every day with the heavy

chores, brought his children to visit with her and then
paid her besides, it was obvious he had earned that place
at the table. He had done more for her mother than she
had over the years, Elizabeth realized, and a wave of
guilt washed over her.

"*Denki*, Mary," Thomas said as he looked at the plate
of food she placed before him. "I am hungrier than I
thought." He smiled at her mother and Elizabeth's heart
melted with the wish that she could be the recipient of
that warmth. She knew the coldness in his tone during
their conversation in the barn was well-deserved. But
that hadn't prevented his words from hurting her.

Elizabeth stayed silent as Thomas ate his meal. She
smiled occasionally as she listened to Thomas and her
mamm discuss the newest antics of his children, and
chat about next spring's planting once the last frost had
gone. She was a polite hostess as she passed plates of
food and served coffee, but her mind wandered, was
constantly mired in days gone by and useless musings
of what-ifs.

"Elizabeth?" The surprised and stern tone in her
mother's voice pulled her out of her reverie. "Thomas
asked you a question."

"What?" Her gaze flew from her mother to Thomas.
"I'm sorry. My mind wandered. What did you ask,
Thomas?"

"I asked about Hannah. Did the two of you remain
friends after you both left our community?"

Elizabeth's heart seized. "*Ja*, we did. We were more
like sisters than friends."

"How is she—" Mary asked.

"Will she be returning to Sunny Creek, too?"
Thomas interrupted, his tone more accusatory than

questioning. The intensity of his gaze made Elizabeth lower hers.

"No." She hoped the softness in her voice would hide the high anxiety storming through her body. Her hands trembled so she immediately folded them in her lap.

"I'm surprised," Mary said. "I know Hannah was happy here until her mother died. I always believed that one day she would return." Her mother sent her a puzzled look. "Is the *Englisch* way so appealing that it is worth leaving everything and everyone she knew behind?"

Elizabeth lightly covered her mother's hand with her own. "Hannah loved the Amish way, *Mamm*. Always. The appeal of the *Englisch* was never the reason we left. You know that."

"Then why?" An icy edge took hold in Thomas's voice.

Elizabeth and her mother gave each other a telling glance but remained silent, keeping a secret between them that neither woman was ready to share.

"It is a simple question, Elizabeth. This sister of yours, if she did not leave for love of the *Englisch*, then why isn't she returning, too?

Elizabeth squared her shoulders and met his gaze unflinchingly. She saw the anger, pain and confusion in his eyes, and she felt sorry for him. His question wasn't about Hannah. It was about them and her betrayal. Yes, she owed him an explanation. But not now. Not yet. The time wasn't right. She wondered if the time would ever be right. She offered him a gentle smile and spoke softly. "As I said, Thomas. Hannah won't be returning home."

"Then she couldn't have loved our way of life as much as you say," he said.

"Leaving Sunny Creek was one of the hardest things Hannah ever did."

"Couldn't have been too hard. She left. You both did."

Elizabeth remained silent beneath the verbal slap of his tone. She knew it was pain speaking.

Mary stood and gathered up some of the empty platters. "What does it matter now, Thomas? It happened so many years ago. Elizabeth has *kumm* home. Let us be happy about that."

"I am sorry if I upset you, Mary. But I am confused." Again he turned his focus on Elizabeth. "Why is asking a simple question so difficult to answer? If Hannah loved it here as much as you say, if you are as close as sisters, then why hasn't Hannah returned with you?"

"Because Hannah's dead."

Mary gasped. "What? Hannah died?" She placed the platters back onto the table and sank down into her chair.

Elizabeth's words caused a heavy silence to descend on the room for several seconds.

Thomas, appearing surprised and chagrined, spoke more softly. "I am sorry you lost your friend. That must have been very difficult for you."

"She was so young," Mary said. "You never told me she was ill. I would have told you to bring her home. I would have helped care for her. When did this happen?"

Elizabeth knew she'd have to tell them the details. She should have told her mother last night, when she showed up on her doorstep unannounced. But she'd played mind games with herself, pretending that if she didn't say the words out loud then they wouldn't be true.

She folded her hands together again and braced herself. "Hannah wasn't ill, *Mamm*. She was murdered."

Neither Mary nor Thomas spoke, they simply glanced at each other then back at Elizabeth and waited.

Her thoughts did a somersault through her mind. How much should she tell them? How much was their right to know versus her desire to dump this heavy burden on other shoulders, too? With every passing second she was certain it had been selfish to come home and bring a potential danger with her. What had she been thinking?

She hadn't been thinking. She'd simply known the Amish community always took care of their own, and her love of that community, her need for their guidance and their help, had brought her home.

"Tell us what happened." Thomas's calm tone soothed her. His strength gave her courage.

"Hannah and I had just rented a condo together. I was helping move some of her things. I came in the back door and—and…"

Mary reached over and clasped Elizabeth's hand.

Elizabeth glanced back and forth between her mother and Thomas. She only saw empathy and kindness looking back. She inhaled deeply then continued the story. "I saw Hannah lying motionless on the floor of the kitchen. A man was bent over her, his hands around her throat."

Mary cried out and offered a quick prayer.

"Go on, Elizabeth." Thomas's entire demeanor offered her encouragement and strength.

"I screamed when I saw what was happening. The

man stood up and raced toward me. I turned and ran as fast as I could. He almost caught up with me but I got away."

"How?" Mary asked.

"I learned how to drive while I was gone, *Mamm*. I jumped in my car and drove away."

"And Hannah?" Mary asked.

"I called the police and then doubled back to the complex. Shortly after I got back, I saw them carry her body out on a gurney to the coroner's van. There was nothing more I could do for her so…" She threw a glance between them. "I came home."

Mary got up and threw her arms around her daughter. "As you should have." She tilted Elizabeth's chin to look at her. "Why didn't you tell me?"

"I should have," Elizabeth replied. "I'm sorry, *Mamm*."

"Now I understand." Thomas's voice caught both women's attention. "The man who attacked you in the barn. He murdered Hannah and he followed you here."

Elizabeth nodded.

Mary gasped again. "Is that who you were looking out the window for this morning?"

Elizabeth hugged her mother tightly. "I'm sorry. I wasn't thinking. I never should have come home."

"Nonsense."

"You don't understand, *Mamm*. I have brought danger home to you, to this community." Elizabeth sprang to her feet. "I need to leave."

Mary caught her hand and stopped her. "Leave? Where would you go? What would you do? You cannot face this terrible thing alone."

"Mary is right." Thomas gestured to the seat Elizabeth had vacated. "Sit. Have another cup of coffee. We'll talk and together we'll decide what the right thing is to do."

"Thomas." Elizabeth's eyes pooled with tears. "The man knows I can identify him. He can't afford to let me get away."

"What do you think he will do?" Mary asked. "Do you think he will try to kill you, again?"

"Ja, Mamm." Elizabeth lowered herself back into her chair. "And anyone else who tries to help me. That's why I have to go. I was wrong to come and it would be wrong to stay."

"It is wrong to leave." The iron steeliness crept back into Thomas's voice. "Running is not the answer to problems. I would have hoped you'd have learned that lesson by now."

A heated flush painted her cheeks. She knew his words had a double meaning. She hadn't run away before. She had chosen to leave. For him. For his happiness. But she knew he couldn't know that.

"I won't be able to live with myself if anyone gets hurt because of me." Her eyes pleaded with him to understand.

"No one will get hurt. The Amish community takes care of its own and you are still one of us, Elizabeth. We will talk to the bishop and ask his guidance. Everything will be all right."

"Thomas is right. The bishop will have sound advice." Mary sat down again. "Don't worry. *Gott* will protect us."

"He didn't protect Hannah." Elizabeth regretted the words the moment they left her lips.

"You must not question *Gott*," Mary said, reprimand-

ing her. "It was His will that Hannah be called home.
And we must place this problem in His hands. He loves
us. He has a plan for our lives. Whatever happens it will
be His will. Trust Him, Elizabeth, always."

She lowered her eyes in chagrin. "I do, *Mamm*. I
shouldn't have said that. I'm sorry."

"Finish your coffee." Thomas gestured to her mug.
"Tell us everything. We will make a plan to keep you
safe." Thomas's resolve remained solid and steady.

Elizabeth dared to relax a moment, to allow someone else to help her carry the burden. The ghost of a
smile crossed her lips as she looked at Thomas. He had
always been there for her. He was there for her now.
But she couldn't miss his thundercloud expression as
he said one more thing.

"This plan, Elizabeth, will not include running
away."

Chapter Three

Elizabeth moved quickly through the barn toward the rear exit.

"Where are you going?" Thomas stepped out of the shadows.

She startled and spun in his direction. "Don't creep up on me. You're going to give me a heart attack."

"You're too young for a heart attack. And I'm not the one who appears to be creeping around."

"Don't be foolish. I'm not creeping anywhere."

"I thought you'd be in the kitchen helping Mary clean up," Thomas said.

"And I thought you'd left for home."

"I was leaving." He came closer. "But I remembered one of the horses has a sore on his leg and I wanted to take a second look at it." He grinned. "Your turn. What are you doing scampering through the barn?"

"I don't scamper."

He raised an eyebrow and grinned. The Elizabeth he had known all his life never walked if she could avoid it. She scampered, scurried, skipped and frolicked through life. It did his heart good to see that some things about her hadn't changed.

"I was going to check on my car." She waved her hand toward the rear barn doors. "I've got it under a tarp behind the barn."

"And you think one of the livestock took it for a joyride?"

Elizabeth laughed at his foolishness, which was exactly what he wanted. He'd always tried to make her happy and her life carefree. He knew she needed a heavy dose of that now. Besides, he had always loved to hear the tinkling sound of her giggles and was not disappointed to hear them now.

"That is a ridiculous notion and you know it." But she covered her mouth to stop a giggle anyway and he smiled. "If I am going to stay, I have to get the car ship-shape and ready to sell."

"If you stay?" he asked.

"We haven't spoken to the bishop yet. He might not want me to stay."

Thomas grinned. He didn't speak but sent her a knowing glance.

"Okay. So he's probably going to let me stay. But I'll still have to sell my car."

"How did it feel to be able to drive your own car?"

"I must admit that is one of the *Englisch* luxuries I really enjoyed."

"Will you miss it?"

"Nah. If I feel like driving, I'll climb on one of the plows and take a spin in the fields with the horses."

Now Thomas had to laugh, as his mind painted a picture of that event.

"I find it hard to picture you behind the wheel of a car," he said. "You seem more the buggy type."

"I am the buggy type. Always have been. But I loved my little Honda Fit, with its racing stripes on the side."

"Honda Fit?"

"Yep. C'mon. I'll show it to you."

Like a flash she was off, scampering across the barn floor toward the back exit. Thomas chuckled, pushed off from the stall he'd been leaning against and lumbered after her.

"Thomas."

The urgency in her voice made his blood run cold. What if that man had returned? He raced toward the back of the barn. When he cleared the open doorway, he skidded to a stop.

Elizabeth stood to his right, leaning heavily against the barn wall.

Thomas shot a hurried glance in every other direction, trying to find the danger or intruder, but saw nothing. His eyes moved back toward Elizabeth and his heart squeezed. She looked so fragile and small and scared. Her body trembled and the piece of paper she held in her hand rattled.

"Elizabeth? What's wrong?"

The blood had drained from her face. She was almost as white as the paper she held in her hands. Fear widened her eyes and she didn't speak. Shakily, she held out the note.

He slid it from her fingers. Anger coursed through his body when he read the words:

I want what is mine. I will contact you again soon with a time and place to meet. Tell no one. I warn you, give it to me or die.

* * *

"*Kumm* in. Sit down." Bishop Eli Schwartz ushered Thomas, Elizabeth and Mary into the front room. His wife, Sarah, offered them tea and cookies, which they gratefully accepted. Once his wife had left the room, the bishop turned his attention to his guests.

"Welcome back, Elizabeth. It is good to see you again. I heard you were back. Are you here for a visit or are you planning to stay?"

Elizabeth wasn't surprised he had heard she was back. Nothing traveled faster in the Amish community than news. She tried unsuccessfully not to squirm in her seat. Instead she attempted to hide her nervousness by clasping her fingers tightly in her lap.

"My intention, Bishop, was to be baptized and move back permanently."

"Wonderful." The bishop's gaze flew from one to the other before it settled on Elizabeth. He raised a brow. "And now?"

Thomas glanced at her for permission and when she nodded he took over the conversation. She listened with only half an ear as he filled in the bishop on everything that had happened in the past twenty-four hours.

She released a breath and relaxed. She knew she shouldn't be relying on Thomas. She should be explaining the circumstances to the bishop on her own. She was strong, independent and hadn't needed a man's help for seven years. She didn't need a man to speak for her now.

But having someone to talk to, someone to comfort her, someone to make her feel protected and safe, even if just for a little while—was that really so bad?

"Elizabeth?"

She startled at the sound of her name.

"The piece of paper?" The bishop held out his hand.

Elizabeth drew the folded paper from her apron pocket and handed it over.

The older man studied it, deep furrows appearing in his forehead and at the sides of his mouth. Then he folded the paper and handed it back to her.

"Who else knows about this?" he asked.

"No one."

The bishop nodded, leaned back in his chair and silently stroked his beard.

"I am willing to leave, Bishop, if you think it would be best for everyone else," Elizabeth said.

"I am sure *Gott* has waited patiently for you to return, to repent and be baptized." The bishop smiled, sipped his tea and then placed the cup back down on the side table. "I know your *mamm* has waited many years for you to find your way home. Now you are here. That is a *gut* thing. Who am I to send you away?"

"But this man?"

"We will deal with him. I will speak with the elders and tell them what is going on. Meanwhile, you need to go home. Keep your eyes open. Don't go anywhere alone. Don't do anything foolish."

"Should we tell the sheriff?" Thomas asked.

Elizabeth knew it was hard for him to ask that question of the bishop because the Amish do not like to involve the *Englisch*, especially law enforcement, in their lives.

"I don't think that is necessary yet." The bishop nodded toward Elizabeth's pocket, which housed the note. "The man wants to meet with Elizabeth. Until he contacts her again, I do not believe she is in any immediate danger." He stroked his beard again. "What do you have that he wants? What did Hannah give you?"

"She didn't give me anything. I don't know what this man wants." Elizabeth tried to remember every conversation between them on the day of Hannah's death.

"Wait!" She leaned forward. "I have a carton of Hannah's belongings. I dropped the one I was carrying into the condo when I ran for my life, but I had another one still in my car." She couldn't keep the excitement and hope out of her voice. "That must be it! Whatever the man wants must be in that box."

"Where is this box?" the bishop asked.

"On the floor of the backseat of my car." She shot a hurried glance at each one of them. "I completely forgot about it. It has to be in the box. I don't have anything else."

"Gut." The bishop's lips twisted in a wry grin. "For now, we will play his game. We will let him think we are willing to return this elusive item. No sheriff. Not yet. Let me discuss it with the elders first. You go home and search through that box. Whatever was worth killing poor Hannah over should be easy to recognize. When we know what we are dealing with we will decide the proper way to proceed."

The bishop stood, indicating the meeting was over. Thomas, Elizabeth and Mary stood, as well.

"Denki," Bishop Schwartz, for seeing us without notice. We appreciate it," Thomas said. He placed a hand under Elizabeth's elbow. "I will do my best to keep an eye on things at the farm the best I can and I will try to keep Elizabeth and Mary safe."

"Gut." The bishop nodded. "I will speak with the others and get back with you shortly. Elizabeth, if there

are any problems, ring the porch triangle and we will all *kumm* running."

Elizabeth smiled and nodded. "Thank you, Bishop."

"Meanwhile, stay safe. Go about your business. Prepare for your repentance and baptism. Let us pray about what the next move should be. And let me know immediately if there are any more letters."

"*Denki.* I feel better already."

Thomas helped both women into the buggy, then went around to the other side. After nodding goodbye to the bishop, he clicked the reins and guided the horse back toward the main road.

"See, Elizabeth," Mary said. "The bishop will know what to do. Everything will be all right."

They'd traveled about a quarter of a mile when Thomas spoke. "I thought the meeting went well. I told you the bishop would not ask you to leave."

"It's not that. I knew Bishop Schwartz would allow me to stay. He has known me and my family since I was born."

"Then what is it?"

"The danger is real, Thomas. I am not afraid for myself, but what have I brought to the community?"

Thomas placed his hand over hers. A pleasant tingling sensation raced up her arms. Even now, she could still be affected by the mere touch of his hand.

"We will keep you safe, Elizabeth. The whole community will be watching for strangers and things that are out of place."

"I know." A pounding headache formed in the sinus area above her eyes. "But what if it isn't enough? What if he hurts someone?"

"Maybe we will find what he wants in that box in

your car. We will give it to him and he will go back to Philadelphia."

"Do you really believe he will take the box and leave?"

"If he wanted you dead, he had the few extra minutes to do it in the barn before I could reach you."

Elizabeth felt the blood drain from her face as she realized the truth of his words. He could have killed her in the barn. Almost did. But a sense of dread filled her. What if he was lying? What if he had no intention of letting her live once he'd gotten what he came for? She'd seen his face. She was a witness to his crime. She'd lived in the *Englisch* world long enough to know criminals didn't leave witnesses behind.

"What you have is more important to him right now than you dead."

The truth of his words gave her a little inner peace.

"What do you think Hannah put in the box?" he asked.

"That's just it, Thomas, I don't know. And I'm scared to death to find out."

The steady clopping of the horse's hooves was the only sound for several more miles as Thomas pondered the day's events. He'd make sure Elizabeth and Mary were settled in and then he'd have to head home. His former in-laws would be bringing the *kinner* home soon.

A smile bowed his lips at the mental image of his two precious children. *Gott* had blessed him with two precious gifts—his smile widened—even if one of those gifts was perpetually drawn to dirt and mire.

His smile didn't last. How was he going to keep Elizabeth and Mary safe when he was miles away on his own farm?

He couldn't and that was unacceptable. He had to find a way to protect them daily. But how?

"You're awfully quiet, Thomas. Is something wrong?" Elizabeth studied him closely.

Something wrong? Everything's wrong.

When he woke this morning his only thought was getting his chores finished for Mary in time to get back home to take care of his own farm and his *kinner*. He'd never expected his world to be turned upside down. But the unexpected events in this life reminded him that he was not in control, *Gott* was.

"Nothing's wrong, Elizabeth. Just thinking through the day's events," Thomas replied.

When Elizabeth smiled at him, his heart skipped a beat. After all these years she could still stir deep feelings in him and, for a moment, he hated himself for that weakness.

"It's been a crazy day," she admitted.

"Ja."

"Denki, Thomas."

He glanced her way and for an instant was lost in the sky-blue depths of her eyes.

"I know you weren't expecting to see me," she said. "And…well, I am grateful for all you have done. Helping my mother on the farm. Taking me to see the bishop. You didn't have to do any of it and I want you to know I appreciate it."

Thomas nodded. "Many things have passed between us, Elizabeth, and many years. But not so many that we can't consider each other a friend."

Did her smile dim when he called her a friend? Was

it possible she harbored deeper feelings, too? No. His mind played games with his hopes. If she'd cared for him as he'd cared for her, she would never have left.

She twisted her hands in her lap and gazed off in the distance.

"Elizabeth?"

She sighed deeply. "I'm sorry. I can't stop thinking about the note."

"The note is keeping you safe," Mary said. "It's giving you time to find out what this mystery item is. There is nothing to worry about. *Gott* will protect us."

"Mary's right," Thomas said. "I'd say the man got what he wanted for now. He frightened you. He put you on edge. He has you looking over your shoulder at every shadow and jumping at every sound."

Thomas clicked the reins and the horse broke into a trot as their buggy turned onto the dirt path leading to the house.

"This will be over soon, Elizabeth," Thomas assured her. "The first thing we need to do is search the box." He pulled the buggy in front of the porch and helped both women down. Mary climbed the steps to the house, while Elizabeth almost ran toward the barn.

Thomas tied the reins to the porch railing then walked toward the barn, where Elizabeth had disappeared only moments before. Could the words he'd offered her for comfort turn out true? Would it be that easy? Give the man what he wants and he'll leave them alone? What could be so important it was worth killing an innocent woman to get? His curiosity grew with each step as he neared the barn.

Mary cried out. "Thomas. Elizabeth. *Kumm* quickly."

Thomas spun back toward the house and ran. He

burst inside. The older woman was pressed against the wall, her knees nearly buckling.

"Mary?"

"Mamm?" Elizabeth whooshed through the doorway and came up short behind him. "Are you all right? What's wrong?"

Mary lifted a trembling hand and pointed.

"Oh, no!" Elizabeth whispered as both of them looked in the direction Mary had indicated.

The house had been ransacked. The cushions of the sofa and chairs had been gutted with something sharp and stuffing covered every surface. The end tables were overturned, some broken.

The destruction spilled into the kitchen. Every cabinet door hung open. Every drawer was pulled out and emptied. Silverware and cooking utensils had been carelessly tossed across the linoleum. Canisters of flour and sugar were emptied onto the floor. Pots and pans had been thrown haphazardly into the messy concoction.

Every nook and cranny had been searched, every chance to destroy something had been taken.

"He was here," Mary whispered. "That evil man was in our home."

Elizabeth rushed to her mother's side and wrapped her arms around her. "It's okay, *Mamm*. We're okay. We aren't hurt. This is just stuff. We can fix stuff, right?"

Mary nodded, a stunned expression still deeply etched on her face.

Although Thomas knew Elizabeth was doing her best to comfort her mother and ease her fears, she couldn't hide the tremor in her own voice from him. He knew her too well. She was terrified.

Both women looked at the destruction surrounding them and remained speechless.

Suddenly Mary headed toward the stairs. "He must have gone upstairs, too."

Thomas stopped her before she could reach the bottom step. "I will *kumm* back and take care of whatever damage was done. Right now we have to leave."

"Leave?" Elizabeth threw him a questioning glance. "Where will we go?"

"Home. With me." Thomas shot Elizabeth a look that let her know he would not take no for an answer. "But not before we retrieve that box and take it with us. It's time to see what is so important inside."

Chapter Four

Elizabeth couldn't stop tapping her toe or fumbling with her fingers in her lap. The steady sound of the horse's hooves clomping up the lane did little to calm her frayed nerves.

"It will be all right, Elizabeth." Thomas smiled and she assumed he was trying to reassure her. "That man does not know where you are going. You and Mary will be safe with me."

If he only knew. The stranger wasn't what made her pulse race and her body tremble with nervous energy. It was seeing his family home, meeting his children. Witnessing a life she'd always wanted but couldn't allow herself to hope for.

"I'm not afraid, Thomas. I know you will do your best to protect us."

The buggy turned onto a dirt lane between two white picket fences and her heart stuttered. She could see a two-story white clapboard house in the distance, with a large front porch. Two adults sat in rocking chairs watching a young boy run around the yard. She saw all of them turn their way as the buggy approached.

"Whoa." Thomas stopped the buggy at the edge of the porch, then leaped out and reached up a hand to help Mary down from the back seat.

Elizabeth stepped down and came around the buggy just in time to see a towheaded boy barrel across the yard and fling himself at Thomas.

"*Daed—Daed, kumm* here. Hurry. I found a little cat hiding in the barn. Can I keep him? *Kumm* see." The boy tugged on his father's hand.

"Benjamin, mind your manners. We have company." He tousled his son's hair. "Say hello. We can go to look at the cat in a little while."

The boy peered around his father and seemed surprised to see Elizabeth. His enthusiasm for the cat was tempered and he peered at her with the cutest look of curiosity on his face.

"Who are you?" He let go of his *daed*'s hand and came closer to her. "I don't know you. Where did you come from?"

"Benjamin. Manners." His father's warning tone caused the boy to lower his eyes and stop talking.

"It's okay," Elizabeth assured Thomas. She squatted down to be eye level with the child. When he looked into her face, her heart seized. He was the spitting image of his father. "Hello, Benjamin. My name is Elizabeth. I am Mary's daughter and I am a friend of your *daed*'s."

The boy's eyes grew wide. He glanced at Mary and then back to her. "I didn't know Miss Mary could have old *kinners*. I thought all *kinners* were little like me."

Elizabeth laughed. "Little *kinners* grow up. You will, too, someday." She offered him her hand. She grinned as he placed his little fingers in her grasp and shook her hand. "Nice to meet you, Benjamin."

He took back his hand. "Do you like cats?"

Elizabeth stood and smiled down at the boy. "I do like cats. When I was little like you, my *daed* let me keep a whole family of kittens in our barn. When they grew up to be adult cats they earned their keep by keeping the field mice away from the barn."

Benjamin grinned and grabbed her hand. "*Kumm* with me. There's a cat in our barn. I'll show you."

"Benjamin, what did I say?" Thomas placed his hands on his son's shoulders. "There will be time for that later, *sohn*. Miss Mary and Miss Elizabeth have things to do right now. You go play in the barn with your cat. We will join you soon."

Benjamin didn't need any extra urging. He was off in a flash, running across the yard toward the barn.

"He's adorable." Elizabeth smiled at Thomas and the look of pride in his eyes made her heart swell.

"Kumm." He placed a hand on her elbow. "Meet the rest of my family."

Mary had already gone up on the porch and was in deep conversation with the two people sitting there. As Elizabeth climbed the stairs, they stood. The man welcomed her first.

"*Gut* afternoon. My name is Isaac. I am sorry to hear of your troubles." He looped his fingers in his suspenders and moved to the side. "This is my wife, Rebecca."

"Hello." The woman stepped forward. "Welcome." She held a toddler in her arms, and she was one of the most beautiful little girls Elizabeth had ever seen. The child sucked on her index finger and stared at her with stunningly blue eyes. Thomas's eyes.

Elizabeth's eyes burned with tears and she fought hard not to shed them.

This is Thomas's family. This is what I had always wanted for him. So why, Lord, does it hurt so much?

"Hello, little one." She smiled and clasped the child's free fingers. "You must be Rachel."

"*Ja.* This is my precious one." Thomas took her from Rebecca's arms. The child giggled in his arms and pulled at his beard. Absently, he placed a kiss on her forehead.

Elizabeth's insides melted as she watched. He was a good *daed.* She knew he would be.

"Let's go inside. I started a fresh pot of coffee. It should be ready by now," Rebecca said. She looked at the two women. "Dinner will be ready shortly. There is plenty of food. You are welcome to join us."

"*Ja,* thank you, Rebecca. Mary and Elizabeth will be joining us for all meals for a while. I have invited them to stay in the *dawdi haus* for a short time. You and Isaac are no longer needing it now that you've bought a farm of your own. My parents stay in the main house with me six months out of the year. It was built for family. Seems foolish to let it stand empty. Mary and Elizabeth need a place to stay so I am offering it to them."

A surprised expression flashed across Rebecca's face, but she covered her reaction quickly. She smiled at the two women. "Both of you are welcome." She reached out her arms to Thomas for Rachel. "*Kumm.* I will set out mugs for us.

Thomas handed his daughter back to her. "*Ja.* We have much to discuss." He turned to his guests. "Right after dinner I will show you to the *dawdi haus.* Usually there is a connecting door and a small bedroom in these in-law apartments but I actually had a small house added on to my own. There is a connecting door off the kitchen. But you will also find a living room, two bedrooms, a kitchen and a bathroom inside. Now that Isaac and Rebecca have chosen to purchase their own farm, it is sitting empty. You are both welcome to use it for as long as you need."

"*Denki*, Thomas. We are grateful for the help." Mary put her arms around Elizabeth's waist and steered her toward the kitchen. Without a word passing between them, Elizabeth knew her *mamm* understood how awkward and difficult meeting Thomas's family was for her. Her mother's secure touch around her waist let Elizabeth know she wasn't going through any of it alone. Again, her eyes burned with threatening tears. She had missed her *mamm*…so much.

"I will bring in your bags from the buggy and, of course, the box. I am anxious to see what great secret is inside." Thomas bounded down the porch steps before anyone could reply.

Thomas had done most of the talking as he brought his in-laws up-to-date on the day's events. Even as he spoke he had to admit being surprised with how much had transpired in only a day's time. He wasn't surprised, however, at their kindness toward Elizabeth, or their sincere desire to help in any way they could. They were good people and he was honored to have them as family.

Crash!

Finishing his second cup of coffee, Thomas pushed it aside, jumped to his feet and ran in the direction of the trouble, closely followed by the rest of the adults.

Benjamin stood in the middle of the room. He had overturned the box Thomas had placed on the sofa and its contents had scattered across the wooden floor. Benjamin's lips puckered and his eyes welled with tears as if he might cry at any moment. "I'm sorry, *Daed*. Don't be mad at me. It was an accident."

"I am not mad, *sohn*. But you know better than to touch things that do not belong to you."

Everyone helped to pick up the strewn items. There were half a dozen books, a couple of plants, a set of sheets, some bath towels, a few knickknacks and even a few small framed pictures.

Thomas held one photo in his hand and stared at it. "This is a picture of Hannah. The Amish do not take pictures of themselves. Maybe Hannah became more *Englisch* than you thought in the years you were gone."

"That is one vice Hannah did like," Elizabeth said. "She took pictures. Lots of them. She wanted to have something besides her mind to record her memories. I think she felt it was concrete proof that she belonged somewhere with people she cared about and who cared about her, after feeling for so many years that she didn't."

"And you?" Thomas asked as he handed the small picture frame to Elizabeth. "Did you take pictures of yourself, too?"

"Not really." Elizabeth took the frame from his hand, looked at it and smiled at the image of her friend. "Hannah snapped one or two of me over the years when I was doing something with her group of friends." She shrugged. "But it was different for me. I always knew who I was and where I came from. I did not need reminders."

One by one, the adults handed various items to Elizabeth as she repacked the carton.

Once most of the items had been cleaned up, Mary

and Rebecca returned to the kitchen to finish getting dinner ready and Isaac excused himself to tend to the animals in the barn, leaving the children with Thomas and Elizabeth.

"I'm sure Benjamin meant no harm, Thomas." She kneeled down so she could be on eye level with the upset child. "You were probably curious, weren't you? Wondering what I had in the box."

The boy nodded.

"Why don't you help me pick up the few things that are left and put them back in the box? Can you do that?"

Benjamin nodded and grinned. He picked up a few things and threw them into the carton.

Thomas eyed every item going back into the box. A key chain. More pictures. Even a small stuffed rabbit. When there were no items left on the floor for the boy to retrieve, he patted his son's rump. "Go, Benjamin. Get washed up for dinner."

The boy scampered off.

"I don't understand." Thomas placed the last item he'd been holding in his hand on the top of the carton. "I don't see anything unusual. Certainly nothing worth harming someone to get back."

Elizabeth sat back on her heels. "I know. I was thinking the same thing. I can't imagine what that man thinks is so important." She picked up two of the books and briefly leafed through their pages. "No notes tucked inside." She rummaged through the box, making sure she hadn't missed something. "And no journals or anything else that would expose this man's identity."

"We must be missing something."

"Maybe the missing item was inside the box I dropped at the condo."

Thomas shook his head. "I am sure the man searched that box before he came all this way." He reached out a hand and helped Elizabeth to her feet. "I've been wondering about that, too. Are you sure you don't remember seeing him before? How would he even begin to know where you might have gone? It doesn't make sense that he would show up on an Amish farm looking for you. I thought you and Hannah had given up the Amish life. Why would he think of looking for you here?"

"We had. No one knew of our past."

"You are wrong, Elizabeth. This man knew."

"Hannah must have told him. But I don't know why she would do such a thing." Elizabeth sighed heavily. "There are many things I don't understand. Hannah and I were best friends. I didn't think we kept secrets from each other."

Thomas saw great sadness in her eyes when she looked at him. "I wish she hadn't kept this man a secret. Maybe I could have helped her. Maybe she wouldn't have been murdered."

Thomas frowned. "There has to be something here. What about the pictures? Anything special? Is the man in any of them?"

Elizabeth took a second look. "No. They are photos of friends Hannah made at the restaurant where she worked." She held one in particular in her hand. "She had just started dating this young man." Elizabeth showed Thomas a photo of Hannah and a young *Englisch* man, their heads together, eating cotton candy at a fair and grinning into the camera. "I hadn't met him yet. She'd only gone out with him a few times. But she spoke well of him. I think she was starting to really like him." Her expression clouded. "I wonder if anyone told him about her death. The police, maybe?"

Thomas handed her back the picture. "I am sorry, Elizabeth. I know it must pain you to have lost your friend."

Elizabeth remained silent, lost in her own thoughts, but grief was etched in her features. She startled him when she suddenly darted across the room. "No, honey. Don't put that in your mouth."

Rachel, sitting on the floor next to a bookshelf, had something in her hands headed directly for her mouth. She'd been so quiet the adults had overlooked her.

Thomas quickly reached his daughter and took the item from the child's hands, and her cries instantly filled the room. "What is this?" He held up a small plastic white dog with black spots on its back and wearing a red collar.

Elizabeth glanced at it and laughed. "It's a toy dog from a popular comic strip. Hannah loved this character. She had pictures, a key ring, even a stuffed animal just like this."

Rachel's wailing continued. She stood up and pulled on her father's pant leg. "Doggy." Rachel held out her hand for the toy.

"Can I give it back to her?" Elizabeth asked. "It's too large for her to swallow and there are no rough edges. She can't get hurt. It's simply a plastic toy. A decoration for Hannah's desk or bookshelf. She collected them all the time."

"If you think it best." Thomas handed the small plastic toy to Elizabeth and watched as she bent down to offer it to his daughter. His breath caught in his throat at the tenderness in her expression. Once, many years ago, he had imagined Elizabeth softly mothering a house full of *kinner*, his *kinner*. Now she was here. In his living room, with his daughter—his and Margaret's daughter—and a wave of guilt washed over him.

What's the matter with me? I shouldn't be thinking about days past, about dreams long gone. I shouldn't be thinking of any other woman and sullying Margaret's memory.

Feeling angry and confused, he tried to distract himself. "Let me move the bookcase. Maybe something else rolled under it." Thomas pulled the wood case out from the wall but found nothing.

The youngster, content with having the plastic dog returned, banged it up and down on the floor and made woofing sounds as she played.

Elizabeth straightened and silently watched the child. She wrapped her arms around her body. Her worried expression concerned him.

"Are you *allrecht*?"

"Yes, I'm fine." She faced him, her troubled expression evident. "What should we do, Thomas? I can't find anything in the box of any importance. Certainly nothing significant enough to cost Hannah her life. I don't think we have what this man wants."

"We will deliver the box and its contents to him."

Her eyes widened. "I don't understand. You told us we would be safe here. How will he find us? He couldn't know I would come here."

"We will find him."

Elizabeth's mouth formed a perfect *O*. "Find *him*? How?"

"I left a note on your mother's door before we left. I told him I was taking you and your mother to a safe place but I promised him I would bring the box to the house tomorrow morning. If all goes well, he will *kumm* back to the house, read the note and wait."

"Did you sign it?"

"Of course not, Elizabeth. That would have defeated the purpose of bringing you here to keep you safe."

Elizabeth nodded. "You're right. I'm not thinking clearly."

Thomas grinned. "We know. That is why you have a whole community working together to keep you and your mother safe."

His words did little to soothe her. She looked more worried than ever.

"What if we don't have what he wants?"

He raised an eyebrow. "I have heard many what-ifs from you. You never used to question things so much before."

"I never witnessed my best friend get murdered or found myself running for my life before, either." She wrapped her arms tighter, as if she had felt a chill. "Seriously, Thomas, what if we don't have what he wants?"

"Hopefully, even if what he wants is not inside the box, he will believe you don't have it and he will go away."

Her eyes darkened. "And if he doesn't go away?"

"We will cross that bridge when we *kumm* to it. No sense worrying. We cannot change what is. Trust in the Lord. He will guide us on the right path."

Elizabeth didn't respond right away. She sat on the sofa and pretended to be watching Rachel play on the floor. But Thomas knew her too well. He could see she was thinking hard about the situation. He knew she was determined not to bring harm to him or his family or anyone in the community if she could help it. He offered a silent prayer that her solution wouldn't be to run away like she had seven years ago.

Finally, she glanced up at him.

"I will do as you say, Thomas. For now."

Chapter Five

Elizabeth held up her lantern. "Thomas? Is that you?"
She moved closer to the porch steps and held her lantern higher.

Thomas heard the fear in her voice and hurried to reassure her. "*Ja*, it's me." He knew she was thinking about the stranger who had stepped out of the darkness and wrapped his hands around her throat.

"*Guder mariye*, Elizabeth. I'm sorry if I startled you."

"Good morning to you, too. You didn't scare me. I am scaring myself, Thomas, with foolish thoughts."

But her thoughts were far from foolish. Lord, thank You for keeping her safe. Thank You for putting me in the right place at the right time to help. Grant me the wisdom and strength to continue to keep them safe.

Thomas, leading his mare out of the barn and approaching the buggy already parked in front of the house, stopped at the bottom of the porch steps. "Did you and Mary sleep well?"

"*Ja*, we did. *Denki*. It is a fine house, Thomas. We are very comfortable. I am grateful for your kindness."

She came down the few steps from the *dawdi haus* and stood beside him as he fastened the horse in place.

"Where are you going so early?"

"I am leaving for your mother's farm. The cows need milking and the stalls will not clean themselves."

"Of course, how could I forget? You go there every morning." She glanced over her shoulder toward the house. "Wait for me. I'll tell *Mamm* and go with you."

Fear no longer laced her words. She actually sounded a little happy, maybe even excited to be joining him.

"What? No." He shook his head. "You are not going with me."

She planted her hands on her hips.

Uh-oh. He couldn't miss the glare she shot his way even with only the light from the lantern illuminating the darkness. He recognized that stance. He'd seen it several times when they were younger. She'd dig in her heels like a mule not wanting to move to pasture. He released a heavy sigh. He knew there would be a battle ahead. What a way to start his day! Maybe he should have tried to sneak away earlier.

"You are not going to the farm without me, Thomas. I am home now. It is my responsibility to help my mother take care of her livestock and her farm."

"It is a man's work. You can stay and prepare a *gut* breakfast for me. I will have worked up an appetite by the time I *kumm* home."

She bristled at his words. "I can't believe you just said that to me. I am perfectly capable of cleaning out stalls, laying hay and milking cows. Maybe you should stay here and fix breakfast for *me*. That is, if you know how to cook at all."

Thomas chuckled under his breath. Yep, this is the

Elizabeth he knew. Fiercely independent. Always demanding to be treated as an equal. Wanting to be a partner in every endeavor and more times than not getting her way because no one had the energy necessary to oppose her and win.

"Ahh, I was wondering if the old you still existed. You never did like being told what to do. I've been surprised you've been as cooperative as you've been."

"I've matured. I don't get as upset as I did when I was younger at the foolishness of men's words. And I've been grateful for your help and your kindness. But don't confuse gratitude with weakness, Thomas. I am capable of doing many things, not just cooking."

He finished harnessing the mare and acted like he hadn't heard a word she said. "You will be safe here. I will not be more than a few hours." He put his foot on the buggy step and hoisted himself up to the bench seat.

Elizabeth held the lantern closer. The light illuminated the carton tucked neatly behind on the floor. "You are taking the box with you. You are hoping to give it to that horrible man."

He didn't reply. He knew she wouldn't listen to reason. He reached for the reins.

Elizabeth hurried in front of the horse, grabbed the bit and blocked the path forward. "You must not do this thing alone, Thomas. I will not let you."

He raised an eyebrow. "You will not *let* me?"

"This man killed Hannah. He can kill you, too. You have *kinner*. Think of them. Speaking of which, where are the *kinner* now?"

"Isaac picked them up about a half hour ago as he does every morning."

"Okay. Fine, then." She glanced over her shoulder toward the house and then back to the buggy.

He tried to hide the grin pulling at the corners of his mouth. She wanted to tell Mary where she was going, but she didn't trust him to stay where he was when she ran inside. The indecision was killing her and he had to admit he found the whole situation funny. She'd already won. He had always given in to her if she wanted something badly enough. Only once had he ever told her no. Only once had he refused to accept her decision. Yet, she'd left anyway.

Elizabeth could be a formidable force when she wanted to be. It was one of the things that aggravated him the most and also one of the many things that he admired and drew him to her. Such strength! Like watching dark clouds gathering on the horizon and knowing you could not stop the storm.

"Let me run and tell *Mamm* where I am going. I will be right back. Do not leave without me, Thomas. If you do, I will follow on my own."

"Why are you doing this? You think you can keep me safe?" He chuckled. "Really? It wasn't me who was being choked in the barn yesterday."

Elizabeth chewed on her lower lip, embarrassment evident in her expression. "The man will find it more difficult to do harm if there is more than one person present. Two against one. I like those odds much better than you out there all by yourself."

"Elizabeth…"

She ignored the exasperation in his tone. "With two of us working together we can finish the chores in half the time and be back here safe and sound before the sun rises."

He pushed his hat back on his head and stared down at her. "You will not let this go, will you?"

"No."

"And you will follow me if I don't take you with me?"

"Absolutely."

Thomas shook his head. "I had forgotten how stubborn you can be. Hurry. Tell Mary and get back here. I will not wait much longer."

Her feet flew across the yard.

Thomas's heart pounded in his chest, a little from a healthy dose of anxiety about running into the man who wanted only to harm Elizabeth and the people she loved, but he had to be honest and admit to himself that part of that pounding was excitement about spending the morning working with her at his side. Seven years disappeared in an instant and he remembered what his life had been like with her in it. Now he had another opportunity. He would be spending the morning with his best friend. Working. Laughing. Talking together almost like the years had never come between them. But years had passed and he had to remember that you can't go back in time—no matter how much you wish you could.

The sound of her boots clomping across the wooden porch drew his attention. He saw the door to the house fly open.

"Mamm..."

He could hear the excitement in her voice. He wasn't the only one anticipating this outing together. He knew it would only be for a few hours. He knew it wouldn't change the past and he was equally certain it couldn't change the future. Too much had happened. Too much time had passed. They were different people now with different lives.

But they had today. They had now. And that would have to be enough.

He could hear the women's voices, but it was too far to make out their words. Within seconds, Elizabeth was back on the porch and bounding down the steps toward the buggy.

Thomas leaned back in his seat and grinned.

Where was Thomas? He'd been gone for over an hour. So much for keeping a close eye on her.

She brushed the beaded sweat from her brow with the back of her hand. She hadn't had to do this much physical labor in years. It was exhilarating but also exhausting. She knew her muscles would be sore and achy tomorrow. Maybe she should have swallowed her pride and stayed home to fix breakfast after all.

Drops of icy cold water splashed her face.

Elizabeth reached up to touch the wetness while simultaneously trying to find the source.

Another splash of ice-cold wetness hit her cheek and traced a path down her neck.

She spun around and spied Thomas only a moment before he spritzed her again.

"Don't!" Elizabeth squealed and tried unsuccessfully to move out of the way.

Thomas laughed and spritzed her from the pail in his hand once again.

"Stop!" She held her hands up in front of her face. She didn't dare laugh. That is exactly what he wanted her to do and if she let him see her laugh he would come after her with no mercy. She choked on her laughter but couldn't contain a series of giggles.

"No, Thomas. Don't you dare." Trapped between the hard edge of the sink and the large, hulking man standing in front of her, she feinted one way and then the other, trying to outmaneuver him. "You're drenching my dress. I'm going to freeze to death."

Thomas barred her escape by setting down the pail, stepping closer and blocking her escape by placing an arm on either side of her against the sink. The warmth of his breath fanned her face. His smile vanished and his expression became serious.

They stared at each other, not speaking, not moving.

"Do you think I would let you freeze?" His smoldering gaze caused visible goose bumps to race up her arms.

Their emotions spoke the words their voices couldn't. The moment became heated and uncomfortable and dangerous.

Before things could move into an area neither one of them wanted, Thomas took charge. Slowly he bent to wet his hand in the pail at their feet and a mischievous grin pulled at the corners of his mouth.

"Stop it!" She laughed and pushed his hand away. "What's the matter with you? You're acting like a child."

His grin widened. "If memory serves, you used to enjoy our childish romps."

She thought her bones would melt into puddles if she stared into those blue eyes even one second more. "We are not children anymore, Thomas."

She started to turn and he clasped her upper arm so she couldn't move. "Hold still."

With his other hand he picked a piece of hay from

her *kapp*. He dabbed away a drop of mud from her cheek with his thumb. "You look like you've been rolling around in the hay."

"I have been." She laughed and stepped around him. "I've cleaned four stalls and laid fresh hay in each. I should look a bit unkempt." She crossed her arms. "By the way, where have you been? You disappeared about two stalls ago."

He sobered and nodded toward the house. "I checked on the house. Made sure nothing more was broken or stolen. Picked up what I could so Mary wouldn't return to her home in disarray. I didn't see any footprints around the house. I think he came once, searched the place, and he hasn't been back."

Elizabeth looked out the barn door, her gaze instantly landing on a familiar object. "You've put the box on the porch."

"*Ja*, just as I said I would. *Gott* willing, he will return, take the box and leave." Thomas moved past her and washed his hands in the sink. "We need to get going. Our work here is done. We told Mary we'd be home by sunrise."

Elizabeth allowed him to help her into the buggy. When he'd walked around and climbed into the seat beside her, she put a hand on his forearm. She felt his muscles flex beneath her touch and a little chill danced up her spine. "*Denki*, Thomas, for letting me come with you today."

"As if I had a choice," he teased, then snapped the reins and turned the buggy toward home. "Besides, I have to admit you were a big help. We finished our chores in record time. But you must never tell anyone," he warned. "It will not rest well with the elders if they knew I allowed you to do heavy work. They will not understand your stubbornness. Me? I know to get out of your way when you want something."

She smiled, knowing he was trying to take her mind off of the box sitting on the porch. She shot one final glance that way as their buggy moved past the house and down the dirt lane.

"Besides," Thomas said, "it is easier to keep you safe if I keep you in sight and not leave you to your own schemes."

Elizabeth heard his words but her mind remained lost in thought.

Would the man come back for the box? And if he did, would he go away, as Thomas hoped?

A restlessness tormented her. She didn't believe it would be that easy. Leave the box and have the bad guy disappear from their lives? Her feminine intuition told her a different story—and it rarely steered her wrong.

"What?" Thomas shot her a questioning look. "I know when your mind is running a mile a minute. What is bothering you? You can talk to me, Elizabeth. I will help any way that I can."

"I know, Thomas. You are a good man...and a good friend."

"So talk to me. What troubles you?"

"I need to go into town later today. I need to talk to the sheriff."

Thomas's expression sobered. "Why? The bishop asked us to let him decide when and if we bring in the *Englisch* law."

"I know. I understand. But I can't let this man get away with what he did to Hannah." She caught and held his gaze. "I can identify him, Thomas. He knows that. I don't believe he ever intended on letting me go free. He plans to kill me once he has the information he thinks I possess."

Thomas's grim expression bordered on anger. "I will not let that happen."

"I know you will try. I know you will do your best to protect me." She patted his arm. "But you are one man—one unarmed, peaceful man who does not think in evil ways. This man will try to kill me and we both have to prepare that he might succeed."

She sat back and folded both her hands in her lap. "That is why I need to tell the police what I saw, what he looks like, while I still can. I need to help the police catch this man."

"It is not your place, Elizabeth."

"Hooey on that. Whose place is it? I saw him with his hands on Hannah's throat. I felt his hands on mine. I cannot let him get away with what he has done."

"Vengeance belongs to the Lord. Not you."

"It's not vengeance, Thomas. It's justice. Hannah was my best friend. He stole her life. He is going on with his life and not paying any consequence for his actions. How do I know he isn't going to do something like this again? And if he harms another woman and I say nothing to try and stop him, whose fault is it then?"

"What can you do? So you tell the police what he looks like. Doesn't he look like every other *Englisch* man?"

"Not any more than every Amish man looks alike."

Thomas frowned and snapped the reins, encouraging the horse to go faster.

"The police have special artists that work with victims of crime," she explained. "In the seven years I lived in the *Englisch* world, I often saw them flash these pictures on the television. I was always surprised how much the pictures looked like the people when they found them. I must do this, Thomas. For Hannah. For myself. And for my conscience. I do not believe the Lord let me see Hannah's murder, let me live through the attempt on my own life, only to remain quiet. I believe I am meant to help solve this case."

She saw a mix of emotions play across Thomas's face. She pressed home her final point. "How is trying to protect other people from being hurt any different than you trying to protect me?"

She heard him release a heavy sigh and knew deep down he agreed with her, but she also knew he wasn't ready to defy the bishop.

"Let me think on this, Elizabeth. Pray about it. If I feel it is the right thing to do, I will speak with the bishop again."

"*Denki*, Thomas." She remained silent the rest of the ride home. It was enough for now.

Chapter Six

It had been a pleasant, quiet, normal day, for which Elizabeth was grateful.

The *kinner* came home around noon. Isaac and Rebecca joined them for the midday meal that she and her mother had prepared. The men left for a while on horseback. Elizabeth, Mary and Rebecca had cleaned the kitchen then took the *kinner* outside to watch them play.

Rebecca darned her husband's socks. Mary kept a watchful eye on the *kinner*. Elizabeth crocheted a chain of loops to begin an afghan for Mary. She was into her second row when a huge smile tugged at her. She wished Thomas could see her now. She was doing "women's work" and doing it well.

Later, Rebecca took Rachel inside for a short afternoon nap. Benjamin busied himself filling a puddle with water and then running and splashing in the mud.

"I told you about that one," Mary said with a laugh as she kept an eagle's eye on the youngster. "Made up of mud, mayhem and mischief."

"I think he's adorable." Elizabeth paused from her crochet work and watched the child playing.

"That he is. But you can never take your eyes off of him. He gets into the mischief of ten *kinner*, that one." Mary stood and shielded her eyes against the setting afternoon sun. "Benjamin. *Kumm.* Your *daed* will be home any minute. You have to get washed up for dinner."

Surprisingly, the boy didn't complain or hesitate. He ran up to Mary as soon as she called him. Clasping the boy with one hand, Mary looked at her daughter. "Will you be coming inside?"

"Soon. I just want to sit here and rock for a few more minutes. It's so calm and peaceful here."

Mary smiled. "*Ja*, it is. But we are also losing the day's light. Do you want me to bring you a lantern?"

"No, *denki*. I'll be okay. I'll be in in a few minutes."

"Can I stay out here with Miss Elizabeth?" Benjamin asked.

"You have to get cleaned up for dinner, young man. Now scoot." Mary playfully swatted his butt and followed the child into the house.

The shadows elongated across the yard as the sun slipped quietly behind the distant trees.

She was home. With her family. With Thomas's family. And she was happy. Truly happy.

Thank You, Lord.

Admittedly, it was a short prayer, but *Gott* knew her heart and the depth of her gratitude.

Darkness crept in like a black cat and Elizabeth knew she should move inside now and help the other two women prepare the evening meal. She started to get up when the sudden movement of the rocking chair caused her to drop a skein of yarn. She bent over to pick it up.

Whoosh!

Something flew past her ear so closely that loose tendrils of hair blew in the breeze of its wake.

Thump!

What was that? What had just happened?

Rebecca sprang to her feet and spun toward the noise. Simultaneously, Mary swung open the front door. "I heard a loud thump. Did you fall? Is everything *all-recht*?" Then her mother gasped as both women peered at the door still standing open and illuminated by the battery-powered lamps inside.

"Oh! Lord, help us." Mary pulled Elizabeth into the house, careful not to touch the door continuing to stand ajar and then yelled for Rebecca.

All three women stood stone-faced as they stared at the knife and the white paper it had embedded in the wood.

Elizabeth's blood drained out of her face and her legs wobbled beneath her.

If I hadn't dropped the yarn… If I hadn't stooped over at that very moment…that knife would have found its mark in me.

"Elizabeth." Rebecca threw a shawl around her shoulders. "You're shaking like a leaf in a storm."

"I'm fine, Rebecca." But she didn't feel fine. She stood there calmly staring at the knife in the wood of the door, not because it fascinated her but simply because she knew if she tried to move she would fall flat on her face.

"What happened? What's going on?" Thomas sprinted up the porch steps, Isaac on his heels. Within seconds, he assessed the scene and hurried the women farther inside. He pulled out the knife and the note and moved into the house, closing the door behind him.

"Was anybody hurt?" His gaze swept the room. He saw his *kinner* playing on the floor. The two older women looked shaken up, but didn't appear to be injured. When he turned his attention to Elizabeth, his heart turned over. Her deathly pale skin and glassy eyes told him all he needed to know.

He reached out and pulled her into his arms and held her tightly against him. He didn't worry about what Isaac or Rebecca thought. He didn't feel guilt at this public display of affection. He only knew that Elizabeth needed him and he was going to be there for her.

"You're all right." He cradled the back of her head against his shoulder and held her quietly until her bones stopped shaking. "Shhh. It's going to be all right. *Gott* is *gut*. No one was hurt."

After a few moments, her rigid body relaxed in his arms and her breathing slowed. When he felt she'd be able to stand on her own two feet, he released her and took a step away. He lifted her chin so he could see into her eyes.

The glazed look was gone. He saw fear. *Ja*. But he also saw anger and determination. Good for her. He could deal with her anger and determination much more than he could face her fear.

"What happened?" he asked.

All three women spoke at once.

"Wait?" Isaac raised his hand in the air. "Let Elizabeth speak."

All eyes turned toward her.

"I was rocking on the porch. It was getting dark and

I decided to come inside and help with dinner, but—but…"

She paled even more, if possible. Thomas's blood boiled. He wanted to find this man and make him pay for the fear he caused. He knew he shouldn't have those feelings. He knew he'd have to repent. But maybe just this once he could repent after he taught this man to see the evil of his ways.

"A skein of yarn slid off of my lap. I leaned forward to pick it up. Something made a whooshing sound by my ear and then I heard a loud thud behind me. I turned to look at the door and couldn't believe what I saw." She gave a lame smile. "Who would have thought I would be grateful for having a clumsy moment? It probably saved my life. I am certain that knife was aimed at me."

She placed her hand on Thomas's wrist and nodded at the paper.

"What does it say?"

Thomas hesitated. He didn't want to upset her further.

"Tell her, Thomas." Mary put her hands on her daughter's shoulders. "She needs to know. We all do."

Several sets of eyes stared at him as he read the paper. Even the children seemed to sense the seriousness of the moment and sat quietly watching the adults. The words hit him in the solar plexus and he found it difficult to breathe. He glanced at the worried look of the adults staring back at him. Slowly, he read the words out loud.

"'The box was filled with junk. You played me for a fool. Now you die.'"

* * *

Several hours had passed since the ominous note incident. Dinner had been eaten mostly in silence. The women cleaned up. The men finished the chores in the barn. The children were bathed and tucked into bed for the night. Isaac and Rebecca left for their own home. Everyone went about their business as usual.

But nothing was usual or normal anymore.

Elizabeth stood in the doorway of the house and listened to the quiet of the night. Even the rustling of the creatures and critters had silenced hours earlier.

Elizabeth snatched a shawl from the wooden peg on the wall and stepped onto the porch. She walked over to where her mother sat, rocking quietly.

"I thought you might need this." She tucked the shawl around her mother's shoulders.

"Denki." Mary pulled the shawl tighter.

"It's gotten quite chilly. Don't you think you should come inside?"

"In a minute."

Elizabeth sat down in the rocker next to her. The flickering light of the lantern on the small table between the chairs was their only light. "Are you okay, *Mamm*? You haven't said two words since dinner."

"I should be asking you that question." Her voice trembled and Elizabeth realized the woman had been crying.

"Oh, no. Don't be upset. I'm *allrecht*. And I'm going to continue to be *allrecht*. Don't worry." She reached over and covered her mother's hand with her own. "Look at me."

When the older woman did, Elizabeth smiled. "Really, *Mamm*. I'm fine."

Mary huffed. "Well, I'm not."

Elizabeth released her mother's hand and sat back. Both women rocked for a few minutes in silence while Elizabeth tried to choose her words with care.

"Maybe I shouldn't have come back. Maybe it would be better for everyone if I left." She held her breath, waiting for her mother's reply.

"That is nonsense. This is your home. This is where you belong." The older woman closed her eyes and leaned her head against the back of the rocker. "I probably should have tried harder to keep both of you here. Neither one of you should have ever left."

"*Mamm*, you know why I left. After my operation, I felt I had no choice."

"Yes, I do know. And I was wrong to allow it. Thomas is a *gut* man. He would have understood."

Elizabeth's eyes teared up. "That is exactly why I left. He is a good man. He would have stood by me. And then what? Would my circumstance have been fair to him?"

Mary shook her head. "I don't know. Maybe we should have left it in *Gott*'s hands instead of trying to make the decision on our own." She looked directly into Elizabeth's eyes. "If it had been only you, I would never have let you go. But I sent Hannah away, too. I believed if you were together it would be for the best. Both of you would help each other. You'd be happy…and safe."

"We were, *Mamm*. We made a *gut* life for ourselves. We made a happy life."

"Happy life? Without your family? Just the two of you alone in an evil world? Hannah is dead. And now someone is hunting you." She cradled her face in her hands. "I made a terrible mistake."

"Stop it." Elizabeth kneeled beside her mother's rocker and put her arms around the woman. "None of this is your fault. Why do you blame yourself?"

It took a few minutes for Mary to compose herself. When she looked up, grief and regret were etched in every line of her face.

"The floor is cold, child. Get up. Sit."

Elizabeth did as directed then waited for her mother to tell her why she was so upset. Instead she asked more questions.

"Do you know who this man is, Elizabeth?"

"No. Of course not. I told you I have no idea who he is."

Mary frowned. "Are you sure? You never saw him before? You never saw him with Hannah?"

"No. Never. Why?"

Mary twisted her hands in her lap. "Did Hannah ever mention this man to you? Tell you anything about him?"

"No. The first time I ever saw him or knew of his existence was the day I saw him standing over Hannah's dead body."

"How old is he?" Mary asked.

"*Mamm*, you're scaring me. Where is this going? What do you know or think you know that I do not?"

"How old?" her mother insisted.

Elizabeth stared at her mother, her confusion growing by the second. "I'm not sure. In his early forties maybe."

Mary nodded as if she had expected that answer. "I wonder why Hannah never told you about him." The question was merely a whisper and Elizabeth felt it wasn't directed at her to answer, but was merely her mother thinking out loud.

She could not remember a time she had seen her mother so upset. She kept her tone kind and her voice soft so as not to upset her further. "If you know something, *Mamm*, please tell me."

The older woman slowly nodded her head. "I will tell you everything I know. But I have one last question."

"Anything. I have no secrets from you."

"Did Hannah act differently before her death? Did you think she might be keeping secrets from you? Did she go out without telling you where she was going or who she was seeing?"

Elizabeth seriously pondered the question. It hadn't seemed strange at the time but hindsight had twenty-twenty vision and now that she was forced to think about it, she knew her mother was right. Hannah had become quieter, kept to herself more. Elizabeth hadn't thought much about it. She knew Hannah had a new boyfriend and thought maybe her mind was on him. And, of course, they were in the middle of a move to the condo, so things were hectic. There hadn't been much time to sit and chat.

"Now that I think about it Hannah hadn't been herself lately. Quieter. A bit preoccupied maybe. But nothing that made me feel something was wrong." She stopped rocking and stared at her mother. "What do you know, *Mamm*? Do you think you know who this man is?"

Fresh tears rolled down Mary's face.

"You do!" Elizabeth's breath caught in her throat. "How do you know? Who is it, *Mamm*?"

"I believe the man is her father."

Chapter Seven

Elizabeth's chest felt like a fifty-pound weight was crushing the breath right out of her. She couldn't believe her ears. Hannah's father? That was absurd. Elizabeth knew Hannah's father. Her family had farmed the property right next to theirs. That's how Hannah and she had become good friends. They'd grown up together. She'd known Hannah's family as well as she'd known her own.

Was her mother losing her mind?

Poor *Mamm*. The stress must be getting to her. Was her health failing? Had more than a few gray hairs crept up on her mother in the years apart? Her heart filled with compassion. What should she do? How could she help? Did Thomas know? Was that why he had gone out of his way to take care of her mother after her father died?

She reached out and clasped her mother's hand. "Why don't you come inside now? It is dark and getting quite cold. I'll make us a cup of hot tea before we go to bed."

Mary pulled her hand away. "Don't treat me like I'm daft. I know what I know."

"I believe you." Elizabeth stood. "And I have a million questions, but I am too cold to continue talking out here. Let's go inside. I'll fix us tea and you can tell me how you know this is Hannah's father."

Her words seemed to appease her mother and the woman stood, picked up the lantern and preceded Elizabeth inside.

Elizabeth took advantage of the time it took to boil the water for tea. She busied herself setting out two mugs and putting a few cookies on a plate. On the surface she tried to keep a calm outward appearance, but her insides were a different matter. Her stomach muscles clenched so tightly they hurt. Her temples throbbed. Her mind flitted from one crazy thought to another as she tried to piece together what her mother had told her.

Once they were situated at the table, tea and cookies in front of each of them, Elizabeth smiled and broached the subject again.

"*Mamm,* I am a little confused. I know that Hannah and her father did not get along well, particularly after Hannah's mother died. That was the main reason Hannah wanted to leave home. Daniel Hofsteadter had remarried. He had young *kinner* now and he mistreated Hannah terribly. I can still remember seeing the bruises his fingerprints made on her arms. I know that the black eye he gave her was the final straw for you. That was the reason you helped us leave and secretly gave us money to hold us over while we found jobs and a place to live in Philadelphia. We both always appreciated your help."

"I didn't act alone. Your father knew about the money. He couldn't let the bishop or community know and we never spoke of it, but he knew. And approved. He loved you, Elizabeth." Mary remained quiet and sipped her tea.

"I don't understand. The Hofsteadters moved to Ohio years ago. Why would you think Hannah's father would come back and want to harm her now? Besides, *Mamm*, I got a good look at the man who attacked me in the barn. It wasn't Hannah's father."

"Daniel Hofsteadter is not Hannah's father. Not her biological father, anyway. That is why he mistreated her after Naomi died. He let the community believe she was his daughter. But she wasn't and he resented her for her entire life because of it." Mary shook her head. "It was such a sad situation. Hannah was a wonderful little girl. I never could understand how Daniel could not see past the circumstances of her birth and love the beautiful child she was."

Elizabeth fell back in her chair. Her teeth chattered and chills raced up and down her spine, but it had nothing to do with the weather and everything to do with the intense shock attacking her system.

How could this be? Hannah had a different father? Had she known? Why had Hannah kept it a secret from her? They were best friends.

Elizabeth didn't know whether to feel sad for her friend or angry at her betrayal of their friendship.

Almost as if Mary could read her mind, she said, "Don't be upset with Hannah for not telling you. She didn't know until I told her and that wasn't until after Daniel gave her that black eye. I'm sure she would have

told you someday. But some secrets get easier to cling
to as time passes and it becomes harder to reveal them."

Elizabeth could tell from the look in her mother's eye
that they were no longer speaking about Hannah and
her father. They were talking about her and Thomas.

"Does Thomas know about Hannah's father?"

"Some of it. Just like he knows some of the reason
you left. He knows Hannah had a different biological
father. And he knows you left with Hannah because she
was your best friend and you wanted to help her adjust
to the *Englisch* world. But he doesn't know the entire
truth of either situation. I had your father tell him only
what I felt he needed to know to help him understand
why you girls left so he could move on with his life."

She took another sip of her tea. "If I had it to do over,
I would not have hidden either truth. No good can *kumm*
from secrets. No good at all."

"Who is Hannah's father? How do you know him?
And why do you think he would kill his own daughter?
None of this makes any sense."

"All of it makes perfect sense, child." She sighed
deeply and stood up. "I am going to bed now."

"But you can't! You can't drop a bombshell like that
on me and then say good-night. You have to tell me what
you know. We have to stop this man."

"I agree. But there is much to tell and it is late. I
will tell both you and Thomas everything I know over
breakfast tomorrow morning."

"Thomas?"

"Yes, Elizabeth. The time for secrets is over. We
will tell Thomas the truth, all of the truth, about both
you and Hannah. And with *Gott*'s help, he will know
what we should do."

Elizabeth watched her mother cross the room and disappear behind her bedroom door.

Tell Thomas the truth? All of it? Maybe her mother was ready, but was she?

"You are quiet this morning, Elizabeth. Is everything all right?" Thomas stared at her over the rim of his coffee cup.

"I'm fine, Thomas. Just a little tired this morning. I didn't sleep well last night."

Assuming her lack of sleep was due to the knife in the door, he decided not to probe further. Maybe this day could begin on a more positive note.

"I changed the bandage on your horse's leg, Mary." Thomas smiled. "I do not think he will be lame. He looks like he is healing nicely."

"*Denki*, Thomas. That is good to hear." She refilled his cup and joined them at the table.

"And I have more *gut* news." He grinned like a Cheshire cat. "I spoke with our milkman and negotiated a ten-percent increase in what he is paying for our milk. It isn't much but it is a little extra."

"That is also *gut* news. Pennies add up to dollars if you are frugal with them," Mary said.

Thomas took a sip of the coffee and eyed both women. Mary seemed unusually nervous. Coupled with Elizabeth's uncharacteristic silence, Thomas knew that something was wrong and he feared it was more than the knife incident from the night before.

He noted the taut lines around Elizabeth's mouth, her downward gaze and her mother's nonstop nervous fingers tapping everything in sight.

What could be worse than having a knife thrown at you?

He glanced from one woman to the other, pushed his empty breakfast plate away and sat back in his chair.

"Which one of you is going to tell me what is wrong?"

The women lowered their eyes and remained silent.

"Enough. I can't sit here all day. There is work to be done. What is going on between the two of you?"

Elizabeth cleared her throat. "*Mamm… Mamm* believes she knows who killed Hannah."

His eyes shot to the older woman then back to Elizabeth.

"She thinks it's Hannah's biological father." Elizabeth's hands trembled when she lifted her coffee mug.

His pulse quickened. "You know Hannah's secret?" His eyes bored into her.

She nodded. "Yes. *Mamm* told me last night. She said we are not to have any more secrets."

"Wise counsel. Secrets do no one good. The truth will always surface."

Again both women shot telling glances at each other.

"Mary, why do you think this man may be Hannah's biological father? Why would he come looking for her after all these years and then try to harm her? It makes no sense."

"Because I don't believe he came looking for her. I believe Hannah found him. And I don't think he wanted to be found."

"Who is this man? What is his name? Is it someone from our community?" Thomas, upset by the information, threw out one question after another, giving her no time to respond.

"Thomas." Elizabeth placed a hand on top of his. "Give her a moment. She will tell us everything in her own time. This is difficult for her."

Thomas reined in his temper and they both waited for Mary to speak. When she did, he could hardly believe what she told him.

"I don't know the man's name. But I believe Naomi may have written it in one of her journals. I never read them because they were Naomi's very private, heartfelt thoughts. I found them when I was helping clean out her personal belongings after her death. Daniel didn't want them and allowed me to take them. I gave them to Hannah the day she left."

Thomas tried hard to process this new information. "Even so, Mary, it is quite a leap to believe this man would kill his own daughter just because she found him. Wouldn't he just tell her to go away and leave him alone if he didn't want to know her?"

"He wasn't a *gut* man." Mary wrung her hands and found it difficult to look at either of them. Her voice dropped to a mere whisper. "He was a rapist."

Elizabeth dropped her coffee cup. Hot coffee fell into her lap and she pushed her chair back from the table. Her mother grabbed a towel and began sopping up the hot liquid.

Elizabeth stilled her mother's hands, took the towel and finished wiping up the hot brew. Then she stared at her mother, shock and concern written all over her face. "Rapist? Hannah was a product of rape?"

Mary nodded. "It happened during our *rumspringa*. Naomi and I were best friends just as you and Hannah grew to be. We were in town together. Thinking we were all grown up and capable of making all the right decisions just because we could stay out past our curfew and were allowed to hang out in town with the other teenagers without punishment or repercussions."

Her eyes took on a sadness and far-away quality as she remembered those long-ago days.

"We were standing on the corner in front of the general store. Not doing anything special, really. Just talking." She fidgeted with her hands. "Some *Englisch* boys approached us. They were a few years older than us. One of them took a liking to Naomi. He flirted with her. He asked her to go for a walk with him in the moonlight."

Mary shook her head. "I tried to talk her out of it. I could smell liquor on his breath. And his friends seemed rowdy and liquored up, too. But she enjoyed the attention. I can still remember her saying, 'What harm is it to take a walk in the moonlight, Mary? Go home. I will see you tomorrow.' So I did."

"The next day she did not *kumm* to the house as she had said she would, so I went to see her. Her parents told me she wasn't feeling well and was in her room. When I went in to see her, she broke down sobbing and told me what had happened. He had pulled her into a field, raped her and left her lying there."

Mary cried softly. "She swore me to secrecy. She said she couldn't live with the shame if everyone knew. Shortly afterward she found out she was with child."

"Did Daniel know?" Thomas asked. He had never liked Daniel, but maybe he had been a better man than Thomas had given him credit for.

"Ja." Mary folded her hands on the table. "Daniel had proposed to Naomi once before and she had turned him down. He asked again. This time she broke

down and told him what had happened. He told her he would keep her secret. That they would marry and he would raise her child as his own. Being afraid and not knowing what else to do, she accepted and they married soon after."

Mary looked at both of them with such sadness in her eyes that Thomas wondered how she could carry such a burden. "She was a good *frau* to Daniel. She was grateful for his help and determined to be the best wife she knew how to be. But he never let her forget that she had turned down his earlier proposal and only accepted his second one because of the pregnancy, and even though he had always wanted her for his wife, he had never been able to forgive her for not loving him in return."

A heavy silence filled the room.

After several intense moments, Elizabeth spoke. "Did Naomi know her attacker's name?"

"Yes. He told her his name. He told her he lived in Pennsylvania. But she knew little more than that. I wasn't even sure she'd put the information into her journals." Mary looked at them both. "Now I wish I had read them. What if the man's name was hidden in those books and Hannah used it to track down her biological father? He may have killed Hannah so she wouldn't expose him."

Mary sobbed. "It's all my fault. I never should have told Hannah the truth. I never should have given her those journals. I couldn't stand how Hannah blamed herself for Daniel's cruelty. I couldn't continue to let her think there was something inferior or wrong with her. I thought it was important for her to understand why Daniel treated her differently from his other *kinner*."

"Did Hannah know she was a product of rape?" Thomas asked.

Mary nodded. "I told her that during *rumspringa* her mother met an older *Englisch* boy who flattered her and that things had gotten out of control. Hannah left here believing her father was a young man who had had too much to drink and didn't listen to the word *no*. Not that that was acceptable. It wasn't under any circumstances. But I believed it was a one-time incident. A terrible choice made by an intoxicated boy. Now, I'm wondering if his identity was in the pages of those journals. Maybe he wasn't just a misguided boy, but was truly an evil man. Now she's dead. And now my daughter's life is in danger, too. What have I done?"

"You have helped us more than you know, *Mamm*." Elizabeth stood and wrapped her arm around her mother's shoulders. "The police need to know about those journals. They will be able to find Hannah's real father now and figure out if he is the killer."

Thomas sprang to his feet and headed to the door.

"Where are you going?" Elizabeth asked.

Thomas grabbed his hat from the peg by the door and placed it on his head. "To talk to the bishop."

"He's been gone a long time." Elizabeth continued to break the defrosted green beans into the bowl on her lap, but she could hardly pry her eyes from watching the lane for Thomas's buggy.

"He will be gone as long as it takes." Mary continued to rock Rachel to sleep.

"What do you think will happen? Do you think the bishop will give us permission to go to the police?" Elizabeth tensed and shot a determined look at her mother.

"I am going to go to the police whether the bishop gives his blessing or not. It is the right thing to do."

Mary frowned. "And you don't think the bishop knows how to do the right thing?"

"Of course I do. But just in case he doesn't…"

"Elizabeth, must you always solve all the problems of the world on your own? It is a lighter burden when you turn your troubles over to *Gott* and ask Him to guide you. Trust in Him."

She held her tongue and pondered her mother's words. When had she moved so far away from the Lord? When had she decided, consciously or not, that she needed to control her own life because she didn't like the way He did?

Had it been when she felt forced to leave Thomas, her parents and her Amish roots behind because of the medical problems He allowed her to have? Was it the empty holidays she'd spent alone, or family gatherings she had missed? Had it been not finding out about her father's death in time to attend his funeral? Or seeing Hannah's death? Or running for her own life?

Had she lost her faith completely?

She believed in *Gott*. Of course she did. But when was the last time she trusted in Him and prayed for His help and guidance?

Mary rose from the rocker, the toddler nestled in her arms. "I'm going to go in and lay her down for her nap," she whispered.

Elizabeth nodded and continued breaking the beans into the pot in preparation for making her green-bean casserole. It had always been her father's favorite… and Thomas's.

She stared up at the sky. In a few hours the sun

would begin to set and breathtaking streaks of orange and gold would paint the horizon. *Gott* created such beauty in nature.

Dear Lord, I believe. Help me with my unbelief.

It was so peaceful and calm here. Unlike the bustling energy of Philadelphia. She had enjoyed the sense of excitement, the sound of the elevator trains, the bustle of the people, crowds of shoppers in the stores. She had savored every second of the experience.

But here she felt an inner peace. A quietness. A calmness. A connection with something more.

She smiled, closed her eyes and quietly rocked to and fro.

She could hear the sound of birds flying over the ice-covered pond. She could hear the rustling of the last dead leaves of autumn being tossed across the empty fields. It was so peaceful. So quiet.

Quiet!

She sat up straight and her eyes shot open.

Where was Benjamin?

She placed the pot of beans on the side table, jumped to her feet and her eyes searched the yard.

He'd been playing with his toy tractor just a minute ago not ten feet away.

Had it been just a minute ago? How long had she been lost in her own thoughts and not paying attention to the child left to her care?

"Benjamin!" She cupped her hand over her eyes and peered into the glare of the sun. No answer. No sign of the boy. Panic seized her throat and she could barely breathe.

She raced down the porch steps, stood in the middle

of the yard and yelled his name again. Still no answer or sign of the child.

Had he run off into the field or snuck off near the pond? She had caught him earlier trying to walk on the ice-crusted surface, not realizing the pond wasn't frozen solid. It could have been a tragedy if she hadn't followed to see what he was up to. She'd warned him to play nearby. So where was he?

She ran as fast as she could to the pond, relieved he wasn't there and the ice was still intact, but frustrated that he still hadn't answered her calls or shown himself. She gazed out over the empty field, saw no sign of the missing child and turned back toward the house.

Where had he gone? Had somebody taken him? The fleeting thought that somehow that man had snatched him right from under her nose turned her blood to ice.

Calm down, Elizabeth. You're letting your imagination get the better of you. No one snatched the child. He's simply off playing somewhere. But where?

The barn.

Of course. He had to be in the barn.

Her feet slammed against the hard, dirt-packed ground as she raced toward the building. She burst through the door and pulled up short, shock and fear freezing her in place.

"Benjamin King! What are you doing? Why didn't you answer me?" She ran across the floor and pulled him off the third rung of the ladder to the loft. "Get down from there. You can fall and get hurt."

The fright in her voice must have sounded like anger to the child because he looked tense and teary.

"Didn't you hear me call you?"

He shook his head.

"What are you doing climbing your *daed*'s ladder? You could get hurt."

"I'm trying to get my cat. The big cat grabbed it by the neck and carried it up there." He lifted his head and pointed to the loft.

Elizabeth glanced up. She saw a mother cat with two kittens poking their heads out from beneath her peering down at them.

"That's their *mamm*, Benjamin. It's probably time for her to feed them."

"They've been up there a long time. I've been sitting here watching them and waiting for her to bring my kitty back down but she hasn't."

"She'll bring your kitten down when she's ready. That doesn't mean you should climb up after it."

Benjamin sniffed and tears rolled down his cheeks. "My kitty is going to fall if I don't get her down. She's going to get hurt."

"Her *mamm* won't let that happen."

"She will. She can't always be looking. You weren't always looking or you would have seen me come into the barn and you wouldn't be so mad at me."

The corners of her mouth turned down.

Out of the mouths of babes.

"Okay. I'll go up and get the kitten. But only if you promise me you will never, ever try to climb into the loft again. I don't care if the mother cat takes her babies up there. You, young man, are not allowed to follow them. Understand?"

Benjamin nodded vigorously and dragged his hand across his tear-streaked face and dripping nose.

Elizabeth started to climb the ladder.

What are you doing? Are you crazy? You think that mamma cat is going to just let you snatch her kitten?

She stopped and decided to go back down when she looked below and saw Benjamin's grinning face staring up at her.

"You can do it, Miss Elizabeth. You're almost to the top. You can get my kitty for me."

Great! How was she going to say no to such an endearing, hopeful little face? She wasn't.

She was on the next-to-the-last rung when she heard an ominous cracking sound. She looked down at her foot and her eyes widened. A wide gap in both sides of the ladder rail told her the wood had been cut. When she had moved her hands up the rail and pulled her weight up the rung, it splintered beneath her hold and the top of the ladder split and folded in on itself. The wood hit her on the head and the speed of the collapse made it impossible for her to regain safe footing.

Elizabeth tried to grab the edge of the loft but had no time to save herself. Within seconds she felt herself hurtling backward through the air and she screamed. Pain was her last conscious thought as her body slammed into the barn floor.

Chapter Eight

Elizabeth's body floated on a cloud. Soft. Welcoming. So why did every inch of her body ache? She tried to open her eyes but they refused to obey her brain's command.

Where am I? What happened?

She heard voices. Muffled. Far away. But definitely voices.

She tried again to open her eyes. They fluttered once, twice, then finally she was able to see.

She wasn't on a cloud. She was lying on a soft mattress. A battery-powered lamp rested on the table beside her bed. She glanced around the room. This was her room. Temporarily, of course. She was in the *dawdi haus*. But how did she get here and why did her muscles ache?

Then she remembered.

Everything.

She sprang upright and then moaned and grabbed her forehead as pain shot through her temple.

A light tap and then the door opened.

"*Gut.* You're awake." Thomas stepped into the room with her *mamm* and Benjamin in tow.

Benjamin ran to her side, his little hand patting her arm. "I'm sorry, Miss Elizabeth. I didn't want you to fall. I shouldn't have asked you to go up and get my kitty."

Elizabeth gingerly turned to look at him and tried to ignore the sharp pain that seized her every time she tried to move her head. She patted his tiny hand. "It's *allrecht,* Benjamin. You didn't do anything wrong."

"Did you get hurt?" His lower lip quivered.

"*Neh,* sweetheart. I got a couple of little bumps and bruises, but I will be fine."

Her answer made him grin.

"Okay, *sohn.* I told you I would let you see her. Now you have and you can see that she is going to be *allrecht.* Go with Miss Mary and get ready for bed. I will be up shortly."

Mary touched her daughter's hand. "Are you truly okay? The doctor said you would be *allrecht* but doctors don't know everything."

"Doctor?"

"*Ja.* Thomas paid extra for Dr. Bridges to make a house call. He left a little over an hour ago."

Elizabeth tried to sit up but her mother put a hand out to stop her. "*Neh,* you rest. I will help Thomas get the *kinner* ready for bed and then I will be back. I will bring some soup. You have been asleep for several hours. You missed dinner." With a final pat on her arm, her mother hurried out of the room.

Thomas stepped out of the shadows. He handed Rachel over to Mary and then approached the side of the bed.

They stared at each other in silence. So many things to say. So difficult to find the words to say them.

"Are you really *allrecht*?" Thomas's expression held more than concern. If she didn't know better, she would have thought he was afraid.

"I'm fine." She sat up and leaned against the headboard. "My head aches a little if I move too fast." She moved her arms and her legs. "I'm achy here and there. Probably have a bruise or two. But I will be fine."

Thomas's face still looked pale and his features grim.

"Really, Thomas. Don't worry. I'm fine."

He nodded and pulled over a straight-back chair. "May I sit for a minute?"

"Of course." She reached up, straightened her *kapp* and smoothed the apron still in place over her dress. "*Denki* for calling the doctor out here. I am sure it was less frightening for my *mamm* than if I had to go into town or to the hospital."

"What happened, Elizabeth? Were you truly foolish enough to climb into the loft for a kitten?"

"Better me than Benjamin." She bristled beneath his criticism even though she knew it came from fear not anger. "The boy tried to climb the ladder to the loft after his kitten. I took him off the lower rungs and went up in his place." She groused under her breath. "I should have left the kitten up there."

Thomas scratched his beard. "I don't understand. The ladder was brand-new. It should not have had a broken rung."

Elizabeth sighed. "Someone sawed ninety percent through the sides of the top railing bordering the last few rungs. Any adult weight would snap it as they climbed. I didn't see the damage until it was too late and I didn't have time to try and break my fall because the top of the ladder collapsed in on itself."

"Sawn through? Are you sure?" Shock claimed his features. "You could have been killed."

"But I wasn't." She smiled even though it took great effort. "A little banged-up, maybe, but okay."

"Falling from that height and not getting hurt? *Gott* is *gut*."

"What can I say? The little extra weight around my hips must have padded my landing."

Thomas didn't laugh. "It isn't funny. You could have broken your back or, *Gott* forbid, snapped your neck."

"But I didn't."

"It was that man again, *ja*?"

"Probably."

"Why did he saw through the ladder? What made him think you would be climbing into the loft?"

Elizabeth sent him a steady gaze but stayed silent.

His eyes registered understanding. "The fall wasn't meant for you. It was meant for me." He squeezed her hand. "I am so sorry."

"Sorry that you didn't fall or get maimed or killed?" She smiled. "I'm not."

"Why is he doing this terrible thing? Why would he want me dead?"

Elizabeth, moved with compassion for the confusion and hurt she saw in his eyes, wanted to wrap her arms around him in comfort. But she knew that was something she shouldn't do…couldn't do. Thomas was no longer hers to comfort, depend on, or love. She'd have to be cautious and keep reminding herself of that fact. She tried to explain.

"Because he is afraid. He is angry and not thinking clearly. He is acting in desperation."

"What is he afraid of? We have not harmed him."

"But he knows we can." Elizabeth swung her legs over and sat on the edge of the bed. "He believes I know his identity and, thanks to *Mamm*, I believe he's right. We do. I believe this man is Hannah's biological father. He thinks I have the proof. Maybe the journals? He does not know who I have told so he is trying to destroy everyone in close proximity to me."

Thomas waved his hand in the air and paced the floor. "Why doesn't he just shoot us all and be done with it?"

"*Neh*, Thomas. Don't say such a thing!"

"Well? Would it be worse than this slow torture he is putting us through?"

"He wants to make it look like accidents so the police don't get involved. He does not want an investigation. He wants to make sure his secret stays secret."

"Throwing a knife at the door with a note that says he wants you dead isn't an accident in my mind."

"I told you. He's desperate...and afraid. He isn't thinking logically and that makes him even more dangerous."

"He is a coward hiding in the shadows."

Elizabeth did not see Thomas get angry often. He was angry now and she empathized with his current frustration.

"I am so sorry, Thomas."

He had a puzzled expression on his face. "Sorry? For what? You have done nothing wrong."

"I brought danger with me when I came home. I am afraid someone is going to get hurt, somebody that I love, somebody completely innocent in all of this mess. And I will be to blame."

"Nonsense. If anyone does get hurt, it will be that man's doing, Elizabeth, not yours." He stopped pacing and stood squarely in the middle of the room. His stature erect, his shoulders back, as if bracing for an attack, his determination was evident in every muscle. *"Ich verschreck net graad."*

"I don't scare easily, either." She parroted him in English instead of repeating his Amish words. "But I am not foolish enough to ignore the danger we're in."

"Neither am I," Thomas said. "It is up to all of us to do what we must do to make sure that nothing happens to harm anyone. And we will."

A glimmer of hope fluttered in her chest. "Did you speak with the bishop?"

"Ja. He is coming here first thing in the morning. He wants to go with us to speak with the sheriff."

"Then he agrees it is the right thing to do?"

Thomas nodded. "When I showed him the note and the knife, he knew we had no choice. We must do everything we can as a community to keep you safe and try to stop this man."

"Does he know what happened here today?"

"Neh. When we tell him in the morning, he will be more determined than ever to stop this man."

Mary appeared in the open doorway with a tray of hot soup and tea.

"Gut," she said, not at all apologetic for listening in on their conversation. "I told you the bishop would do the right thing, Elizabeth. Now *kumm.* Have something to eat before it gets cold." She glanced at Thomas.

"The *kinner* are in their beds and waiting for you to say *gut necht*."

"*Denki*, Mary. I will go to them now." He paused in the doorway and glanced back at Elizabeth. "It is *gut* that you came back to us. Do not ever question it. Get some rest. We will talk again in the morning."

She watched him leave. Her *mamm* gestured for Elizabeth to join her in the kitchen. She reached the kitchen just as she heard the sound of the front door closing.

Thomas had told her the bishop and the rest of the community wanted her to stay and would help to keep her safe. No wonder she considered this place her home and these people her family. Even Thomas wanted her to stay despite the pain she had caused him years ago. He'd made that evident by doing everything in his power to keep her safe. Would it be selfish of her to stay and possibly bring more harm to their community? Or would it be selfish to leave, depending only on her own wits and discounting the feelings of everyone who had ever cared for her?

She stared at the closed door.

Despite the problems and danger, everyone in the community seemed to want her to stay.

Even Thomas.

And her heart filled with hope.

Thomas stepped quietly into Rachel's room and crossed to her bed. He stared down at his sleeping daughter, shining the light from the portable lamp he carried across her form. She was lying on her back, her right arm carelessly slung over her head, her long lashes curled at the edges, her cheeks blushing a soft rosy hue against the tender softness of her cheeks, her lips puckered as she sucked on an imaginary pacifier in her dreams. Lost in sleep, she looked so much like her mother.

A pang of grief seized him.

Two years since he'd been able to sit with Margaret in the quiet of the evening and share the details of his day, enjoy the warmth of her home cooking, smell the lemon freshness of her hair and feel her petite form curled in his arms in bed at night.

Two years.

Sometimes it seemed as if it had been only yesterday. Sometimes it seemed like another life, a thousand years ago.

Rachel would never know her mother's love. But she would know her mother. He would speak of her often and keep her alive in the child's mind.

Thomas gently pressed his lips against his sleeping daughter's forehead and quietly left the room.

He wasn't surprised to see light shining beneath Benjamin's door. He pushed the door ajar. The battery-powered lamp on the table beside his bed lit the room. A huge tented mound of blankets lit from the inside by flashlight let him know instantly that his *sohn* was not asleep, but on some incredible imaginary adventure beneath the tentlike structure.

Where did this child get his never-ending energy? Not from him, he thought, as he placed a hand over the yawn that claimed him.

"Benjamin, *kumm*. It is time to sleep."

Thomas lifted the edge of the covers and was momentarily taken aback. Benjamin had used a feather duster braced against a block of wood from the fireplace to brace the blankets up as a tent. The child sat cross-legged and crouched over, the flashlight he held shining its beam upward on his chin and highlighting his small freckled face in the cloaked darkness of the blankets.

Thomas couldn't help but laugh. What was an Amish man to do with so much creativity? How was he to direct his son to use *Gott*'s gifts in a more practical way? He scratched his chin beneath his beard. Maybe that wasn't his job. Maybe his job was to encourage his boy to follow *Gott*'s direction in his life no matter where that path might lead. At one time, Amish people never wore bright colors. It changed over the years. Maybe his Benjamin would bring more change—good, creative change—to his people. *Gott* created this wonderful, intriguing, energetic boy. Thomas could hardly wait to see what *Gott* had planned for his *sohn*'s life.

"Look, *Daed*." Benjamin grinned at his father. "There is a great storm coming. A tornado with darkness and winds. I have built a safe place inside this tent for the animals." Benjamin held up the hand-carved cow and horses that Thomas had crafted for the boy last Christmas.

He smiled and his heart seized. He loved this little boy so much. He had lost Margaret, but *Gott* had blessed him with two beautiful, unique *kinner*. His gratitude knew no bounds.

"Let's put the animals to sleep." Thomas took the wooden toys from his hands. "And it is past time for you to go to sleep, too. Have you said your prayers?"

Benjamin nodded. "Miss Mary and I prayed together."

"Gut." He removed the duster and wood from beneath the blankets and again smiled at the child's creativity.

"We prayed for *Grossmammi* Rebecca and *Grossdaedi* Isaac," Benjamin said as he crawled to the top of his bed and flopped his head down on his pillow. "And for *Grossmammi* and *Grossdaedi* in Florida. And for you and Rachel. And I even prayed for Miss Mary and Miss Elizabeth."

"I am sure *Gott* was happy to hear from you tonight."

"I even asked *Gott* to say *gut necht* to *mamm* and tell her I love her and I miss her."

Thomas paused, a bittersweet pang stealing his breath. "You are a *gut sohn*. Now close your eyes and get some sleep." He ran his hand across Benjamin's silky hair and tucked the blanket around his shoulders.

He doused the lights and stepped out of the room.

He entered his bedroom, crossed to the small chest at the end of the bed, sat down and pulled off his boots. He ran his hand across the wood. He'd made this chest as a wedding gift for Margaret to keep her quilts in after they had married.

He slid open a drawer to remove fresh clothes for tomorrow and his hand fell upon a crisp, white prayer *kapp*. He pulled it out and sat back down on the chest.

This is Margaret's kapp. I kept it for Rachel so she would have something of her mother, so I could hold it in my hands and show it to her when I talk to her about what a wunderbaar *woman her mother was.*

He twisted the fabric in his hands. The edges of his mouth turned down.

What is wrong with me tonight? Why am I feeling more nostalgic than normal? What is it that bothers me?

Gently, he folded the fabric.

Elizabeth. That is why.

He placed the *kapp* back into the corner of the top drawer.

My mind wanders to another woman and I feel guilty and afraid I will forget my Margaret.

His eyes burned.

Please, Margaret. Don't be upset with me. I cannot help it. You and I spoke many times about Elizabeth. Neither of us ever believed she'd be back home again. But she is. And my heart remembers days past no matter how much my mind cautions against it.

Thomas put on fresh long johns and climbed beneath the covers. He placed his hand on the empty pillowcase beside him.

I will not forget you, Margaret. And I will continue to speak often and lovingly of you to our kinner.

He rolled onto his back and spoke aloud in the darkness.

"I think you would have liked her, Margaret. You are very different women, but deep down your hearts are the same." He placed his arm across his forehead and whispered his deepest fears. "But I am frightened. Bad things are happening. Things I cannot control. What if I cannot keep her safe? What if she knows it and decides to run away again? My heart broke when I lost you. I am afraid of what will happen to the last shards of my heart if Elizabeth runs and I lose her again."

He stared into the darkness for long patches of time. Then he began to pray.

Chapter Nine

❧

Thomas coughed. Restlessly he rolled over in bed. His mind tried to wake him while his tired body wanted only to burrow farther beneath the covers. It couldn't possibly be time to get up. Hadn't he just fallen asleep?

He opened his eyes and turned his head toward the window.

Pitch-black.

Exactly what he'd expect in the middle of the night. He glanced at his wind-up clock. Three thirty.

He was right. It wasn't time to get up yet.

So what was it that disturbed him?

A dream must have pulled him from his slumber. He plumped his pillow, settled into a comfortable position on his side and gave himself permission to return to sleep.

Until he coughed again.

He sat up in bed.

His chest tightened and his eyes burned. He grabbed a flashlight he kept in the drawer beside his bed and aimed the light toward the bedroom door.

Smoke!

A light gray mist—a toxic mist—seeped under the door and floated into the air.

Thomas jumped out of the bed. Grabbing his shirt and pants from the peg beside the bedroom door, he dressed faster than he knew possible and rushed into the hall. The thicker, denser smoke in the hallway knocked his heart rate up a notch. He ran with as much speed as he could muster to Benjamin's room.

"Get up, *sohn*. We must go. Now!" He lifted the boy from the bed, clasping the confused and half-asleep child in his arms, and raced for his daughter's room.

Rachel was already awake. She was standing on the bed, rubbing her eyes and crying.

He snatched her up.

"Hold fast to my neck. We must hurry and get out of here." With a child in each arm he bolted toward the stairs. The closer he got to the stairwell, the thicker the smoke. A blast of heat met him at the top of the stairs, but thankfully, he did not see any fire. As he moved cautiously but quickly down the stairs into the heavier smoke, the three of them struggled with spasms of coughing.

Benjamin started to cry.

"Shhh, little ones. It's going to be *allrecht*. We're going to be outside in a minute. Bury your faces in my shirt so you don't smell the smoke."

Both children did as he instructed.

A sense of relief washed over him when he made it to the front door. Before he could lower Benjamin to the floor so he could free his hand to clasp the door-knob, it flew open.

"Oh, thank You, *Gott*." Elizabeth reached over the

threshold and pulled Rachel from his arms. "Hurry. We have to get the *kinner* outside."

Thomas, both arms clasping Benjamin against his chest, ran out the door behind her.

Thomas cleared the porch and was about fifty feet from the house before he dared to stop. He placed Benjamin down and stood beside Elizabeth and Rachel.

He looked back. Thick black smoke plumed to the heavens. The ominous whooshing and crackling of the bright orange flames filled the night air and the intense heat seared his face despite the distance from the blaze. The acrid smell scorched his throat and burned his eyes. One quick glance at the others and he saw the heat affected them, too, noting their red cheeks from the heat and tears streaming down their faces.

Thomas quickly examined both his children to make sure they were unharmed. Only then did he take a deep, cleansing breath to try and clear his smoke-filled lungs.

"What—what happened?" he asked, choking on his words.

He looked again at the burning *dawdi haus*.

"Mary? Where is Mary?" A sense of panic laced his words. He moved to run toward the house and Elizabeth grabbed his arm.

"She's out. She's safe."

"Are you sure you and your *mamm* are unharmed?" His eyes searched Elizabeth from head to toe for any injury and found none. "How did this happen? Did the wind knock over a lantern?"

Before Elizabeth could reply they heard a repetitive, sharp clanging sound pierce the stillness of the night air. Thomas glanced over at the far end of his porch and saw Mary ringing the triangle over and over again, calling the community for help.

Shortly after Mary had stopped ringing the triangle, the nearest neighbors began to arrive quickly followed by others.

The closest ones ran through the icy fields. Others arrived in buggies. They came over the hills in droves, sleep long gone from their minds.

Thomas knew the fire department wouldn't be far behind. Many of his Amish neighbors were volunteer firemen for the Sunny Creek unit. But someone had to take charge and organize the people who were here now. Rachel was cradled safely in Elizabeth's arms. Thomas quickly kneeled before his crying boy.

"I know this is a scary thing, Benjamin, but try not to be afraid. No one is hurt. *Gott* is protecting us." He glanced up at Elizabeth and then back to his son. "I need you to stay here with Miss Elizabeth while I go and help the other adults put out the fire." He grabbed his son's shoulders and made eye contact. "Do you understand? I mean it. You must not move from this spot unless Miss Elizabeth tells you to. This is not a time for you to wander away."

The boy nodded.

Thomas stood up. "I've got to get Mary off of that porch. She's too close to the fire."

"Look," Elizabeth pointed in that direction. "She's coming this way now."

Assured that all his loved ones were safe, he placed Benjamin's hand in Elizabeth's. "I have to go. Please take care of my *kinner.*"

"I will, Thomas. Be safe."

He turned and ran toward the crowd, which had already formed a water line from the trough by the horse corral. They were handing buckets of water as quickly as possible from one man to another in an attempt to put out the flames.

Isaac suddenly appeared out of the darkness. "*Mein Gott*, what has happened? Is everyone safe?"

His clothes unkempt and hair disheveled, he wore a sleepy look of disbelief on his face. Rebecca ran up right behind him.

"Where are the children?" she asked.

Thomas pointed toward Elizabeth and Mary. Rebecca ran in their direction.

Thomas slapped Isaac on the shoulder. "*Kumm* with me. I've got two hoses in the barn." Within minutes, both men were dousing the flames with streams of water but one look at the destruction and Thomas knew it was a losing battle. The *dawdi haus* was lost. The most important thing now was to keep the flames from reaching the main house. Already Thomas could see a couple of the panels of siding on his front porch melted and scorched.

Sirens wailed in the distance, growing louder by the second. Within minutes red and blue strobe lights flashed across the yard and flitted across the still standing porch of the main house. Help had arrived. It was one of the most welcome sights Thomas could remember seeing in a long time.

Elizabeth took her first deep relaxing breaths. The firemen extinguished the flames. Only misty white smoke hovering above smoldering ashes remained. She adjusted her back against the tree she'd been leaning on in an attempt to get more comfortable. Thankfully, the flames hadn't claimed the main house. She hoped she'd be able to move the children out of the cold and into the warmth of the house soon.

"Do you want me to take her?" Rebecca whispered, gesturing toward Rachel, who was asleep in Elizabeth's arms. "You haven't had a break for hours. You must be exhausted."

Elizabeth glanced down at Benjamin, his head lying on her thigh while he slept. She adjusted Rachel's sleeping body in her arms and smiled. She was falling in love with these children and at this moment couldn't think of anyplace else she wanted them to be.

"No thank you, Rebecca. They're fine. I don't want to wake them."

Rebecca smiled, a knowing look in her eyes. "If you change your mind, I will be sitting on what's left of the porch with Mary. She won't move. She insists on sitting in one of the rocking chairs, and even though I offered to move it off the porch and over closer to you, she still insists on staying on the porch. What does she think? If she sits there, the fire won't touch the house?"

Elizabeth chuckled. "It is one of her favorite things to do, rock on a porch and watch the world pass by. Now that the firemen have contained the blaze, it probably makes her feel safe to sit there, like some things are still normal in this crazy world."

Rebecca placed a comforting pat on her shoulder. "I am sure you are right." She leaned over and placed a mug of hot tea on the ground beside her.

"Denki."

"I'll go and keep her company. I could use a little 'normal' right now, myself."

She watched the woman cross the yard and join her mother on the porch.

The scent of cinnamon teased her nostrils and was a welcome change to the acrid smell of burned wood. Elizabeth glanced down at the hot mug of tea. Now if she could only figure out a way to pick it up without waking Rachel.

"Let me help."

Thomas.

What a welcome sight! She'd tried to keep track of him during the fire, but in the darkness with so many men fighting the flames she hadn't been able to single him out of the crowd. Now he stood near her feet, the hint of dawn lighting the sky behind him.

Her eyes took a quick inventory for any burns or injuries.

He appeared unhurt.

Denki, Gott.

Black soot and sweat covered him from top to toe. He wore weariness and concern in every crease in his face, but stood before her confident and strong. A far cry from the tall, lanky young man she had left seven years ago. Farming, hard physical labor and a few years had honed his muscles and finished his transition from boy to man.

Dirty. Unkempt. Tired. And she'd never found him more attractive.

Thomas crouched down beside her and lifted his sleeping daughter from her arms.

"Put her here," Elizabeth whispered and scooted to make room on the quilts she had thrown on the cold ground while trying not to disturb Benjamin. She adjusted the other quilts she had placed over the three of them to keep them warm and lifted an edge for Thomas.

He settled on the ground beside her and covered his daughter's back with the excess blanket to keep her warm.

"I'm sorry, Thomas."

"Again, you apologize. For what?"

She gestured to the still smoking ashes of what had once been part of his home. "You've lost everything."

"Not everything. The people I love are unharmed. The main house is untouched. We are fortunate my parents are in Sarasota for the winter. You and Mary can move into their rooms on the main floor. I will have a new *dawdi haus* built before they return and all will be well." He smiled at her, his teeth appearing extra white against the black soot smeared on his skin. "You are the one who lost everything. I'm sorry, Elizabeth. There was no way to recover any of your belongings."

"That's all they were, Thomas. Belongings. Nothing that can't be replaced." She smiled back at him. "Here. You look like you need this more than I do." She picked up the mug and handed it to him.

He lifted the cup to his lips, took a long, healthy swallow and handed it back.

"*Denki.* I needed that. My throat is dry from breathing in all that smoke."

He leaned his head back against the tree trunk and closed his eyes.

As seconds of silence became minutes, Elizabeth thought he had fallen asleep until he spoke.

"The fire wasn't caused by an overturned lantern, was it?" He still didn't open his eyes or move.

"No."

"When is this going to stop?" The question seemed more rhetorical than one that demanded an answer. More a whisper of pain and troubled thoughts.

"When we do what we have to do to stop this man. *Ja?*"

Both Elizabeth and Thomas turned their heads to see the speaker. Bishop Schwartz, his face as sooty as Thomas's, his features as drawn and tired, stared down at them.

"Bishop Schwartz, I didn't see you in the chaos and confusion." Thomas stood, stretched out a hand and shook the elderly man's in gratitude. "*Denki* for coming."

"Where else would I be? You know we band together and help our own, Thomas."

"*Ja.* 'Tis true."

"And it is time now for the community to band together and get rid of the weed that has infiltrated our lives before any more damage occurs."

"I wanted to speak with you, Bishop." Elizabeth gently eased Benjamin's head off of her leg and stood up, too. "I was going to ask Thomas to bring me over later today."

"Speak, child."

"Yesterday afternoon, in the barn..."

"*Ja, ja*, I know. The sawn-through ladder. I was told and I am grateful you were not seriously injured."

"Then tonight...the fire..." She could sense Thomas tense beside her, almost as if he knew what she was about to say. The bishop shot her a quizzical look but did not interrupt.

"I don't want anyone hurt."

"Of course not, child. No one wants anyone hurt."

"But being here is dangerous for everyone. This man is intent on destroying me and everyone I come in contact with. I could not bear it if my being here causes someone to get injured or perhaps lose their life." She gestured toward the smoldering ashes of the *dawdi haus*. "I have already caused Thomas the loss of a large part of his home."

"What are you trying to say, Elizabeth?" the bishop asked.

"I wonder if it is time for me to leave—past time—before anything more happens."

She wrapped her arms tightly around her trembling body, unsure whether her shuddering was from the cold or from anticipation of his answer.

The bishop arched an eyebrow. "Did you set the fire?"

"Neh."

"Do you believe you are *Gott* or that you have the power to control another's actions?"

Elizabeth's cheeks flamed and she lowered her eyes. "Of course not."

"This is the second time I have heard this question from you and I do not want to hear it again." He spoke sternly but his tone held compassion as well. "What Thomas told you before is correct. You cannot solve problems by running away from them. They only follow you and cause more problems." He stepped closer and placed a comforting hand on her shoulder.

"*Gott* will help us deal with this man. I have prayed for His guidance. I suggest you do the same. I do not believe when He answers your prayers that He will tell you to leave your family and community now that you have found your way home. Understand?"

Elizabeth nodded.

"*Gut*. Now I am going home to clean up, change my clothing and take a brief rest. I am not as young as I used to be." He chuckled. "Although I held my own with the younger men fighting that fire." He gestured over his shoulder. "I am sure I will feel it in my bones today. But that will be a *gut* thing. A little ache in my bones will remind me that I am still alive and useful."

He smiled at Elizabeth. "I will return later this morning to pick you up. It is time we speak to the sheriff together. He will do what he needs to do and I will do what I need to do. When we return, I will call the men to a community meeting. We will form a plan and develop a schedule so our community is protected and everyone is kept as safe as possible while the *Englisch* law brings this man to justice."

"*Gut* to hear, Bishop," Thomas said.

The bishop nodded toward both of them and left.

Thomas looked at her and shook his head. "Will there ever be a time, Elizabeth, when you will stop believing that running away is the answer?"

Her eyes widened and she couldn't contain the anger and frustration in her voice. "Do you think it would be easy to leave? You act like running away is a selfish thing."

"Isn't it?"

"No!" She railed at him. "Leaving is hard. Sometimes it is the hardest thing you ever do in your entire life, but you do it. Not for yourself. But for the good of others."

"And you know what is best for others?" He threw his hands up in the air in frustration. "It is not your place to play *Gott*, Elizabeth. What gives you the right to make people's decisions for them? *Neh*, it is not your right." He stared her down. "It was never your right."

His jaw tightened and his eyes flashed his pain.

Her *mamm* and Rebecca had approached when they saw the bishop walk over to speak to them. Now they stood quietly to the side, watching. The discomfort in their body language and the way they both shot glances everywhere but at her told Elizabeth that they'd overheard their argument.

Mary spoke first. "We will take the children inside now. It is cold out here and it is time they get some warm food in their bellies."

Rebecca was already lifting Rachel into her arms.

"Take your time. Finish your conversation," Mary said. "Rebecca and I will have a hot breakfast waiting for both of you when you come inside."

After they left with the children, Elizabeth glanced over at Thomas.

Now is the time to tell him. Make him understand why you hurt him so much.

She wanted to. The words rested on the tip of her tongue. But she couldn't. Not yet. Maybe not ever. After all these years, what would it change?

Thomas looked like he was also struggling to find words that might ease the tension between them. Finally, he spoke.

"We are fortunate it is *Gott*'s will that the main house remains standing. We will all have a roof over our heads, warmth against the cold, food to eat. *Gott* is good."

His acceptance of the situation, his laid-back attitude, made her snap.

"Is that what you think, Thomas? This was *Gott*'s

will? And that's enough for you? No anger. No fear. No remorse. And, of course, let's not even consider that nasty word *vengeance*. After all, the Amish are perfect people in a perfect world. They never blame anyone for anything. They just plop it in *Gott*'s hands and go on with everyday business. Right?"

She practically screamed the words at him and then covered her mouth with her hands. She couldn't believe what she'd said. It was fear talking. And anger. Frustration. Maybe a little bit of hopelessness. Definitely helplessness. But she, too, was Amish. She didn't believe those horrible words that poured out of her mouth, did she? Had she been gone from the Amish so long that her heart had hardened and her faith had disappeared?

Thomas stared at her long and hard. When he spoke, weariness and maybe even a little resignation laced his words.

"Do you think being Amish makes me, what—less than human? That I have no feelings? I have feelings, Elizabeth. Too many feelings sometimes." His eyes flashed with anger.

"I didn't mean…"

"Neh?" He paced back and forth and then pulled to an abrupt stop in front of her. He slapped a hand against his chest, practically spitting his words out. "I *feel*, Elizabeth. The grief I felt—deep, soul-wrenching grief—when I lost my Margaret brought me to my knees too many nights to count." He stomped his foot and pointed his arm toward the horizon. "And that evil man who did this? I am not ashamed to say I am angry— red-hot, boiling-in-my-very-soul angry. Do you think it is easy for me to try to keep everyone I care about,

everyone who claims my heart, free from the clutches of this evil man?"

He took several deep breaths and struggled to control himself. When he turned to look at her, she could see something had changed. When he spoke again, his tone of voice had softened. "And I've known sorrow, Elizabeth—dull, aching pain that I have felt for years. It started the day you left me."

"Thomas." Her heart seized as she witnessed the raw emotions flashing across his face. She wanted to reach out to comfort him but forced herself to remain still.

"How do you see me?" His eyes searched hers. "I am *human*, Elizabeth, as well as Amish. I hurt and get angry and suffer and, *ja*, sometimes I feel afraid and unsure of myself."

He clasped her hands in his.

"But I have also known great joy. The day I held Benjamin in my arms for the first time and later, Rachel, I thought *Gott* had blessed me with a little piece of heaven." He smiled into her eyes. "I had a *wunderbaar* life with a good, solid, kind, loving woman. I have experienced laughter, and happiness…and love. So far it has been a *gut* life. Ups and downs, but *gut*."

His eyes darkened with an emotion that frightened yet exhilarated her at the same time. He still had feelings for her. Deep feelings. She couldn't pretend anymore that they were merely friends.

"Sometimes it is difficult for me to say 'It is *Gott*'s will' and mean it." He chuckled mirthlessly. "Many times when I am frustrated and, *ja*, maybe even mad at Him, I have told *Gott* that we need to have a long talk when we meet in person so He can explain why He allowed my life to unfold the way it did." He softly traced the pad of his thumb down her cheek. "But then some-times He surprises me. He answers my prayers before I even pray them."

He pulled her close.

"I have lived long enough to look back on my life and see how each thing that happened, *gut* or bad, led to another. How I wouldn't have turned down one path if *Gott* hadn't allowed an obstacle to block another."

He smiled down on her.

"So, *ja*, I trust *Gott*, Elizabeth. With everything."

He pressed his lips against her forehead for several heartbeats, then stepped back.

"*Gott* is waiting for you to trust Him, too, *lieb*. Think about it. Better still, pray about it."

He released her and walked toward the house.

Chapter Ten

The autumn sun bathed her cheeks in warmth despite the chill in the air. Elizabeth searched the sky. Gray clouds looming on the horizon warned of the first snowstorm of the season quickly approaching. She pulled her shawl tightly around her shoulders.

"I thought I might find you out here." Her mother approached, pulling her own shawl tighter as she came and stood beside her on the porch.

"I can't believe the *dawdi haus* is gone." Elizabeth glanced over at the blackened pile of ashes. "There is nothing left, *Mamm*. Thomas built the *dawdi haus* and now he's lost everything in it, furniture, house goods, everything."

"*Neh*, not everything. What matters to his heart is still here, alive and well. People matter to Thomas. *Kinner*. Family. Friends. Things can be replaced and rebuilt, *ja*?" She smiled and wrapped an arm around her daughter's waist. "How did your conversation go with Thomas after we left? Did you finally tell him the truth about why you left?"

"No." She released a deep sigh. "I wanted to. I almost did."

"What stopped you?"

"What good would it do? It happened seven years ago. How can it possibly matter now?"

"It matters to Thomas."

"Why?"

"Because it is an open wound that has not been able to heal. He has never understood. He has blamed himself for you leaving, but he's not even sure what he blames himself for." Mary tilted Elizabeth's chin with her index finger. "You must tell him, child. He has a right to know."

"It will make me look like I am making excuses or asking his forgiveness."

"Aren't you?"

"Yes." She smiled at her mother. "And no."

A perplexed expression flashed across Mary's face.

"Yes, of course, I wish his forgiveness," Elizabeth said. "I caused him so much pain and my leaving was supposed to do just the opposite. But I am not going to use my medical condition as an excuse or to play on his sympathies. If I had it to do over again, I would make the same choice."

Mary tilted her head and her mouth fell open. "You would?"

Elizabeth laughed. "After I told Thomas everything, of course. That part I would do differently. I wouldn't have made him wonder all these years. I would have made sure he understood my choice."

Mary nodded. "*Gut.* It is nice to know living in an *Englisch* world for so many years has not hardened your heart so much that you cannot see the mistakes you have made. We both have made mistakes. It is time now to tell the truth. No more secrets."

"No more secrets."

Mary hugged her daughter.

"Where is Thomas?" Elizabeth glanced over Mary's shoulder toward the house and then looked out toward the barn.

Mary smiled. "He knew he was not the only one who lost everything in the fire. So he left to try and fix it."

"What do you mean?"

"Everything you owned in this world was in your suitcases inside the *dawdi haus*. You have nothing left but the clothes on your back. So I gave him permission to go back to my house and bring the rest of my clothing here. I am sure we can find some clothes we can fix to fit you. I even asked him to bring a few extra *kapps* and my comb and brush set."

Elizabeth's eyes widened and her heart raced. "Oh, no! You didn't let him go. That's exactly what this man will expect. He'll know we lost everything. He'll expect us to go back to the house. He'll be watching." She started to move toward the barn. "I have to stop Thomas. He's in danger."

Mary clutched her daughter's arm and held her in place. "Thomas is a grown man. A smart man. You think he didn't think of these things, too?"

"And he still went?"

"Elizabeth, you have been gone for many years. Thomas is not the young boy you left behind. He is a strong, intelligent, hard-working, kind man. I trust him to take care of himself—and to take care of us." She looked deeply into Elizabeth's eyes. "Do you?"

Elizabeth hesitated, her mother's words hitting home.

She suddenly realized she was still trying to control other people's lives. When was she going to learn that *Gott* was in charge? The only thing she could control was how she reacts to life's situations. And right now she wasn't doing a very good job.

Please, Lord, forgive me. Help me to be better. Help me to mature into the woman You have planned for me to be.

"Look." Mary gestured to the gravel lane leading to the house. "Maybe that is Thomas now."

They watched the buggy approach. As it drew nearer, both women could see Bishop Schwartz holding the reins. He circled wide and pulled to a stop with the buggy facing down the lane. Then he stepped down and fastened the reins to the rail in front of the porch.

"Is this a *gut* time to go see the sheriff? I would like to get into town and back as quickly as possible. It looks like we will soon be having snow."

All eyes searched the sky. The dark clouds on the horizon had moved closer and now hung heavily overhead, giving the sky the ominous appearance of an impending storm.

"*Kumm* inside for a few minutes and warm up, Bishop," Mary said. "I will fix you a hot cup of coffee before you go and pack another in a thermos for your trip home."

The bishop grinned. "I don't suppose it would be polite to refuse just one cup. And cookies, *ja*? You have fresh-baked cookies?"

Elizabeth laughed. "We have two different kinds to choose from. How about one of each?"

The bishop rubbed his hands together. "Lead the way. Hopefully, the snow will wait a little longer."

* * *

"When were you attacked?" the sheriff asked. He scribbled down her name, the current date and the rest Elizabeth couldn't quite make out from the angle where she was seated.

"Three days ago."

"And you've waited until now to come in?" The sheriff frowned at the bishop. "I know you folks like to handle things amongst yourselves. But don't you think this is a little bit out of your league? This isn't tipping cows or slinging eggs at houses."

"*Ja*, that is why we are here," the bishop replied.

The sheriff turned his attention to Elizabeth. He leaned back and rocked in his desk chair. "You say you got a good look at this man's face?"

"Too good a look. His hands were around my throat at the time and his face was only inches away." Elizabeth, her hands folded in her lap, sat across from the sheriff, Bishop Schwartz seated by her side.

The bishop patted Elizabeth's hand. "She has much to tell you, sheriff. It is a tale of rape. Murder. Attempted murder. Knives. Threatening notes. Burning a house to the ground."

The sheriff's mouth fell open and he stared at them in disbelief. "Nothing happens in Sunny Creek. Certainly nothing like this. And you say all of this has happened in the past three days?"

"Almost all of it," the bishop said. "Some of it may be the reason the rest has been happening." He waved at the paper beneath the sheriff's hands. "Maybe you should pay close attention and listen, sir, before you start to write. I wouldn't want you to miss anything. And I am sure you will have many questions."

The sheriff laid down his pen. He reached into his top drawer, withdrew a small tape recorder and hit the record button. "Today is Thursday, November first, and we are in my office...er, the sheriff's office in Sunny Creek, Pennsylvania, Lancaster County. This is Sheriff Tyler speaking. I am in the room with Elizabeth Lapp and Bishop Schwartz. I am about to record their statements." He pushed the recorder into the center of the desk. "State your consent to be recorded. Then whenever you're ready, Elizabeth, you can begin telling me your story."

Both Elizabeth and the bishop stated their consent.

"What brought you into my office this morning?" The sheriff leaned back in his chair. The expression on his face almost made her smile. He looked like he was hanging on to her every word. He was right. Things didn't happen in Sunny Creek. Until now.

An hour and half later the sheriff hung up his phone after speaking with the Philadelphia police and swiveled back to face them. He slid the completed recording back into the top drawer of his desk. "I am amazed at this story, Miss Lapp. I am sincerely sorry you have been going through all this." He nodded in the bishop's direction. "And I am grateful you counseled her to bring the matter to me. This is a dangerous situation and definitely not one you should be trying to handle on your own."

"Ja." The bishop acknowledged his words. "It is your job to find this man and bring him to justice. It is our job as a community to stay informed and to be vigilant and help keep one another safe."

"I understand." The sheriff wore a worried look on his face. "And the extra help from the community regarding keeping an eye out and keeping each other safe will be greatly appreciated. As you know, I only have a four-man police force plus myself. Although I will order more frequent patrols of your farms, to be honest it will be a great help to all of us if your community is made aware of the dangers and helps to monitor the area, as well."

The sheriff shifted in his chair and made direct eye contact with the bishop. "The one thing I must insist on, however, is that if you do see something or someone out of the ordinary, that you make it to a phone shanty and call it in to me. This man is dangerous and this situation is in my wheelhouse. Understand?"

Both of them nodded.

The sheriff slid a business card with his office number, cell-phone number and home number written across the back to the bishop, and then gave a second one to Elizabeth.

"I cannot stress enough the importance of avoiding contact with this man if you see him. I don't want anyone hurt or killed."

"We have no desire to confront or try to capture this criminal, Sheriff," the bishop assured him. "If we see him, we will call you. Our desire is simply to keep the members of our community informed and safe while you do your job."

"Good. Then we are in agreement." The sheriff turned his attention to Elizabeth. "The Philadelphia police are sending one of their detectives and a police sketch artist out here first thing tomorrow morning."

Elizabeth nodded. "Thank you, Sheriff."

"They weren't happy that you took off without telling them you witnessed Hannah's murder, but they sure are happy you've surfaced now. They've hit a brick wall. It was turning into a cold case. This is going to break everything wide open."

"I hope so." Elizabeth stood and the bishop joined her. "The sooner this man is behind bars, the better it will be for everyone."

"I've been sheriff of Sunny Creek for the past five years and nothing like this has ever happened here. I'm simply blown away. Let's work together as a community. I assure you we'll catch this guy. And I must confess I won't mind if it's another twenty years before I see anything like this come to our doors again." The sheriff stood and shook both their hands. "Thank you for coming in. You're doing the right thing."

"You're welcome, Sheriff," Elizabeth said. "And I'm sorry I didn't come in sooner."

"Well, you're here now and that's what counts." He tucked his thumbs into his belt. "He's got to be hiding out in someone's barn or sleeping in a field to be able to keep such a close eye on you. The last three nights have been mighty cold. I bet this guy is miserable and in a big hurry to get out of here. Snow is forecast for today. That should flush him out and when it does we'll be ready for him."

"I hope so, Sheriff. He's been pretty clever so far," Elizabeth said.

"No. No one has been looking for him. Things are about to change. Bishop Schwartz is going to put the Amish community on alert. Our local police force is going to be patrolling your farms. And help is on the way from Philadelphia. I even asked for a little extra man power besides the detective and the police sketch artist. I'd say time is no longer on this guy's side."

"Maybe he will decide to leave on his own." Even the bishop didn't look like he believed his own words.

"Or he will become more desperate, making him even more dangerous." Elizabeth shot a worried look between the two men.

"Try not to worry," the sheriff said. "Stay indoors for the rest of today if you can. Keep vigilant. And I'll see you here in my office at nine o'clock tomorrow morning. You can give your description to the police artist. We'll get it out to the media as soon as possible." He came around the desk to escort them to the door. "I don't think it will be much longer before we have this man in custody."

A sudden gust of wind blew the door open with a bang and a tall man, shaking snow from his hat, loomed on the threshold.

Instinctively the sheriff's hand flew to his gun.

"No! Relax, Sheriff. He's with me." Elizabeth laughed. "Hello, Thomas. What took you so long?"

After a quick summary of what he had missed and what the current plans would be, Thomas held open the door of the sheriff's office and accompanied Bishop Schwartz and Elizabeth outside.

"*Denki*, Thomas, for coming," the bishop said. "This snow doesn't look like it plans on stopping anytime soon."

Thomas glanced at the sky and turned up the collar of his coat.

That's an understatement if I ever heard one!

This first snow of the season looked more like a full-blown blizzard rather than a storm. The snow was blowing sideways, making visibility poor, and the cold temperature was seeping straight into his bones. If this was any indication, it was going to be a long, hard winter.

"We better get home soon. The roads are already covered with snow. The horses will find it difficult to pull a buggy through this mess if we don't get a move on."

No sooner had he spoken than a strong gust of wind blew the bishop's hat from his head and Thomas scurried to retrieve it.

"*Denki*, again." The bishop placed the hat back on. "Looks like we have accumulated two inches already. I admit I am anxious to get home."

"I saw no reason for you to have to make a third trip to my farm in one day. You have helped enough. Go home, Bishop. I will see that Elizabeth gets home safely."

The bishop climbed into his buggy. "I will stop by Levi's place and ask him to come over this evening to keep watch. He is young and sturdy. This storm won't deter him. I'll wait until after tomorrow's meeting with the police before I call a formal men's meeting and set up a schedule for the rest of us to help keep watch. I believe even this monster will seek shelter in this storm."

After watching the elderly man click the reins and pull out in the direction of his home, Thomas rechecked that the windshields on his buggy were properly fastened, then stepped up and slid onto the bench beside Elizabeth.

"I hope you will be warm enough. The wind is cold and blowing hard."

Thomas settled in. He offered a silent prayer that they would make it home safely as he often did in bad weather. He reached over and tucked a large blanket over their legs. Without further delay, he snapped the reins and pulled into the street.

"Some of the men have put propane-powered heaters in their buggies," he said as the buggy moved down Main Street. "But I am afraid to use them in such close quarters. What if a car rear-ended me?"

"I understand."

"I have looked at the heater, though. It would mount in the front, here in the middle." He pointed to a spot between them. "The tubing and propane tank would have to be in back with the *kinner*. Knowing Benjamin, that would not be safe."

"For sure." Elizabeth chuckled and adjusted the blanket. "What is this made from, Thomas? Fur does not normally weigh this much."

"I ordered it special. It is fur on both sides and has insulation within the front and back covers."

"Well, it is certainly warm." She pulled it up and covered her shoulders, too. "You don't need a heater. This is *wunderbaar*."

He grinned. He wanted her to be comfortable and had felt bad that she might be cold.

They had traveled in a companionable silence for several miles when he shot a glance her way and asked, "What's that song I heard you singing to the *kinner* earlier this morning?"

"You heard that? I was trying to lift their spirits and calm them after the fire. I hope you don't mind."

"It was a cute song. Dashing through snow or something like that?"

Elizabeth laughed. "Something like that."

"Well, this qualifies as snow and we are definitely

dashing home. Since the *kinner* are not here why don't you sing to me, Elizabeth?"

He grinned when a rosy blush colored her cheeks. She smiled coyly at him, which touched his heart. She was strong and independent, *ja*. But she was also feminine and soft and vulnerable. He liked that about her. His feelings for her were definitely not dead and gone. They'd hibernated like a bear in winter. Now that she had returned, so had his feelings, whether he wanted them to or not.

She studied him almost as if she wondered if he had been sincere when he'd asked her to sing, or if he was simply teasing her. Once she'd made up her mind, a low, pleasant hum filled the buggy and soon the words he'd heard her singing to Rachel and Benjamin followed. She had a soft, high, melodious voice. This morning he had stood in the doorway of the living room and watched his *kinner*. For once, his ever-active son sat quietly at Elizabeth's feet, playing with a wooden cow and horse while he listened to the song. His daughter, holding the plastic dog toy Elizabeth had let her keep, had sat on Elizabeth's lap. The child had barely moved and stared raptly up into her face. Apparently, she liked to listen to Elizabeth sing.

So did he.

Thomas clicked the reins and urged his mare down the street and toward the highway leading home.

Chapter Eleven

When the song ended, Elizabeth sang another. When she finished singing, they traveled in companionable silence. It was good having her home again.

After several minutes, he asked, "Now that you've seen the sheriff, do you feel better?"

Elizabeth nodded. "It's a load off my mind. After I help the police artist with the sketch of the suspect tomorrow, I can wash my hands of this whole mess. It won't be my responsibility anymore. I can relax and let the professionals handle things."

"It was never your responsibility."

She sighed heavily. "I know, Thomas. You want me to believe it's not my fault that a lunatic is trying to kill me and everyone close to me. I get it." She smiled at him. "But it sure feels like it's my fault. He did follow me here."

"*Ja.* And the snow is following me home. Is the snow my fault?"

Elizabeth laughed. "Point made, Thomas."

The snow grew heavier and visibility became difficult as dusk settled into darkness.

"I can see the highway up ahead. A few miles on it and we will be able to pull onto less traveled roads." Thomas wondered if he was reassuring her or himself.

Elizabeth remained burrowed beneath the blanket and quiet. He knew she was concerned about the fierceness of the storm, as well.

The sudden roar of an approaching car engine filled the air.

Both Thomas and Elizabeth looked ahead and then behind the buggy to locate the vehicle.

"Who would be crazy enough to drive his car at such a high speed in this weather?" The words tumbled from his mouth seconds before headlights of an approaching vehicle appeared on the dark country road at the top of the upcoming hill.

The mare, skittish already from the punishing storm, snorted and raised her head. The buggy swayed slightly from left to right, then back again.

"Whoa, girl. It's *allrecht*. Take it easy." Thomas tried to keep his voice calm and authoritative with the animal. The last thing he needed was his mare to break out of a trot and run freely toward the open highway. He pulled back slightly on the reins, trying to keep her in check.

The approaching car put on its bright lights and gunned the motor, picking up speed. Its tires spun a shower of snow into the air as it crested the hill. The vehicle, taking the bend in the road too quickly, slipped and slid in the freshly fallen snow.

"Thomas, be careful." Thomas could feel Elizabeth's tension as she moved closer to him, straightened her back, inhaled sharply and placed a hand on his knee. "Maybe we should pull over and let this idiot pass by."

Thomas didn't disagree, but where was there a safe

place to pull over? Snowdrifts were already forming on the sides of the road and he couldn't risk the buggy getting stuck.

The car's headlights blinded them as the driver lost control and careened from his lane into theirs. The driver hit the brakes but not in time. The roaring approach of the car terrified their horse. The mare slid in the snow. The buggy swayed violently. Thomas's heartbeat kicked up several notches as he fought to keep the buggy from tilting and crashing onto the side of the road.

"Easy, girl. Take it easy."

The horse threw up her head and tried to raise up on her hind legs. Her nostrils flared and her eyes widened with fear.

The buggy tilted on two wheels.

Elizabeth let out a short scream but quickly stifled it.

Thomas banged his head on the roof. Both of them slid across the seat with the out-of-control swaying of the buggy and their bodies slammed painfully into each other.

Would he be able to stop the buggy before they hit the main intersection leading into open highway? Granted, in this weather and at this time of night traffic would be at a minimum, but it would only take one car or truck to send them careening into a ditch or worse.

Elizabeth slid her arm under his, buried her face against his sleeve and held on tight.

Thomas braced his feet against the floorboards and pulled back hard on the reins. "Whoa, girl! Stop!"

But it was too late.

The terrified horse broke into a full gallop and within seconds they burst into oncoming traffic.

The sound of someone laying on a car horn blasted

so loudly Thomas thought the car was in the buggy with them. Headlights blinded them and he raised his arm to shield his eyes seconds before the car veered into the other lane, sliding and fishtailing in a deadly spin.

The signature ear-shattering blast of a semitruck's horn sounded as its driver fought for control and with expert driving skills maneuvered his rig between the buggy and the car in his lane without striking either of them.

Thomas's horse ran into a snowdrift on the side of the road. It must have felt safer in the knee-deep snow than on the road because the buggy came to an abrupt stop and the mare stayed right where she was. A quick glance showed the truck had never paused. The car had stopped for a few minutes and then had also continued on. Thomas sat for a moment in the darkness and bowed his head.

Denki, Lord. Only You could have moved that semi out of the way.

Elizabeth had never let go of his arm. Now that they were stopped and safe, he felt her lift her head from his sleeve.

"Are you *allrecht*?" he asked.

She nodded. "Are you?"

"Ja." He held up a hand and purposely let it tremble. "A little shaken maybe, but not hurt. Think this shaking will ever go away or will I have to learn a new way to feed myself?"

Elizabeth chuckled and the tension in the cab eased for a moment. Then she looked hurriedly in every direction.

"Where is he?"

"Who?"

"You know who. This wasn't an accident. We were forced off the road. It was him."

"Not necessarily. It might have been a foolish driver going much too fast for the weather and road conditions."

She didn't look convinced and continued to stare over her shoulder. "I know it was him."

He caught and held her gaze. "I don't know who the driver was. What I do know is *Gott* was with us. We are safe and unharmed. But we are sideways in the middle of a highway. We have to move immediately before something bad does happen."

With that said, Thomas jumped out of the cab and hurried forward to see to his mare. He stroked her and spoke to her in a calm, soothing voice. Then he grabbed her bit and led her out of the snowdrift and placed her in the right direction back onto the highway.

Hopping up on the step and back into the cab, he quickly threw the blanket over his legs. The cold chilled him to the bone. His trousers had been soaked through with snow in parts both from earlier in the storm and now from climbing through knee-high snow to reach his horse. His body shuddered.

He didn't think the driver had been Hannah's killer. The man might be desperate but Thomas didn't believe he was stupid. If it had been him, he had ample opportunity to slam into their buggy and finish off both of them and he hadn't.

No.

Most likely it had been an inexperienced driver going much too fast on unfamiliar roads in inclement weather.

However, it didn't change how terrifying the incident had been.

Thomas refused to allow Elizabeth to see how badly it had shaken him. He'd rather she believe it was the weather that caused his trembling.

He shot her a reassuring grin.

"Homeward bound. I could use some time in front of a roaring fire with a hot cup of coffee." He winked at her. "And one of your homemade cookies for sure."

Thomas clicked the reins.

Mary approached carrying two mugs. "Mind if I sit with you? I brought both of us some hot tea."

Elizabeth accepted the mug. "*Denki*. Of course I'd enjoy your company." She gestured to the rocking chair beside her. "Sit with me."

"You've been very quiet lately, spending most of your evenings sitting on this porch until everyone else has long gone to bed."

Elizabeth sipped her tea and then tossed her mother a smile. "Is there a question in there someplace?"

"No questions. Observations."

Elizabeth continued to drink her tea.

"It's been two weeks since you met with the police artist. Thomas tells me there is still no news from Philadelphia, no new leads or clues to Hannah's killer."

"True. The last I heard they were unable to find her mother's journals. They must have been in the box I dropped when I ran from the condo and that criminal probably found them. Without those journals the police have been unable to discover the man's name or confirm the story I told them of Hannah's conception. So they're right back where they started. No leads. No clues. Nothing."

"They have the picture they made from your description."

Elizabeth shrugged. "It hasn't done much good. The sheriff told me the Philadelphia police gave it to the media. They also made flyers and hung them in bus stops, airports, rail stations, post offices and other crowded areas, but nothing of substance came from them.

"I'm not surprised, though." She looked at her mother. "I tried, *Mamm.* I did my best to work with the artist. But the composite drawing... I don't know. It resembled him in some ways, but something was off and I couldn't put my finger on it. Yes, it looked like the man. But do I think it was a close enough replication of him to be easily recognized? No. I don't. It was too generic. The likeness could have been one of a hundred men. Maybe that's why the police didn't get any viable calls."

"You did your best. That is all anyone can expect of you."

"It wasn't enough."

"Elizabeth, your best is always enough."

"But he's still out there somewhere."

Mary reached over and patted her hand. "It's been more than two weeks since anyone has seen or heard anything out of the ordinary. For whatever reason, I think the man decided to leave. I believe we are safe now."

Elizabeth chewed on her lower lip. "As long as he is free and not behind bars we will never be safe."

"Time will tell, child. But Thomas agrees with me. Even the bishop thinks we are safe. The men in the community are no longer taking shifts through the night keeping watch. He released them yesterday. He feels something more would have happened by now if the man was still here."

"I agree. I think he left, too. I'm just not sure why he would. He's a desperate man and I did not give him what he was looking for. It doesn't make sense to me that he would leave." She sighed. "On the other hand, I can't see him hiding out in people's barns or sleeping in the fields for this amount of time. In town the inns have his picture and the sheriff told them to notify him immediately if this guy shows up. So, yes, I think he left. But that doesn't mean he won't come back…and probably when we've let our guard down and least expect it."

Mary scolded her. "Is this what you plan to do? Spend the rest of your life keeping guard at night? Being afraid? Looking over your shoulder? That is not life, Elizabeth."

She stamped her foot on the porch floor to gain Elizabeth's full attention. "You are letting him win, *ja*? You are so afraid he will steal your life you don't see that he already has and you are continuing to let him do it." She waited until they made eye contact. "Elizabeth, listen to me, please. Life is short. Don't make it shorter. Be grateful to *Gott* that you have today—for that is all we are promised, *ja*? Make the most of your life. I fear you have already missed so much."

Mary pointed to the sky. "Look at those stars! Aren't they beautiful? *Gott* placed each and every one of them in their own special spot. He has planned for our special spot in this life, too." She smiled. "Daughter, I want the best for you. Enjoy the sun on your face. Laugh with the *kinner*. Work hard and enjoy the fruits of your labor in a fine feast you've prepared for the church service, or a quilt you made and put in your hope chest. Help others who are not as fortunate as yourself. There are many people who need an extra hand or are alone and lonely."

Mary leaned forward in her rocker and drilled her point home. "Live your life, Elizabeth, with gratitude and joy and a serving heart. Do that and I am sure *Gott* will bless you with peace and happiness."

"Sometimes, *Mamm*, that is not so easy to do." Elizabeth stared up at the sky. "But you're right about those stars. It is, indeed, a beautiful sight."

"Don't waste the time *Gott* has given you. It will be over all too soon."

Elizabeth frowned and studied her mother more closely. "Are you all right, *Mamm*? Your health, I mean. Are you well?"

Mary laughed. "What? You think I am dying because I am trying to encourage you to live?" She shook her head. "I am fine. But it hurts my heart to watch you nervous and fearful and spending your nights alone staring into the darkness."

"You're right. It's time I allow the police to worry about this criminal," Elizabeth said. "And past time to turn the entire situation over to *Gott*."

"Gut." Mary smiled widely.

They spent the next hour talking in generalities about the latest antics of the *kinner*, the weather, even who was going to make what dish for the upcoming Thanksgiving feast only a couple of weeks away. It was time to move inside when her mother pinned her with another question.

"I feel there is more on your mind than this evil man who no longer seems to be a threat to us. We said no more secrets. What else is bothering you?"

Elizabeth sighed heavily. Her mother didn't miss much as far as she was concerned, never had. She folded her hands in her lap and forced herself to say the words she hadn't even wanted to think about.

"It's time we leave, *Mamm*."

"Leave? Thomas has not said anything like that to me. Has he mentioned it to you?"

"No, of course not. He is too kind to ask us to go. But we cannot continue to live in his home. This is his home, *Mamm*. His *kinner*. His family. Not ours."

Mary nodded. "This is true." She slowly pushed the rocker with her toe. "It's just been *wunderbaar* to be a part of a family again." Her voice sounded wistful. She glanced over at Elizabeth. "I have been lonely sometimes without you and your father in the house. And, I must admit, I enjoy the *kinner*."

Mary stood and picked up the empty mugs.

"But you are right. This is not our family. It is time to go home. We will leave in the morning."

Before her mother turned and went inside, Elizabeth thought she'd seen tears glistening in her mother's eyes—or were they her own?

Chapter Twelve

Thomas stood at the far end by the tack room and was washing up in the sink. His eyes lit on Elizabeth the moment she stepped inside the barn.

"*Guder mariye*, Thomas."

"*Guder mariye*, Elizabeth."

"Breakfast is ready when you are."

He turned to face her and wiped his hands on a towel. "I am always ready for one of your meals. You and Mary spoil me." He patted his stomach. "I am getting fat."

Elizabeth laughed and the sound of it sent a warmth through him. "Then I'll have to find more chores to burn off the extra calories because I made cinnamon rolls especially for you today."

"Cinnamon rolls!" He placed his hands on his heart. "*Denki*. You have made my day." He crossed the barn floor and followed her into the house.

He wondered if it had been as difficult on her as it had been on him since she'd moved back to her mother's house almost two weeks ago. He knew she'd been happy in his home and he'd done everything he could to make her feel welcome. And the *kinner* missed her.

He had brought the *kinner* to visit a couple of times each week when he came to do the heavier chores for her mother.

But it wasn't the same.

He had to admit he had enjoyed seeing her at every meal. Sitting with her in the evenings on the porch. Playing together with the *kinner*.

It had been easy to pretend they were a family. It had felt *gut* to be a family again. And it had been devastatingly hard to acknowledge that they weren't family and it was time for her to leave.

Thomas hung his hat on the peg by the door and slipped past her into the kitchen.

"*Guder mariye*, Mary. Something smells good."

Her mother smiled. "You say that every morning, Thomas."

"And I mean it every morning, Mary."

They both laughed and he pulled out the chair at the head of the table and sat down.

"*Kumm*, Elizabeth, before it gets cold." Thomas beckoned her over his shoulder. "I am not going to be polite this morning. I will claim all the bacon if you don't fill your plate before I do." He pulled out the chair beside him, then turned his attention back to Mary.

"Rebecca asked me to remind you to make your egg custard for Thanksgiving dinner tomorrow. It is one of her favorites."

Elizabeth sat in the chair beside him.

He grinned at her and wiggled his eyebrows. "And I would not mind if you make your green-bean casserole. Your *daed* and I used to challenge each other for the last scoop."

"I remember."

Her smile seemed bittersweet and Thomas wondered if she was thinking of her father and missing him. Probably missing Hannah, too. He sensed a bit of loneliness in the wistfulness of her voice. He'd caught that same longing in Mary's voice a time or two over the years.

He reached into his trouser pocket and extended his hand toward Mary. "And I was asked to deliver this to you. It was included in a package I received from my parents."

He held out a letter.

Mary took it and quickly shoved it into her apron pocket.

"Mamm?" Elizabeth seemed surprised and shot her a questioning look.

"What?" The woman tried to evade Elizabeth's penetrating stare. "It's simply a letter from a friend."

Thomas grinned at the telltale blush in Mary's cheeks and almost laughed out loud at the astonished look on Elizabeth's face.

"A male friend?" Elizabeth's words were a whisper.

"His name is Joshua. He is a widower. He lost his wife the same year I lost your father. He goes to Sarasota every winter along with Thomas's parents."

"Have I ever met him?"

"Neh. I think he and his wife moved here the year after you left."

"Why haven't you mentioned him to me before?" Elizabeth grinned.

Mary sent a censuring look her way. "What's there to mention? We are simply friends. It is nothing you need to concern yourself with."

But Mary's blush deepened and she couldn't seem to

make eye contact with either one of them. She quickly changed the subject.

"Thomas, Elizabeth and I need to go to town later today. Do you have time to take us?"

"*Mamm!* Thomas does enough for us. I am perfectly capable of driving the buggy into town."

Thomas ignored Elizabeth's outburst. "I will be happy to take the two of you. I'll come back right after lunch to pick you up."

"Thomas, I can drive a buggy…"

There she goes again. Hands on hips. Eyes flashing. Heels dug in and ready for a fight. Boy, he had missed her. She's as ornery as an old mule at times.

"Don't get your feathers in an uproar. I know you can drive a buggy. And you can muck a stall and feed chickens and milk cows." He placed his hand over hers on the table. "But it doesn't mean you have to. You have a man more than willing and able to do it for you." He removed his hand, lifted his mug and took a swig of coffee. "Besides, I was hoping you and your mother would help me in return."

Elizabeth looked at him suspiciously. "What do you need from us?"

"Both of the *kinner* need new boots. I am not good with shopping unless it is for farm supplies or something I need for the horses. I was hoping you would help me with that chore."

"We'd love to help," Mary said before Elizabeth could open her mouth.

"*Gut*, it's settled." He stood and headed for the door before Elizabeth could protest some more. "Be back around one."

He slipped outside, skipped down the steps and found

himself humming as he climbed into his buggy to head home and do his own chores.

He loved getting Elizabeth all riled up. It was fun.

He loved the glint in her eyes, her stubbornness, her determination to prove she was as good as any man… or any*one* for that matter.

He loved her strength and independence.

He loved…

Shock raced through his body as he realized the direction his thoughts had gone and he immediately made himself think about something else.

"Watch me, Miss Elizabeth. Watch how fast I can run in my new boots." Benjamin ran across the front porch of the general store with his little sister skipping right behind him.

"Don't go too far," Elizabeth called. "I want both of you to stay with me."

They turned and raced back again, the sound of their boots clomping across the wooden planks.

Benjamin pulled to a stop in front of her. "Aren't these boots fast?"

Elizabeth smiled. He was such an adorable little imp. "*Ja*, Benjamin. I think you picked out the fastest boots in the entire store."

"I have boots, too." Rachel held up one foot.

"*Ja*, sweetie. You have new boots, too." Elizabeth reached out for the girl's hand, but before she could clasp it, the child pulled away, let out a cry and started running away.

"Rachel, stop." She moved quickly and fastened her hold on the girl's shoulders. "Where are you going? We have to stay here and wait for your *daed*."

Rachel pointed and started to whine. "Doggy!"

Elizabeth's gaze went in the direction the child pointed. She had dropped the little plastic toy and it had rolled off the porch and was lying in the street.

"You wait right here! Don't move." She hurried down and snatched up the toy only moments before she heard the clumping of hooves behind her and knew Thomas's buggy was right behind her. She ran to the steps, grabbed the edge of her skirt and hopped onto the planking. She grinned when Rachel clasped the dog to her chest. She really loved that little plastic toy.

"Here, let's put it in your pocket until we get home." She slid it into the pocket of Rachel's apron. "It's time for the doggy to take a nap. He'll be safe in your pocket and you can play with him when you get home."

Rachel grinned and patted her pocket. "Night, night, doggy."

"*Daed*, look at my new boots. They're the fastest boots in the store." Benjamin took off again, running back and forth across the porch, skirting customers and making zooming noises as he rushed by.

Thomas grabbed him on his second pass. "Whoa, partner. You're a little too fast. You don't want to get in the way of the store's customers, do you?"

The boy looked at the other adults milling in and out of the store as if it was the first time he'd even noticed them.

"When we get home," his father said, "you can run as fast and as much as you want on our front porch. How's that?"

"Yippee." Benjamin jumped up and down. "Can we go home now, *Daed*?"

"I don't know. Can we?" Thomas looked their way. "Are you ladies finished with your shopping?"

"Almost, Thomas," Mary replied. "I forgot to buy a spice I need."

"I could use some new material for a dress, too. I didn't have a chance to look while I was watching the *kinner*," Elizabeth added.

"Sounds to me like the ladies need some lady shopping time." He hoisted Rachel up on his shoulders and grabbed Benjamin's hand. "Why don't the three of us go over to Millie's café and get some hot chocolate with whipped cream. What do you say?"

The kids cheered.

"That settles it, then. You ladies enjoy your shopping. Take your time. We'll be right across the street. Come join us when you're done."

Elizabeth thanked him and watched them cross the street and disappear inside the café.

"He's a good *daed*. Those *kinner* are blessed," Mary said.

Elizabeth agreed.

"You still haven't told him your secret even though you said you would. Why?"

"I will, *Mamm*. I'm not trying to keep it a secret anymore. Honestly, I'm not. But after we moved home... well, there hasn't been an opportunity. What am I supposed to do? Follow him out to the barn and drop the news on him while he's milking the cows?" She locked eyes with her mother. "You know I haven't had any alone time with him since we moved back. This is a sensitive and personal subject. The timing has to be right."

Her *mamm*'s lips twisted in a wry grin. "Thanksgiving is in two days. I am sure you will be able to find a few minutes to talk with him privately. And I am equally sure you will both be grateful that you did."

Elizabeth put her arm around her mother's shoulders and steered her toward the store. "Okay. You're right. No more excuses. I'll pull him aside and tell him right after the Thanksgiving meal."

"Gut."

They were almost to the store entrance when Elizabeth froze. She couldn't move a muscle if her life depended upon it. Her breathing quickened and a sick tightening grasped her chest. Despite the winter weather a bead of sweat broke out on her forehead and the pulse at her temples throbbed.

Calm down. You're having a panic attack. That's all it is.

Unfortunately her body didn't want to listen to her mind. The blood drained out of her face and her knees wobbled.

Stop this before it gets worse. Inhale sharply and exhale slowly. C'mon, you can do it.

"Elizabeth, what is it? What's wrong?"

She closed her eyes, took a deep breath, pursed her lips and exhaled as slowly as she could.

"Elizabeth, answer me. What's wrong? You're scaring me."

She took another calming breath, opened her eyes and looked at her mother. "It's him."

"Who?" Her mother tossed looks in every direction.

"The killer." Her words were a mere whisper.

Mary grabbed her arm and held on tight. "Where, child? Where is he? We need to run and get Thomas."

Mary started to pull her toward the steps but Elizabeth stood her ground. "No, *Mamm*. He's not here in person. That's his picture."

She pointed to a newspaper in a display rack near the entrance of the general store. She didn't know how she'd missed it earlier. She'd probably been so busy paying attention to the children that she didn't notice her surroundings.

Mary stepped forward and peered at the paper behind the glass.

The headline read, The President Arrives in Philadelphia.

"The president?" Mary's voice quavered and she looked at her daughter as though she had lost her mind.

"No, *Mamm*. Of course not." Elizabeth jabbed the glass with her index finger. "Him. The man in the background."

"Which one? There are several men standing behind him."

"The one on the end of the podium standing by the flag."

Elizabeth rummaged in her purse to find enough change to purchase the paper. When she did, she opened the glass covering and pulled out the newspaper. With trembling hands, she held it up for a closer look.

Her mother peered over her arm. "Who is he? Does it tell you his name?"

Elizabeth scanned the caption. "Oh, dear heavenly Father, help us. No wonder he was so desperate not to be identified."

"Why? Who is he?" Her mother pulled on her arm and tried to read the paper herself.

Elizabeth gave a long, heavy sigh. "His name is Richard Dolan. He's a Pennsylvania senator."

"Senator? That can't be, can it?" Mary grabbed her daughter's arm and forced Elizabeth to look at her. "You're telling me a senator may have raped my best friend and killed his own daughter?"

The anguish Elizabeth saw in her mother's face made her realize she wasn't the only one who had lost a dear friend or others she'd cared about. She wasn't the only one hurting and afraid.

"Well, obviously he wouldn't have been a senator all those years ago, but he is now."

"Are you certain it's him?"

"I wish I wasn't, *Mamm*. But this is the man who killed Hannah. Now we know why he left. He only had a couple of weeks to return home, make things appear normal and prepare for his arrangements to be with the president in Philadelphia for this big fund-raiser. He couldn't be missing in action. He had to go home."

Her hands shook and she almost dropped the paper.

"Once the president has returned to Washington, Senator Dolan is free to come and go as he pleases." She shot a glance at her mother and knew she couldn't hide her terror. "He's coming back, *Mamm*. I know he is."

"Don't panic. At least we'll be prepared this time. We'll tell Thomas and the bishop what we know and what we suspect."

"*Ja*, but first I have to tell the sheriff." She faced her mother and clasped her forearms. "I need you to go across the street and tell Thomas what's happened and where I am." Elizabeth stepped back and clutched the paper against her chest. "This newspaper went to press last night in order to be on the stands today. We have to hurry. Dolan could already be here."

Chapter Thirteen

"Ms. Lapp, come in." The sheriff stood and came around his desk as Elizabeth stomped the snow from her boots on the doormat. The heat in the room was a welcome change from the frigid temperatures outside and the smell of fresh coffee almost made her drool.

"Please, have a seat. I planned to drive out later today to talk to you. You've just saved me the trip."

Elizabeth strode into the room and stood in front of the sheriff. "You were coming to see me? Why? Did they catch him?"

"Please." He pulled out the chair. "Sit down."

She did as he requested.

The sheriff went back behind his desk, sat in his well-worn brown leather chair and folded his hands on his desk.

"May I offer you a cup of coffee?"

"No, *denki*." As much as she'd love to take him up on the offer, this wasn't a social call and she couldn't help feeling the sheriff was stalling for some reason.

"Did you find him?" Elizabeth asked again.

"No. Not yet."

"Then why were you coming to see me?"

"The Philadelphia police called and…uh, asked me to speak with you."

He squirmed in his chair, the leather squeaking beneath his excess weight. He fumbled with a pencil on his desk and seemed to be having difficulty making eye contact with her.

"There's no easy way to tell you…"

"Yes there is, Sheriff. Say it straight out. I've lived in your world for the past seven years. There isn't much that surprises me anymore."

He studied her face and gave a curt nod. "Very well. The Philadelphia police gave a press conference earlier today. They announced that they believe they have a witness to the murder who has just agreed to come forward with physical evidence identifying Hannah Fischer's killer. If the information is viable, they expect to be able to make an arrest shortly."

"What?" Elizabeth fell back in her chair and her mouth gaped open. "I never agreed to any such thing."

"We know. It's a ploy. That's why I was coming out to your place. They want me to pick you up and put you in protective custody for a few weeks so that you won't be in the line of fire when the killer returns and tries to silence you."

"A ploy?" Elizabeth couldn't contain her shock. She leaned her forearms against the desktop. "Let me get this straight. You were coming out to my home to snatch me up a day and a half before Thanksgiving to hide me away because the Philadelphia police decided to use me as bait."

His neck colored and he squirmed even more.

"They're hoping the fish will come after the bait only to find an empty hook. Is that what you're doing?"

"Not me, Ms. Lapp. The higher-ups made that decision." He cleared his throat. "I understand why you're upset. I'd be, too, if someone dangled me on the end of a fishing line to catch a killer. Particularly without my knowledge or permission." He sat back in his seat.

"But what can I say? You're all we've got. The composite drawing didn't help. You are the only witness to the crime. All roads turned stone-cold. They thought this would flush him out."

"I'm sure it will." Elizabeth didn't know whether to be furious or grateful that law enforcement was so invested in solving the case.

The sheriff's mouth twisted. "Truthfully, I agree with them." He held his palms out to prevent her from protesting. "Not that I like the way they did it. Not telling you or anything. But it probably will make him show up in Sunny Creek again. Soon. That's why I can't let you leave my office today. I've got to put you in protective custody."

Before Elizabeth could protest, Thomas opened the door. He removed his hat as he entered, nodded to the sheriff and pulled out the chair beside Elizabeth.

"Are you *allrecht*?" he asked her. "Mary just told me."

"I'm fine, Thomas." She glared at the man sitting across from her. "Aren't I, Sheriff?"

Thomas shot a quizzical look at both Elizabeth and the sheriff but remained quiet.

"Law enforcement decided to take matters into their own hands." Although she spoke to Thomas, she never took her eyes from the sheriff. "They decided to use me as bait—without my knowledge or permission, of course."

"What do you mean 'bait'?"

The sheriff quickly brought Thomas up to speed on what had happened. "So we're going to take her into protective custody for a week or two and see what happens."

Both of them spoke simultaneously.

"*Neh.* You can't do that," Thomas said.

"I am not staying in protective custody," Elizabeth said.

The sheriff sighed. "Look…"

"No, Sheriff. You look. I came here today for a reason." Elizabeth leaned back in her chair. "I am about to break this case wide open for you. I know the name of the killer and where you can find him." She smiled at the astonished look on the man's face.

The sheriff looked from one to the other, then settled his gaze on Elizabeth.

"Maybe you should tell me what evidence you have. Then we'll discuss the custody situation."

Elizabeth placed the newspaper on the sheriff's desk and jabbed her index finger on the picture of the man standing on the platform. "That is the man you're looking for, Sheriff. His name is Richard Dolan."

The sheriff picked up the paper, looked at the picture and laughed.

"That's funny, Ms. Lapp. Guess you're entitled to at least one joke after what we're asking of you."

The sheriff's grin dissipated when he realized that neither Thomas nor Elizabeth were laughing with him.

"Wait a minute." He tossed the paper back onto the desk. "You're serious? You're trying to tell me that

Richard Dolan—Senator Richard Dolan—is the man who attacked you in the barn? That this man—" he shook the edges of the newspaper "—killed Hannah Fischer."

"That's exactly what she's saying, Sheriff." Thomas stared hard at the man, almost daring him to contradict Elizabeth.

The grin, although a weak one, was back on the sheriff's face. He glanced back and forth between them then turned his attention to Elizabeth.

"Ms. Lapp, I am sure you *think* this is your culprit, but I assure you that you're wrong."

"Really? Tell me, Sheriff, was it you who got a good look at his face while he was trying to choke you to death? Or was it me?"

The sheriff shook his head, apparently having great difficulty wrapping his mind around her words. "Ms. Lapp, this man has built his entire political career based on family values. It's even rumored he's going to run for president in the next election."

"Well, that certainly sounds like motive to me." Elizabeth folded her hands in her lap and stared him down.

The sheriff's disbelief of Elizabeth's words irritated Thomas and he couldn't keep silent any longer. "Elizabeth would never lie to you about this. If she says this is the man, I believe her."

Elizabeth smiled at him.

The sheriff rummaged in his file drawer and withdrew a copy of the composite picture. He placed the newspaper and the drawing side by side and spun them around to face them.

"I'll admit that there are some similarities. I'll give

you that. But there's no way the man in this picture is the same man in the newspaper."

Thomas slid the pictures closer to Elizabeth. "What do you think?"

"I agree with the sheriff. That's why we didn't get any leads when the media ran with it. The drawing isn't accurate." She studied them for a few minutes, then looked up at him with a grin. "I knew something was wrong with this drawing, Thomas, but I couldn't put my finger on what it was."

Excitement sounded in her voice. "Look!" She jabbed her index finger on the papers and then locked her gaze with the sheriff's. "The chin is different. So are the eyes. This drawing is too generic. It could fit the description of a multitude of men. That's why no one recognized him." She slid the papers back. "But Senator Richard Dolan is the man who killed Hannah. He is the same man who tried to choke me to death." She sat back and stared at him. "Now I want to know what you intend to do about it."

The sheriff released a slow, heavy sigh. "Ms. Lapp, do you have any idea what the Philadelphia police are going to do when I call them? They're going to laugh me right out of my job."

"Why's that, Sheriff?" Thomas asked. "Don't you think powerful people can be bad people?" He leaned forward to emphasize his point. "Do you know your Bible, sir? There are many leaders in the Bible who did terrible, evil things. Some killed two-year-old babies. Others ordered the murder of Christ, *Gott*'s *sohn*. Is this senator more important than any of those men?

The sheriff ran a hand across his balding scalp. "Okay, I'll make the call. I just can't promise they'll take her seriously." He turned his attention to Elizabeth. "Now what's this about not staying here in protective custody?"

"The day after tomorrow is Thanksgiving. I intend to spend the day with my family and friends."

"I can't keep you safe if you're walking around out there, Ms. Lapp. I think I'd skip Thanksgiving dinner this year in return for being alive to eat it next year."

"You don't understand."

"Enlighten me."

"I have no doubt you will keep me safe if I follow your plan and let you stash me someplace under armed guard." Elizabeth stood and pointed, again, to the man in the picture. "And what do you think this man will do if he can't get to me?" She squared her shoulders and looked him right in the eye. "He will be furious. He will seek revenge on me and he will hurt the people I care about, the people he can get near. I refuse to let that happen."

"If you walk out those doors, I can't promise I can keep you safe."

"I understand. But I know you'll try. And I know the Philadelphia police are on their way and they intend to help catch Mr. Dolan. The rest is in *Gott*'s hands and that's good enough for me."

"Ms. Lapp, I don't think you fully understand the danger you are in, particularly after today's press conference. If you are correct and our culprit is Mr. Dolan, then he will stop at nothing to get to you. You threaten his current career and any aspirations for a higher one."

"Has anyone considered picking up Mr. Dolan for custody now before he comes to Sunny Creek?" Thomas asked. "Seems to me prevention is better than hoping for a cure. Get the man. Lock him up. Problem solved."

The sheriff grimaced. "I wish it could be that easy. I'll call the Philadelphia police in just a minute. But I'm more worried about the timing. If Ms. Lapp is correct about Mr. Dolan, then he isn't sitting around waiting for us to knock on his door. He's making a beeline for Sunny Creek to shut her up before she can bring him down."

Worry and fear tore at Thomas's gut. What if he couldn't keep her safe? He clasped her hand. "Elizabeth, maybe I was wrong. Maybe you should consider going into this protective custody the sheriff is talking about."

"*Neh*, Thomas." She patted his hand and then spoke directly to the sheriff.

"If you want to use me as bait, then use me. I intend to stay right out in the open, where he can easily find me. I will not allow him to hurt any of the people I love. I'm done with running away." She smiled at Thomas and her voice softened. "I've learned that running away never solves anything."

Thomas took a moment to let her words register and then grinned when he realized her words had a deeper, personal meaning.

She returned the grin then faced the sheriff.

"No, Sheriff. I'm not hiding. I'm not running. This has to end. I want my life back and the lives of the people in my community to return to normal. This man has stolen enough from us. I won't let him steal anything more."

Thomas stood and placed his hand lightly on her shoulder. "We will protect her, Sheriff. That is our job."

He put his hat back on his head. "It is your job to catch this man. We hope you will do your job…soon."

Without another word, they turned and walked out of the sheriff's office.

Thomas drew her close as they walked down the street to the café, where Mary and the *kinner* waited. She smiled at him and did her best to look unaffected but he could feel an occasional shudder and he didn't believe it was from the cold.

She seemed skittish at every sudden sound and wary of every approaching man on the street.

He almost wished he could turn her around, march her back into the sheriff's office and call the whole thing off. But he knew she was doing the right thing. The brave thing. It had to be done. It was time for this terrorizing to end.

He lowered his head and said a silent prayer while they walked.

Heavenly Father, give me the courage and strength and wisdom to face the battle ahead beside her. Help me keep her safe.

They had reached the café when Thomas caught her arm and stopped her from entering. Surprised, she turned and looked at him.

"It is normal to be afraid, Elizabeth." He smiled down at her. "We will be afraid together. No matter what happens, this terrible situation has to end. Now. *Ja?*"

"*Ja*, Thomas."

"And you will not have to face this man alone. I will be by your side. And we will have extra help from the men in our community, too."

She reached up and caressed his face. "*Denki*, Thomas."

"Remember, Elizabeth, he is just a man, not a giant or a monster. Men make mistakes. This man will make one and the sheriff will arrest him."

Elizabeth smiled. "Even if he is a giant, Thomas, we know how to handle that, don't we? David slew the giant, Goliath, with a slingshot and a stone." She clasped his hand, pulled him toward the door to the café and tossed a question over her shoulder. "By the way, Thomas, do you happen to know where I can buy a slingshot?"

Chapter Fourteen

Thanksgiving dawned clear, crisp and cold. The remaining snow from the last storm had formed ice crystals that glistened in the sun's morning rays. The temperature had risen slightly. It would be a good day to bundle up the *kinner* to play outside. Maybe they could go sledding. Her mother's field had undulating small hills that would be perfect for it.

Elizabeth crossed to the barn to bring in some mason jars of corn and green beans for the dinner preparation. She startled and almost dropped them when she turned and saw the sheriff standing by the barn door.

He removed his hat. "Sorry to scare you, Ms. Lapp. I thought you'd heard me pull up."

"That's all right, Sheriff. I startle easily these days. How can I help you?"

The sheriff had stopped by twice in the past day and a half and a patrol car had come by at least four times. Today's visit was the first time he had actually stopped to talk. Something must be up.

"I thought I'd stop and bring you up-to-date on the investigation."

"I'd appreciate that."

He told her that the Philadelphia police had reacted as he had initially said they would. But after a series of jokes and jibes, when they realized he was serious, they got to work. They went to the senator's Pennsylvania residence to speak with him and were told by his wife that he had flown to Washington on business. A check of the airlines proved that was untrue.

They did not question his wife about his whereabouts on the day of Hannah Fischer's murder, or the attempts on Elizabeth's life, because they didn't want to tip their hand that he was being investigated just yet.

They were unable to get current contact information from his office assistant other than his personal cell-phone number. She didn't seem to be aware of any business appointments in Washington. The assistant assumed the appointments must be of a personal nature.

The police hit pay dirt, though, with further questioning. The senator's assistant had recognized a picture they showed her of Hannah. Upon further questioning, she remembered the young woman had been in the office. She checked the calendar and confirmed that Hannah had had an appointment with the senator a month before her death. The assistant didn't know what they'd discussed, but she remembered that there had been an argument between the senator and the woman. She'd heard raised voices coming from his office, but had been unable to make out any of the words. The young woman stormed out of the senator's office appearing angry and upset. The senator had slammed his office door. He'd never confided in his assistant about what the young woman wanted or what the argument had been about. He dismissed her questions and nothing else ever came of the encounter.

The police weren't laughing anymore. Senator Richard Dolan had suddenly become the number-one person of interest in this case.

Elizabeth took a deep breath and processed the new information. She nodded. "Thank you, Sheriff. I appreciate the update."

The sheriff donned his hat. "Happy to do it."

"I guess things will start moving pretty quickly now," Elizabeth said. "Either the law will locate him and bring him in for questioning, or he will show up here and attempt to finish what he started."

The sheriff frowned. "That's about the size of it, Miss Lapp. Are you sure you don't want to take me up on that offer of protective custody?"

Of course I do. I want to hole up somewhere and stay safe until this whole mess is over.

Every bone in her body shivered with fear. But she knew she couldn't do it. She couldn't leave her community exposed to a madman who was looking for her.

"Thank you, Sheriff. I'll be fine."

He nodded. "Well, you'll see a few extra people around. We have undercover agents posing as your mail carrier, your milkman and an extra unmarked car making a patrol round or two, so don't get skittish if you don't see the regular people."

"Thanks, again. I appreciate the heads-up."

She watched him turn to leave and started toward the house when Thomas appeared in his wake. "Are you *allrecht*? What did the sheriff want?"

Elizabeth smiled. Thomas, true to his word, had been like her shadow ever since they'd left the sheriff's office the day before yesterday. He tried to stay out of her way as she went about her day, but she was well aware that he was always close by. And when he had to leave, he made sure one of the other men in their community dogged her every step.

Elizabeth had to laugh. She wasn't sure whether the men were more afraid of the elusive villain or of Thomas's wrath if they let her out of their sight.

"I can't stay out here in the barn talking. I have to get started on that green-bean casserole you like so much if I hope to have it ready for our Thanksgiving dinner. Our guests will be arriving before you know it."

"Elizabeth, I need to know…"

"*Ja*, I know, Thomas. *Kumm* inside with me. *Mamm* is going to want to know what the sheriff said, too. I'll fill you both in over a hot cup of coffee."

True to her word, Elizabeth updated them on the sheriff's visit. They tossed worried looks at each other but neither said anything negative to Elizabeth. Nevertheless an uneasy expectancy settled over the room. He was coming. The three of them knew it and there was little anyone could do about it.

At Mary's suggestion, they clasped hands and prayed.

The rest of the morning passed in a hurried blur of cooking, cleaning and more cooking.

Thomas played outside in the snow with the *kinner* but Elizabeth noticed how he stayed even closer to the house since the sheriff's news.

By midafternoon buggies filled the yard as the other families began to arrive. The sound of *kinner*'s laughter and high-pitched voices filled the air as games of tag and softball ensued. The women gathered in the kitchen. Many had brought casseroles or homemade bread. Several women brought fresh-baked pies. The men worked together to move aside the living-room furniture and set up multiple long tables and benches, while Bishop Schwartz claimed the chore of starting a fire in the fireplace and keeping it stoked.

The meal came together in perfect harmony. The aromas of fresh breads, roasted chicken, stuffing, vegetable casseroles and a variety of pies caused more than one stomach to rumble and everyone to sniff the air with pleasure.

While they all ate to the point of overeating, the room buzzed with robust conversations. The men could be heard talking about spring crops, weather predictions and even Lucah's problem with a lame horse. The women spoke of new quilting patterns, recipes and Agnes Hofsteadter's upcoming baby shower.

No one mentioned the subject that Elizabeth was sure wore on everyone's minds, and she was grateful. It gave her the opportunity to relax for a little while. She joined the various conversations, filled her plate more than once, laughed at a child's antics and thanked *Gott* multiple times that she had finally come home again.

When the meal ended and everyone scattered to help clean up, Elizabeth slipped up beside Thomas. He was getting ready to help carry a bench out to the waiting buggy.

Surreptitiously, Elizabeth grabbed his sleeve and held him in place. Lowering her voice to a mere whisper, she asked, "Thomas, do you think when you're finished that you and I could take a walk for a few minutes. I have something important I need to discuss with you."

His brow wrinkled in concern. "Is everything *all-recht*?"

"*Ja*, no worries." She smiled confidently at him even though her pulse raced like a thoroughbred's at the opening shot. "I have something I need to say that is best said in private."

His concerned, puzzled look didn't go away, but he nodded.

Elizabeth turned the corner and stood for a second leaning against the hall wall.

Now or never, Elizabeth. No more secrets. You can do this.

She took a deep breath and exhaled long and hard.

Please, Lord, give him the grace to forgive me.

As if today wasn't stressful enough, she had told her mother she would be open and honest with Thomas.

A killer on the loose with her in his crosshairs. Long-buried secrets about to be exposed. Today couldn't get much better.

Elizabeth's shoulders stooped as if she carried the weight of the world on them. Oh, well. She'd find out soon enough if this day would, indeed, be one to be thankful for. She pushed off from the wall and headed into the kitchen to help the women clean up.

"Will you be home before I go to bed? I want you to say my night prayers with me."

"I don't know, *sohn*. It is already getting late and there is still much for me to do here." Thomas ruffled Benjamin's hair. "Did you have a *gut* time today?"

"It was *wunderbaar, Daed*. I hit two of the balls Levi threw to me. I tagged Henry and John and Micah. And Miss Mary let me have an extra piece of apple pie." He rubbed his small, rotund belly. "I am full up." His grin barely fit his face and his eyes shone with excitement. "She even gave me a scoop of vanilla ice cream on my second piece of pie."

Thomas laughed loudly. "Well, let's hope, *sohn*, that your belly doesn't protest later tonight that you shoved too many goodies into it."

Rachel sat on Rebecca's lap in the buggy with Benjamin tucked in beside her, and Thomas pressed a kiss onto his daughter's forehead. Clasping both of his children's hands, he said, "Why don't we say a prayer together now just in case I can't get home before bedtime."

The children joined him in prayer, then gave him hugs and multiple kisses before he stepped away from the buggy. He nodded to Isaac to pull away and waved goodbye. It was the last buggy to leave for the day, and he watched as it slowly ambled down the gravel lane.

This had definitely been a day to be thankful to the *gut* Lord. Each day he got to spend with those *wunderbaar* children was a day to be thankful.

When the buggy was no longer in sight, his thoughts strayed to Elizabeth. He wondered what was so important that she had taken him aside and requested a private moment. She had smiled and hadn't seemed worried or upset. Maybe it would be good news of some kind and he could add it to the things to be grateful for today. There had been enough bad news lately. Too much.

Patting his own groaning, overfed stomach, he turned and went in search of Elizabeth. A walk would do him good. And a walk with Elizabeth would ease not only his stomach, but also his heart.

Elizabeth spun around as Thomas approached her on the porch.

"I'm sorry," Thomas said. "I didn't mean to startle you. I should have stomped my feet or coughed or something."

She grinned. "Not your fault, Thomas. I'm finding myself jumping at anything and everything."

He stepped closer. "It was a *gut* day, *ja*?"

She nodded.

He stepped even closer and clasped her hand in his.

"But the day's not over." He glanced at the sun as it began its descent behind the trees, leaving long streaks of red and orange and gold in its wake. "I do believe I was asked to accompany a certain young woman on a walk. We should go now before it gets dark."

She smiled into his eyes. "Let's do it."

Hand-in-hand they stepped off the porch, strolled across the yard and moved into the nearby field. The snow crunched beneath their boots and the chill in the twilight air put a rosy glow on their cheeks.

They rehashed the afternoon's events and conversations as they walked. Elizabeth knew the Amish rarely gave compliments to anyone, but Elizabeth bragged about the two softball hits she'd seen Benjamin get. He couldn't help the wave of pride he felt for his *sohn*. And he didn't hold back complimenting her on the chocolate-and-marshmallow dessert she had surprised everyone with.

Thomas reveled in both the conversation and the walk.

It had been a very long time—years—since he'd taken a stroll with a woman after an evening meal. Yet, here he was. Strolling. Talking. Smiling. And doing it with Elizabeth. Something he would have never believed possible.

Sometimes hurts and regrets from the past threatened to surface and spoil the moment. But he'd mentally remind himself of all the good years he had spent with Margaret. If things hadn't happened the way they did, he wouldn't have had those years—or the children, who were the fruit of that union. He had finally chosen to forgive Elizabeth. What had happened years ago had happened. He might never understand why she'd made the choices she had, but so be it. She needed his help now and that was all that mattered.

Thomas smiled. He was glad he wasn't *Gott* and wondered why anyone in their right mind would ever try to apply for the job. Controlling lives was a full-time and difficult chore.

The sun had almost set and night was not far behind.

"It is time we go back to the house." He didn't want to break the peaceful moment or bring up a sore subject, but felt he had no choice. "I don't think it wise for you to be outside once it is dark."

She agreed but her steps faltered and he sensed her hesitation.

"Elizabeth?" He stopped and faced her. "You have something you want to tell me? I find it is always best to just say what is on your mind. *Ja?*"

Elizabeth took a deep breath. Whatever it was weighed heavily on her. He wondered if he should be concerned. When she looked up at him, her eyes glistened with unshed tears.

"I'm sorry, Thomas, that I hurt you so badly." She released her hand from his. "I never meant to." She clasped her hands together tightly. "I mean I knew you'd be hurt when I left. We both would. But I had no idea how much."

* * *

Elizabeth studied Thomas to gauge the impact of her words. His posture stiffened and his body language told her he was battling to keep calm and appear unruffled. He looked like he wanted to say a thousand things but he refrained. When he did speak, he simply shrugged. "It was a very long time ago, Elizabeth. There is nothing we can do about the past."

"Ja." She reached out and gently touched his arm. "But the wounds haven't healed yet. For either one of us."

His eyes shifted and he couldn't seem to look at her. He spoke quietly and gently, but she knew raw emotion tumbled inside him. He touched her cheek and smiled into her eyes. Then he lowered his hand. "I loved you, Elizabeth. That's why it hurt so much. You left with nothing more than a scribbled note saying goodbye, no explanation or reason, and that you hoped I'd have a good life. You didn't respect me enough to tell me in person. You left a note after the fact so I couldn't try and talk you out of it. Your parents had to give it to me."

Repressed anger and hurt surfaced in his voice and it broke her heart.

"I deserved better." His eyes couldn't hide his pain.

"Ja, you did."

He didn't seem to know what to say to that. Finally he looked her straight in the eyes and asked the question that she knew had troubled him for years.

"Why, Elizabeth? What terrible thing did I do to chase you away? I thought we loved each other. Was I the only one who felt that way?"

Unable to hold back the tears anymore, she shook

her head until she could clear the sob from her throat and find her voice.

"I left because I loved you, Thomas. More than you realize."

He threw a hand in the air. "That makes no sense."

"I wanted you to have a good life and I knew I couldn't give it to you. You think it is cowardice to run away. Sometimes it is courage. Sometimes you love another person so much that their happiness means more to you than your own. You're not running away, Thomas. You're crawling away because your heart is shattered into a million pieces and you can barely move. That's how much I loved you. And that is why I left." She stretched up on her toes and kissed him. The salty taste of her tears mingled on their lips.

Chapter Fifteen

Thomas didn't say anything. He smiled at her with all the tenderness he could muster. There were so many questions and he was grateful that she was finally ready to give him the answers he craved. But not here. Not in the dark in the middle of a field when a known predator hung in the shadows.

"We have to get you back inside. It is not safe."

She didn't protest when he clasped her hand and led her back to the house.

When they walked through the door, Mary looked up from her sewing. One glance at the expression on her face and Thomas knew she was aware of the conversation they'd been having. He'd believed for years that she'd known the real reason Elizabeth had left, but he'd never been able to get her to tell him.

"If you don't mind, Mary, Elizabeth and I are going to go into the kitchen to talk. Would you like me to bring anything out to you?"

Mary smiled. "No, Thomas. I had plenty to eat and drink today. If you don't mind, I'll sit here and finish my sewing. Elizabeth knows where everything is."

He acknowledged her statement with a nod and led Elizabeth into the kitchen.

Elizabeth put on a kettle for tea. She seemed more nervous standing in a well-lit kitchen baring her soul than she did in a twilight-dimmed field.

He hurried to reassure her. "*Denki*, Elizabeth. I am grateful you are willing to talk to me about this. I have had many questions for many years." He sat at the table and pulled her down into the chair beside him. "I still don't know why you made the choices you made—and I want to understand." He clasped her hand on the tabletop. "Tell me everything."

When she began talking it was as if a dam broke. The words tumbled out fast.

"Do you remember that I had to go into the hospital for an operation?"

"*Ja*. You had a cyst on your ovary. I visited you every day."

"Yes, you did."

"The surgery went well. I even remember the nurses had you up and walking the hospital halls the same day."

"True. What you didn't know was what the doctors found during the operation. They had to remove my right ovary because it was riddled with cysts and ineffective. But the left ovary had problems, too. I have a condition called endometriosis."

"What is that?"

"A medical condition that changed everything between us."

"I don't understand."

"Think of it as having a weed, the worst weed, growing in your fields. You can try to cut it out but you can't get it all, it keeps coming back, and it chokes your crop."

He sat quietly and listened.

She pulled her hand away and folded both hands in front of her. "Endometriosis is my weed. It is choking my insides. It is making it impossible for me to have a child." She took a deep breath. "Amish people love large families. And I knew how good a *daed* you would be. I couldn't stay here and marry you. I couldn't deprive you of a family, Thomas. So I left."

Thomas's mouth gaped open in shock. "That's why you left? Because of your health?"

Elizabeth nodded.

"But I would have married you anyway. Didn't you know that?"

She smiled at him and reached out to stroke his hand. "I knew you would because you are a *gut* man. That's why I didn't tell you. I didn't want to ruin your life."

"You should have spoken to me about this." Thomas tried to control his anger but it was getting harder by the second. "If I had had a medical condition or maybe been injured and couldn't work the farm, would you have left me?"

"Neh," she said softly.

"Why? Because you are a better person than me?"

"Neh, Thomas. I loved you. I would have stayed by your side always."

"That's my point, Elizabeth."

She lowered her eyes and seemed unable to face him.

"You made the choice for both of us and you had no right to do that. You are not *Gott* and yet you try to control others as if you know what is best for them."

Seven years. She threw away seven years of their lives together—and for what?

He struggled with a myriad of emotions, not knowing what to say or how to act.

"I'm sorry, Thomas. I should have told you. I should have given you the choice or, at the very least, let you understand why I was leaving. I hurt you. More than I thought I would. More than I ever wanted to." Her eyes pleaded with him to try and understand. "If it is any consolation, you are not the only one who suffered. These past seven years have been difficult for me, too."

He realized she was right.

Yes, he'd been hurt. But he'd also been able to move on. *Gott* blessed him with Margaret and then added the gift of two *kinner*.

What had Elizabeth gained?

She'd been apart from him. But she'd also been apart from her family, her friends, her community. She hadn't even been able to attend her own father's funeral and he knew that loss still cut deep.

She'd made a foolish decision but he understood now that she'd done it out of love, not malice. And she'd paid a heavy price. It wasn't his place to hold grudges against her—not anymore.

A sense of relief washed over him. He realized that this month together, keeping her safe from harm, had helped him come to grips with his pain. He'd been able to forgive her even before she'd told him the truth tonight.

He stood, came around the table and pulled her to her feet. He swept a strand of hair off her cheek. "You have nothing to be sorry for, Elizabeth. You did what you thought was right at the time. It is over. It can't be undone." He folded her in his arms. "But we can both learn from past mistakes. We must trust one another.

We must be open and talk with each other. No more secrets."

Elizabeth smiled and when she did it was like a ray of sunshine peeking out from behind a dark cloud.

"*Denki*, Thomas."

"*Neh. Denki* to you. You have answered questions that bothered me for years. Now I know the truth. Now I am at peace with it."

"*Mamm* was right." She glanced over Thomas's shoulder. "Don't ever tell her I said that, though, or I'll never hear the end of it." She chuckled. "She said if I told you the entire story that we both would have something to be grateful for on this Thanksgiving Day."

He leaned forward and claimed her lips. When the kiss ended, he tilted her chin and smiled into her eyes. "*Ja*, Mary is right. I have much to be thankful for on this day. *Gott* is *gut*."

"Ahem."

Both of them jumped and pulled apart.

"Levi, I didn't see you standing there," Thomas said.

"Obviously not." The man grinned from ear to ear. "I have *kumm* to do my watch shift. You can leave now." His grin widened. "If you want to, that is."

Elizabeth giggled like a schoolgirl and the sound of it warmed his heart. "Levi is right, Thomas. The *kinner* will be waiting for you. I am in good hands."

Thomas shot a look between them. "Fine." He stepped close to Levi and lowered his voice as he passed. "Don't take your eyes off of her."

Levi, one of the younger single men in their community, grinned again. "Don't worry, Thomas. I will care for her as if she was my own."

Thomas raised an eyebrow. "Don't get any crazy ideas in your head. Just keep a careful watch."

Both Levi and Elizabeth laughed.

"Go home, Thomas." Elizabeth stepped forward and gave him a peck on the cheek. "I will see you tomorrow."

Grumbling under his breath, Thomas planted his hat on top of his head, grabbed his coat and headed for the door.

Elizabeth sat on the bed combing out her hair when she heard a knock on her bedroom door.

"Come in." She smiled as her mother entered the room. She'd wondered how long it would take her to come and pepper her with a dozen questions. She was surprised the dear woman had waited this long.

"I brought you an extra quilt." She laid it at the foot of the bed. "It might get very cold this evening. Thomas said he thinks we will soon have more snow."

Elizabeth grinned. She knew what her *mamm* wanted and it had nothing to do with keeping her warm. She couldn't resist stringing her along just a little longer.

"*Denki.* I will be warm as toast."

Her mother stood in the middle of the room looking awkward but not making any effort to leave.

"Would you like me to help you comb your hair?" her mother asked. "I used to do the back for you when you were a teenager. Remember? We had some of the best conversations during those special mother-daughter times."

Elizabeth couldn't hold back any longer and laughed out loud. "No, *Mamm*, I don't need help with my hair." She patted a place on the bed beside her. "But you're welcome to *kumm* and sit beside me. It is a *gut* night for a mother-daughter talk."

Her mother didn't need a second invitation. She plopped on the bed, folded her hands on her lap and got straight to the point.

"You told Thomas."

"Ja."

"I thought so. And how did he take it? What did he say?" Her mother looked intently at her, clearly anxious to hear every detail.

Elizabeth laughed again. "Weren't you standing in the hallway straining your ears to hear every word?"

Her mother's cheeks colored.

She had been standing in the hall!

Elizabeth hugged her mother and laughed with abandon. "I was only kidding but you really did creep into the hallway and try to listen, didn't you?"

Her mother pulled out of her arms and tried not to appear as flustered as she really was.

"I'm sorry. I couldn't just sit there with my sewing and pretend I didn't know what was going on." She looked chagrined. "But if it's any consolation, I couldn't hear a single word. And then Levi came in and caught me snooping and I had to rush back to my chair before he made an issue of it."

Elizabeth's grin was so wide her face hurt.

"What do you want me to say, *Mamm*? That you were right? That I should have told Thomas the entire truth in the beginning? That nothing good comes from secrets?"

Elizabeth threw her hands up in the air. "Well, you were right, *Mamm*." She hugged her mother again. When she released her, she smiled into her eyes. *"Denki, Mamm.* You gave me good advice."

Her mother smiled back. "How did Thomas react? Was he upset? Angry?"

"Maybe a little…at first." She pleated her hair into a braid that hung down her back. "I'd hurt him. Deeply."

Her mother nodded.

"But eventually he understood my choice even if he didn't agree with it." Elizabeth smiled. "He forgave me." She looked at her mother and said, "And then he kissed me."

Mary's mouth dropped open. Then she grinned and clapped her hands. "See? I was right. I told you Thomas is a *gut* man. I knew he would forgive you."

Elizabeth leaned to the side and purposely bumped her mother. "And Levi caught us."

Her mother laughed and the two of them giggled like schoolgirls. It brought back memories—good memories—and Elizabeth wished she had never left home. This was where she belonged, with her *mamm*, with the new friends she was making in the community and with Thomas. Suddenly the whole world seemed filled with opportunities and she couldn't remember ever being happier.

"Well, I am glad, child, that you did the right thing. Now it is no longer a secret. Wounds can heal. And who knows what *Gott* has in store for the two of you."

"Whoa, *Mamm*. Don't get ahead of yourself. Just because Thomas and I had this conversation and he said he forgave me, doesn't mean that we will be anything more than good friends."

Elizabeth crossed to the window and reached up to pull the curtain closed.

"Good friends who kiss each other," her mother teased.

Elizabeth chuckled. "*Ja*, I must admit the kissing part was fun. I wouldn't mind trying that again."

Elizabeth tugged again on the curtain but it stuck and wouldn't slide across the wooden rod. "What's with this curtain?" She looked up, couldn't see anything in the way and tugged it again.

"We need a new rod. There's a little spur on the top and if you don't pull it just the right way, the material gets stuck." Her mother came toward her. "Here, let me show you."

Mary stepped in front of Elizabeth and reached up to twist the material.

At that exact moment the window exploded and shards of glass flew everywhere. Both Mary and Elizabeth cried out and fell to the floor.

Elizabeth covered her face with her hands to protect against the flying glass. And she could feel little slivers bite into her hands, her neck and the little unexposed skin of her face.

Disoriented and confused, she sat up. She instinctively brushed the splintered glass off her face, shoulders and chest, while her mind tried to process what had happened. She was shaking broken glass out of her hair when she looked over at her mother.

Mary lay in a crumpled heap on the floor.

For a moment, Elizabeth thought she had curled into that position to shield herself from the flying glass.

"Mamm?"

When she didn't answer or move, Elizabeth quickly crawled across the few feet to her mother's side. Gingerly, she placed her hand on her back. "Are you *all-recht*? Did any of the glass cut you?"

She heard the thundering sound of someone racing up the stairs.

"Mamm?"

Gently, Elizabeth eased her mother over onto her back.

Her hands flew to her face and she screamed at the same moment the bedroom door burst open and Levi rushed into the room.

"What happened? What's going on?" Levi hurried to their side.

Her mother's blood smeared Elizabeth's face and covered her hands. "It's *Mamm*. I think she's dead."

Chapter Sixteen

Thomas hurried down the hospital corridor with Rachel clutched in his arms as he dragged Benjamin as fast as his little legs would go.

He hated hospitals.

He didn't know if it was the fluorescent lighting that always seemed unnatural and too bright, or the smell of antiseptic mingling with illness, or the sound of tears and hushed voices from the rooms he passed.

He had visited several members of the community over the years within these walls. And he had sat by Margaret's bed in this place and held her hand as she died.

Neh. He definitely did not like hospitals.

As he reached the final corridor, the waiting room came into view. His eyes found Elizabeth immediately. She sat slightly apart from the others, head bowed. Not far from her was Levi, as well as Bishop Schwartz and his wife, Sarah, and Isaac and Rebecca. The bishop had called him on the cell phone he was allowed to keep for business. He told Thomas to come to the hospital immediately. When asked why, he'd said only that Mary had been hurt and he would give him the details when he arrived. Then the bishop had told him where they would be.

Apparently Thomas was the last to arrive. But no surprise there. His farm was the farthest from the hospital and none of the others had two sleepy children to wake up and get dressed. But he was here now. His heart galloped in his chest, whether from the anxiety of having to hurry or the fear of what awaited him, or both, he wasn't sure.

Rebecca spotted him immediately and came down the hall toward him, while Benjamin let go of Thomas's hand and ran to join the others in the waiting room.

When Rebecca reached his side, she lifted Rachel, who had fallen back to sleep during the buggy ride, from his arms. "Give her to me, Thomas. Isaac and I will take care of the *kinner*. You will have other things you must do."

Rebecca glanced over her shoulder and when she turned back, she lowered her voice. "Go to her, Thomas. She needs you now."

"I will. But first, how is Mary? What happened? Is she ill? Did she have a heart attack or a bad fall or what?" he asked.

"Somebody shot her."

"What?" Shock roared through his body like a tsunami. "Who? How?" His thoughts flew in a million different directions. He felt helpless and confused—and angry to the bone. He shook his head as if that would make it all disappear.

"Where is Mary now?" he asked.

"She's in surgery. It is bad, Thomas. The doctor told

us he would do his best but we should prepare ourselves for the worst."

Thomas tried to absorb the information. "I don't understand. How did this happen?"

Before she could answer Thomas peered around her and saw the sheriff standing next to Elizabeth. He was asking her questions and writing her answers in his small notepad.

His eyes shot back to Rebecca. "It's that man Dolan, isn't it? He's back. Did he shoot Mary?" He was shocked. "Why would he do that? What did Mary ever do to him? She was no threat."

"We don't know for sure it was him. There were no witnesses, but who else would do such a thing?" Rebecca glanced back at the sheriff then returned her attention to Thomas. "The sheriff believes it was Mr. Dolan. He called his people to put out an alert."

Thomas gritted his teeth. "Tell me what happened."

"Elizabeth was at her bedroom window. She tried to pull the curtain closed but it got stuck. Mary came over to help. She stepped in front of Elizabeth just as a bullet smashed through the glass."

Thomas's stomach turned over.

That bullet was meant for Elizabeth!

"Was Elizabeth hurt?"

"Some cuts on her face and hands from flying glass. A bruise from hitting her knee when she fell onto the wood floor. But nothing serious." Rebecca looked sad and concerned. "Elizabeth's wounds go much deeper than the physical ones."

Dear Lord, denki for sparing Elizabeth. Please, Lord, don't let Mary die in her place. Mary is a gut woman, still young, and one of your faithful servants.

She has had much heartache in her life. Please spare her an early death.

Thomas took one long look at Elizabeth's bowed head, her slumped shoulders and her hands covering her face.

Lord, we both know if Mary dies that Elizabeth will never be able to forgive herself. Please, Lord, be merciful.

Thomas remembered not too long ago having a conversation with Elizabeth about how he was human and he had feelings. Well, he had feelings now. Deep, dark ugly ones. He hoped the sheriff found this horrible man before he did.

"Tell me about Mary. Where did he hit her? How bad were her injuries?" He took a deep breath, trying to steel himself for the answer while his mind screamed out against the scenario unfolding right in front of him.

Mary. Shot?

He couldn't wrap his head around it. He loved Mary like another mother.

Rebecca answered honestly and directly. "From what I was told, Mary stretched her arm over her head to reach the curtain. The bullet entered through her side under her arm. The doctor said it barely missed her heart. It did splinter a piece of her sternum and the fractured bone pieces caused additional damage to other tissue as well. She lost much blood before we were able to get her to the hospital."

When Thomas looked over again, he saw that the sheriff had left. He stared at the back of Elizabeth's bowed head for several long moments. She looked frail, broken, almost as if something as soft as a whisper could blow her over. His heart ached for her. But he couldn't go to her. Not yet. Not with all these dark, angry feelings roiling inside.

He glanced at his sleeping daughter, who was nestled in Rebecca's arms, and it brought a ghost of a smile to his lips. There was still good in this world.

He placed a hand on Rebecca's shoulder. "*Denki* for taking care of the *kinner* for me." He turned and started to walk away.

"Wait!" Rebecca said in a hushed voice. "Thomas, where are you going? You should be with Elizabeth. I believe your presence will be a calming influence on her."

Thomas smiled fondly at his former mother-in-law. She had never questioned his feelings for this new woman in his life or even that he had any, which was more than he could say for himself. She had never shown any signs of remorse or jealousy that Margaret might be replaced in his heart, in his *kinner*'s heart. But then, his mother-in-law seemed to know what he already knew. Margaret would always have a place in his heart and a presence in the lives of his *kinner*. Still, her kindness and empathy touched him.

"You are a kind woman, Rebecca. I appreciate all you do for me."

"We are family, Thomas. We will always be family." Her eyes glistened with unshed tears.

Thomas knew Margaret was right there with them, at this very moment. He could almost feel her presence and she was very much on both their minds.

"*Ja*, Rebecca. Always."

The moment passed and Thomas glanced at Elizabeth again. She seemed to be purposely keeping the others at bay. He knew her well enough to know what was going on in her mind and in her heart. She believed she was the reason Mary was shot and she didn't want anyone else close enough to her to be hurt.

"You're right. Even if Elizabeth doesn't think she needs me, even if she tries to push me away, I need to be with her. I can't let her go through this alone. But not yet. I have someplace else I need to be."

Without another word, he turned and moved swiftly down the hospital corridor. He knew exactly where he was going and he couldn't get there fast enough. He had passed a set of double doors on his way in and took note of the small sign posted outside.

Within minutes he had reached his destination and pushed open the chapel doors.

The wee hours of the morning became dawn and then daylight. And yet there was still no word from the doctors about her mother. Elizabeth didn't think she had a tear left in her body. Her mother couldn't die. She couldn't lose her. Not now. Not when they'd just been reunited. And not from a bullet that had been meant for her.

"Elizabeth."

The sound of Thomas's voice flowed over her nerve endings like a healing balm. She turned to face him. He offered her a paper cup of hot coffee, presumably from one of the hospital vending machines. A swift look around the room showed more and more of their community arriving as the day progressed and word traveled from farm to farm and house to house.

She accepted the coffee gratefully.

"Can I get you something to eat? The hospital cafeteria's open. Isaac and Rebecca just got back from taking the *kinner* downstairs for some breakfast. It took them a little extra time. Benjamin decided to hit every button in the elevator before Isaac could stop him so they paused on every floor."

Elizabeth smiled for the first time in the past twelve hours. That was so like Benjamin. "*Neh*, I'm not hungry."

"Elizabeth, you have to have something. The last thing anyone needs is for you to get weak or sick, too."

"*Mamm* isn't sick, Thomas. She's shot. That horrible, evil man shot her." She looked up at him and wondered if her expression mirrored the shell-shocked emptiness she felt inside.

"I can't believe *Mamm* is fighting for her life from a bullet that was meant for me," she whispered.

Thomas didn't try to dissuade her. He simply sat beside her and clasped her hand, offering empathy and understanding. She didn't know how she'd be getting through all this if she hadn't been able to lean on his rock-solid calmness.

"We should hear something soon." He squeezed her hand. "In the meantime, you need to eat."

She shook her head. "I can't. Food would only get lodged in my throat and choke me." She squeezed his hand in return. "I'm *allrecht*. Truly. I'll eat when I need to."

She leaned her head against his shoulder. She knew she shouldn't. She knew the Amish frowned on personal contact or affection in public. And she knew she had no right to assume a more personal relationship than Thomas might be willing to offer. They'd been an item years ago. That didn't mean Thomas wanted to rekindle old flames.

Still.

She needed him. She needed his strength, his presence, his fortitude.

And, thank the good Lord, he was giving it to her.

It doesn't matter right now if he is offering me friendship or if there is a possibility for more. He's here. Thank You, Lord.

She nestled closer, inhaling the faint scent of hay on his coat, which he'd thrown over the back of his chair. She absorbed the heat of his body through his flannel shirt as he drew her closer and wrapped his arm around her back.

"Thomas?"

"Ja?"

The sound of his voice rumbled in his chest beneath her ear and she smiled.

She raised her head and looked into his face.

"Why can't they find him? They know who he is. They know where he works, where he lives. He is a public figure. Many people know him. Why hasn't anyone spotted him yet?"

"They will. He cannot hide forever."

"He should have been arrested days ago." She looked him straight in the eye. "Do you think they are really looking for him? I know they all thought it was a big joke in the beginning. That a simple Amish woman would mistakenly identify a revered senator as the perpetrator of such heinous crimes."

She gently pushed off him and sat up. "But they can't still be thinking I'm crazy, can they? They have to be looking for him, right? Especially now. How can they think that *Mamm* being shot is a coincidence or was done by someone else?"

"Shh, calm down." He pulled her close again, and wrapped his arm around her shoulders. "Of course they believe you. I spoke to the sheriff myself. They know he did this. Everyone does and they are looking everywhere for him. They will find him…soon. How can they not? He is flesh and blood like the rest of us. Someone will see him." He reached down and clasped her hands. "Will you pray with me?"

She nodded and was taken aback a little when she saw surprise register on his face. Did he think she didn't believe in *Gott*? Or did he still believe she was trying to control the world?

She bowed her head and clasped his hands.

They prayed together for a long while, fervently, and Elizabeth couldn't deny the sense of peace that descended upon her. No matter what happened, she knew it would be *Gott*'s will and that He would be by her side helping her through the hard times every step of the way. The thought calmed her more than anything or anyone. She had come home. Not just to her Amish roots. She had repented and returned to *Gott*.

"Ms. Lapp?"

Elizabeth and Thomas turned toward the man standing in the doorway. "I'm Dr. Gardner. I wanted to let you know your mother made it through the surgery. It is still touch-and-go, though. It was a much longer and more difficult surgery than we expected. There was extensive internal damage. We had to remove her spleen and a small part of her liver due to damage from the ricocheting bone fragments. But I've been told she's a fighter. I hope they were right because that's what we need her to be right now."

"Can we see her?" Thomas stood and faced the doctor.

"Only for a few minutes. Her body needs to rest so it will be strong enough to fight to recuperate."

"We understand." Elizabeth rose. "We won't stay long but I do want her to know we're here."

The doctor nodded and they followed him down the hall.

When he pushed open the door, Elizabeth just stood in the doorway. She couldn't make her legs propel her forward. Her mother looked so small and frail lying in that hospital bed. Tubes and wires seemed to be connected to every available piece of her flesh, even tubing in her nose. Two large machines on either side of the bed whooshed and beeped as they monitored her blood pressure, heart rate and oxygen levels. She had never seen her mother so vulnerable and it tore at her heart.

Thomas thanked the doctor as he left and gently guided her into the room.

Elizabeth crossed directly to the bed. She reached down and, careful not to disturb any of the apparatus, lifted her mother's hand to her lips. When she put it back down, one of her tears fell onto her mother's skin.

"Mamm," she whispered. "Thomas and I are here. You made it through the surgery. You're going to be just fine." She reached into her pocket, withdrew a white prayer *kapp* and positioned it on her mother's head. Smiling at Thomas, she said, "This will make her feel better when she wakes up. She would feel naked without her prayer *kapp*."

They stood by the bedside for a few moments longer, staring down at her pale, still form. Thomas leaned forward and planted a kiss on the woman's forehead.

Thomas's devotion, his tenderness toward her

mother, touched Elizabeth's heart and she knew her eyes glistened with unshed tears at the sight.

"She loves you, you know," she told Thomas. "For an Amish woman who is not known for giving compliments, she sings your praises night and day."

Thomas chuckled. "I think she's pretty special, too."

He came around and clasped Elizabeth's elbow. "*Kumm.* We told the doctor we would not stay long." He gently steered her toward the door. They were just about to leave the room when they heard a very faint voice call out.

Elizabeth rushed back to her mother's side and grinned when she saw the woman open her eyes.

"Hi, *Mamm.*" She clasped her mother's hand and, careful not to disturb the IV tubing, squeezed gently. "You gave us a pretty good scare." She leaned forward and pressed her lips against her mother's brow and then straightened. "The doctor said the surgery went well but you're not out of the woods yet. He said you have to fight to get better, *Mamm.* I know you can do it. You're one of the strongest women I know."

Mary slowly looked from Elizabeth to Thomas, blinking frequently as if trying to orient herself to her situation and surroundings, and then her gaze settled back on Elizabeth.

"What do doctors know?" she asked in a hoarse whisper. "They are not *Gott.* I have already spoken to *Gott.* I don't believe He wants me to come home yet."

Thomas and Elizabeth shot glances at each other and chuckled.

"Good to hear," Thomas said, "because I'm not ready to say goodbye."

Mary had a spasm of coughing, enough to make

the monitors signal the nurse, who ushered them away from the bed and told them they had to leave and let her have her rest.

They were at the door to go when Mary spoke again.

"Thomas." He turned and looked her way. "Everyone must band together and find where this man is hiding. He must not be allowed to hurt anyone else."

Thomas nodded. "Don't worry, Mary. We are all working together—our community, the local police, the Philadelphia police. There is no place left for the man to hide."

"Promise me?"

Thomas raised an eyebrow.

Elizabeth knew her mother had surprised him as well as herself. The Amish didn't make promises. They simply said they would do something or they would not. They didn't ever want to promise something they might not be able to deliver. That would be the same as lying.

Elizabeth watched as Thomas straightened to his full height, his broad shoulders filling most of the open doorway. His eyes glittered with a fierce determination and his mouth looked carved in granite. He looked her mother straight in the eye when he spoke.

"I promise, Mary."

Chapter Seventeen

❧

"I have to go now, Thomas."

Thomas stood up from the sofa, where he'd been watching the *kinner* play with their toys on the hardwood floor.

"I still don't understand why you refuse to stay with us. Haven't you ever heard the phrase *there is safety in numbers*? You will not be safe all alone at your place."

His arm swept the room. "We have plenty of room. You can have your old room back. Stay, Elizabeth. At least until Mary is released from the hospital."

Rebecca looked up from her sewing and uncharacteristically inserted herself into the conversation.

"You might even decide to stay a little longer than planned. Once Mary is well enough to come home, she is still going to be weak and need extra care for quite a while. If you stay here, you won't have to do it all alone."

Elizabeth smiled at her. Both of the women knew it wouldn't matter where Mary stayed when she got out of the hospital. The women in the community would band together and help with her care, with housekeeping and cooking whether she was in her own home or in someone else's. That's what their Amish family did for each other.

No. Rebecca was matchmaking.

Elizabeth could see the hint of a smile on the woman's lips and took note how she was careful not to make eye contact with either one of them so as not to tip her hand.

Elizabeth's smile widened.

Considering that Rebecca was Margaret's mother, Elizabeth felt humbled and happy that the woman not only approved of her possible place in their lives, but also seemed to be inviting it, hoping Thomas would take the bait with proximity.

All the more reason for her to go.

"*Neh*, Thomas. I appreciate the offer but I want to go home."

Thomas nailed her feet to the floor with his intense gaze. "Running away again, Elizabeth?"

She bristled beneath his words and felt defensive and on guard. "That was uncalled for."

"Well? What do you call it?" Thomas asked. "You have been doing your best for days now to stay as far away from all of us as possible. You are skittish and nervous all the time. You constantly look over your shoulder and jump at the slightest sound. And yet you refuse to let any of us help you. I'm surprised you accepted the buggy ride here and actually came inside for a hot meal."

"I had no choice. I had no other transportation and I am sure you were the one responsible for everyone else being suddenly busy."

Elizabeth smiled at Rebecca. "*Denki*, for the meal, Rebecca. I hadn't eaten anything of substance for two days. I needed a home-cooked meal." Elizabeth moved toward the door. "But I really need to be getting home."

Thomas's eyes glittered like an iceberg in the middle of the ocean. His voice deepened and a tone of censure coated his words.

"You said you would never run away again." He pierced her with his gaze. "Why do I feel like you're running, Elizabeth?"

As they stared long and hard at each other, Rebecca lowered her eyes and pretended to concentrate on her sewing.

"My *mamm* is still in the intensive care unit. Do you really think I would abandon her when she needs me?"

Now, there was silence.

Elizabeth knew this had nothing to do with her mother, and only a little to do with her going back to her own house. Once Mary had opened her eyes, spoken, and seemed to be on the mend, Elizabeth had started subtly pushing away Thomas. Not because she didn't care. But because she did. She was poison right now to anyone in her community and she had to protect them even if they wouldn't protect themselves.

But it wasn't until this moment, when she heard the anger in his tone and saw the fear in his eyes, that she realized Thomas had taken it the wrong way and believed she was pushing *him* away because she didn't care rather than because she wanted him safe. He was afraid to open up to her. Afraid she would break his trust and abandon him again without a word.

She had no one to blame but herself for that misconception.

When was she going to learn how to talk to him, really communicate, so he would know that she never, ever would hurt him like that again?

Immediately she crossed to his side, placed a comforting hand on his arm and smiled up at him. "Thomas, I am not running away. I will never run away again. I promise."

His eyes widened.

She knew those final two words held incredible weight with him. The same weight he'd given them when he'd promised Mary that Dolan would be found.

He reached out and clasped her arms in turn. "You are safer here. You are safer with me."

She cupped his face. "*Ja*, Thomas. I know I am safe with you. You would protect me with your life. I know that. I trust that."

She gave him her sweetest, most tender smile. "But I don't want that."

Elizabeth looked over at the children playing on the floor. Benjamin had built a corral out of twigs for his carved horse and cow and was playing with them. Rachel held her little plastic dog. She'd tied a piece of yellow ribbon around its neck and was playing at taking it for a walk across the hardwood floor. Elizabeth had to chuckle because it certainly looked more like dragging and banging than walking.

"Look at those precious, beautiful *kinner*, Thomas. They are your priority. They are the ones you must protect at all costs. And keeping me here, in their presence, is dangerous." She forced him to make eye contact with her. "I cannot allow what happened to my *mamm* to happen to these *kinner*, or you, or Rebecca or Isaac." She kissed his cheek. "And neither can you."

She stepped back and his tormented expression

wrenched her heart. She knew he recognized the truth of her words but she knew him well enough to know he also wanted to be there for her and he was finding it difficult to do both safely for everyone.

"I'll be *allrecht*, Thomas. I can take care of myself."

"All alone?"

"I won't be alone."

He raised a brow.

"I am in *Gott*'s hands. *Ja?*" She smiled softly. "And I've given *Gott* a little bit of help. I've agreed to allow the sheriff to put me in protective custody until Dolan is captured."

He looked shocked, but as he stood mulling over her words, she saw he understood the logic of the decision.

"When did you make this arrangement? You've been with me and I haven't seen you speak with the sheriff."

"I wasn't sure how you would react so I discussed my plans with the bishop. He thought it was the safest thing to do and agreed to go and speak to the sheriff for me." Her smile widened. "Matter of fact, I expect either the deputy or the sheriff is waiting for me at my house right now. I told them I would return there to gather some of my things as soon as I had dinner here. That would give them time to prepare and…" She paused long enough to clamp control over her emotions. "It would give me time to say a proper goodbye."

Rebecca's head jerked up. She looked concerned but she didn't interrupt them.

Thomas pondered the information a little longer.

"How long do you think you will be gone?"

"Not long. As you, yourself, said Thomas, this man cannot hide much longer."

Although a frown pulled at the corners of his mouth, Thomas nodded his head.

"*Denki*, Thomas, for understanding. Please believe me, this is difficult for me, too. But I must protect the people I love. You understand that, *ja*?"

Tears surprisingly glistened in his eyes. He gave her a bittersweet smile.

"I need you to do one other thing for me," she said.

"Anything."

"I need you to check in on *Mamm* every day. Make her understand why I am not there and assure her that I am safe."

"There is no need to ask for something I will do anyway."

"And there's one other thing." She grinned. "Lend me a horse so I can get home. I will tend to him and leave him in the barn for you to pick up later."

"I can…"

"You can stay here with your family, Thomas, where you belong."

He stared at her for a long, hard minute and then he nodded. "I will get the horse ready."

He had just started to move toward the door when Rachel broke out in heart-wrenchingly loud wailing. All eyes turned toward the child.

Thomas was at her side and squatting beside her in a heartbeat. "What, darling? What's wrong?" His hands smoothed her hair while his eyes searched her for injury.

"Doggy's broken," she cried.

She held her pudgy little hands high. One part of the dog hung suspended from the ribbon she'd used as a leash and the other part of the dog was fisted in her other hand.

"That's okay," Thomas assured her. "Let *Daed* see. Maybe I can fix the doggy for you."

He took both pieces from her and looked at them strangely. "What…?"

Elizabeth moved in for a closer look.

"Thomas," she exclaimed. "That's not one of Hannah's toy knickknacks. I didn't look at it closely before. It's a flash drive."

"A flash what?"

"A flash drive! A flash drive! It's a portable computer file. You wouldn't believe the things you can store on one of these." She yanked the piece with the silver protrusion from his hand and held it up in front of her face for a closer look. She could barely contain her excitement as she bounced and spun around. "I can't believe I didn't look at this closer. I thought it was a knickknack. Hannah had dozens of little toys she kept around. Most flash drives are flat and rectangular. I never suspected one could be inside something that looked like a toy. Unbelievable! *Denki, Gott!*"

"I don't understand. Why are you so excited over this—this flash drive thing?"

"Don't you see? This is it!" she said, tossing glances at both Thomas and Rebecca. "This is what Dolan has been looking for. Hannah must have put something incriminating on this drive. Something he knows law enforcement can use to put him behind bars for life." She whooped and hollered and both children, not sure why they were doing it, whooped and cheered with her.

She stopped her spinning and held the flash drive in front of Thomas's face. "This is our freedom, Thomas. Hannah gave us the gift of freedom." She threw her arms around Thomas and then kissed him soundly.

"Elizabeth…"

She grabbed his hand and started to pull him toward the door. "*Kumm*, Thomas. We have to get it to the sheriff right away."

"Whoa! Slow down." Thomas clasped her arm and made her sit down on the sofa. Elizabeth's excitement was contagious but he'd learned through life's experience to err on the side of caution. Until he understood what was happening, he wasn't going anywhere. "I know you're excited but I have questions."

"So do I," said Rebecca.

Rebecca came over and sat on one side of Elizabeth while Thomas sat on the other. The children, having fun with their whooping and hollering, continued to spin themselves until they got dizzy and collapsed on the floor laughing.

"May I?" Rebecca asked as she took the flash drive out of Elizabeth's hands and stared at it quizzically. "You said there are files stored on this toy?" She turned it one way, then another. "I don't understand how this can hold anything? Where would it be? How could it be of any help?"

Elizabeth reclaimed the drive and held it protectively in her fisted hand. "It's a piece of technology they use every day in the *Englisch* world. I know you don't understand, but trust me. I honestly believe this is the missing piece. This is what Hannah told Dolan I had in my possession. It has to be! There was nothing else of value in that box."

She started to spring to her feet. "I've got to get this to the sheriff."

Thomas stopped her from rising. "Wait!" When he

had her attention, he said, "I agree. We should get this to the sheriff. But not before we know what, if anything, is on it."

"What?" Elizabeth shot him a puzzled look. "Why? How can we find out what's on the file without giving it to the sheriff first?"

"I have Mennonite friends that run the hardware store in town. They use a computer in their business. I will take it to my friend. John will put it in his computer for me and tell me what is on it." Thomas slid the drive out of her hand and placed it in his shirt pocket. "If you are right, Elizabeth, and this holds information about Dolan, I will make sure the sheriff gets it right away." He looked at her and his heart was heavy. She was so excited. So sure this would be the answer. How could he face her disappointment if she was wrong? He had to slow her down and buy both of them some time to think things through.

"Elizabeth, don't you think we should know what is on this thing before we hand it over sight unseen to the sheriff? It is possibly the only evidence against this man. We owe it to Hannah to be smart, be logical and do the right thing."

"Are you certain your friend can help us?"

"*Ja*, I am sure. He will be happy to do it. But that is not what concerns me." He stared into her eyes. "I'm sorry. I know you are excited and you don't want to delay, but Dolan is a prominent man in the *Englisch* world. I don't trust that it is a safe or wise thing to hand over the only proof of wrongdoing we have without knowing what that proof might be. Do you?"

Thomas could see her take a deep breath and slowly she calmed down.

"You're right, Thomas. We need to know what is on that drive. When you take it to your friend, ask him to make a copy for us. He can save it on his computer and put it on another flash drive for us. If your Mennonite friend owns a computer, he will know how to do that easily."

Thomas nodded. "*Allrecht*, I will drop you at your house and then I will drive the buggy into town to see my friend."

"*Denki.*"

"Will you care for the *kinner*, Rebecca?" Thomas asked.

"Certainly. I am as anxious as both of you to help catch this man before he can hurt anyone else."

Elizabeth grinned and sprang to her feet.

Thomas rose a bit slower. He didn't feel right about leaving Elizabeth at the house. Danger clung to her heels like a person's shadow.

"Are you certain the sheriff or his deputy will be there to keep you safe while I am gone?" he asked.

"I am sure."

"Fine. Then I will get the buggy ready." He paused in the doorway. "And if the sheriff is not at your house when we arrive, I will take you into town with me. Understand? I am in no mood to deal with your stubbornness right now."

Elizabeth laughed. "No problem, Thomas. I want to know what's on that drive as much as you do. I'm only going to the house to try and draw Dolan to me and away from you."

"That is supposed to make me feel better?" His insides twisted into knots. He didn't want to leave Elizabeth's side. But he didn't want to put his family in danger, either. And he couldn't think of any other way to find out what was on this contraption in his pocket than to leave them both. He prayed to *Gott* that he wasn't making a terrible mistake.

"Don't worry, Thomas. If the sheriff isn't there, we won't have a choice. We will have to go into town together." She clasped her hands in front of her chest, "But please—" her gaze pleaded with him "—we must hurry."

Without any further discussion, he grabbed his hat from the peg by the door and hurried toward the barn.

Chapter Eighteen

"See! I told you, Thomas. Everything is going to be okay."

Thomas pulled the buggy to a stop next to the police car parked in front of Elizabeth's front porch. An officer got out as they pulled up.

"Good afternoon, Ms. Lapp." He extended a hand to help her descend from the buggy. "I'm Deputy Benson."

Elizabeth had to stifle a smile. This young man didn't look old enough to be a deputy or anything else in law enforcement. He looked like a teenager playing dress up. But the gun hanging on his belt wasn't a toy so she supposed she was in good hands.

"Nice to meet you, Deputy Benson. Thank you for helping us."

He touched the brim of his hat and nodded. "The sheriff said I'm not to leave your side. He wants you to pack a couple of bags and then I'm to bring you into the station."

Thomas leaned across the passenger seat of the buggy. "Have you checked the property, Deputy Benson? Are you sure no one is here?"

"I did."

"The barn, too?"

"Sir…"

The young deputy bristled beneath Thomas's questioning. "The barn was the first place I looked. I know how to do my job."

"He didn't mean anything by it, Deputy." Elizabeth hurried to defuse the male testosterone creating tension where there shouldn't be any. "This man has been too clever for all of us. Thomas is only trying to help."

The deputy looked over at Thomas and patted his gun. "She'll be fine. No one is going to get past me."

Thomas didn't look relieved. If anything, the lines on his brow and around his mouth deepened.

"Thomas, the sooner you leave, the sooner you'll have what we need and you'll come back." She waved him away. "Hurry, okay?"

Thomas shot one more frown at the deputy before snapping the reins, then he turned the buggy around and headed back down the gravel lane.

Maybe I'm imagining things, but that buggy sure seems to be leaving a lot faster than it got here.

Elizabeth smiled to herself. It felt good to have Thomas be protective and caring. But nothing could make her more excited at the moment than the discovery of the flash drive. She didn't know what was on it, but she had no doubt it was the missing piece. Soon this would all be over and then…

Elizabeth's smile widened as she pondered the possibilities.

"Ms. Lapp."

She turned at the sound of her name.

"Let's get you inside. You'll be safer if you're not

standing out in the open." The deputy glanced around. "I've checked out the area but it is still a good idea to move you inside."

The deputy stepped to the side and swept a hand toward the house. "Besides, you have to get busy and pack. It'll be dark soon and I know the sheriff wants to get you settled in for the night."

Elizabeth nodded and preceded the deputy into the house.

Now all she had to do was stall the deputy for a couple of hours to give Thomas enough time to complete his task and get back here. Somehow she thought she had the more difficult assignment.

Thomas clicked the reins urging the horse faster.

He hadn't wanted to leave Elizabeth with that deputy. The man didn't look older than some of the teenagers working the fields. And the officer patted the gun on his hip as though that should make Thomas feel more confident in his ability to protect her.

Well, it didn't.

It had the opposite effect if truth be told. He looked like a young man dressed up in costume who itched for the opportunity to pull out that gun and use it. The officer's bravado showed no respect for the power and the responsibility of the weapon he wore.

But what choice did Thomas have? Rebecca was alone at his homestead with his precious children. Elizabeth was alone with a man-child pretending to be a cop. He was alone in a buggy on a dark road heading to a friend's house to find out what was on a toy.

Meanwhile a killer lurked in the darkness, able

to strike anytime, anywhere, and there was nothing Thomas could do about it.

Tears burned at the back of his eyes. Hot tears. Angry tears. Helpless tears.

How would he ever survive if something happened to his *kinner* while he was off chasing down the files on a toy?

He clenched his teeth.

Was he doing the right thing?

An image of Elizabeth popped into his mind. The hope in her eyes. The excitement in her voice. Her certainty that the toy in his pocket held their freedom.

But what if this plastic dog was nothing more than a toy? Or didn't hold any valuable information after all?

And, worse, what if the killer took this opportunity to make his final move?

Thomas's stomach soured.

Fear crept up his spine and almost paralyzed him. He'd never felt soul-deep fear. He'd been startled a time or two. Sure. Everyone had. And he'd had a sinking fear when Mary had been shot that she might not survive her injury because of her age. But this was different.

This fear was accompanied by a sense of impending doom, a mental preview of unbearable loss, a hopelessness unlike anything he'd ever experienced before.

His chest seized with panic and his breathing came in shallow bursts.

"Help me, *Gott*."

That's all he could say. That's all he could cry out. But it was all he needed. An inner peace came over him and filled him up from his toes to the top of his head.

No matter what happened this night, Thomas had to

remember that *Gott* was the one in control and as much as Thomas loved his *kinner* and loved Elizabeth, *Gott* loved all of them more. Thomas found great solace in that belief.

As his buggy moved down Main Street he could still see lights in the office window of his friend's business.

Denki, Gott, that I got here before he left for home.

He hitched his horse to the porch railing, sprang up the porch steps of his friend's business, and pushed open the door.

John, sitting behind a desk, looked up when the bell over the door tinkled.

"Thomas. *Gut* to see you. What brings you out at this time of night?"

Thomas crossed directly to the counter housing one of the computers and John got up and met him there.

"Is everything *allrecht*?"

"It will be if you can help me." Thomas withdrew the flash drive from his shirt pocket and slid it across the counter toward his friend. "I need to know what is on this toy."

John picked up the dog and studied the metal prongs of the flash drive. "I've never seen a flash drive disguised as a toy. Where did you get this?"

"Please, John, it does not matter right now. I need to know the secrets hidden inside it, and every second that passes puts my family in grave danger. Can you help me?"

John's face blanched at the mention of danger, but he didn't hesitate. He immediately turned on his computer and slid the dog into an opening on the side of the machine. He hit a button once. Twice. Then blinked at the screen and turned the laptop to face Thomas.

"Take a look, Thomas. Is this what you're looking for?"

Chapter Nineteen

The deputy pushed his chair back and patted his stomach. "That was delicious, Ms. Lapp, I haven't had a home-cooked meal that good in years."

"Thank you."

He started to get up.

Elizabeth put her hand on his forearm to stop him and then pulled back. "Wait, officer. Let me refill that coffee cup for you. It'll only take me a few minutes to brew a fresh pot."

"Sorry, Ms. Lapp." He glanced at his watch. "We should have been on the road two and a half hours ago."

"I have pie." She hurried over to the counter and brought back an apple pie. "Now don't tell me you can't squeeze in a few minutes for a cup of coffee and a slice of pie."

The young man stared at the golden pastry and his conflicting emotions warred across his face. "I'll tell you what. You go upstairs and pack while I go outside and take another check around the house and the barn. When I come back, if the coffee is ready, we'll have a quick cup and a slice of that delicious-looking pie and then hit the road."

Elizabeth knew she'd stalled as long as she could and he wouldn't tolerate much more. She smiled sweetly. "It's a deal."

As soon as the deputy left, she put on another pot of coffee, ran upstairs to throw a few dresses and other needed items into a bag and made it back to the kitchen in record time.

She glanced out the kitchen window into the darkness.

Where are you, Thomas? I'm running out of ideas. Please. Hurry.

The smell of freshly brewed coffee filled the room and Elizabeth hoped the young deputy would find it enticing. If he was in such a big hurry, he should have been back by now. Maybe he was still sensitive about Thomas questioning him and was doing an extra-thorough job.

Or maybe he was on his car radio trying to explain to the sheriff why they weren't in town yet.

She finished washing the last of the dishes when she heard the front door open and close.

She wiped her hands on the towel next to the dish drainer, smiled as brightly as she could and turned to face the deputy.

"Your timing is perfect. The coffee…"

The words died on her lips as she faced Richard Dolan, standing in the doorway with a gun pointed directly at her chest.

She made a dash for the back door.

He moved faster and pushed her against the counter. "Just where do you think you're going, huh?" He grabbed her arm with his left hand and twisted it behind her painfully. "I'm tired of playing games with you. We're ending this right now." He pushed the gun into her stomach. "Am I making myself clear?"

Her heart beat double time and she nodded.

He saw her glance toward the kitchen entrance. "Looking for your policeman bodyguard to come to your rescue?" He gave her a menacing sneer. "I can't believe how long it took for him to finally come outside. What were you two doing in here all that time?" The evilness of his grin sickened her.

She squirmed beneath his hands. "Get away from me. Let me go."

The gun pressed into her abdomen harder.

"Don't worry, honey. I'm not interested in anything you have to offer. One of you Amish women tempted me years ago but it's not going to happen again."

Elizabeth's heart seized as his words reminded her of the broad scope of the crimes he'd committed against good, innocent people. Her mother had been right. This had to be Hannah's father. Her stomach turned and she thought she was going to be sick. She threw another look at the door.

"Look all you want. He's not coming, lady. You've run out of time. It's just you and me now."

His fingers dug into the flesh of her arm and he practically threw her into the closest chair. He leaned close and said in a soft, menacing tone, "Let me explain how this works. I'm going to ask you for the last time to give me the evidence that Hannah passed on to you. And, if you're smart, you're going to give it to me."

"How do I know you aren't going to kill me anyway?"

"You don't." He sat down next to her and slid the

muzzle of his gun under her chin. "But it's the only chance you have." She took a breath of relief when he removed the gun and sat back in his chair. "Now, where is it?"

"You killed Hannah."

He blinked. "Are you kidding me? You know I did. You were there. What game are you playing?" He pointed the gun at her chest. "Are you just plain stupid? I'm not fooling around. Give me what's mine. Now."

Elizabeth's heart ached for Hannah. The last few moments of her life she knew she was dying. And she knew it was her own father killing her. Tears rolled down Elizabeth's face.

"Will it do any good if I say it was an accident?" Dolan asked. "I didn't mean to kill her. All I wanted was the evidence she'd collected against me. We started arguing. She started hitting me and tried to run away. I grabbed her by the throat to stop her." A flash of remorse made him look almost human for a moment. "Do you think I wanted to kill my own daughter? I was angry and I squeezed too tight. By the time I realized it, she had already stopped breathing."

"You might have still been able to save her. If you had tried to revive her…if you had called 911."

He slapped her across the face. The blow stunned her and hot pain shot through her left cheek.

"You ruined everything!" He screamed at her, spittle from his words hitting her face. "You came in the door, saw what had happened and took off. I didn't have any time to think things through. I had to react. I went after you and by the time I got back…"

"You shot my mother, too. You almost killed her."

"You and I both know that shot was meant for you." He shrugged. "She got in the way."

"And you sawed through the ladder. You could have killed Thomas."

His face contorted with rage. "What did you expect? Did you think I was going to let you and your friends destroy me and everything I spent my entire life working for?"

He pushed the muzzle of his gun beneath her chin so hard she didn't dare move or even breathe for fear he'd pull the trigger.

He glared at her with an intensity that frightened her to her soul.

Please help me, Lord.

He took several deep breaths and then stepped back. "I thought it was over." He sank into the chair opposite her. "When the police published the composite drawing I thought I was in the clear. No one would be able to identify me from that stupid drawing. Didn't look like me at all. The box you gave me didn't have anything in it but junk. So I began to think maybe you really didn't have anything and I didn't have to worry about you identifying me. You'd already tried and it was a dismal failure."

Elizabeth, afraid to anger him more, remained quiet while he ranted.

"I went through the box you dropped in the doorway of Hannah's condo and I found the journals. I was named as her mother's rapist."

He looked at her incredulously "Rapist? Is that what Hannah believed?" He flailed his arm as he spoke, the gun moving wildly with each movement. "I was a drunken twenty-two-year-old young man. Okay, I didn't stop when her mother said no. I get that. But we were kids. Kids do stupid things. It doesn't make me a rapist."

"It does if she said no."

He straightened and glared at Elizabeth.

"I tried to reason with Hannah. I tried to explain. She wouldn't have any of it. She told me that I'd ruined her mother's life and forced her to marry a man she hadn't loved. And that I ruined her life because that man never accepted her for his own."

He waved his arm again as he spoke.

"Why couldn't she leave it alone?" He stared at her. "I convinced myself that I had the evidence against me in those journals. The composite was a joke. I was free and clear, so I went home."

Again, the gun pointed her way. "But then the police said a witness was coming forward with evidence so I realized I wasn't in the clear after all." He hit her again. "You deserve everything that is going to happen to you. We both could have gone on with our lives in peace if you didn't decide to go to the police.

"When Hannah came to my office to confront me, I denied everything. We argued. I threw her out. But not before she'd grabbed my coffee cup from my desk." He inched closer. "She had a DNA test run, didn't she? That's the evidence you're planning on using against me."

He sprang up, overturning his chair with a loud bang that made Elizabeth flinch.

"I can't let you ruin me. My marriage and family. My future run for president. My entire life hangs in the hands of a stupid, Amish fool." He outstretched his hand. "Time's up. Give it to me. Now."

"I will." She barely moved her lips, not wanting her chin to press against the barrel of the gun.

He looked surprised for a moment. Then he grinned and moved the gun away. "Good. Now you're talking intelligently." He held out his left hand, palm up. "Where is it?"

"I don't have it on me." She threw her hands up to protect her face when she saw his angry expression. "What? Do you think I'd carry something so important around in my apron pocket? I'll—I'll get it for you."

"You better." He dragged her to her feet and shook her hard, his fingers digging into her flesh. "What evidence do you have?"

"Hannah put everything on a flash drive."

"Where is it?"

"Right here." Thomas stepped into the kitchen. His heart pounded in his chest at the sight of his worst nightmare. The armed man dragged Elizabeth to her feet and Thomas could tell from the pained expression on her face that his fingers were digging into her arms.

Neither of them must have heard the buggy pulling up, or Thomas letting himself into the house. He had a moment of self-doubt. Maybe he shouldn't have made his presence known. Maybe he should have run to the barn for a pitchfork or shovel to use as a weapon. But once he saw Dolan with his hands on Elizabeth he couldn't turn away.

And where was the deputy? He'd been right. The man hadn't been sufficient protection at all.

Elizabeth's gaze locked with his and he saw a flash of hope. But just as quickly it changed to one of fear and regret. He knew she believed Dolan was going to kill them and she didn't want him here.

Dolan pulled Elizabeth in front of him as a shield and put the muzzle of the gun under her chin. "Stay back or I'll kill her."

Thomas raised both his hands. "Relax. I'm no threat. There's no need for you to hurt anyone."

"Do you have the flash drive?"

"Ja." Thomas held up the drive in his right hand.

Dolan looked at it and then got angrier. "Do you think I'm stupid? That's a kid's toy!" Without hesitation he lowered the gun and shot Elizabeth in the shoulder.

She screamed out with pain and collapsed onto the floor.

"No!" Thomas began to move toward her when Dolan lifted the muzzle of the gun and pointed it at Elizabeth.

"Stay where you are or I'll shoot her in the head and be done with it."

Thomas froze in place, slowly raising his hands again. "This is the flash drive. We thought it was a toy, too. That's why we didn't put it in the box we gave you. I let one of my *kinner* play with it but it isn't a toy. Let me prove it."

Dolan nodded his permission.

Slowly, Thomas pulled apart the toy, revealing the flash-drive mechanism.

Dolan looked surprised, then relieved. "Give it to me."

"Gladly." Thomas threw the flash drive as hard as he could, hitting Dolan in the right eye. Dolan instinctively raised his right hand to his eye and pulled the gun away from Elizabeth while Thomas rushed forward and slammed into the man. They smashed against the counter, bounced off of it and fell entwined to the floor.

Thomas fought desperately to subdue the man while still trying to pull the gun from his hand.

As they fought, Elizabeth's hands joined the mix and she, too, tried to pry the gun away.

"Hold it! Don't move!" Deputy Benson rushed forward and placed his gun against Dolan's temple. "Give me a reason to pull this trigger."

Dolan, realizing he didn't have a chance, released his hold on both Thomas and the gun.

Thomas rolled away then squatted beside Elizabeth. "He shot you. How badly are you hurt?"

Both of them looked at the large circle of blood on the left side of her dress.

"Let me see. We need to stop the bleeding."

"*Neh*, Thomas. It'll be fine. Let's get the flash drive to the sheriff."

Red and blue strobe lights shone through the kitchen window.

"That's him, now," Thomas said. "I sent my friend to get him while I hurried back here. We have to get you to a hospital."

The sheriff, followed by one of his other deputies, barged into the room and quickly assessed the situation.

"Lie still, Ms. Lapp. I'll radio for an ambulance unless you want my deputy to take you. It will be quicker than waiting for the ambulance."

Elizabeth sat up. "No. I'm all right. I don't need an ambulance."

He helped Thomas lift Elizabeth to her feet.

She looked at Thomas. "Was I right? What was on the flash drive?"

Thomas put an arm behind her back and supported her with his strength. "A DNA report, copies of her mother's journal pages, a birth certificate. Everything you need."

Elizabeth smiled at him. "*Denki*, Thomas." Her voice riddled with pain she nodded at the sheriff. "Give the sheriff the flash drive."

He did.

The sheriff looked at the plastic dog in his hand. "Who would have thought this was anything other than a toy?" He turned to his deputy. "Take Ms. Lapp to the hospital." He gestured toward the others. "But first, cuff Dolan and put him in the back of my car. I'll take him in and book him myself."

Once the deputy dragged Dolan out of the room, the sheriff patted Deputy Benson on the shoulder. "You better go with them. Looks like the back of your head is going to need a few stitches."

Elizabeth leaned heavily against Thomas's body and smiled at the young deputy and sheriff.

It was over.

Finally.

The following morning, Elizabeth sat in a wheelchair beside her mother's bed.

"Are you sure you're going to be *allrecht*?" Mary asked.

"That's what I should be asking you," Elizabeth replied.

"They are moving me out of ICU today and into a regular room. I should be able to come home in no time."

"*Ja*, I know. I'm your new roommate. I had to have

surgery last night to remove the bullet from my left shoulder. The doctor wants me to stay in the hospital for a couple more days so I asked him to put me in a room with you. I begged Thomas to bring me here to see you so I could tell you myself."

"Against my better judgment," Thomas said. "But you know how stubborn this one can be. I figured if I grabbed a wheelchair and brought her down here for a minute, I could get her to go back to her room and rest."

"*Gut*, now go. You see I am better. They will bring me to the room soon. Go back and rest because when they move me I am going to want to hear all the details about what happened."

Thomas and Elizabeth laughed.

Neither of them spoke as Thomas wheeled her back to her room. He helped her get into bed and pulled the covers up over her sling.

Elizabeth grimaced.

"You're in pain."

"Some."

"See. The doctors know what they are talking about. You should be in bed."

"I am in bed, Thomas."

"*Ja*, and you are going to stay there. I am planning a large wedding in three weeks' time. If you keep getting out of this bed, you won't heal and I will have to marry you in your wheelchair. I don't think you will be happy."

Elizabeth blinked and then blinked again.

"What did you say?"

Thomas clasped her right hand. "You heard me. I spoke to the bishop and he gave us permission. The week before Christmas will be a perfect time for a wedding. No one else has asked for those dates."

He sat on the edge of the hospital bed, still clasping her hand in his. "Rebecca and some of the other women are already making the plans."

"Aren't you forgetting something?" Elizabeth's heart pounded against her chest. She was thrilled and scared all at the same time.

"What? That I didn't properly ask you? *Neh*, I asked you seven years ago. You haven't properly answered."

"Thomas, nothing has changed. I have endometriosis. We will never be able to have children."

"We have *kinner*, Elizabeth. Two *kinner* who need a *mamm* and already love you. Do you love them?"

"You know I do."

"Besides, I spoke with the doctor about this endometriosis. Some women are still able to have *kinner*. Maybe you will be one of those women."

"And if I can't?"

"It is not up to us, Elizabeth. It is in *Gott*'s hands. I trust whatever His plan is for our lives." He kissed her hand. "I love you, Elizabeth. I am not marrying you to breed you like cattle. I am marrying you because I have never met anyone as stubborn or independent or vulnerable and loving and kind as you. I want to spend the rest of my life with *you*. What *Gott* chooses to do with our lives, I accept."

He leaned forward and kissed her, sweetly, lovingly. "Will you be my wife?" he whispered against her lips.

"*Ja*, Thomas, but only because you asked properly." She smiled up into his eyes. "And also because I love you. I have always loved you. And I will love you for the rest of my life." Then she leaned forward and kissed him right back.

Epilogue

First day of summer
Eighteen months later

"*Neh*, Benjamin!" Thomas yelled, then shook his head when he realized his words were too late. He watched his son splash in a mud hole on the side of the barn. "He's going to be seven soon. When will he start being more responsible?"

Elizabeth cupped her husband's chin and turned his face toward hers. "He is a six-year-old boy right now, Thomas. This is what *kinner* do. They play. They explore. And they get dirty."

"*Ja*, but not when we are going to church service. He knows better."

"You're right." Elizabeth reached into her bag and showed him an extra pair of trousers. "But with Benjamin I am always prepared. I'll take him inside to change. And I will be sure he knows neither one of us is happy with what he has done."

Her lips twitched as she tried not to grin.

"Elizabeth." He spoke in his sternest tone, but seeing

the look on Elizabeth's face he suspected Benjamin's chastising wasn't going to be too tough.

"I know, *lieb*. It's not funny. He must stay clean at least long enough for church. He can play with the other *kinner* after service and get dirty then if he wants. I will tell him."

Thomas leaned forward and kissed her lips. "Have I told you what a good *frau* and *mamm* you are?"

"*Neh*. But I try to be."

"You are."

"*Denki*, husband."

"At least I told you how much I love you."

"*Neh*, not today."

"What? Well I have to do something about that." He stepped forward and clasped her in his arms. She fit perfectly, like a missing puzzle piece. The top of his chin rested on her *kapp*. She pressed her face against his chest.

"I love you, Elizabeth King." She smiled up at him and he kissed her, deeply, lovingly. "You have my heart."

"I love you, too" she whispered.

"Yuck! Stop it! You're squeezing me." Rachel, caught between them during their embrace, pushed her way clear of Elizabeth's skirts and moved to the side. She put her hands on her little four-year-old hips and scolded her father. "You should look and make sure I'm not standing in front of *Mamm* when you kiss her, *Daed*. You squeezed me."

Both of them laughed.

Thomas dropped to one knee. "You are right, little one." He pulled her into his arms, gave her a kiss and a snuggle, then tickled her with his beard until her giggles filled the air. "Am I forgiven?"

She threw her arms around his neck and squeezed hard. "Just don't do it again. Okay?"

Thomas grinned. "Okay."

"Rachel, come with me." She took the girl's hand. "We have to get Benjamin changed before the church service begins."

Before he joined the men, Thomas stood for a moment and watched his family walk into the house. He offered a silent prayer of thanks. He didn't know why *Gott* had chosen to bless him twice with two wonderful wives in his life, but he would be forever grateful.

Benjamin behaved during the two-hour service. Elizabeth must have spoken to him. When the service ended and everyone moved outside, Benjamin looked at him and said, "I am sorry, *Daed*, for getting dirty before church. I won't do it again."

Thomas crouched down to be eye level with the lad. "You are growing into a young man now, Benjamin. You are not a baby or toddler anymore. Did your *mamm* speak to you about the mud?"

"Yes, sir."

"Then you have been corrected enough. You may go now and play tag with the other boys. We will be spreading our picnic blanket under that tree." Thomas pointed to a tree slightly away from the others in the middle of the field.

"When I wave, *kumm* and eat with us."

"Yes, *Daed*." Benjamin turned and ran off with several of his friends.

Usually the families ate together after the service, but today Elizabeth had requested they have their own picnic. She'd spoken to the other women first and got their blessing.

As he started to walk toward the field where Elizabeth waited for him, he noticed the other women watching him and giggling and whispering to each other.

He politely nodded his head as he passed them. He wished Elizabeth had not made this request. He felt awkward sitting alone in the field while everyone else gathered for a feast at the house. But she'd been insistent that she wanted to have this private family picnic and there was little he would deny her.

He plopped down on the blanket beside her. She'd already set out fried chicken, mashed potatoes and gravy, corn and hot rolls. The tantalizing aromas almost made him forget his awkwardness at being apart from the others.

Almost.

"Where is Rachel?" he asked as she handed him a plate full of his favorite foods.

"Your *mamm* has her. They are sitting with Isaac and Rebecca up at the house."

"Elizabeth, tell me again why we are eating apart from the others?" He did not want to upset her but he was getting more uncomfortable by the minute. They could have a picnic another time. Right now they should be at the tables set up outside the main house with the others.

"It's the first day of summer, Thomas. It is a perfect day for a picnic."

"*Ja*, it is a perfect day." He tossed a glance around. "Well, at least we aren't the only ones going separate from the others today."

Elizabeth shot him a questioning glance.

"Look." He pointed to the silhouettes of two people talking under a tree at the other end of the field. "I believe that is Mary and Joshua."

Elizabeth strained to see past his shoulder. "So it is." She smiled. "What do you think they are talking about that is so important it needs to be done privately?"

Thomas shrugged. "You know I am not one to gossip."

"*Ja*, but?" Elizabeth's smile widened.

Thomas appeased her. "Joshua happened to mention to me that he might not be going to Sarasota this winter. That there might be a good reason for him to stay here."

Elizabeth clapped her hands. "Oh, Thomas, that would be *wunderbaar*. My mother is still in her prime. Fifties is not old these days. It has bothered me terribly that she is all alone. Especially since she said there were enough older adults in our lives once your parents returned, and insisted on staying in her own home."

"*Ja*, that's where you get your stubbornness."

Ignoring the barb, she said, "I've liked Joshua from the moment I met him last spring, when he returned with your parents. I've been praying that *Gott* would make a path for these two people to each other." She raised her hands to ward off any chastising from him about trying to control people's lives. "*Gott* willing, of course."

Thomas shook his head and wagged his finger at her. Then he glanced again toward the house and couldn't help but notice that not just the women, but many of the men also looked their way. "Elizabeth, you are right. It is a perfect day. But I am not sure this is the perfect time for a picnic." He gestured toward the house. "Our place is with the others. We can have a picnic another time."

"I spoke to the bishop and the other women. No one minds, Thomas."

"I mind. It does not feel right." He glanced again at the community, who all seemed to be watching them.

"Don't be silly, husband. You are allowed to have a picnic with your wife, aren't you? I made your favorites."

He took a bite of the chicken. The tender meat almost melted in his mouth.

"This is very *gut*."

"Denki."

He took another bite. "Why aren't you eating?"

"I will have some soup later. My stomach is unsettled right now."

He looked at her hard, concern making his pulse quicken. "Are you ill?"

"No, *lieb*. I am not ill." Her eyes shone and she smiled.

"I don't understand."

"Yesterday was the last day of spring and already we are beginning summer. But it has been a beautiful spring this year, hasn't it? It is the beginning of new life, Thomas. You have already planted our fields and with *Gott's* favor we will have a good harvest this year. The flowers have poked their heads through ground that is no longer frozen and the buds have blossomed. Leaves are again covering the trees. *Gott* is showing the world that nothing is impossible. Even after the dead of winter there can be new life."

He resisted the urge to touch her forehead and see if she had a fever. She had not been herself for weeks but this recent behavior was upsetting. Later today he would make a point to talk with Mary. Maybe she would be able to help him understand why Elizabeth was acting so strangely.

"Do you understand what I'm trying to tell you, Thomas?"

He stared at her blankly.

He really wasn't happy he had agreed to this picnic. But he didn't want to upset her, either. Women. Sometimes they are so difficult. Why don't they just speak frankly and clearly like men?

He placed his plate down on the blanket. He couldn't play this game with her any longer.

"No, Elizabeth. I don't understand. I don't want to hurt you or make you angry but I should not have agreed to this picnic. We do not belong here. We belong with the others. It doesn't matter that spring has just ended and summer begins. This happens every year. This year is no different."

"Ahh, Thomas, but this spring was very different. *Gott* blessed me with new life, too. I am pregnant."

It took a moment for his mind to understand what she had just told him.

"What did you just say?" Confusion, surprise and excitement all tumbled together inside him.

"I'm going to have a *boppli*."

"Are you sure? I thought the doctors said…"

"I am sure. I have seen a doctor." She clasped his hand in hers. "You were right, Thomas. *Gott* is in control. He has a plan for our lives. And He knows better than the doctors." She stroked his cheek. "We are having a child, Thomas. A gift from *Gott*."

His heart exploded with joy. He wrapped her in his arms and kissed her soundly.

Thomas could hear cheering and calls of congratulations drifting across the field. It seemed he was the last one to know about this secret. He turned and waved to the others before turning his attention back to Elizabeth.

The others could wait.

He was having a picnic with his wife.

* * * * *

If you enjoyed The Amish Witness, *look for these other great books from author Diane Burke, available now.*

The Marshal's Runaway Witness
Hidden in Plain View
Silent Witness
Bounty Hunter Guardian
Double Identity
Midnight Caller

Find more great reads at www.LoveInspired.com

WE HOPE YOU
ENJOYED THESE
LOVE INSPIRED®
AND
LOVE INSPIRED®
SUSPENSE
BOOKS.

Whether you prefer heartwarming contemporary romance or heart-pounding suspense, Love Inspired® books has it all!

Look for 6 new titles available every month from both Love Inspired® and Love Inspired® Suspense.

Save $1.00

on the purchase of any
Love Inspired® or Love Inspired®
Suspense book.

Available wherever books are sold,
including most bookstores, supermarkets,
drugstores and discount stores.

✂

Save $1.00

on the purchase of any Love Inspired® or
Love Inspired® Suspense book.

Toby was sure something was bothering Sarah.

He thought through their conversation among her family's Christmas trees. She'd been distressed by how Summerhays and his wife paid too little attention to their *kinder*, but she'd been ready to speak her mind on that subject.

So what was bothering her?

You.

The voice in his head startled him. He'd heard it clearly and, for once, it wasn't warning him away from becoming too close to someone. Instead, it was telling him the reason why there might be a wall between him and Sarah.

Maybe it was for the best. Every day he lingered was another drawing him into the community. Each moment he spent with Sarah enticed him to look forward

LIEXP0918

to the next time they could be together. In spite of his determination, his life was being linked to hers and her neighbors.

That would change once his coworker's trailer pulled up to take him back to Texas.

Sarah gestured toward the *kinder*. "They're hungry for love."

"You're worried they're going to be hurt when I go back to Texas."

"Ja."

He wanted to ask how she would feel when he left, but he'd hurt his ankle, not his head, so he didn't have an excuse to ask a stupid question.

"The *kinder* will be upset when you go, but won't it be better to give them nice memories of your times together to enjoy when they think about you after you've left?"

Nice memories of times together? Maybe that would be sufficient for the *kinder*, but he doubted it would be enough for him.

Don't miss
The Amish Christmas Cowboy *by Jo Ann Brown,*
available October 2018 wherever
Love Inspired® *books and ebooks are sold.*

www.LoveInspired.com